THE PENGUIN CLASSICS

FOUNDER EDITOR (1944–64): E. V. RIEU

ALEXANDER SERGEYEVICH PUSHKIN was born in Moscow in 1799. He was liberally educated and left school in 1817. Given a sinecure in the Foreign Office he spent three dissipated years in St Petersburg writing light, erotic and highly polished verse. He flirted with several pre-Decembrist societies composing the mildly revolutionary verses which led to his disgrace and exile in 1820. After a stay in the Caucasus and the Crimea, he was sent to Bessarabia, where he wrote *The Prisoner of the Caucasus* and *Bachisaraysky Fontan*. His work took a more serious turn during the last year of his southern exile when he began *Tsygany* and *Eugene Onegin*. In 1824 he moved to his parents' estate at Mikhaylovskoye in north-west Russia and spent two fruitful years during which he wrote his great historical drama *Boris Godunov*, continued *Eugene Onegin* and finished *Tsygany*. With the failure of the Decembrists' rising in 1825 and the succession of a new tsar, Pushkin recovered his freedom. During the next three years he wandered restlessly between St Petersburg and Moscow. He wrote an epic poem, *Poltava*, but little else. In 1829 he went with the Russian army to Transcaucasia, and the following year he retired to a family estate at Boldino, completing *Eugene Onegin*. In 1831 he wrote his experimental little tragedies, *Povesti Belkina*, in prose; and married the beautiful Natalia Goncharova. The rest of his life was harried by debts and the malice of his enemies. His literary output slackened, but he wrote two prose works, *The Captain's Daughter* and *The Queen of Spades*, and one folk poem, *The Golden Cockerel*. Towards the end of 1836 anonymous letters goaded Pushkin into challenging a troublesome admirer of his wife in the Horse Guards, to a duel. Pushkin was mortally wounded and died in January 1837.

Rosemary Edmonds was born in London and studied English, Russian, French, Italian and Old Church Slavonic at universities in England, France and Italy. During the war she was translator to General de Gaulle at Fighting France Headquarters in London and, after the liberation, in Paris. She went on to study Russian Orthodox Spirituality, and has translated Archimandrite Sophrony's *The Undistorted Image* (now published in two volumes as *The Monk of Mount Athos* and *The Wisdom from Mount Athos*) and *His Life is Mine*. She has also translated Tolstoy's *War and Peace*, *Anna Karenina*, *The Cossacks*, *Resurrection*, *Childhood*, *Boyhood*, *Youth* and Turgenev's *Fathers and Sons*. Her other translations include works by Gogol and Leskov. She is at present researching into Old Church Slavonic texts.

ALEXANDER PUSHKIN

THE QUEEN OF SPADES

THE NEGRO OF PETER THE GREAT
DUBROVSKY
THE CAPTAIN'S DAUGHTER

Translated with an Introduction by
ROSEMARY EDMONDS

PENGUIN BOOKS

Penguin Books Ltd, Harmondsworth, Middlesex, England
Penguin Books, 625 Madison Avenue, New York, New York 10022, U.S.A.
Penguin Books Australia Ltd, Ringwood, Victoria, Australia
Penguin Books Canada Ltd, 2801 John Street, Markham, Ontario, Canada L3R 1B4
Penguin Books (N.Z.) Ltd, 182–190 Wairau Road, Auckland 10, New Zealand

—

The Captain's Daughter and
The Negro of Peter the Great published by Neville Spearman 1958
This collection published in Penguin Books 1962
Reprinted 1968, 1978, 1979, 1982

—

Copyright © Rosemary Edmonds, 1958, 1962
All rights reserved

—

Set, printed and bound in Great Britain by
Cox & Wyman Ltd, Reading
Set in Monotype Garamond

*The wood-engravings in the book
are by George Buday*

CONTENTS

INTRODUCTION

ALEXANDER SERGEYEVICH PUSHKIN (1799–1837), the greatest name in Russian literature, was born in the reign of Paul I – who closed down all private printing-presses in Russia and prohibited *inter alia* the importation of foreign literature, travelling by Russians abroad and even French fashions. Pushkin's father belonged to the nobility, while his mother inherited Abyssinian blood, her grandmother being the daughter of the 'negro', Hannibal, whom Peter the Great bought from a Turkish seraglio. As a schoolboy the young Pushkin shared the high hopes of a new era which swept Russia after the Napoleonic débâcle of 1812, and experienced the disappointment which followed. A very daring *Ode to Liberty* written while he was an official in the Ministry of Foreign Affairs, and circulated in manuscript in Petersburg, was brought to the notice of the police and caused his banishment to the south of Russia before his twenty-first birthday. In the summer of 1824 he was transferred to his mother's estate in the province of Pskov and put under the supervision of the local governor, the marshal of nobility who requested his father to open the young man's correspondence and spy on him generally, and the archimandrite of the neighbouring monastery of Svyatogorsk.

During his coronation festivities Nicolas I suddenly decided to send for the exiled poet. An order was signed obliging Pushkin to travel under the escort of the imperial courier, but 'not in the position of a prisoner'. (In a sense, this was to be his status for the rest of his life.) In Moscow the Emperor ordered him to 'send me all your writings from now on: it is I who shall be your censor'. Nicolas never ceased to be suspicious of Pushkin and every move the latter made was observed and reported to the police. Nor did the Tsar's censorship exempt his works from that imposed upon all writers by the Third Section and its chief, Count Benckendorff, to whom Pushkin complained: 'Not a single Russian author is more oppressed than I. Having been approved by the Emperor my writings are yet stopped when they appear; they are printed with the censors' wilful corrections, while all my protestations are ignored.' He was refused permission to visit France and Italy, or to join a mission going to China, and his private letters continued to be opened and censored. 'It was a devil's trick to let me be born with a soul and talent in Russia,' he wrote to his wife, whom he married in 1831.

Natalia Goncharova possessed unusual beauty but a shallow, uncultured mind. The pair settled in Petersburg, and the Tsar, who admired Natalia and wished her to attend Court, made Pushkin a gentleman of the chamber – a rank suitable for a youth of eighteen but an insult to a man of standing, which compromised the poet in the eyes of the liberal younger generation. The adopted son of the Dutch minister at Petersburg, Baron George Heckeren d'Anthès, paid persistent attention to Natalia, until anonymous letters goaded Pushkin into challenging him to a duel, in which the poet was mortally wounded. His death was recognized by the people as a national calamity, and the house where his body lay was besieged by mourners. The Tsar and his police became alarmed. After a secret funeral service the remains were removed by night in a coffin covered with straw, which was driven in an ordinary sledge under an escort of gendarmes to the Svyatogorsky monastery.

Of Pushkin's short life six years were spent in exile. As we have seen, his writings were subjected to the severest censorship, and oppression by the police and gendarmerie was unremitting. Almost from his schooldays he felt that he lived *hors la loi* and deprived of legal justice.

Pushkin began his prose work in 1827 with an historical

narrative, *The Negro of Peter the Great*. It was the age of the great historical romances of Walter Scott, the age of new ideas on history. 'In our day', wrote Pushkin, 'the word *novel* means an historical epoch developed in the form of an imaginary story.' In *The Negro of Peter the Great* Pushkin strove for a new understanding of history. He brought history nearer to himself and to his readers by giving it biographical interest. 'The plot of the story', he said, 'centres about the Negro's wife, who is unfaithful to her husband, gives birth to a white child, and is punished by being shut up in a convent.' The novel opens with a striking picture of the morals and manners of French society in the first quarter of the eighteenth century. 'Nothing could equal the frivolity, folly and luxury of the French of that period. . . . Greed for money was united to a thirst for pleasure and dissipation; estates were squandered; morals foundered; the French laughed and speculated – and the State was going to ruin to the lively refrain of satirical vaudevilles.' In contrast to the decay of France under the Regent, Pushkin vividly portrays youthful Petrine Russia, the stern simplicity of the Petersburg Court and Peter's 'progressive' outlook and concern for his Empire. 'Russia seemed to Ibrahim one huge work-room where only machines were moving and every worker was occupied with his job in accordance with a fixed plan.' Ibrahim was one of Peter's collaborators, a courtier who recognized his responsibility to the country. A feeling of duty and not dread of the Tsar or any motive of personal ambition brought him home from the brilliant if frivolous *ambiance* of the nobility of France. For the sake of duty, for the sake of the honour of helping a great man, Ibrahim sacrificed gaiety and pleasure, exchanging a life of refinement for one of austerity and toil. 'He felt that he, too, ought to be labouring at his appointed task, and tried to regret as little as possible the gaieties of Parisian life.'

It was natural that Pushkin should feel drawn to a monarch whose work he understood in all its implications. 'Peter was undoubtedly a revolutionary by God's grace,' he wrote the year before his death. 'The tremendous revolution achieved by his autocratic power abolished the old system of life, and European influences spread all over Russia. Russia entered Europe like a launched vessel, amid the hammering of axes and the thunder of cannon ... As the executioner of an era which no longer corresponded to the nation's needs, the Tsar brought us culture and enlightenment, which in the end must bring us freedom too.'

'Had this novel [*The Negro of Peter the Great*] been completed ... we should have a supreme Russian historical novel, depicting the manners and customs of the greatest epoch of Russian history,' was the verdict of the eminent critic Belinsky.

Dubrovsky, the tale of a young officer whose father, like Naboth, is ousted from his small estate by an unscrupulous neighbour, is one of Pushkin's masterpieces. Melodramatic in subject, it is extremely simple in style. The fairly elaborate plot develops swiftly against a background which presents an illuminating picture of rural conditions in Russia and of Russian legal procedure under Catherine II. The two noblemen, Troyekurov and Vereisky, with the Byronic hero, the young Dubrovsky, are impressive creations in Pushkin's portrait gallery. The heroine is more of a lay figure – in all his prose stories except the historical ones Pushkin seems to have been more interested in his men than in his women characters. An almost exclusive diet of a little gentle music, a great many French novels, and no companionship, makes them eager to Suffer in one role after another – any role so long as they can dramatize themselves into the centre of the stage. This time the heroine goes to the altar to wed her elderly suitor, expecting until the last second to be rescued and carried off by the brigand. But the brigand arrives late and unhesitatingly she switches into the new part of the loyal wife.

A word as to Pushkin's use of landscape, which he introduces only when it is needed as a physical setting. For him nature is a visual phenomenon, never to be endowed with emotional content in order to add to a mood. In *Dubrovsky* there is an almost laconic description of the Volga: 'The Volga flowed past outside; loaded barges under full sail floated by, and little fishing boats ... flashed here and there. Beyond the river stretched hills and fields, and several small villages enlivened the landscape.' That is all: and there is no further mention of the Volga. It is the river itself that interests Pushkin. He describes it *qua* river, and the Volga does not appear again.

Of Pushkin's shorter stories *The Queen of Spades* is perhaps the most entertaining. It was certainly the most popular in his lifetime. Card-players punted on the three, the seven and the ace; and critics – Dostoyevsky was one of the first – wrote enthusiastically, declaring that in it Russian literary language had been created. Certainly in the person of Hermann a new type emerged in Russian literature.

In *The Queen of Spades* Pushkin again attains great simplicity of language. An almost total absence of adjectives excludes rhetorical cadence. The dry energetic sentences – as cold and relentless as the hero himself – are saved from jerkiness by the use of semi-colons instead of full stops. Consider the rhythm here: 'It was a frightful night: the wind howled, wet snow fell in big flakes; the street lamps burned dimly; the streets were deserted.' The phrases are not so much linked together as confronted with one another. A common impulse and the pressure which they exert one on the other carry them forward. Continuity of thought welds a series of abrupt phrases into a smooth whole: the author has his story perfectly worked out and knows exactly what he is doing. *The Queen of Spades* is remarkable for the range of its dramatic action and its economy of words – Pushkin's masters are the French for whom the crowning virtue of prose is conciseness. The opening paragraph – it is one of Pushkin's famous openings – plunges the reader into the heart of the matter. The card game is over, the company are having supper and chatting. 'The long winter night had passed unnoticed; it was after four in the morning when the company sat down to supper.' And there follows without delay the conversation bringing in the young man and the old woman, the two principal protagonists.

From first to last a tinge of fantasy pervades the story, looming over the whole plot like some mysterious and fatal curse. By contrast, the epigrams at the beginning of each chapter tend to restore the everyday world. Drawn for the most part from popular ballads, conversations between friends or personal correspondence – the only exception is the quotation from Swedenborg preceding Chapter 5 – they provide a foil to Pushkin's consummate literary style (whereas the more usual function of the epigram is to point the text with brilliance). The epigram to the shortest chapter – '*Homme sans mœurs et sans religion*' – offers an ironic forecast of the reader's verdict on Hermann. For Pushkin Hermann was not a hero but he recognized him as a man of the future – the theme of the poor young man resolved *coûte que coûte* to wrest for himself a place in the sun was already familiar in the works of artist and poet. Dostoyevsky called him a 'colossal figure' and went on to create Raskolnikov. (It was no accident that Pushkin invested Hermann with a physical likeness to Napoleon. The type of young man determined on success was bound up in contemporary understanding with the person of Napoleon. Pushkin makes Hermann resemble Napoleon and at the same time describes him as a mean character.)

What is the *primum mobile* of *The Queen of Spades*? The compelling power of chance events and circumstances? The idea of fatality? Is it a tragedy of destiny or a tragedy of personality? Or is Pushkin merely telling us a story having no special significance? ... Tchaikovsky's opera has given persuasive expression to one of these interpretations but, occupied as it is with only one of a whole series of motive forces, it does not measure up adequately to Pushkin's creation, which is both more and less than a tragedy of fatality. *The Queen of Spades* may be described as a psychological tale without psychology.

Pushkin's last prose narrative, *The Captain's Daughter*, was born of his interest in the rebellion against Catherine II in 1773, under the leadership of the illiterate Cossack, Emelian Pugachev (who claimed to be Peter III, the husband Catherine had 'liquidated'). In preparation for a history of Pugachev himself Pushkin had collected material from the State Archives, and journeyed to the Urals and the Lower Volga, the centres of the revolt; but Nicolas I objected to the project on the ground that a rebel like Pugachev 'has no history'. *The Captain's Daughter* combines historical accuracy with superb character drawing. As Gogol pointed out: 'For the first time characters that are truly Russian come into being: the simple commander of a fortress, his wife, his young lieutenant, the fortress itself with its single cannon, the confusion of the period, and the modest greatness of ordinary people.'

'The history of the people is the province of the Poet,' wrote Pushkin in 1825. For him the poet's imagination, his invention in general, did not entail an inevitable distortion of history. In his novels, as in Walter Scott's, historical events are interwoven with personal memoirs or a family chronicle in which the imaginary heroes occupy the foreground. The historical figures appear only in the background but they are drawn into the circle of everyday human relationships and thus lose their traditional grandeur and remoteness. In Pushkin, to quote his own lines on Walter Scott, 'we get to know past times not with the *enflure* of French tragedy, not with the primness of the sentimental novel, not with the *dignité* of history, but as though we were living a day-to-day life in them ourselves.' In thus widening the social basis of literature itself by introducing into it a great variety of characters from Peter the Great and Catherine II to the unassuming Captain Mironov Pushkin proves himself to be the cultural complement of Peter who, just over a century previously, had opened his 'window on to Europe'. Pushkin filled the gap between the literature of his country and that of the world.

Pushkin's plots move forward irresistibly, only very occasionally interrupted by a brief passage of description, such as that of the storm in Chapter 2 of *The Captain's Daughter*. Rarely does he introduce any personal idea, and then never to the detriment of the action. A short paragraph gives us his views on the use of torture, and a single sentence sums up his whole political philosophy – 'The best and most enduring of transformations are those which proceed from an improvement in morals and customs, and not from any violent upheaval.' (In this connexion we may quote the last lines of the same work: 'Heaven send that we may never see such another senseless and merciless rebellion *à la russe*! Those who plan impossible revolutions in Russia are either youngsters who do not know our people or positively heartless men who set little value on their own skins and less still on those of others.')

'Precision and brevity are the principal merits of prose,' wrote Pushkin in 1822, five years before he himself launched into 'humble prose'. 'Prose calls for ideas and more ideas, without which brilliant expressions avail nothing.' He demanded of the writer 'philosophy, objectivity, the statesman-like ideas of the historian, shrewdness, vivid imagination, absence of bias for favourite thoughts, freedom.' In his works the Russian literary language reached its perfection. His prose is as disciplined and mathematical as a Bach fugue. His sentences are short and splendidly chiselled. There is never a blurred outline, never a single superfluous word or unwarranted punctuation mark. He had no taste for 'shabby ornaments'. ('The charm of naked beauty is still so incomprehensible to us that even in prose we pursue shabby ornaments,' he wrote in 1828.)

Pushkin gave the heavy, archaic, uncertain language of his predecessors the purity, elegance and precision of a classical language, creating forms and rhythms for centuries to come.

London, October 1957   ROSEMARY EDMONDS
and October 1960

The footnotes throughout have been added by the translator

The Negro of Peter the Great

I

ONE of the young men sent abroad by Peter the Great to acquire the learning needed by a country in the course of reorganization was his godson, the negro Ibrahim. Ibrahim studied at the Military School in Paris, passed out with the rank of artillery captain, distinguished himself in the Spanish war and, after being dangerously wounded, returned to Paris. In the midst of his voluminous labours the Tsar never failed to inquire after his favourite, and always received flattering reports of Ibrahim's progress and conduct. Peter was exceedingly pleased with him and more than once called him back to Russia, but Ibrahim was in no hurry. He found various excuses for not returning: now it was his wound, now a wish to complete his education, now lack of money – and Peter indulgently complied with his requests, begging him to look after his health, thanking him for his zeal in the pursuit of knowledge, and (although extremely parsimonious over his own expenditure) did not spare his exchequer where his favourite was concerned, the ducats being accompanied with fatherly advice and words of caution.

According to the testimony of all the historical memoirs nothing could equal the frivolity, folly and luxury of the French of that period. The closing years of Louis XIV's reign, which had been distinguished for the strict piety, gravity and decorum of the Court, had left no trace whatsoever. The Duc d'Orléans,[1] who combined many brilliant qualities with all kinds of vices, unfortunately did not know what it was to dissemble. The orgies of the Palais-Royal were no secret in

1. Regent of France from 1715 to 1723.

Paris; the example was infectious. At this time Law[1] appeared upon the scene; greed for money was united to a thirst for pleasure and dissipation; estates were squandered, morals foundered; the French laughed and speculated – and the State was going to ruin to the lively refrain of satirical vaude-villes.

Meanwhile, society presented a most remarkable picture. Culture and the craving for amusement had brought all ranks together. Wealth, charm, renown, talent or mere eccentricity – everything that fed curiosity or promised amusement was received with equal favour. Writers, scholars and philosophers left the quiet of their studies and appeared in high society, to do homage to fashion and to dictate to it. Women reigned, but no longer demanded adoration. Superficial gallantry replaced the profound respect formerly shown to them. The pranks of the Duc de Richelieu,[2] the Alcibiades of the modern Athens, belong to history, and give some idea of the morals of the day.

> *Temps fortuné, marqué par la licence,*
> *Où la folie, agitant son grelot,*
> *D'un pied léger parcourt toute la France,*
> *Où nul mortel ne daigne être dévot,*
> *Où l'on fait tout excepté pénitence.*[3]

Ibrahim's arrival, his looks, culture and natural intelligence, attracted wide attention in Paris. All the ladies were anxious to see *le nègre du Czar* at their houses, and vied with each other in his pursuit. More than once he was invited to the gay evening parties of the Regent; he attended suppers enlivened by the presence of the young Arouet[4] and the old Chaulieu,[5]

1. John Law (1671–1729), projector of financial schemes, organizer of *La Banque Générale* in Paris.

2. Duc de Richelieu (1698–1788), marshal of France and a gay, outstanding figure of the Court of Louis XV.

3. Voltaire: *La Pucelle d'Orléans*, Canto XIII.

4. François Marie Arouet de Voltaire (1694–1778).

5. Guillaume Chaulieu (1639–1720), poet and author of frivolous songs.

by the conversations of Montesquieu[1] and of Fontenelle;[2] he did not miss a single ball, fête or first performance; and abandoned himself to the general whirl with all the ardour of his years and temperament. But it was not only the thought of exchanging this dissipation, these brilliant pastimes, for the simplicity of the Petersburg Court that dismayed Ibrahim: other and more powerful bonds attached him to Paris: the young African was in love.

The Countess L—, although no longer in the first bloom of youth, was still renowned for her beauty. On leaving the convent at the age of seventeen she had been given in marriage to a man with whom she had had no time to fall in love and who afterwards made no effort to win her affection. Gossip ascribed several lovers to her but thanks to the tolerant attitude of society she enjoyed a good reputation, for she could not be reproached with any ridiculous or scandalous adventure. Her house was the most fashionable in town, and the best Parisian society made it their place of *rendez-vous*. Ibrahim was introduced to the Countess by young Merville, who was generally regarded as her latest lover and used every possible means to confirm the report.

The Countess received Ibrahim courteously but without any particular mark of attention: this captivated him. As a rule people viewed the young negro as a sort of phenomenon and, flocking round, overwhelmed him with compliments and questions – and this curiosity, although it had an air of affability, offended his pride. Women's sweet attention – almost the sole aim of our exertions – far from delighting, filled him with bitterness and indignation. He felt that for them he was a kind of rare animal, an alien, peculiar creature, accidentally transported into their world and having nothing in common with them. He actually envied men who were in no way remarkable, and considered them fortunate in their insignificance.

1. Charles-Louis Montesquieu (1689–1735), political publicist and satirist.
2. Bernard Le Bovier de Fontenelle (1657–1757), savant and publicist.

The thought that nature had not intended him for the joys of requited passion saved him from conceit and vain pretensions, and this gave a rare charm to his manner with women. His conversation was simple and dignified; it pleased Countess L—, who had grown tired of the pompous jests and sly insinuations of French wit. Ibrahim frequently visited her. Gradually she became accustomed to the young negro's appearance, and even began to find something agreeable about the curly head that stood out so black among the powdered wigs in her drawing-room. (Ibrahim had been wounded in the head, and wore a bandage instead of a wig.) He was twenty-seven years old, tall and well-proportioned, and more than one society beauty gazed at him with sentiments more flattering than mere curiosity; but the prejudiced Ibrahim either noticed nothing or put it down to coquetry. But when his eyes met those of the Countess his distrust vanished. Her look expressed such amiable good-nature, her manner towards him was so simple, so spontaneous, that it was impossible to suspect her of the faintest shadow of coquettishness or mockery.

The idea of love did not enter his head, but to see the Countess every day had now become a necessity for him. He was always seeking to meet her, and every encounter seemed to him an unexpected gift from Heaven. The Countess divined his feelings sooner than he did. Whatever people may say, love without hopes or demands touches a woman's heart more surely than all the wiles of the seducer. When Ibrahim was present the Countess watched his every movement and took in everything he said; without him she brooded and sank into her habitual absent-minded state. Merville was the first to notice their mutual attraction – and to congratulate Ibrahim. Nothing inflames love so much as an approving remark from an onlooker: love is blind, and, distrusting itself, is quick to snatch at encouragement.

Merville's words roused Ibrahim. The possibility of possessing the woman he loved had never yet occurred to his imagination; the light of hope suddenly flooded his soul; he fell madly in love. In vain did the Countess, alarmed by the frenzy of his passion, combat it with friendly admonishments and wise counsels; she herself was beginning to waver. ... Incautious tokens of approval followed one after another. At last, carried away by the passion she had inspired, the Countess, succumbing to its power, gave herself to the ecstatic Ibrahim.

Nothing can be hidden from the observant eyes of the world. The Countess's new love affair soon became known to everyone. Some ladies marvelled at her choice; to many it seemed perfectly natural. Some laughed, others regarded her conduct as unpardonably indiscreet. In the first intoxication of passion Ibrahim and the Countess noticed nothing; but soon the equivocal jokes of the men and the caustic remarks of the women began to reach their ears. Hitherto Ibrahim's distant, cold manner had protected him from such attacks; he suffered them impatiently and did not know how to ward them off. The Countess, accustomed to the respect of society, could not with equanimity see herself an object of calumny and ridicule. With tears in her eyes she complained to Ibrahim, now bitterly reproaching him, now imploring him not to try to defend her lest by some useless brawl he ruin her completely.

A new circumstance now made her position still more difficult: the consequence of their imprudent love became apparent. The Countess with despair told Ibrahim that she was with child. Comfort, advice, suggestions – all were drained and all rejected. The Countess saw that her ruin was inevitable and in utter misery awaited it.

As soon as the Countess's condition became known gossip began again with renewed vigour; sentimental ladies gave vent to exclamations of horror; men laid wagers as to whether the child would be white or black. There were showers of epigrams at the expense of the husband, who was the only person in the whole of Paris to know and suspect nothing. The fatal moment was approaching. The Countess was distraught. Ibrahim visited her every day. He saw her mental and physical strength gradually failing. Her tears and her terror sprang afresh every moment. At last she felt the first pains. Measures were hastily taken. Means were found for getting the Count out of the way. The doctor arrived. A couple of days before this a poor woman had been persuaded to relinquish her new-born infant into the hands of strangers, and a person of trust had been sent to fetch it. Ibrahim was in the closet next to the bedroom where the unfortunate Countess lay. Not daring to breathe, he listened to her stifled groans, to the maid's whispers and the orders of the doctor.

Her agony lasted several hours. Every groan she uttered rent Ibrahim's soul; every interval of silence filled him with dread. . . . Suddenly he heard the feeble wail of a child and, unable to contain his delight, rushed into the Countess's bedroom. . . . A black baby lay upon the bed at her feet. Ibrahim approached. His heart beat violently. With a trembling hand he blessed his son. The Countess smiled faintly and stretched out a feeble hand to him . . . but the doctor, fearing too much excitement for his patient, drew Ibrahim away from the bed. The new-born child was laid in a covered basket and carried out of the house by a back staircase. The other baby was brought in and its cradle put in the Countess's bedroom. Ibrahim went away, somewhat reassured. The Count was expected. He returned late, learned that his wife had been safely delivered, and was greatly pleased. In this way the public who had been expecting a scandal were deceived in their hopes and obliged to seek consolation in mere malicious gossip. Everything resumed its normal course.

But Ibrahim felt that his fortune was bound to change, and that his relations with the Countess must sooner or later reach her husband's ears. In that case, whatever happened, the Countess's doom would be sealed. Ibrahim loved passionately and was passionately loved in return, but the Countess was wilful and flighty: this was not the first time that she had loved. Disgust and hatred might replace the tenderest feelings in her heart. Ibrahim could already foresee her beginning to cool towards him. Hitherto he had not known jealousy, but with horror he now felt a presentiment of it. Thinking that the pain of parting would be less agonizing, he resolved to break off the ill-starred love affair, leave Paris and return to Russia, whither Peter and a vague sense of duty had long been calling him.

2

DAYS, months went by – and the love-struck Ibrahim still could not make up his mind to leave the woman he had seduced. With every hour that passed, the Countess grew more attached to him. Their son was being brought up in a distant province. Gossip was dying down, and the lovers began to enjoy more peace, silently remembering the past storm and trying not to think of the future.

One day Ibrahim was at the Duc d'Orléans' levee. Walking past him, the Duke stopped and handed him a letter, telling him to read it at his leisure. The missive was from Peter I. Guessing the true cause of his godson's absence, the Tsar had written to the Duke that he did not intend to put the least pressure on Ibrahim, that he left it to his own free will to return to Russia or not, but that in any case he would never forsake his old protégé. This letter touched Ibrahim to the bottom of his heart. From that moment his destiny was decided. The next day he informed the Regent of his intention to set out for Russia without delay.

'Reflect upon what you are doing,' the Duke said to him. 'Russia is not your native country. I do not suppose you will ever see your torrid fatherland again; but your long residence in France has made you equally a stranger to the climate and customs of semi-barbarous Russia. You were not born a subject of Peter. Follow my advice: take advantage of his gracious permission, remain in France for whom you have already shed your blood, and rest assured that here, too, your services and talents will find their due reward.'

Ibrahim thanked the Duke sincerely but clung to his intention.

'I am sorry,' the Regent said to him, 'but I admit you are right.'

He promised to let him retire from the French service, and wrote in full to the Russian Tsar.

Ibrahim was soon ready to leave. On the day before his departure he spent the evening as usual at Countess L—'s. She knew nothing. Ibrahim had not the courage to tell her the truth. The Countess was tranquil and gay. Several times she called him to her side and rallied him upon his pensive mood. After supper the guests departed. Only the Countess, her husband and Ibrahim remained in the drawing-room. The unhappy man would have given everything in the world to have been left alone with her; but Count L— seemed to be so comfortably settled by the fire that there was no hope of getting him out of the room. All three were silent.

'*Bonne nuit!*' the Countess said at last.

Ibrahim's heart sank and he suddenly felt all the pain of parting. He stood stock still.

'*Bonne nuit, messieurs,*' the Countess repeated.

Still he did not move . . . Then his eyes went dim, his head reeled; he was scarcely able to walk out of the room. On arriving home, in a hardly conscious state he wrote the following letter:

I am going away, dear Leonora; I am leaving you for ever. I write to you because I have not the courage to tell you in any other way. My happiness could not have lasted; I have enjoyed it against fate and nature. You are bound to cease loving me; the enchantment must inevitably pass. This thought has always haunted me, even in those moments when I seemed to forget everything at your feet, revelling in your passionate devotion, your infinite tenderness. . . . The careless world unmercifully persecutes that which in theory it allows: its icy derision would sooner or later have vanquished you, would have humbled your ardent soul – until in the end you would have been ashamed of your passion. . . . And what would have become of me then? No, better that I should die, better that I should leave you before that awful moment. . . .

Your peace of mind is more precious to me than anything else: you could enjoy no peace with the eyes of the world fixed upon us. Remember all that you have suffered – all the insults to your pride, all the torments of dread; remember the terrible birth of our son.

Think: is it right that I should subject you any longer to anxiety and peril? Why strive to unite the destiny of so tender and beautiful a being as yourself with the unhappy lot of a negro, a pitiful creature whom people scarcely deign to recognize as human?

Farewell, Leonora; farewell, my dear, my only friend. In leaving you I leave the first and last joy of my life. I have neither fatherland nor kindred; I am going to Russia, where my utter solitude will be a solace to me. Exacting work, to which I shall henceforth devote myself, will, if not stifle, at least distract me from the agonizing memories of days of rapture and bliss. . . . Farewell, Leonora! I tear myself from this letter as though it were from your arms. Farewell, be happy and think sometimes of the poor negro, of your faithful

Ibrahim

That same night he set out for Russia.

The journey did not seem to him so frightful as he had expected. His imagination triumphed over reality. The farther he got from Paris the closer and more vividly he pictured the things that he was leaving for ever.

Before he was aware of it, he had reached the Russian frontier. It was already autumn but in spite of the bad roads he was driven with the speed of the wind, and on the morning of the seventeenth day of his journey arrived at Krasnoe Selo, through which the highway passed in those times.

It was another twenty-eight versts[1] to Petersburg. While the horses were being changed Ibrahim went into the post-house. In a corner a tall man in a green peasant-coat and with a clay pipe in his mouth sat leaning his elbows on the table, reading the Hamburg newspapers. Hearing somebody come in, he raised his head.

'Ah, Ibrahim!' he cried, rising from the bench. 'Good morning to you, godson!'

Recognizing Peter, Ibrahim rushed joyfully towards him but stopped short respectfully. The Tsar approached, embraced him and kissed him on the head.

'I was informed of your coming,' said Peter, 'and came to

1. Eighteen miles.

meet you. I have been waiting for you here since yesterday.'

Ibrahim could not find words to express his gratitude.

'Have your carriage follow on behind,' continued the Tsar, 'and you drive home with me.'

The Tsar's carriage was brought up; he took his place with Ibrahim beside him, and they drove off at a furious pace. An hour and a half later they were in Petersburg. Ibrahim gazed with curiosity at the new-born capital which was rising out of the marsh at the bidding of its monarch. Rough dams, canals without an embankment, wooden bridges everywhere bore witness to the recent triumph of the human will over the reluctant elements. The houses appeared to have been built in a hurry. In the whole town there was nothing magnificent save the Neva, which had not yet received its granite frame but was already full of warships and merchant vessels. The imperial carriage stopped at the palace, which was called the Tsaritsyn Garden.

On the steps Peter was met by a handsome woman of some five and thirty summers, dressed in the latest Paris fashion. After he had kissed her, Peter took Ibrahim by the hand and said:

'Do you recognize my godson, Katinka? Pray love and be kind to him as you used to in the old days.'

Catherine looked at Ibrahim with her penetrating black eyes, and stretched out her hand in a friendly manner. Two young beauties standing behind her, tall, slim and fresh as roses, respectfully approached Peter.

'Liza,' he said to one of them, 'do you remember the little negro boy who used to steal my apples for you at Oranienbaum? This is he: let me introduce him to you.'

The Grand Duchess laughed and blushed. They went into the dining-room. The table had been laid in expectation of Peter's arrival. He sat down to dinner with all his family, inviting Ibrahim to join them. During dinner the Tsar conversed with him on various subjects, questioned him about the Spanish war, about France's internal affairs, and the Regent, whom he liked though disapproved of in many ways.

Ibrahim possessed a precise and observant mind. Peter was much pleased with his answers; he recalled one or two incidents of Ibrahim's childhood and related them with such gaiety and good nature that nobody could have suspected this kind and hospitable host of being the hero of Poltava, and Russia's mighty and formidable reformer.

After dinner the Tsar followed the Russian custom and retired to rest. Ibrahim was left with the Empress and the Grand Duchesses. He did his best to satisfy their curiosity, and described the Parisian mode of life, the festivals that were kept in that capital, and the capriciousness of fashion. In the meantime some of the persons closely associated with the Tsar appeared at the palace. Ibrahim recognized the magnificent Prince Menshikov,[1] who, seeing a negro conversing with Catherine, cast an arrogant sideways glance at him; Prince Yakov Dolgoruky,[2] Peter's gruff councillor; the erudite Bruce[3] whom the people called the 'Russian Faust'; the young Raguzinsky, his former comrade; and others who came to the Tsar to make reports and receive orders.

A couple of hours later the Tsar emerged.

'Let us see whether you have forgotten your old duties,' he said to Ibrahim. 'Take a slate and follow me.'

Peter shut himself up in his work-room and busied himself with state affairs. He worked in turn with Bruce, with Prince Dolgoruky, and with the chief of police, General Deviere, and dictated several ukases and decisions to Ibrahim.

Ibrahim could not sufficiently admire the clarity and quickness of his judgement, the power and flexibility of his mind and the wide range of his activities. When their labours were over, Peter took out a pocket-book in order to see whether all that he had intended to do that day had been accomplished. Then, as they were leaving the room, he said to Ibrahim:

1. Prince Menshikov (1670–1729), general-field-marshal and favourite of Peter the Great.

2. Prince Dolgoruky (1639–1720), senator and close adviser of Peter the Great. Noted for his forthrightness.

3. Y. V. Bruce (1670–1735), of Scottish extraction, mathematician, astronomer and naturalist. Reputed to be a sorcerer.

'It is late; I expect you are tired. Spend the night here as you used to do in the old days. I'll wake you in the morning.'

Left alone, Ibrahim had difficulty in collecting his be-bewildered senses. He was in Petersburg; he was seeing again the great man in whose house, not yet understanding his worth, he had passed his childhood. Almost with remorse he confessed to himself that, for the first time since their parting, the Countess L— had not been his sole thought throughout the day. He perceived that the new mode of life which awaited him – the activity and constant occupation – might revive his soul, wearied by passion, idleness and secret melancholy. The thought of being a great man's fellow-worker and, together with him, influencing a great nation aroused in him for the first time a feeling of noble ambition. In this mood he lay down on the camp-bed that had been prepared for him – and then the familiar dream transported him back to far-off Paris and the arms of his dear Countess.

3

THE next morning Peter woke Ibrahim as promised, and conferred on him the rank of lieutenant-captain in the Grenadier company of the Preobrazhensky regiment. The courtiers crowded round Ibrahim, each in his way trying to make much of the new favourite. The haughty Prince Menshikov pressed his hand in a friendly manner; Sheremetyev[1] inquired after his Parisian acquaintances, and Golovin[2] invited him to dinner. The latter's example was followed by others, too, so that Ibrahim received enough invitations to last him at least a month.

Ibrahim now began to lead an uneventful but busy life – consequently he did not suffer from ennui. He grew daily more attached to the Tsar and better able to apprehend his lofty mind. To follow a great man's thoughts is the most absorbing of studies. Ibrahim saw Peter in the Senate arguing with Buturlin[3] and Dolgoruky on important questions of legislation; at the Board of Admiralty laying the foundations of Russia's naval power; he saw him with Feofan,[4] Gavril Buzhinsky[5] and Kopievich,[6] in his hours of rest examining translations of foreign publications, or visiting some merchant's manufactory, a craftsman's workshop or a learned man's study. Russia seemed to Ibrahim one huge work-room where only machines were moving and every worker was occupied with his job in accordance with a fixed plan. He felt

1. Count Sheremetyev (1652–1719), general-field-marshal.
2. I. M. Golovin (d. 1737), commissary general of the army.
3. I. I. Buturlin (1661–1738), member of the Collegium of War.
4. Feofan Protopovich (1681–1736), archbishop of Novgorod and Peter the Great's closest collaborator in church matters.
5. Gavril Buzhinsky (1680–1731), director of all the printing presses in Moscow and Petersburg.
6. I. F. Kopievich (d. c. 1707), Lutheran pastor, translator and author of text-books.

that he, too, ought to be labouring at his appointed task, and tried to regret as little as possible the gaieties of Parisian life. He found it more difficult to banish from his mind that other dear memory: he often thought of the Countess L—, picturing her legitimate indignation, her tears and her grief. ... But at times a terrible thought oppressed his heart: the distractions of high society, a new intrigue, another happy lover – he shuddered; jealousy began to set his African blood in a ferment, and scalding tears were ready to roll down his dusky cheeks.

One morning as he sat in his study surrounded by business papers he suddenly heard a loud greeting in the French tongue. Ibrahim turned round quickly – and young Korsakov, whom he had left in Paris in the whirl of society life, embraced him with joyful exclamations.

'I have only just arrived,' said Korsakov, 'and have come straight to you. All our Parisian acquaintances send you their greetings, and regret your absence. The Countess L— ordered me to tell you that you must return at all costs, and here is a letter for you from her.'

Ibrahim seized it with tremulous fingers and gazed at the familiar handwriting on the address, not daring to believe his eyes.

'How glad I am that you have not died of tedium in this barbarous Petersburg!' Korsakov went on. 'What do people do here? How do they spend their time? Who is your tailor? Is there at least an opera-house?'

Ibrahim absently replied that probably the Tsar was just then at work in the dockyard. Korsakov laughed.

'I see you have no thoughts to spare for me at present,' he said. 'Some other time we will talk to our hearts' content. I will go and present myself to the Tsar.'

With these words he spun round on his heel and ran out of the room.

Left alone, Ibrahim hastily opened the letter. The Countess reproached him tenderly, accusing him of evasion and lack of trust.

You say [she wrote] *that my peace of mind is more precious than anything in the world to you. Ibrahim, if this were true, could you have brought me to the condition to which the unexpected news of your departure reduced me? You were afraid that I would detain you; believe me that, in spite of my love, I should have known how to sacrifice it to your well-being and to what you regard as your duty.*

The Countess concluded her letter with passionate assurances of love, and adjured him to write to her occasionally – even should there be no hope of their ever meeting again.

Ibrahim read the letter twenty times over, kissing the dear lines with rapture. He was burning with impatience to hear about the Countess, and was just preparing to drive to the Admiralty, in the hope of finding Korsakov still there, when the door opened and Korsakov appeared again in person. He had already paid his respects to the Tsar, and as usual seemed much pleased with himself.

'*Entre nous*,' he said to Ibrahim, 'the Emperor is a very strange man. Imagine, I found him, clad in a sort of linen jacket, on the mast of a new ship, whither I was obliged to clamber with my dispatches. I stood on a rope-ladder, without room to make a decent bow, and became completely confused – a thing which has never happened to me in my life. However, after reading my papers, the Tsar looked me up and down, and no doubt was agreeably impressed by the taste and elegance of my attire; at any rate, he smiled and invited me to the Assembly this evening. But I am a perfect stranger in Petersburg: during the six years I have been away I have quite forgotten the local customs. Pray be my mentor, call for me and introduce me.'

Ibrahim agreed, and hastened to turn the conversation to a subject that held more interest for him.

'Well, and how is the Countess L—?'

'The Countess? Naturally, at first she was very much grieved by your departure; then, of course, she gradually grew reconciled and took unto herself a new lover – do you know whom? That lanky Marquis R—. Why do you stare at me like that with your goggle eyes? Does it seem odd to you? Don't you know that it isn't in human nature, particularly feminine nature, to sorrow for long? Think it out, while I go and rest after my journey; mind you don't forget to call for me.'

What emotions filled Ibrahim's heart? Jealousy? Rage? Despair? No, but profound, overpowering dejection. He kept repeating to himself: 'I foresaw it, it was bound to happen.' Then he opened the Countess's letter, read it through again, bowed his head and wept bitterly. He wept long. The tears relieved his heart. Glancing at the clock, he saw that it was time to go. Ibrahim would have been very glad to stay at home, but an Assembly was a matter of duty and the Tsar strict in demanding the presence of his entourage. He dressed and set out to call for Korsakov.

Korsakov was sitting in his dressing-gown, reading a French novel.

'So early?' he said, when he saw Ibrahim.

'Why, it's half past five,' Ibrahim answered. 'We shall be late. Make haste and dress, and let us go.'

Korsakov started up and rang the bell violently; his servants came running in; he hurriedly began dressing. His French valet handed him slippers with scarlet heels, blue velvet breeches, and a pink coat embroidered with spangles. His peruke was quickly powdered in the ante-room and brought in to him. Korsakov thrust his closely cropped head into it, asked for his sword and gloves, turned round a dozen times before the looking-glass and informed Ibrahim that he was ready. The footmen handed them bearskin cloaks, and they drove off to the Winter Palace.

Korsakov bombarded Ibrahim with questions: Who was the reigning beauty in Petersburg? Who was supposed to be the best dancer? What dance was now in fashion? Ibrahim very reluctantly gratified his curiosity. Meanwhile they reached the palace. A number of long sledges, old-fashioned carriages and gilded coaches were already standing on the rough grass in front. At the steps there was a crowd of liveried coachmen with moustaches; running footmen glittering with gold braid and feathers, and carrying maces; hussars, pages, awkward footmen loaded with their masters' fur cloaks and muffs – a retinue which the noblemen of the period considered essential. At the sight of Ibrahim a general murmur of 'The negro, the negro, the Tsar's negro!' arose among them. He hurriedly led Korsakov through this motley crowd. A palace footman flung the doors wide for them, and they entered the hall. Korsakov was dumbfounded. ... In the great room lit by tallow candles which burned dimly in the clouds of tobacco smoke grandees with blue ribbons across their shoulders, ambassadors, foreign merchants, officers of the Guards in their green uniform, shipbuilders in jackets and striped trousers thronged up and down to the continual music of wind instruments. The ladies sat round the walls, the younger among them decked out in all the splendour of fashion. Their gowns dazzled with gold and silver; out of monstrous farthingales their slender forms rose like the stems of flowers; diamonds sparkled in their ears, in their long curls and round their necks. They glanced gaily to right and left, waiting for their cavaliers and for the dancing to begin. The elderly ladies had made ingenious attempts to combine the new fashions with the now prohibited style of the past: their caps bore a close resemblance to the sable head-dress of the Tsaritsa Natalia Kirilovna,[1] and their gowns and mantillas somehow recalled the *sarafan*[2] and *dushegreika*.[3] They seemed to feel more astonishment than pleasure in being present at these newfangled diversions and looked askance at the wives and daughters of the Dutch skippers who in dimity skirts and red bodices sat knitting their stockings and laughing and chatting among themselves as though they were at home.

Noticing the new arrivals, a servant came up to them with beer and glasses on a tray. Korsakov was completely bewildered.

1. Peter the Great's mother.
2. Russian national dress.
3. A short sleeveless jacket.

'*Que diable est-ce que tout cela?*' he asked Ibrahim in an under-tone. Ibrahim could not help smiling. The Empress and the Grand Duchesses, resplendent with beauty and brilliant attire, walked about among the guests, talking to them graciously. The Tsar was in the next room. Korsakov, anxious to present himself, could hardly make his way through the constantly moving crowd. The next room was mainly full of foreigners, who sat there solemnly smoking their clay pipes and emptying earthenware mugs. On the table were bottles of beer and wine, leather pouches with tobacco, glasses of punch and some chess-boards. At one of the tables Peter was playing draughts with a broad-shouldered English skipper. They zealously saluted one another with volleys of tobacco smoke, and the Tsar was so taken aback by an unforeseen move on his opponent's part that he failed to notice Korsakov for all the latter's shifts. Just then a stout gentleman with a large bouquet on his breast bustled in and announced in a loud voice that dancing had begun. He went out again immediately, and a great number of the guests, Korsakov among them, followed.

The unexpected scene took him by surprise. Ladies and gentlemen stood in two rows facing each other along the whole length of the ball-room; to the sounds of the most mournful music the gentlemen bowed low, the ladies curt-seyed still lower, first to the front, then to the right, then to the left, then straight before them again, to the right, and so on. Korsakov stared wide-eyed at this peculiar way of passing the time, and bit his lips. The curtseying and bowing con-tinued for the best part of half an hour; at last they stopped and the stout gentleman with the bouquet proclaimed that the ceremonial dances were over, and ordered the musicians to play a minuet.

Korsakov was delighted, and prepared to shine. Among the young ladies there was one in particular who appealed to him. She was about sixteen, luxuriously dressed but in good taste, and sat near an elderly man of stern and imposing appearance. Korsakov dashed up to her and asked for the honour of a dance. The young beauty looked at him in confusion, and seemed at a loss for an answer. The gentleman sitting by her side frowned more than ever. Korsakov was waiting for her decision but the gentleman with the bouquet came up to him, and leading him into the middle of the room said pompously:

'My dear sir, you are at fault. In the first place, you approached this young lady without making three bows in the proper fashion, and, in the second, you took it upon yourself to single her out, whereas in the minuet that right belongs to the lady and not to the gentleman. In view of this, you have to be severely punished – that is to say, you must drain the Goblet of the Great Eagle.'

Korsakov felt more and more bewildered. The other guests instantly surrounded him, noisily demanding the immediate fulfilment of the law. Hearing shouts and laughter, Peter came out of the adjoining room, for he was very fond of assisting at such punishments. The crowd made way for him, and he entered the circle, in the centre of which stood the culprit and before him the marshal of the Assembly with a huge goblet filled with malmsey wine. He was vainly trying to persuade the offender to comply willingly with the regulation.

'Aha!' said Peter, seeing Korsakov. 'You are caught, my friend. Come now, monsieur, drink up, and no grimaces.'

There was no help for it: the poor dandy drained the goblet to the dregs without drawing breath, and handed it back to the marshal.

'Hark you, Korsakov,' said Peter to him, 'those breeches of yours are of velvet, such as I myself do not wear, and I am far richer than you. That is extravagance: take care I do not quarrel with you.'

When he heard this reprimand Korsakov tried to make his way out of the circle, but he staggered and almost fell, to the inexpressible delight of the Emperor and the whole merry company. So far from breaking up or spoiling the entertainment, this episode served to enliven it still more. The gentlemen scraped and bowed, while the ladies curtseyed and clicked their heels with more zeal than ever, no longer troubling to keep time with the music. Korsakov was unable to take part in the general gaiety. The lady whom he had selected went up to Ibrahim at the bidding of her father, Gavril Afanassyevich Rzhevsky, and, casting down her blue eyes, timidly gave him her hand. Ibrahim danced the minuet with her and escorted her back to her seat; then, seeking out Korsakov, he led him out of the ball-room, put him in his carriage and saw him home. On the way Korsakov at first kept muttering vaguely: 'That damned Assembly! ... That damned Goblet of the Great Eagle! ...' but soon dropped sound asleep, and was not conscious of arriving home, or of being undressed and put to bed. He awoke the next day with a headache and a dim recollection of the bows, the curtseys, the tobacco-smoke, the gentleman with the bouquet, and the Goblet of the Great Eagle.

4

In times of old our forbears feasted long,
Goblet with foaming beer and silver cup
With sparkling wine passed slowly round the throng.

RUSSLAN AND LUDMILLA

I MUST now introduce my gentle reader to Gavril Afanassyevich Rzhevsky. He came of an ancient boyar family, possessed
vast estates, was hospitable, had a passion for falconry, and
kept a great number of indoor servants: in short, he was a
true Russian nobleman. He could not endure the German
spirit, as he put it, and strove to preserve in his home the old
customs that were so dear to him. His daughter was sixteen
years old. She had lost her mother while still a child. She
had been brought up in the old-fashioned way, that is to say,
surrounded by nurses, playmates and maidservants; she
embroidered in gold, and could not read or write. In spite of
his aversion for everything from abroad her father could not
resist her desire to learn foreign dances from a captive Swedish
officer who lived in their house. This worthy dancing-master
was some fifty years of age; his right leg had been shot
through in the battle of Narva and was consequently not
particularly well qualified for the minuet and the coranto but
the left leg made up for it by executing the most difficult *pas*
with astonishing skill and agility. His pupil did credit to his
efforts. Natalia Gavrilovna was renowned for being the best
dancer at the Assemblies – and this was partly the reason for
Korsakov's offence. He came the next day to apologize to
Gavril Afanassyevich, but the airiness and elegance of the
young fop found no favour in the eyes of the proud old
noble, who satirically nicknamed him the French monkey.

It was a holiday. Gavril Afanassyevich was expecting a
number of relatives and friends. A long table was being laid
in the old-fashioned dining-hall. Visitors were arriving with

their wives and daughters, who had at last been set free from domestic seclusion by edicts of the Emperor and by his own example.[1] Natalia Gavrilovna brought round to each guest a silver tray laden with gold cups, and each man as he drained his regretted that the kiss given in the old days on such occasions was no longer the custom. They sat down to dinner. The place of honour next to the host was taken by his father-in-law, Prince Boris Alexeyevich Lykov, an old man of seventy; the other guests ranged themselves according to the seniority of their family, thus recalling the happy days when birth received due honour. The men sat on one side of the table, the women on the other. The family protégée and companion in her old-fashioned jerkin and peasant head-dress, a prim wrinkled little dwarf of thirty, and the captive dancing-master in his faded blue uniform occupied their usual places at the end. Numerous menials bustled round the table, which was laid with a great many dishes. Among the servants the major-domo was conspicuous for his stern expression, big paunch and lofty immobility. The first few moments of the meal were devoted exclusively to savouring the traditional Russian dishes: the rattling of plates and spoons alone interrupted the general silence. At last, seeing that the time had come for entertaining his guests with pleasant conversation, the host looked about him and said:

'But where is Yekimovna? Summon her here!'

Several servants were about to dash off in different directions but at that moment an old woman, rouged and powdered, wearing a low-cut brocade dress and decked with flowers and tinsel, came into the room, singing and dancing. Her appearance was greeted with pleasure by everyone.

'Good day to you, Yekimovna,' said Prince Lykov. 'How are you getting on?'

'Nicely, nicely, my dear man, with singing and dancing and looking for a sweetheart.'

---

1. Until the reign of Peter the Great (d. 1725) Russian women lived in almost Oriental seclusion, and it was for the purpose of abolishing this custom that Peter established his famous 'Assemblies'.

'Where have you been, you clown?' asked the host.

'I've been dressing up, my dear man, for our welcome guests, for this holy day, by order of the Emperor, by command of my master, in the German fashion, for good people all to laugh at.'

There was a burst of merriment at these words, and the fool took her place behind her master's chair.

'Our fool talks nonsense enough but sometimes she speaks the truth,' remarked Tatiana Afanassyevna, the host's eldest sister, whom he held in great respect. 'The fashions today are indeed enough to make good people laugh. But since you, gentlemen, have shaved off your beards[1] and put on skimpy jackets it is idle to talk about women's clothes; but really it is a pity about the *sarafan*, the maiden's ribbons and the woman's head-dress! Why, just look at the fine ladies nowadays – 'tis enough to cause laughter and tears at one and the same time: hair frizzed like tow, greased and covered with French chalk; stomachs so tightly laced 'tis a wonder they do not break in two; petticoats distended with hoops, so that they have to enter a carriage sideways and bend to go through a door. They can neither stand nor sit nor draw breath – regular martyrs, the poor dears!'

'Ah, Tatiana Afanassyevna, my friend,' said Kirila Petrovich T—, a former governor of Ryazan, where he had acquired, not altogether by fair means, three thousand serfs and a young wife, 'I do not mind what my wife wears: she may dress as she pleases, provided she does not order new gowns every month and throw away her others which are practically new. In the old days the grandmother's *sarafan* formed part of the granddaughter's dowry, but now the gown that the mistress wears today, you will see the maid wearing tomorrow. What is to be done? It spells ruination for the Russian gentry, alas and alack!'

Saying these words, he glanced with a sigh at his wife,

---

1. In his eagerness to introduce the customs of Western Europe into his new Empire Peter the Great had decreed that all Russians (except the clergy) should shave off their beards and wear their hair short.

Maria Ilyinishna, who did not seem to care at all either for their praises of the past or their disparagement of the new. Other ladies shared her displeasure but said nothing, for in those days modesty was considered an indispensable attribute in a young woman.

'And who is to blame?' said Gavril Afanassyevich, filling a tankard with frothy *kvass*. 'Is it not our own fault? Young women play the fool, and we encourage them.'

'But what can we do, if we are not free in the matter?' retorted Kirila Petrovich. 'Many a husband would be only too glad to shut up his wife in the women's apartments at the top of the house, but they come with beating drums to summon her to the Assembly. The husband goes after the whip, but the wife is busy dressing. Ugh, those Assemblies! They're the Lord's punishment for our sins.'

His wife chafed with impatience; her tongue fairly itched to speak. At last she could contain herself no longer and turning to her husband she asked him with a sour smile what harm he saw in the Assemblies.

'Why, this harm,' replied her spouse heatedly, 'since they were instituted husbands no longer have the upper hand of their wives; wives have forgotten the words of the Apostle: "Wives, reverence your husbands." Their minds are taken up not with their domestic affairs but with new clothes; they do not think of how to please their husbands but how to attract the attention of flighty young officers. And is it seemly, Madam, for a Russian noblewoman to be in the same room with tobacco-smoking Germans and their maidservants? And dancing and talking with young men far into the night – it's unheard of! It might be all very well if they were relatives but with perfect strangers – !'

'If I were to speak my true mind – though 'twould be more prudent to hold my tongue – ' said Gavril Afanassyevich, frowning, 'I confess these Assemblies are not to my liking either – before you know where you are you may run up against someone who is drunk, or are made drunk yourself for the amusement of others. Then you have to keep your eyes open that some scapegrace isn't up to mischief with your daughter, and the young people are spoilt beyond words nowadays. At the last Assembly, for instance, young Korsakov made such a commotion over my Natasha that I positively blushed. Next day I see somebody driving right into my courtyard. I thought to myself, Who in the name of heaven is it – Prince Alexander Danilovich, perhaps? Not a bit of it – it was young Korsakov! He could not, if you please, stop his carriage at the gate and take the trouble to walk across to the steps – oh no! He flew in, scraped a leg and started to chatter away – the Lord preserve us! Yekimovna mimics him very amusingly: here, fool, act the foreign monkey for us.'

Yekimovna seized the lid off one of the dishes and, taking it under her arm as though it were a hat, began twisting, scraping and bowing in every direction, repeating 'Mossoo . . . mam'zelle . . . *Assemblée* . . . *pardon.*' Prolonged and general laughter again testified to the guests' appreciation.

'The living image of Korsakov,' said old Prince Lykov, wiping away tears of laughter when eventually quiet was restored. 'But why not admit it? He is not the first, nor will he be the last, to return to Holy Russia from foreign parts transformed into a buffoon. What do our children learn abroad? To scrape a leg, to chatter in goodness knows what gibberish, to treat their elders with disrespect, yes, and to run after other men's wives. Of all the young men who have been educated in foreign lands the Tsar's negro (the Lord forgive me!) is more of a man than any.'

'Dear me, prince!' said Tatiana Afanassyevna. 'I have seen him, seen him quite close . . . what a dreadful visage! I was quite scared.'

'Of course,' Gavril Afanassyevich remarked, 'he is a steady, decent man, not to be compared with that weathercock. . . . But who is it has just driven through the gate into the courtyard? Surely it cannot be that foreign monkey again? Why do you stand gaping there, you idiots?' he continued, turning to the servants. 'Run and stop him, and for the future . . .'

'Are you raving, dunderhead?' interrupted Yekimovna the

fool. 'Or perhaps you are blind? That's the Imperial sledge: the Tsar has come.'

Gavril Afanassyevich hastily got up from the table; everybody rushed to the windows, and, sure enough, they saw the Emperor walking up the steps, leaning on his orderly's shoulder. There was a general hurly-burly. The host rushed to meet Peter; the servants ran hither and thither as if they had gone crazy; the guests took fright – some even thinking how they might depart home as quickly as possible. Suddenly Peter's loud voice was heard on the other side of the door; the room was hushed, and the Tsar entered, accompanied by his host, overcome with joy.

'Good day, ladies and gentlemen!' said Peter gaily.

All made a low bow. The Tsar's sharp eyes sought out the host's daughter in the crowd, and he called her to him. Natalia Gavrilovna advanced boldly enough, though she was blushing not merely to the ears but to the shoulders too.

'You grow prettier every day,' the Emperor said, kissing her upon the head as was his habit. Then, turning to the guests, he added: 'Well, have I disturbed you? Were you dining? Pray be seated again; and give me some aniseed-vodka, Gavril Afanassyevich.'

The host rushed to his stately major-domo, snatched the tray from his hands and, filling a golden goblet, himself handed it with a bow to the Emperor. Peter drank the vodka, ate a dry biscuit, and once more invited the company to go on with their dinner. All resumed their former places except the dwarf and the companion, who did not dare to remain at a table graced by the Tsar's presence. Peter sat down next to Gavril Afanassyevich and asked for some soup. His orderly handed him a wooden spoon with ivory mountings, and a knife and fork with green bone handles, for Peter used no forks and spoons but his own. The dinner which a moment ago had rung with talk and laughter continued in silence and constraint.

The host, out of respect and delight, ate nothing; the guests also stood on ceremony and listened with reverent homage to the Emperor chatting in German to the captive Swede about the campaign of 1701. The fool Yekimovna, whom the Emperor addressed more than once, replied with a sort of timid aloofness, which, be it noted, was in no sense a mark of natural stupidity on her part. At last the dinner came to an end. The Tsar rose, and after him all the other guests.

'Gavril Afanassyevich,' he said to the host, 'I want a word with you in private.' And taking him by the arm he led him into the drawing-room, shutting the door behind them.

The guests stayed in the dining-room, talking in whispers about this unexpected visit and, afraid of being indiscreet, they soon one after another went home, without having thanked the host for his hospitality. His father-in-law, daughter and sister saw them very quietly to the door, and remained alone in the dining-room, waiting for the Emperor to come out.

HALF an hour later the door opened and Peter appeared. With a grave inclination of his head he acknowledged the salutations of Prince Lykov, Tatiana Afanassyevna and Natasha, and walked straight into the ante-room. Rzhevsky helped him on with his red sheepskin coat, accompanied him to the sledge, and on the steps thanked him once more for the honour he had shown him.

Peter drove away.

Returning to the dining-room, Gavril Afanassyevich seemed much preoccupied; he angrily ordered the servants to make haste and clear the table, sent Natasha to her room and saying to his sister and father-in-law that he wanted to talk to them led them into the bedroom where he usually rested after dinner. The old prince stretched himself upon the oak bedstead; Tatiana Afanassyevna settled in the old brocaded arm-chair, drawing up a footstool for her feet; Gavril Afanassyevich locked all the doors, sat down at the foot of the bed by Prince Lykov, and in a low voice began:

'It was not for nothing that the Emperor was graciously pleased to come and see me: guess what he wanted to talk to me about.'

'How can we tell, my dear brother?' said Tatiana Afanassyevna.

'Has the Tsar appointed you governor somewhere?' said his father-in-law. 'It is high time he did so. Or has he offered you an embassy? Why not? It is not only government secretaries who are sent to foreign sovereigns, but persons of quality as well.'

'No,' Rzhevsky answered with a frown. 'I am a man of the old school, and our services are not needed now, although it may be an Orthodox Russian gentleman is worth as much as these modern upstarts, pancake-sellers and heathens. But that is a different matter.'

'Then what did he talk to you about, all that time?' asked Tatiana Afanassyevna. 'Can it be some misfortune has befallen you? The Lord save and defend us!'

'It isn't exactly misfortune, but I confess I was rather taken aback.'

'But what is it, brother? What has happened?'

'It is about Natasha: the Tsar came to make a match for her.'

'Praise be!' said Tatiana Afanassyevna, crossing herself. 'The girl is of marriageable age, and like match-maker, like suitor. God give them love and concord: it is a great honour. For whom does the Tsar ask her hand?'

'H'm!' Gavril Afanassyevich cleared his throat. 'For whom? That's just it – for whom!'

'For whom, then?' repeated Prince Lykov, who was beginning to doze off.

'Guess,' said Gavril Afanassyevich.

'My dear brother,' replied the old lady, 'how can we guess? There are no end of marriageable young men at Court, any one of whom would be glad to take your Natasha to wife. Is it Dolgoruky?'

'No, it isn't Dolgoruky.'

'Just as well: far too high and mighty. Schein, is it? Or Troyekurov?'

'No, neither the one nor the other.'

'No, they are not to my taste either: flighty, they are, and too much infected with the German spirit. Well, is it Miloslavsky?'

'No, not he.'

'And a good thing, too: he is rich and stupid. Who is it then? Yeletsky? Lvov? Surely not Raguzinsky? No, I give it up. For whom, then, does the Tsar want Natasha?'

'For the negro Ibrahim.'

The old lady cried out, clasping her hands. Prince Lykov raised his head from the pillow and repeated in amazement:

'For the negro Ibrahim?'

'My dear brother!' said the old lady in a tearful voice. 'Do not be the ruin of your own dear child – do not deliver poor little Natasha into the clutches of that black devil!'

'But how am I to refuse the Emperor,' objected Gavril Afanassyevich, 'when he promises us his favour, me and all our family?'

'What!' cried the old prince, who was wide awake now. 'Marry Natasha, my granddaughter, to a bought negro slave?'

'He is not a commoner,' said Gavril Afanassyevich. 'He is the son of a negro sultan. The Turks captured him and sold him in Constantinople, and our ambassador rescued him and presented him to the Tsar. Ibrahim's elder brother came to Russia with a considerable ransom and . . .'

'My dear Gavril Afanassyevich!' his sister interrupted him. 'We have heard the fairy-tale about Prince Bova and Yeruslan Lazarevich! You had better tell us what answer you gave to the Emperor.'

'I said that he was our master, and that it was his servants' duty to obey him in all things.'

At that moment there was a noise behind the door. Gavril Afanassyevich went to open it but felt something in the way. He gave a hard push – the door opened and they saw Natasha lying unconscious on the blood-stained floor.

Her heart had swooned away when the Emperor shut himself up with her father; some presentiment whispered to her that the matter concerned her, and when Gavril Afanassyevich sent her away, saying that he must speak to her aunt and grandfather, she had not been able to resist the feminine instinct of curiosity and, stealing quietly through the inner rooms to the bedroom door, had not missed a single word of the whole awful conversation. When she heard her father's last sentence the poor girl fainted and in falling struck her head against one of the iron corners of the chest in which her dowry was kept.

Servants came running in haste; they picked Natasha up, carried her to her room and placed her on the bed. In a little while she regained consciousness and opened her eyes but did not recognize her father or her aunt. She broke out into a high fever; in her delirium she kept raving about the Tsar's negro and the wedding, and then suddenly cried out in a pitiful, piercing voice:

'Valerian, dear Valerian, my life! Save me: here they come, here they come. . . .'

Tatiana Afanassyevna glanced uneasily at her brother, who turned pale, bit his lip and silently left the room. He joined the old prince, who, unable to mount the stairs, had remained below.

'How is Natasha?' he asked.

'Very bad,' replied the distressed father. 'Worse than I thought: she is delirious and raves about Valerian.'

'Who is this Valerian?' asked the old man, alarmed. 'Can it be that orphan, that boy belonging to the Strelitz[1] man, who was brought up in your house?'

'The very same, woe is me!' replied Gavril Afanassyevich. 'His father saved my life during the mutiny of the Strelitz, and the devil put it into my head to take the accursed young wolf-cub into my home. When he was enrolled into the Service two years ago, at his own request, Natasha burst into tears as she said good-bye to him, while he stood as though turned to stone. It struck me as suspicious, and I spoke to my sister about it. But since that time Natasha has not mentioned him, and nothing further was heard of Valerian. I thought she had forgotten him, but it seems she hasn't. . . . But it is settled: she shall marry the negro.'

Prince Lykov did not gainsay him: that would have been useless; he went home. Tatiana Afanassyevna remained by Natasha's bedside; after sending for the doctor Gavril Afanassyevich locked himself in his room, and all was still and mournful in the house.

*

The unexpected offer to make a match for him surprised Ibrahim quite as much as it did Gavril Afanassyevich, if not

1. An ancient Russian body-guard abolished by Peter the Great.

more. This was how it happened. They were engaged on a piece of work together when Peter said to Ibrahim:

'I perceive, my friend, that you are low-spirited. Tell me frankly, what is wrong?'

Ibrahim assured the Tsar that he was content with his lot and wished for nothing better.

'Good!' said the Tsar. 'If you are dejected for no reason, I know how to cheer you up.'

When they had finished work Peter asked Ibrahim:

'Did you like the girl you danced the minuet with at the last Assembly?'

'She is very charming, sire, and seems to be a good and modest girl.'

'Then I will help you to know her better. Would you like to marry her?'

'I, sire? . . .'

'Listen, Ibrahim: you are a lonely man, having neither kith nor kin, a stranger to every one except myself. If I were to die today, what would become of you tomorrow, my poor African? You must get settled while there is still time, find support in new ties, become connected with the Russian nobility.'

'Sire, I am happy under your Majesty's protection and in the possession of your favour. God grant I may not outlive my Tsar and benefactor – that is all I wish. But even if I did think of marrying, would the girl and her relatives consent? My appearance . . .'

'Your appearance? What nonsense! There is nothing wrong with you. A young girl must obey her parents, and we shall see what old Gavril Afanassyevich will say when I come in person to ask his daughter's hand for you!'

With these words the Tsar ordered his sledge, and left Ibrahim plunged deep in thought.

'Get married!' thought the African. 'Why not? Can I be doomed to pass my life in solitude, knowing nothing of the greatest joys and most sacred duties of man, simply because I was born in the tropics? I may not hope to be loved:

a childish objection! As though one could believe in love! As though woman's frivolous heart were capable of love! I have renounced for ever such charming delusions, and chosen other more practical attractions instead. The Tsar is right: I must think of my future. Marriage with Rzhevsky's daughter will unite me with the proud Russian nobility, and I shall cease to be a stranger in my new fatherland. I will not expect love from my wife but be content with her fidelity; and I will win her affection by constant tenderness, trust and devotion.'

Ibrahim tried to go on with his work as usual but his mind was in a turmoil. He left his papers and went for a stroll along the banks of the Neva. Suddenly he heard Peter's voice; he looked round and saw the Tsar, who had dismissed his sledge and was hurrying after him with a beaming countenance.

'It is all settled, my friend!' Peter said, taking him by the arm. 'I have arranged the marriage for you. Go and call on your future father-in-law tomorrow, but see that you humour his family pride: leave your sledge at the gate and walk across the courtyard, talk to him about his services and his noble lineage – and he will dote on you. And now', he went on, shaking his cudgel, 'take me to that rascal Menshikov. I must see him about his latest tricks.'

Cordially thanking Peter for his fatherly solicitude, Ibrahim accompanied him as far as Prince Menshikov's magnificent palace, and then returned home.

6

A LITTLE lamp was burning dimly before the glass case containing the old family icons with their glittering gold and silver mountings. Its flickering flame cast a faint light over the curtained bed and a small table covered with labelled medicine-bottles. Near the stove a servant maid sat at her spinning-wheel, and the slight whirr of the spindle was the only sound that disturbed the stillness of the room.

'Who is there?' asked a weak voice.

The maid got up at once, went over to the bed and gently lifted the curtain.

'Will it soon be daylight?' Natasha asked.

'It's past midday,' the maid answered.

'Gracious me, why is it so dark, then?'

'The shutters are closed, miss.'

'Help me to dress, quick.'

'I can't, miss. Doctor's orders.'

'Am I ill then? Have I been ill long?'

'It's a fortnight now.'

'Is it possible? And it seems to me as if it were only yesterday that I went to bed. . . .'

Natasha was silent; she was trying to collect her scattered thoughts: something had happened to her, but what it was she could not exactly remember. The maid stood awaiting her orders. At that moment a dull noise was heard below.

'What is that?' asked the sick girl.

'They have finished dinner and are getting up from the table,' the maid answered. 'Your aunt will be here directly.'

Natasha seemed pleased at this; with a feeble gesture she dismissed the servant. The maid drew the bed-curtains and sat down again at her spinning-wheel. A few minutes later a head in a broad white cap with dark ribbons appeared in the doorway and a voice asked in an undertone:

'How is Natasha?'

'Good morning, auntie,' the invalid said quietly, and Tatiana Afanassyevna hastened to her.

'Our young lady has regained consciousness,' said the maid, carefully drawing an arm-chair to the side of the bed.

The old lady, with tears in her eyes, kissed her niece's pale, languid face, and sat down beside her. A German doctor in a black coat and learned wig came in after her and, feeling Natasha's pulse, declared first in Latin and then in Russian that she was out of danger. Asking for paper and ink, he wrote out a fresh prescription, and departed. The old lady rose, kissed Natasha once more and hurried downstairs to give the good news to Gavril Afanassyevich.

In the drawing-room the Tsar's negro in full uniform, with sword by his side and hat in his hand, sat respectfully talking to Gavril Afanassyevich. Korsakov, lolling on a soft couch, was listening absent-mindedly to their conversation and teasing a venerable borzoi dog. Becoming tired of this occupation, he went up to the mirror, a familiar recourse of the idle, and in it he saw Tatiana Afanassyevna, standing in the doorway and vainly trying to attract her brother's attention.

'You are wanted, Gavril Afanassyevich,' said Korsakov, turning to him and interrupting Ibrahim.

Gavril Afanassyevich immediately went out to his sister, shutting the door behind him.

'I marvel at your patience,' Korsakov said to Ibrahim. 'You have been listening for a whole hour to all that stuff and nonsense about the antiquity of the Lykov and Rzhevsky families, and have even added your own moral observations! In your place *j'aurais planté là* the old humbug and all his race, including Natalia Gavrilovna, who gives herself airs, pretending to be ill – *une petite santé!* Tell me honestly: surely you aren't in love with the little *mijaurée*?'

'No,' Ibrahim answered: 'I am marrying her not for love, of course, but for practical reasons, and then only if she feels no positive aversion for me.'

'Look here, Ibrahim,' said Korsakov, 'follow my advice

for once: I assure you, I have more sense than would appear. Give up this mad idea – don't marry! I do not think your betrothed has any particular liking for you. All sorts of things happen in this world, you know. Here am I – tolerably good-looking, of course, but it has happened to me to deceive husbands who were in no way inferior to me, I can assure you. And you yourself ... remember our Parisian friend, Count L—? There is no relying on a woman's fidelity: happy are those who do not bother about it. But you ... With your passionate, brooding and suspicious nature, with your flat nose, thick lips and fuzzy hair – for you to rush into the dangers of matrimony! ...'

'I thank you for your friendly advice,' Ibrahim interrupted him coldly, 'but you know the saying: "One does not have to sing lullabies to other people's children" ...'

'Take care, Ibrahim,' Korsakov answered, laughing, 'that you are not called upon some day to prove the truth of that saying in a literal sense.'

But the conversation in the next room was growing heated.

'You will kill her,' the old lady was saying. 'She cannot bear the sight of him.'

'But just consider,' her obstinate brother retorted, 'for a fortnight now he has been coming to the house as her betrothed and has not seen her once yet. He may end by thinking that her illness is mere pretence, and that we are simply seeking to delay matters so as to rid ourselves of him in some way or other. Besides, what will the Tsar say? He has sent three times as it is to inquire after Natasha's health. Protest as you please, but I do not intend to quarrel with him.'

'Merciful heavens, what will become of the poor child!' said Tatiana Afanassyevna. 'At least let me go and prepare her for the visit.'

Gavril Afanassyevich consented, and returned to the drawing-room.

'Thank God, she is out of danger!' he said to Ibrahim. 'Natalia is much better; were it not for leaving our dear guest alone here, I would take you upstairs to have a glimpse of your betrothed.'

Korsakov congratulated Gavril Afanassyevich on his daughter's recovery, begged him not to be uneasy on his account, assured him that he was obliged to go at once, and rushed into the hall, not allowing his host to see him off.

Meanwhile, Tatiana Afanassyevna hastened to prepare the invalid for her terrible visitor. Entering the room, she sat down breathless by the side of the bed and took Natasha's hand, but before she had time to utter a word the door opened. 'Who is it?' Natasha asked. The old lady turned faint. Gavril Afanassyevich drew back the curtain, looked coldly at the invalid and inquired how she was. Natasha tried to smile at him but could not. She was struck by her father's stern expression and a vague feeling of anxiety took possession of her. At that moment it seemed to her that someone was standing at the head of her bed. With an effort she raised her head and suddenly recognized the Tsar's negro. Then she remembered everything, and all the horror of her future presented itself before her. But exhausted nature received no perceptible shock. She let her head sink back on the pillow and closed her eyes ... her heart was beating painfully. Tatiana Afanassyevna signed to her brother that the invalid wanted to sleep, and they all crept quietly out of the room, except the maid-servant, who sat down to her spinning-wheel again.

The unhappy girl opened her eyes and, seeing no one by her bedside, called the maid and asked her to go and fetch the dwarf. But at that moment a little old figure, round as a ball, rolled up to her bed. Lastochka (that was the dwarf's name) had followed Gavril Afanassyevich and Ibrahim upstairs as fast as her short little legs could carry her, and, true to the inquisitiveness natural to the fair sex, had hidden behind the door. Seeing her, Natasha sent the maid away, and the dwarf sat down upon a stool by the bedside.

Never did so tiny a body house so much mental activity. She had a finger in every pie, knew all there was to know, and busied herself with everything. By her cunning and insinuating ways she had succeeded in gaining the affection of her masters and the detestation of the rest of the household, which she dominated completely. Gavril Afanassyevich listened to her tales, complaints and petty requests. Tatiana Afanassyevna was constantly asking her opinion and following her advice, while Natasha cherished a boundless affection for her and confided to her all the thoughts and emotions of her sixteen-year-old heart.

'Do you know, Lastochka,' she said, 'my father is marrying me to the negro.'

The dwarf gave a deep sigh and her wrinkled face became more wrinkled than ever.

'Is there no hope?' Natasha continued. 'Won't father have pity on me?'

The dwarf shook her head, on which she wore a little mob-cap.

'Won't grandfather or auntie intercede for me?'

'No, miss, while you were ill the negro succeeded in bewitching every one. The master raves about him, the prince can talk of no one else, and Tatiana Afanassyevna keeps saying: "'Tis a pity he's a negro, as a better suitor we could not wish for".'

'O God, O God!' moaned poor Natasha.

'Do not grieve, my pretty one,' said the dwarf, kissing her listless hand. 'Even if you are to marry the negro, you will still have your liberty. Things aren't what they used to be in the old days: husbands no longer keep their wives under lock and key. They say the negro is rich: your house will have everything you can think of, and you will be living in clover.'

'Poor Valerian!' said Natasha, but so softly that the dwarf could only guess at the words which she did not hear.

'That's just it, miss,' she said, mysteriously lowering her voice. 'If you had thought less about that boy you would not have talked about him when you were delirious, and your father would not have been angered.'

'What?' cried Natasha in alarm. 'I talked about Valerian? Father heard? He was angry?'

'That's just the trouble,' replied the dwarf. 'If you ask your father now not to marry you to the negro he will think it is because of Valerian. There is no help for it: submit to your father's will, and what is to be will be.'

Natasha made no answer. The thought that her heart's secret was known to her father disturbed her deeply. One hope alone remained: to die before the odious marriage. The idea comforted her. Weak and sad at heart, she resigned herself to her fate.

7

In Gavril Afanassyevich's house, to the right of the entrance-hall, was a small room with one tiny window. A plain bed covered with a blanket of baize stood in this room; in front of the bed there was a deal table on which a tallow candle was burning and some music lay open. An old blue uniform and an equally old three-cornered hat hung on the wall below a rough woodcut of Charles XII on horseback, secured with three nails. Sounds of a flute came from this humble habitation. Its solitary occupant, the captive dancing-master, in a night-cap and a cotton dressing-gown, sought to relieve the tedium of a winter evening by playing some old Swedish marches. Having devoted two whole hours to this exercise, the Swede took his flute to pieces, placed it in its case and began to undress. . . .

Dubrovsky

I

SEVERAL years ago Kiril Petrovich Troyekurov, a Russian gentleman of the old school, was living on one of his country estates. His wealth, distinguished birth and connexions gave him great influence in the province where his property was situated. His neighbours were ready to humour his smallest whim; the officials of the province trembled at his name. Kiril Petrovich accepted all these marks of servility as his rightful due. His house was always full of guests prepared to provide amusement for his lordship's leisure and join in his noisy and sometimes boisterous mirth. No one dared refuse his invitations or fail on certain special days to put in an appearance at Pokrovskoe to pay their respects to him. In his domestic habits Kiril Petrovich manifested all the vices of a man of no education. Completely spoiled by circumstances, he allowed full rein to every impulse of his passionate temperament, and to every caprice of his somewhat limited intellect. He was immensely hospitable, and in spite of a wonderful constitution two or three times a week he suffered from having eaten too much, and every evening was slightly the worse for liquor.

Very few of the serf-girls of his household escaped the amorous attentions of this elderly man of fifty. Moreover, in one of the wings of the house lived sixteen maid-servants engaged in fine sewing, as befitted their sex. The windows of this wing were protected by wooden bars, the doors were kept locked, and Kiril Petrovich held the keys. At appointed hours the young recluses went out for a walk in the garden under the surveillance of two old women. Every now and then Kiril

Petrovich would marry some of them off, and new-comers took their place. He treated his peasants and domestics in a harsh and arbitrary fashion, but this had no effect on their devotion to him: they were proud of their master's wealth and repute, and in their turn took many a liberty with their neighbours, trusting to his powerful protection.

Troyekurov's time was generally spent in driving about his extensive estates, in festive eating and drinking, and in playing practical jokes, of which he would invent a fresh one daily, the victim usually being some new acquaintance, though his old friends could not count on escape, with the exception of one, Andrei Gavrilovich Dubrovsky. This Dubrovsky, a retired lieutenant of the Guards, was his nearest neighbour, and the owner of seventy male serfs. Troyekurov, haughty in his dealings with people of the highest rank, respected Dubrovsky in spite of his humble standing. They had once served together in the same regiment, and Troyekurov knew from experience what a short-tempered and strong-willed man Dubrovsky was. The events of the year 1762 of glorious memory[1] parted them for a long time. Troyekurov, a relative of the Princess Dashkov,[2] received rapid promotion; Dubrovsky, losing most of his fortune, was obliged to resign from the Service and settle down on the one estate he had left. Hearing of this, Kiril Petrovich offered him his patronage; but Dubrovsky thanked him and remained poor and independent. Some years later Troyekurov, retired with the rank of general, came to his country seat; the friends met again and rejoiced to see each other. After that they met every day, and Kiril Petrovich, who had never deigned to visit anybody in his life, would call without ceremony at his old comrade's modest little home. They were of the same age, belonged to the same class by birth, had had the same upbringing, and were to some extent alike in their tastes and temperament. In certain respects their fates too had been similar: both had married for love, both had early become widowers, and both had been left

1. Assassination of Peter III and accession of his wife Catherine II.
2. One of Catherine's adherents in the revolution of 1762.

with an only child. Dubrovsky's son was away at school in Petersburg; Troyekurov's daughter was being brought up under her father's supervision, and Troyekurov often said to his friend: 'You know, Dubrovsky, if your Volodya turns out well I'll marry my Masha to him, even though he is as poor as a church mouse.' Dubrovsky would shake his head and as likely as not reply, 'No, my friend, my Volodya is no match for your daughter. A poor nobleman like him had much better marry a poor girl of good family, and be master in his own house, than become the henchman of some spoilt young woman.'

Everyone envied the harmony that reigned between the haughty Troyekurov and his poor neighbour, and marvelled at the audacity with which the latter, at Troyekurov's table, said just what he thought, not troubling whether his opinion was at variance with that of his host. Some would-be imitators tried to assert their independence too, but Troyekurov gave them such a lesson that they lost all inclination to repeat the experiment, leaving Dubrovsky the only exception to the general rule. Then an unexpected incident upset and altered everything.

One day in the early autumn Kiril Petrovich Troyekurov prepared to go hunting. The grooms and huntsmen were told to be ready by five o'clock next morning. An oven and kitchen-things and a tent were sent on beforehand to the place where Kiril Petrovich was to have dinner. He and his visitors went to look at the kennels, where over five hundred hounds lived in warmth and comfort, singing praises in their canine tongue to Kiril Petrovich's generosity. There was also a hospital for sick dogs under the care of Timoshka, who acted as staff-doctor, and a separate place where bitches could have their pups and suckle them. Kiril Petrovich was proud of his fine establishment, and never missed an opportunity to boast of it to his friends, each of whom had inspected it at least twenty times before. He walked through the kennels surrounded by his guests and accompanied by Timoshka and the head huntsman, inquiring after any of the hounds who were ill; giving some reprimand, more or less harsh and deserved; and calling a few of the hounds to him by name and speaking to them caressingly. His guests felt obliged to go into raptures over Kiril Petrovich's kennels; Dubrovsky alone said nothing and frowned. He was a passionate sportsman, but he could only afford to keep a couple of hounds and a borzoi bitch, and could not help feeling a measure of envy at the sight of this magnificent establishment.

'What are you frowning at, my dear fellow?' Kiril Petrovich asked him. 'Don't you like my kennels?'

'Yes,' replied Dubrovsky abruptly, 'the kennels are wonderful, but I doubt whether your servants live as well as your dogs.'

One of the kennel-men took offence.

'We have nothing to complain of, thanks be to God and our master,' he said, 'but if the truth were known there's a certain noble gentleman who might well exchange his manorhouse for any one of these kennels: he would be warmer here and better fed.'

Kiril Petrovich burst into a roar of laughter at his serf's insolence, and his guests followed suit, although they felt that the quip might equally apply to them. Dubrovsky turned pale and was silent. Just then some new-born puppies were brought up to Kiril Petrovich in a basket; he looked them over, chose two out of the litter and ordered the rest to be drowned. In the meantime Dubrovsky disappeared, no one noticing him go.

Back from the kennels with his guests, Kiril Petrovich sat down to supper, and it was only now that he missed Dubrovsky. The servants informed him that Dubrovsky had gone home. Troyekurov immediately instructed someone to fetch him back without fail. He never went hunting without Dubrovsky, who was a fine connoisseur of a dog's points and an infallible arbiter in all possible disputes connected with sport. The servant dispatched after him returned while they were still at table and reported to his master that Dubrovsky had refused to listen and would not come. Kiril Petrovich, heated as usual with home-made brandy, lost his temper and sent the same servant a second time to tell Dubrovsky that unless he came at once to spend the night at Pokrovskoe he, Troyekurov, would have nothing more to do with him. The servant galloped off again. Kiril Petrovich rose from the table, dismissed his visitors and went to bed.

The first thing he asked next day was, 'Is Dubrovsky here?' He was handed a letter folded in the shape of a triangle. Kiril Petrovich commanded his secretary to read it aloud, and heard the following:

'My dear sir,

I have no intention of returning to Pokrovskoe until you send your huntsman Paramoshka to me with an apology; and it will be for me to punish or forgive him as I see fit. I do not intend to put up with sallies from your serfs, or from yourself either for that matter: I am a gentleman of ancient lineage, not a buffoon.

I remain,
Your obedient servant,
Andrei Dubrovsky'

According to our present-day ideas of etiquette such a letter would be most unseemly. Kiril Petrovich, however, was angered not by its peculiar style and nature, but merely by its substance.

'What!' he shouted, springing barefoot out of bed. 'Send my servants to him with an apology! For him to punish or forgive as he sees fit! What on earth has got into his head? He can't know who he is dealing with! I'll teach him a lesson! I'll make him smart! He shall find out what it is to come up against Troyekurov!'

Nevertheless Kiril Petrovich dressed and set out for the hunt with all his customary splendour. But the shoot was not a success: they only saw one hare the whole day, and it escaped. Dinner in the fields under the tent was no more successful – at least, it was not to the fancy of Kiril Petrovich, who struck the cook, quarrelled with his guests, and on the way home purposely rode with all his party across Dubrovsky's fields.

2

SEVERAL days passed, and the animosity between the two neighbours persisted. Dubrovsky went no more to Pokrovskoe, and Kiril Petrovich, who missed him, vented his spleen by making the most offensive remarks which, thanks to the zeal of the local gentry, reached Dubrovsky's ears improved and supplemented. A fresh incident destroyed the last hope of a reconciliation.

One day Dubrovsky was going the round of his little estate; as he neared the birch copse he heard the blows of an axe and, a minute later, the crash of a falling tree. Hastening to the spot, he came on some of Troyekurov's peasants calmly stealing his wood. Seeing him, they took to flight. Dubrovsky and his coachman caught two of them and, tying their arms, brought them home, at the same time capturing three of the enemy's horses. Dubrovsky was exceedingly angry: hitherto Troyekurov's serfs, notorious rascals, had never dared to get up to their tricks on his estate, aware of his friendship with their master. Dubrovsky now perceived that they were taking advantage of the rupture between him and his neighbour, and, contrary to all the conventions of war, he decided to punish his prisoners with the twigs they had collected for themselves in his copse, and to put the horses to work in his fields along with his own.

News of these events reached Kiril Petrovich the same day. He was beside himself with fury and at first wanted to attack Kistenyovka (as his neighbour's village was called) with all his serfs, and, razing it to the ground, besiege the owner in his very house. Such exploits were nothing out of the way to him; but soon his thoughts took another direction. Pacing up and down the drawing-room with heavy steps, he happened to glance out of the window and see a troika stop at the gates. A little man in a leather travelling-cap and a frieze coat stepped out of the trap and proceeded towards the steward's lodge. Troyekurov recognized Shabashkin, the assessor of the District Court, and sent for him. In a minute Shabashkin was standing before Kiril Petrovich, bowing repeatedly and respectfully waiting to hear what he wanted.

'Good day to you ... what is your name now?' said Troyekurov. 'What are you here for?'

'I was on my way to town, your excellency,' Shabashkin answered, 'and calling at Ivan Demyanov's to see if there were any orders from your excellency.'

'You have come at the right moment. ... What is your name now? I want you. Have a glass of vodka and listen.'

Such a friendly reception pleasantly surprised the assessor. He declined the vodka and listened to Kiril Petrovich with every mark of attention.

'I have a neighbour,' said Troyekurov, 'a petty landowner, an impudent fellow, and I want to take his estate from him. ... What is your view about that?'

'Your excellency, are there any documents or ...'

'Nonsense, my good man, what do you want with documents? The law deals with documents. The point is to take away his estate without regard to law and documents. Wait a minute, though! That estate did belong to us at one time. It was bought from a certain Spitsyn and sold afterwards to Dubrovsky's father. Can't you hang something on that?'

'It's difficult, your excellency; probably the sale was in order.'

'Think, my good man. Try your utmost.'

'If, for example, your excellency could somehow obtain from your neighbour the deeds in virtue of which he holds possession of his estate, then, of course ...'

'Yes, I know, but the trouble is, all his papers were burnt at the time of the fire.'

'What, your excellency? His papers were burnt? Nothing could be better. In that case you have simply to take proceedings according to the law and without the slightest doubt everything can be arranged to your complete satisfaction.'

'You think so? Well, mind then, I rely upon your zeal, and you can rest assured of my gratitude.'

Shabashkin, bowing almost to the ground, took his departure, and that very day began to devote all his energies to the business entrusted to him. Thanks to his dispatch, exactly a fortnight later Dubrovsky received a request from the authorities to furnish forthwith the requisite answer to a petition filed by His Excellency General Troyekurov, alleging that Dubrovsky had no right to the ownership of the village of Kistenyovka.

Dumbfounded by this startling inquiry, Andrei Gavrilovich at once wrote a somewhat rude reply, saying that the village of Kistenyovka had become his on the death of his father, that he held it by right of inheritance, that it was none of Troyekurov's business and that all adventitious pretensions to his property were a fraud and a swindle.

This letter produced an exceedingly agreeable impression on the mind of Shabashkin: he saw, in the first place, that Dubrovsky had very little knowledge of legal business; and, in the second, that it would not be difficult to manoeuvre so incautious and hot-tempered a man into a highly disadvantageous position.

When Andrei Gavrilovich considered the inquiry he had received more coolly he realized that it ought to be answered in greater detail. He wrote out a fairly pertinent statement, but this subsequently proved also to be inadequate.

The business dragged on. Convinced of the righteousness of his case, Andrei Gavrilovich troubled himself very little about the matter: he had neither the inclination nor the means to scatter money about on bribes, and, though he was the first to deride the mercenary consciences of the bureaucratic fraternity, it never occurred to him that he might become the victim of a legal swindle. Troyekurov, for his part, gave equally little thought to winning the case he had set in motion: Shabashkin was acting for him, using his name, threatening and bribing the judges, and quoted and interpreted the ordinances in the most distorted manner possible. At last, on the ninth day of February in the year 18—, Dubrovsky received a summons to appear before the District Court to hear the Court's judgment on the matter of the property disputed between himself, Lieutenant Dubrovsky, and General-in-chief Troyekurov, and to affirm his signature in agreement or disagreement thereto. That day Dubrovsky set out for the town. On the road he was overtaken by Troyekurov; they exchanged haughty glances, and Dubrovsky observed a malicious smile on his adversary's face.

Arriving in town, Dubrovsky put up at the house of a merchant of his acquaintance, and the following morning went to the District Court. Nobody paid any attention to him. Immediately after him Troyekurov appeared: the clerks stood up, putting their quills behind their ears; the lawyers met him with profound servility, and brought an arm-chair for him in consideration for his rank, his years and his corpulence. He sat down; Dubrovsky stood leaning against the wall. A deep silence ensued, and the secretary began in a ringing voice to read the Court's ruling. We quote it in full, believing that everybody will be gratified to learn of one of the methods whereby in Russia we can be deprived of an estate to which we have incontestable rights.[1]

'On the tenth day of February of the year 18— the District Court sitting in the matter of the wrongful possession by Guards-Lieutenant Andrei Dubrovsky, son of Gavril Dubrovsky, of the estate and property belonging to General-in-chief Kiril Troyekurov, son of Piotr Troyekurov, comprising in the province of —— the village of Kistenyovka, — male serfs, together with the land and meadows and appurtenances, in all — acres. Concerning which matter it appears [that] the aforesaid General-in-chief Troyekurov on the ninth day of —— of last year 18— petitioned this Court to hold

1. There follows the complete transcript of a lawsuit in the province of Tambov which dragged on from 1826 to 1832, until finally the Kozlov District Court by an act of glaring injustice deprived a poor landowner of his property in favour of a rich one. Pushkin merely changed the names of the principals in the case to Dubrovsky and Troyekurov and, foreseeing trouble otherwise with the censor, removed the case from contemporary times to the not very distant past.

that his late father, Collegiate-Assessor and Knight Piotr son of Yefim Troyekurov on the fourteenth day of August in the year 17—, at that time holding the office of Provincial Secretary in the Regional Administration of ——, did purchase from Clerk-in-Chancery Fadei Spitsyn, son of Yegor Spitsyn, the property comprising in the neighbourhood of —— the above-mentioned village of Kistenyovka, which village at that time according to the census was styled Kistenyov, having in all according to the fourth census — male serfs with all their peasant holdings, the domain, with the plough- and other land, the woods, the hay-meadows, the fishing in the river known as the Kistenyovka, and with all the appurtenances belonging to the said estate and with the timber manorial house, and in short everything without exception which came to him by inheritance from his father Cossack-Sergeant of the nobility Yegor son of Terenty Spitsyn, and was held by him, not excepting a single serf, or a single parcel of land, at the cost of 2500 roubles, concerning which the deed of purchase was completed on the same day in the chambers of the Court and Tribunal of ——, and his father on that twenty-sixth day of August was let into possession through the rural police-court of —— and a deed of seisin executed. And lastly on the sixth day of September in the year 17— his father by the will of God expired, and during this time he the plaintiff, General-in-chief Troyekurov, at a very early age from the year 17— was serving in the Army and for the most part was campaigning in foreign lands for which reason he was not in a position to receive intelligence alike of the decease of his father and of the estate bequeathed to him. Now however upon his final retirement from the Service and his return to the estate of his father, comprising in the provinces of —— in the districts of —— various villages having in all 3000 serfs, out of this property he finds the afore-mentioned Guards-Lieutenant Andrei Dubrovsky without any legal or other title in possession of the above-listed number of serfs (numbering according to the —— census in that village — serfs) with the land and all appurtenances. Wherefore, presenting together with his petition the original deed of purchase given to his father by the seller Spitsyn, he requests that the afore-mentioned estate be removed from the wrongful possession of Dubrovsky and placed as it should be at the full disposal of himself Troyekurov. And for the said unlawful appropriation and the revenues enjoyed therefrom, following upon proper investigation of these latter, he requests that the due penalty be exacted from him, Dubrovsky, and satisfaction rendered to himself, Troyekurov.

'Investigations made by the —— District Court following upon this said petition revealed: that the afore-mentioned present person in actual possession of the disputed estate, Guards-Lieutenant Dubrovsky, gave the local Nobiliary Assessor the explanation that the estate now in his possession, consisting of the aforesaid village of Kistenyovka, having — serfs, with the land and appurtenances, was inherited by him on the death of his father, Sub-lieutenant in the Artillery Gavril Dubrovsky, son of Evgraf Dubrovsky, who acquired it by purchase from the father of the plaintiff, former Provincial Secretary and afterwards Collegiate-Assessor Troye-kurov, by procuration given by him on the thirtieth day of August in the year 17—, witnessed in the District Court of ——, to Titular-Councillor Grigory Sobolev, son of Vassily Sobolev, according to which [procuration] there must be in existence a deed of purchase of this estate from him to his father, since in it it is precisely stated. that he, Troyekurov, sold all the property acquired by him by purchase from Clerk-in-Chancery Spitsyn, with — serfs and land, to his, Dubrovsky's, father, and that the money agreed on by treaty, that is, 3200 roubles, was received in full from his father without any reduction and he requested the said Sobolev to deliver to his father the statutory deed of purchase. The same procuration moreover stipulated that in consideration of the payment of the whole sum his father should as rightful owner occupy and possess the estate purchased by him and thenceforth dispose of it pending the completion of the said deed, and that from then on neither the seller Troyekurov nor any other person or persons should inter-fere with the property. But when exactly and in which Court this deed of purchase from the said Sobolev was given to his father he, Andrei Dubrovsky, did not know, for at that time he was in his extreme youth, and after the death of his father he could not find any such deed, and supposed that it had been destroyed with other papers and property when the house was burned down in the year 17—, of which happening the local inhabitants knew well. And that since the day of the sale by Troyekurov or the issue to Sobolev of the procuration, to wit, since the year 17—, and after the death of his father in the year 17— and up to the present time they the Dubrovskys had held undisputed possession of the said estate, to all of which the neighbouring residents – fifty-two persons in all – are witness, having on oath testified that in fact, as they well remember, the said disputed estate was first possessed and enjoyed by the said Dubrovskys some seventy years back without any misdoubt whatsoever from any quarter whatsoever but by virtue of some title-deed or procuration of which they are uncertain. Whether the previous purchaser of the estate in question, the former Provincial Secretary Piotr Troyekurov, ever took possession of it [the estate in question] they do not remember. But the Dubrovsky house some thirty years prior to this present time was burned down in a fire which occurred during the night on their estate, and it was generally reckoned that the said disputed estate enjoyed an average annual revenue from that time of 2000 roubles.

'On the other hand General-in-chief Kiril Troyekurov, son of Piotr Troyekurov, on the third day of January of the present year petitioned this Court to find that although the said Guards-Lieutenant Andrei Dubrovsky had put forward in connexion with this affair the procuration issued by his deceased father Gavril Dubrovsky to Titular-Councillor Sobolev referring to the estate sold to him he had not put forward concerning the same either any genuine deed of sale or even any clear evidence of the existence at any time of any such deed as required by the general regulations in Section 19 of the Statute of the twenty-ninth day of November of the year 1752. Wherefore the procuration itself, now, following on the death of its donor, his father, by the provisions of the Statute of the —th day of May of the year 1818 is wholly invalid. Moreover [the Statute requires] that possession of estates in dispute be restored – with the number of serfs enumerated in the purchase deeds, not the number actually found on inspection.

'Concerning this said estate belonging to his father the deeds have been put forward by him in proof of his title, according to which deeds it follows, by reason of the said Statute, that the estate be removed from the wrongful possession of the said Dubrovsky and given back to him as the rightful owner thereof by inheritance. And the said landowner Dubrovsky having possession of property not belonging to him and to which he had no title whatsoever, and having wrongfully enjoyed revenues from the said estate not belonging to him, after calculation of the amount due . . . be required to give to him Troyekurov satisfaction. After consideration of the said matter and of the provisions of the relevant Statutes the —— District Court decrees that:

'Whereas it appears that General-in-chief Kiril Troyekurov, son of Piotr Troyekurov, concerning the said disputed estate now in possession of Guards-Lieutenant Andrei Dubrovsky, son of Gavril

Dubrovsky, comprising the village of Kistenyovka, having, according to the current — census — male serfs, together with land and appurtenances, has put forward a genuine deed of sale of the same to his late father, Provincial Secretary, afterwards Collegiate-Assessor, in the year 17— by Clerk-in-Chancery Fadei Spitsyn of the nobility. And Whereas the said purchaser, as appears from the signature on the said title deed, was in the same year introduced into possession by the District Court of ——, such estate having been already bequeathed to him. And Whereas in denial of this Guards-Lieutenant Andrei Dubrovsky has put forward a deed of procuration delivered by the deceased purchaser Troyekurov to Titular-Councillor Sobolev for the completion of the deed of purchase in the name of his father, Dubrovsky. And Whereas the —— Statute not only prohibits the confirmation by such means of ownership of such real estate, but also prohibits any provisional entering into possession [thereof]. And Whereas the deed of procuration itself is completely annulled by the death of the donor – And Whereas in addition to this Dubrovsky since the beginning of the inquiry, that is, from the year 18— has to this day put forward no clear evidence that any title in respect of the said disputed estate was ever at any time or place actually completed in accordance with the deed of procuration – Now therefore this Court decrees that the said estate, with — serfs, land and appurtenances, wherever they may now be, be confirmed in favour of General-in-chief Troyekurov in accordance with the deed of procuration by a deed of purchase; be removed from the disposal of the said Guards-Lieutenant Dubrovsky and placed in the possession of the rightful owner, Troyekurov, and seisin granted to him as by right of inheritance, and [the said estate] be registered at the District Court of ——. And Whereas General-in-chief Troyekurov further requests recovery from Guards-Lieutenant Dubrovsky in respect of his unlawful possession of the estate inherited by him and his enjoyment of the revenues therefrom. And Whereas this said estate, according to the testimony of the old inhabitants, was held for a period of years in undisputed and undisturbed possession by the Dubrovskys. And Whereas it does not appear that Troyekurov has until the present time put forward any petition concerning such unlawful possession by the Dubrovskys of the said estate, And Whereas the law requires that

'In the case where a man shall sow the ground of another or fence round his land, and humble petition be made concerning his unlawful seizure,

*and the matter be thoroughly investigated, then the said land shall be
restored to the rightful owner together with the emplements and the fencing
and the outbuildings thereof,*

'Now therefore this Court decrees in the claim made against
Guards-Lieutenant Dubrovsky that seisin be given to General-in-
chief Troyekurov and the estate returned into his possession in its
entirety, without reservation or exception. And that upon his
taking possession the whole be returned to him without reservation
or exception, General-in-chief Troyekurov having the right to
petition the Court in case of need and to put in such further
legitimate evidence as he may possess. The Court having notified
plaintiff and defendant alike that its ruling is based on legal principles, and is in accordance with legal form, summons both the
one and the other to attend for the hearing of this ruling and to
sign their satisfaction or dissatisfaction through the appropriate
channels.

'This ruling has been signed by all present at this Court.'

The secretary finished. The assessor stood up and with a
low bow turned to Troyekurov, inviting him to sign the
paper which he held out. The triumphant Troyekurov, taking
the pen from him, wrote beneath the decision of the Court
that he was completely satisfied with it.

It was Dubrovsky's turn. The secretary handed him the
document, but Dubrovsky stood stock-still with bent head.
The secretary repeated his invitation 'to subscribe his full
and complete satisfaction, or his thorough dissatisfaction, if,
contrary to expectation, his conscience told him that his case
was a righteous one, and he intended within the appointed
time to appeal against the decision of the Court'.

Dubrovsky said nothing. . . . Suddenly he raised his head,
his eyes flashed, he stamped his foot, pushed the secretary
with such force that the man fell, seized the inkstand and
hurled it at the assessor, shouting in a wild voice: 'Have you
no respect for the church of God! Out of my sight, you
offspring of Ham!' Then, turning to Kiril Petrovich, 'It is
unheard of, your excellency! Huntsmen bring their hounds
into the church of God! Dogs run about in church! I'll
teach you!'

Everybody was appalled. The ushers came in on hearing the uproar and with difficulty managed to overpower him. He was taken out and put on his sledge. Troyekurov walked out after him, accompanied by all the officials. Dubrovsky's sudden madness was a great shock to him and it spoiled his triumph. The justices, who had counted upon his gratitude, were not honoured with one single affable word. He went straight back to Pokrovskoe, smitten with secret remorse and not altogether enjoying the gratification of his hatred. Dubrovsky, meanwhile, lay on a bed. The district doctor (luckily not entirely an ignoramus) bled him and applied leeches, and blistered him with Spanish flies. Towards evening he began to feel better, and the next day he was taken to Kistenyovka, which scarcely belonged to him any more.

3

SOME time elapsed but poor Dubrovsky was still far from
well. True, there were no more attacks of madness but his
strength was visibly failing. He forgot his former occupations,
rarely left his room and for days together sat lost in thought.
Yegorovna, a kind-hearted old woman who had once nursed
his son, now tended him. She cared for him as though he
were a child, reminded him when it was time to eat or sleep,
fed him and even put him to bed. Dubrovsky obeyed her and
had nothing to do with any one else. He was in no state to
think about his affairs or to look after his property, and
Yegorovna decided that she must lay the whole situation
before young Dubrovsky, who was then serving in one of the
regiments of Foot Guards stationed in Petersburg. And so,
tearing a leaf from an account-book, she dictated a letter
to Hariton the cook, who was the only person in Kistenyovka
who could read and write, and sent it into town that same
day to be posted.

But it is time for the reader to become acquainted with the
real hero of our story.

Vladimir Dubrovsky had been brought up in the Cadet
Corps,[1] and had joined the Guards with the rank of cornet.
His father spared nothing to keep him as befitted his position,
and the young man received more money from home than
he had any right to expect. Irresponsible and ambitious, he
indulged in extravagant habits, played cards, ran into debt
and troubled himself very little about the future. Occasionally
the thought crossed his mind that sooner or later he would be
obliged to take to himself a rich bride.

One evening, while several fellow officers were sprawling
about on the couches in his rooms and smoking his pipes
with amber mouth-pieces, Grisha his valet handed him a

1. Military academy reserved for the sons of the aristocracy.

letter. The seal and the handwriting of the address at once attracted the young man's attention. He opened it hastily and read as follows:

Our dear Master Vladimir Andreyevich,

I, your old nurse, venture to inform you of the health of your papa. He is very poorly, and sometimes wanders in his talk, and sits all day long like a foolish child – but life and death are in the hands of God. Come home to us, my dearie, we will send the horses to meet you at Pesotchnoe. They tell us the District Court is coming to hand us over to Kiril Petrovich Troyekurov, because they say we belong to him – but we have always belonged to you and have always heard so ever since we can remember. Living in Petersburg you could tell our Father the Tsar about this, and he would not let us be wronged. It has been raining here these two weeks now, and Rodya the shepherd died on St Nicolas day. I send a mother's blessing to Grisha. Does he serve you well? I remain yours truly, your faithful servant

Nurse Arina Yegorovna Buzireva.

Vladimir Dubrovsky read these somewhat confused lines several times with profound emotion. He had lost his mother in early childhood and hardly knew his father, having been taken to Petersburg at the age of eight. Nevertheless, he felt a romantic attachment to him and an affection for family life all the stronger for having had so little opportunity to enjoy its peaceful pleasures.

The thought of losing his father distressed him acutely, and the condition of the sick man, which he guessed from his old nurse's letter, horrified him. He pictured his father left helpless in an out-of-the-way village in the hands of a foolish old woman and the other servants, threatened with some calamity and gradually sinking in physical and mental agony. Vladimir reproached himself with criminal neglect. Although it was months since he had had news of his father he had not thought of inquiring after him, imagining he was away somewhere or busy about the estate. That same evening he took steps to obtain leave of absence, and two days later set out in the stage coach, accompanied by his faithful Grisha.

Vladimir Andreyevich neared the post-station where he had to turn off for Kistenyovka. His heart was full of sad forebodings; he feared that he would no longer find his father alive. His imagination conjured up visions of the melancholy existence awaiting him in the country: a desolate village, no neighbours, poverty and business responsibilities to which he was an utter stranger. Arriving at the station, he went to the post-master and asked if there were any horses for hire. When the post-master heard where he was bound for he said that horses from Kistenyovka had been waiting for him for the last four days. Presently Anton, the old coachman who used to look after his pony and take him round the stables, came up. Anton's eyes filled with tears when he saw Vladimir. Bowing very low, he told him that the old master was still alive, and then ran to harness the horses. Vladimir refused the offer of something to eat, anxious to be on the road. Anton drove him along cart-tracks across country, and they started to talk.

'Tell me, Anton, what is this lawsuit between my father and Troyekurov?'

'The Lord only knows, Vladimir Andreyevich, sir. Our master, they say, fell out with Kiril Petrovich, and that one went to law about it, though often enough he takes the law into his own hands. 'Tis not for us servants to try to understand our betters but really and truly a mistake it was for your father to cross Kiril Petrovich: you might just as well go knocking your head against a brick wall.'

'It seems, then, that this Kiril Petrovich Troyekurov can do just what he likes with you all?'

'That's the way of it, sir: they say he don't care a fig for the Governor, and the police-captain is at his beck and call; the gentry dance attendance on him. "Set down a trough, and the pigs will come," as the saying is.'

'Is it true that he wants to take our estate from us?'

'That's what we have heard, sir. T'other day the sacristan from Pokrovskoe said at the christening in our foreman's house: "Your good times are over! Kiril Petrovich is taking you in hand!" And Nikita the blacksmith answered him: "Come now, Savelish, don't go grieving our host and upsetting the guests. Kiril Petrovich is what he is, and Andrei Gavrilovich is what he is, and all of us are God's people and the Tsar's." But you can't shut other people's mouths.'

'So you don't want to go to Troyekurov?'

'Go to Kiril Petrovich? God save us and preserve us! His own serfs fare bad enough, and if he got his hands on other people's he'd not only flay the skin off their backs but rip the flesh away too. No, God grant long life to Andrei Gavrilovich; and if he is taken we don't want no master but you, our benefactor. Don't you be giving us up, and we will stay by you.'

With these words Anton flourished his whip, gave the reins a shake, and the horses broke into a brisk trot.

Touched by the devotion of the old coachman, Dubrovsky fell silent and settled down to his own reflections. An hour or more passed; suddenly Grisha roused him by exclaiming: 'There's Pokrovskoe!' Dubrovsky looked up. They were driving along the bank of a broad lake, from which a little river flowed, winding among the hills and disappearing in the distance. On one of the hills, above the thick verdure of the trees, rose the green roof and the belvedere of a huge stone house. On another hill there was a church with five cupolas and an ancient belfry, and round about were peasant huts with their wells and kitchen-gardens. Dubrovsky recognized the place: he remembered that he used to play on that very hill with little Masha Troyekurov, who was two years younger than he and who even then gave promise of turning into a beauty. He wanted to ask Anton about her, but a sort of shyness restrained him.

As they were driving past the manor-house he had a glimpse of a white frock flitting between the trees in the garden. At that moment Anton whipped up the horses and, impelled by the vanity which possesses town cab-drivers and country coachmen alike, dashed headlong across the bridge and past the garden. Leaving the village behind, they drove up a hill, and Vladimir caught sight of the copse of birch-trees and, in an open space to the left, the little grey house with its red roof. His heart began to beat – Kistenyovka and his father's shabby dwelling lay before him.

Ten minutes later he was driving into the courtyard. He looked about him with indescribable emotion: it was twelve years since he had seen his birthplace. The birch-saplings which had then only just been planted along the fence had grown into tall spreading trees. The courtyard, formerly adorned with three symmetrical flower-beds with a wide carefully swept path between them, was now a meadow with long grass where a tethered horse was grazing. The dogs began to bark but, recognizing Anton, subsided and wagged their shaggy tails. The servants came rushing out of their cottages to surround their young master with noisy manifestations of joy. He had difficulty in squeezing through the eager crowd to run up the dilapidated steps. Yegorovna met him in the porch and threw herself weeping on his neck.

'Well, nurse, well!' he repeated, pressing the worthy old woman to his heart. 'And my father? Where is he? How is he?'

At that moment a tall old man in a dressing-gown and night-cap, pale and thin, came into the room, dragging one foot after the other.

'Where is my Vladimir?' he said in a weak voice, and Vladimir warmly embraced his father.

The joy proved too much for the invalid. He faltered, his legs gave way under him, and but for his son's support he would have fallen.

'Why did you get out of bed?' Yegorovna said to him. 'He can't stand on his feet and yet he had to be doing the same as other people and going where they do.'

The old man was carried back to his bedroom. He tried to talk to his son but his thoughts were confused and there was no coherence in what he said. He dropped into silence and dozed off. Vladimir was shocked by his condition. He had his things brought into his father's room and asked to be left alone with him. The servants obeyed and turned their attentions to Grisha, who was led away to the servants' hall, to be plied with food and overwhelmed with questions and greetings.

4

A coffin now lies on the table
Where once the board was festive and gay.[1]

A FEW days after his arrival young Dubrovsky would have
liked to find out how matters stood with regard to the estate,
but his father was not able to give him the necessary information, and Andrei Gavrilovich had no lawyer. Going through
the various papers, Vladimir found only the assessor's first
letter and the rough draft of his father's reply. This was not
enough to give him any clear idea of the case, and he decided
to await developments, trusting to the righteousness of his
father's cause.

Meanwhile Andrei Gavrilovich was sinking hourly.
Vladimir saw that the end was not far off, and he never left
the old man, who had become quite senile.

By now the time for lodging an appeal had expired and
nothing had been done about it. Kistenyovka belonged to
Troyekurov. Shabashkin came to him to present his respects
and congratulations, and to ask when his excellency intended
to take possession of his newly acquired property – and would
he do so in person or would he commission someone else
to act as his representative? Kiril Petrovich felt troubled. He
was not grasping by nature; his desire for revenge had carried
him too far; his conscience was uneasy. He knew the state
his adversary, the old comrade of his youth, was in, and his
victory brought no joy to his heart. He glared at Shabashkin,
seeking for some pretext to abuse him, but finding none
said angrily:

1. Lines from Derzhavin's ode *On the Death of Prince Meshchersky*,
written at Petersburgh in 1780. (In Russia when a person died the body
was lifted on to the table to lie in state until taken to church for the
funeral.)

'Be off! I have no time for you!'

Shabashkin saw that he was in a bad temper, bowed and hastened to withdraw. Left alone, Kiril Petrovich began pacing up and down the room whistling 'Thunder of victory, resound!',[1] always a sure sign with him of extreme mental disturbance.

At last he ordered a droshky,[2] put on a warm coat (it was the end of September), and drove out, himself taking the reins.

Soon he caught sight of Andrei Gavrilovich's house. His soul was full of conflicting emotions. Satisfied vengeance and love of power to a certain extent stifled his nobler feelings, but at last these latter prevailed. He resolved to effect a re-conciliation with his old neighbour, wipe out all traces of their quarrel and restore his property to him. Having eased his soul with these good intentions, Kiril Petrovich set off at a trot for his neighbour's house, and drove straight into the courtyard.

The sick man happened to be sitting at his bedroom window. He recognized Kiril Petrovich, and a dreadful look of agitation came into his face: a livid flush replaced his usual pallor, his eyes flashed and he uttered some unintelligible sounds. His son, who was in the room poring over account-books, raised his head and was alarmed at his condition. The sick man was pointing with his finger to the courtyard with an expression of rage and horror. At that moment Yegorovna's heavy steps were heard.

'Master, master!' she cried. 'Kiril Petrovich has come, Kiril Petrovich is at the door! Lord God!' she gasped. 'What is it? What is the matter with him?'

Andrei Gavrilovich had hastily gathered up the skirts of his dressing-gown, meaning to rise from his arm-chair. He half got to his feet – and then suddenly fell. His son rushed towards him; the old man lay unconscious, hardly breathing; he had had a stroke.

1. Opening line of a poem by Derzhavin, set to music by Kozlovsky, celebrating the taking of Ismail in 1791, during the Russo-Turkish war.
2. A low four-wheeled carriage.

'Quick, quick, send into the town for a doctor!' Vladimir shouted.

'Kiril Petrovich Troyekurov would like to see you,' announced a servant, coming into the room.

Vladimir cast him a fearful look.

'Tell Kiril Petrovich to take himself off before I have him turned out – now go!'

The man delightedly hurried away to execute his master's bidding. Yegorovna threw up her hands in despair.

'Dearie!' she shrieked. 'You'll be the ruin of us! Kiril Petrovich will eat us alive!'

'Quiet, nurse!' said Vladimir angrily. 'Make haste and send Anton for the doctor.'

Yegorovna went out. There was no one in the hall: all the servants had run to the courtyard to look at Kiril Petrovich. She came out on to the steps and heard Grisha deliver the young master's message. Kiril Petrovich listened, seated in the droshky; his face went black as night; he smiled haughtily, scowled menacingly at the assembled servants and drove slowly round the courtyard. He looked in at the window where Andrei Gavrilovich had been sitting a minute or two before, but he was no longer there. The old nurse stood on the steps, forgetful of her master's orders. The servants were noisily discussing what had just occurred. Suddenly Vladimir appeared in the midst of them and said abruptly: 'There is no need for a doctor – my father is dead!'

Confusion followed. The servants rushed into the old master's room. He was lying in the arm-chair where Vladimir had carried him; his right arm hung down to the floor, his head was bent forward upon his chest – there was no sign of life in the body, which, though not yet cold, was already disfigured by death. Yegorovna set up a wail. The other servants crowded round the corpse left to their care; they washed it, dressed it in a uniform made in 1797, and laid it out on the same table at which for so many years they had waited upon their master.

5

THE funeral took place three days later. The poor old man's body, wrapped in a shroud, lay in the coffin surrounded by lighted candles. The dining-room was crowded with serfs ready to follow the funeral procession. Vladimir and some of the men lifted the coffin. The priest walked in front, and after him his clerk, singing the burial prayers. The master of Kistenyovka crossed the threshold of his house for the last time. The coffin was carried through the copse – the church was on the other side of it. It was a bright, cold day; the autumn leaves were falling from the trees. Emerging from the wood, they saw before them the timber church and the churchyard shaded by the old lime-trees. The mortal remains of Vladimir's mother rested there, and there, beside her tomb, a new grave had been dug the day before. The church was packed with the Kistenyovka peasants come to render the last homage to their master. Young Dubrovsky stood by the ikonostasis; he did not weep or pray but the expression on his face was terrible. The sad ceremony came to an end. Vladimir was the first to give the farewell kiss to the dead; the manor serfs approached after him. The lid was brought and nailed on the coffin. The women wailed aloud, the men frequently wiped their eyes with their fists. Vladimir and the same three servants as before carried the coffin to the churchyard, accompanied by the whole village. The coffin was lowered into the ground; all who were present threw a handful of earth on to it; the grave was filled up, they bowed before it and went home. Vladimir walked away hastily and, leaving the others behind, disappeared into the Kistenyovka wood.

Yegorovna, in his name, invited the priest and the other clerics to the funeral dinner, saying that the young master would not be coming. Father Anissim, his wife Fedorovna and the clerk made their way to the house, discoursing with

Yegorovna upon the virtues of the deceased and the future that in all probability awaited his heir. (Troyekurov's visit and the reception given to him were already known to the whole neighbourhood, and the local politicians predicted serious consequences therefrom.)

'What will be, will be,' said the priest's wife, 'but I shall be sorry if Vladimir Andreyevich is not master here. He is a fine young fellow, there is no denying that.'

'But who else can be our master?' Yegorovna interrupted her. 'It is no good Kiril Petrovich getting into a temper – he has a brave one to deal with. My young falcon can stand up for himself, and please God his high-born friends will not forsake him. Kiril Petrovich is far too puffed up, that's what he is. He did slink away, though, with his tail between his legs, when my Grisha shouted to him: "Be off, you old cur! Get away from here."'

'Mercy on us, Yegorovna,' said the clerk. 'How ever could Grisha bring himself to say such things? I believe I'd as soon venture to lay a complaint against my lord bishop as make a wry face at Kiril Petrovich. The instant I set eyes on him I go all of a tremble. And my back bends of its own accord before I know where I am. . . .'

'Vanity of vanities!' said the priest. 'They will sing "May his memory live for ever!" when Kiril Petrovich dies just the same as they did today for Andrei Gavrilovich. The funeral may be grander, and more people be invited to the house afterwards, but it will be all one in the sight of God.'

'Oh, father, we wanted to invite all the neighbourhood but Vladimir Andreyevich wouldn't hear of it. It isn't that there's not enough to entertain people with . . . but what could we do? At all events, with only a few of you coming back you can eat to your heart's content.'

This kindly promise and the hope of finding a toothsome pie waiting for them caused the party to quicken their steps. They arrived safely back at the house, where the table was already laid and vodka served.

Meanwhile Vladimir advanced further into the depths of the

wood, hoping to tire himself out and thus deaden his sorrow. He walked on, not looking where he was going; branches caught and scratched him at every step, his feet continually sank into the bog – but he was oblivious. At last he reached a little glen surrounded on all sides by the forest; a brook wound silently among the trees half stripped of their leaves by the autumn. Vladimir stopped, sat down on the cold turf, and thoughts, each one gloomier than the last, oppressed his soul. . . . He was painfully aware of being alone in the world; terrible storm-clouds menaced the future. The quarrel with Troyekurov foreboded fresh misfortunes. His modest heritage might be taken from him, in which case he would be completely destitute. For a long while he sat in the same spot without moving, watching the gentle flow of the stream bearing away a few withered leaves, and it struck him as being very much like life: the analogy was so true, so homely. At last he realized that it was growing dusk; he got to his feet and began to look for the way back, but for a long time he wandered about the unfamiliar wood before stumbling upon the path which led straight to his courtyard gates.

The priest and his party were coming towards him. This was a bad omen.[1] Automatically he turned aside and hid behind the trees. They did not see him, and continued talking earnestly among themselves.

'Avoid evil and do good,' the priest was saying to his wife. 'There is no need for us to stay here. It does not concern us, however the business may end.'

The priest's wife made some reply but Vladimir could not hear what she said.

Approaching the house, he saw a number of people, peasants and house-serfs, crowding into the courtyard. From where he was he could hear unusual noise and a hubbub of voices. Two troikas waited by the coach-house. On the steps several unknown men in official uniforms seemed to be talking together.

'What does this mean?' he asked angrily of Anton, who

1. To meet a priest was considered a bad omen in Russia.

ran forward to meet him. 'Who are these people, and what do they want?'

'Oh, Vladimir Andreyevich, my dear,' the old man answered breathlessly, 'it's Court officials. They are giving us over to Troyekurov, they are taking us from your honour! ...'

Vladimir's head drooped; the serfs surrounded their luckless master.

'You are our lord and master,' they cried, kissing his hands. 'We don't want any master but you. We will die, but we will not leave you. Say the word, sir, and we'll settle them.'

Vladimir looked at them, and dark thoughts surged in his mind.

'Quiet,' he said. 'I will speak to the officers.'

'That's it – you speak to them, sir,' some of them shouted from the crowd. 'Put the wretches to shame!'

Vladimir went up to the officials. Shabashkin with his cap on his head stood, arms akimbo, staring arrogantly about him. The police-captain, a tall stout man of some fifty years of age, with a red face and a moustache, cleared his throat when he saw Dubrovsky, and pronounced in a hoarse voice:

'Thus I repeat what I have said to you already, by the decision of the District Court from this day forth you belong to Kiril Petrovich Troyekurov, who is here represented by Mr Shabashkin. Obey him in all things, whatever he may order you; and you, women, love and honour him, for he is very partial to you.'

At this witticism the police-captain burst into a laugh, and Shabashkin and the other officials followed suit. Vladimir boiled with indignation.

'Allow me to inquire, what does this mean?' he asked the jocular police-captain with affected composure.

'Why, it means this,' the resourceful official answered, 'that we have come to place Kiril Petrovich Troyekurov in possession of this estate, and to request certain others to take themselves off for good and all!'

'But you might, I should have thought, communicate with

me first, rather than with my peasants, and inform the owner that his estate no longer belongs to him. . . .'

'The former owner, Andrei, son of Gavril Dubrovsky, by the will of God is dead; but who are you?' said Shabashkin with an insolent stare. 'We do not know you, nor have we any wish to do so either.'

'Your honour, that's Vladimir Andreyevich, our young master,' a voice called out from the crowd.

'Who dared to open his mouth?' said the police-captain threateningly. 'What master? Who is this Vladimir Andreyevich? Kiril Petrovich Troyekurov is your master. . . . You hear that, you blockheads?'

'Nothing of the kind!' said the same voice.

'Why, this is defiance!' the police-captain shouted. 'Hey, elder, come here!'

The village elder stepped forward.

'Find out at once who it was that dared speak to me. I'll give him – '

The elder turned to the crowd and asked who it was had spoken. But every one was silent. Soon there was a murmur at the back of the crowd; it grew louder and in a minute broke into fearful yells. The police-captain dropped his voice and was about to try persuasion.

'Why stand looking at him?' the peasants cried. 'Come on, seize 'em, lads!' And the crowd surged forward.

Shabashkin and his group rushed into the vestibule and slammed the door behind them.

'Push, lads!' shouted the same voice, and the crowd pressed against the door.

'Stop!' Dubrovsky cried. 'Fools! What are you doing? You will destroy yourselves and me too. Go home, all of you, and leave me alone. Don't be afraid, the Tsar is merciful. I will appeal to him – he will not see us wronged, we are all his children. But how is he to take our part if you start rebelling and behaving like brigands?'

Young Dubrovsky's words, his ringing voice and impressive appearance produced the desired effect. The crowd calmed down and dispersed. The courtyard emptied, the officials stayed in the house. Vladimir walked sadly up the steps. Shabashkin opened the door and with obsequious bows began to thank Dubrovsky for his kind intervention.

Vladimir listened to him with contempt and made no answer.

'We have decided', continued the assessor, 'with your permission to remain here for the night, as it is already dark and your peasants might attack us on the way. Be kind enough to have some hay spread on the parlour floor for us; as soon as it is daylight we will take our departure.'

'Do what you please,' Dubrovsky answered dryly: 'I am no longer master here.'

With these words he went into his father's room and shut the door.

6

'AND so all is over!' Vladimir said to himself. 'Only this morning I had a home and was provided for; tomorrow I shall have to leave the house where I was born. My father, the ground where he rests, will belong to the hateful man who caused his death and beggared me. . . .' Vladimir clenched his teeth; his eyes rested on a portrait of his mother. The artist had painted her leaning against a balustrade, in a white morning dress with a red rose in her hair. 'This portrait, too, will fall into our enemy's hands,' Vladimir thought. 'It will be thrown into a lumber room together with broken chairs, or hung in the hall for his kennel-men to laugh at and pass remarks about; and her bedroom, the room where my father died, will be given to his steward or his harem. No, no! He shall not have this house of mourning from which he is driving me out!' Vladimir set his teeth; murderous thoughts rose in his mind. He heard the voices of the petty officials; they were giving their orders and making themselves at home, demanding first one thing and then another, and outraging his melancholy reflections. At last all was quiet.

Vladimir unlocked the chests and drawers and started sorting out his father's papers. They consisted for the most part of farming accounts and letters connected with various matters of business. Vladimir tore them up unread. Among them he came across a packet with the inscription: '*Letters from my wife.*' With profound emotion Vladimir took them up. They had been written during the Turkish campaign,[1] and were addressed to the army from Kistenyovka. She described to her husband her life in the country and her household occupations, tenderly complained of being parted from him, and implored him to return home as soon as possible to the embraces of his loving wife. In one of the letters she expressed

1. i.e. during the Russo-Turkish war, 1787–91.

her anxiety concerning the health of little Vladimir; in another she rejoiced at the aptitudes he showed, and predicted a happy and brilliant future for him. He read on, engrossed to the exclusion of all else, absorbed in a world of domestic bliss, and did not notice how the time passed. The clock on the wall struck eleven. Putting the letters into his pocket, Vladimir took a candle and left the room. The officials were asleep on the parlour floor. On the table were the tumblers they had emptied, and a strong smell of rum pervaded the entire room. Vladimir stepped past them in disgust, and went into the hall. There all was dark. Seeing a light, somebody rushed into a corner. Turning towards him with the candle, Vladimir recognized Arhip the blacksmith.

'What are you doing here?' he asked in surprise.

'I wanted . . . I came to find out if they were all in the house,' stammered Arhip in a low voice.

'But why have you got your axe?'

'Why have I got my axe? A man can't go about without an axe these days. These Court people are such wicked folk, you never know – '

'You are drunk. Put down the axe now, and go and sleep it off.'

'Me drunk? Vladimir Andreyevich, sir, God is my witness I haven't touched a drop . . . is it likely, at a time like this? It's unheard of – quill-drivers taking possession of us, turning our masters out of their houses . . . How they snore, the brutes! I'd like to make an end of 'em in a single go, and no one the wiser.'

Dubrovsky frowned.

'Listen, Arhip,' he said after a pause. 'You must put such ideas out of your head. It's not the fault of these men here. Light the lantern and follow me.'

Arhip took the candle from his master's hand, found a lantern behind the stove, lit it, and the pair went quietly down the steps and walked along the side of the courtyard. The watchman's rattle sounded; the dogs barked.

'Who is on the watch?' asked Dubrovsky.

'We are, sir,' replied a piping voice. 'Vassilissa and Lukerya.'

'Go back to your homes,' Dubrovsky said. 'There is no need for you to stay here.'

'Knock off,' added Arhip.

'Thank you, sir,' the women answered, and repaired home at once.

Dubrovsky walked on. Two men approached. They challenged him, and Dubrovsky recognized Anton's and Grisha's voices.

'Why aren't you asleep?' he asked them.

'How could we sleep?' Anton answered. 'To think we have lived to see this! . . .'

'Hush,' interrupted Dubrovsky. 'Where is Yegorovna?'

'In the big house, upstairs in her room.'

'Go and fetch her, and get all our people out of the house. See that not a soul is left indoors except the officials. And you, Anton, have a cart ready.'

Grisha departed, and a minute later appeared with his mother. The old woman had not undressed that night; with the exception of the officials nobody had closed an eye.

'Are you all here?' Dubrovsky asked. 'Nobody left in the house?'

'Nobody except the clerks,' Grisha answered.

'Bring me some hay or some straw,' said Dubrovsky.

The men ran to the stables and returned with armfuls of hay.

'Put it under the steps – that's right. Now, lads, a light!'

Arhip opened the lantern and Dubrovsky kindled a splinter of wood.

'Wait,' he said to Arhip. 'I believe in my haste I shut the doors into the hall. Hurry and open them.'

Arhip ran into the vestibule – the inner doors were open. He locked them, muttering in an undertone: 'Open them, indeed! Not likely!' and returned to Dubrovsky.

Dubrovsky applied the lighted splinter to the hay, which burst into a blaze; the flames leaped up, lighting the whole courtyard.

'A-ah!' wailed Yegorovna. 'Vladimir Andreyevich, what are you doing?'

'Quiet!' said Dubrovsky. 'Now, children, farewell! I go where God may lead me; be happy with your new master!'

'You are our dear master,' cried the peasants. 'We will die rather than leave you – we are coming with you!'

The horses were brought up. Dubrovsky took his seat in the cart with Grisha. Anton applied the whip and they drove out of the courtyard.

In a minute the whole house was in flames. The floors crackled and gave way; burning beams began to fall; red smoke curled above the roof; pitiful wails and cries of 'Help! help!' were heard.

'Not likely!' said Arhip, watching the fire with a malicious smile.

'Arhip, son, save them, the scoundrels,' Yegorovna said to him. 'God will reward you.'

'Not I,' the blacksmith answered.

Just then the officials appeared at the window, trying to smash the double frames. But at the same instant the roof crashed down – and the screams stopped.

Soon all the house-serfs came pouring into the courtyard. The women with loud cries hastened to save their belongings; the children skipped about, delighted with the blaze. Sparks flew up in a fiery shower, setting light to the peasant-huts.

'Now all is as it should be,' said Arhip. 'Burns well, eh? It must be a fine sight from Pokrovskoe.'

At that moment a new apparition attracted his attention: a cat was running about the roof of the burning barn, not knowing where to jump. Flames were on all sides of it. The poor creature mewed plaintively for help; the small boys yelled with laughter, watching the animal's despair.

'What are you laughing at, you little devils?' the blacksmith said to them angrily. 'Aren't you ashamed? One of God's creatures perishing, and you little fools pleased about it!' – and putting a ladder against the burning roof he climbed up to save the cat. It understood his intention and with grateful eagerness clutched at his sleeve. The blacksmith, half scorched, descended with his burden.

'Well, lads, good-bye,' he said to the crowd, which was somewhat abashed. 'There is nothing more for me to do here. Good luck to you. Think kindly of me.'

The blacksmith went off. The fire continued to rage for some time but subsided at last. Piles of red-hot embers glowed brightly in the darkness, while round about them wandered the inhabitants of Kistenyovka who had lost their all in the conflagration.

7

THE next day news of the fire spread throughout the neighbourhood. Everybody explained it in a different way, making various guesses and surmises. Some maintained that Dubrovsky's servants, having got drunk at the funeral, had set the house on fire through their carelessness; others accused the officials, who had taken a drop too much in their new quarters. Some guessed the truth, asserting that the author of the terrible calamity was none other than Dubrovsky, moved by anger and despair. Many declared that he had himself perished in the flames, together with the officials and all his servants. Troyekurov drove over next morning to the scene of the fire, and personally conducted the inquiry. It seemed that the police-captain, the assessor of the District Court and two clerks, as well as Vladimir Dubrovsky, the old nurse Yegorovna, his man Grisha, the coachman Anton and the blacksmith Arhip had disappeared nobody knew where. All the servants testified that the officials perished when the roof fell in. Their charred remains were in fact discovered. The women Vassilissa and Lukeria told how they had seen Dubrovsky and Arhip the blacksmith a few minutes before the conflagration. The blacksmith, according to the general showing, was alive, and was probably the chief, if not the sole person responsible for the fire. Grave suspicions rested on Dubrovsky. Kiril Petrovich sent the Governor a detailed account of all that had happened, and the law was brought into action again.

Soon other reports gave fresh food for curiosity and gossip. Brigands appeared, spreading terror throughout the countryside. Measures taken against them by the district authorities proved unavailing. Robberies, each more daring than the last, followed one after another. There was no safety either on the high road or in the villages. Brigands drove about in troikas in broad daylight all over the province, holding up travellers and the mail. They went into the villages, robbed and set fire to the manor-houses. The chief of the band gained a reputation for his cleverness, his daring and a sort of generosity. Extraordinary things were related of him. The name of Dubrovsky was on every lip. All were convinced that he and no other was the leader of the fearless villains. The only wonder was that Troyekurov's estates had been spared: the brigands had not attacked a single barn of his, or stopped a single cart belonging to him. With his usual arrogance Troyekurov attributed this exception to the awe and dread which he inspired throughout the province, as well as to the excellent police-watch which he had organized in his villages. At first Troyekurov's neighbours laughed at his presumption, and everyone waited for the uninvited guests to visit Pokrovskoe, where they would find plenty to loot, but at last they had to agree with him and admit that even robbers treated him with unaccountable respect. Troyekurov was triumphant, and at the news of each fresh exploit on the part of Dubrovsky he indulged in reflections at the expense of the Governor, the police-officers of the district and the company commanders, who always allowed Dubrovsky to escape with impunity.

Meanwhile the first of October arrived, and with it the patronal festival of the church in Troyekurov's village. But before we proceed to describe the events that followed we must introduce the reader to characters who are new to him, or whom we mentioned only briefly at the beginning of our tale.

8

THE reader has probably already guessed that Kiril Petrovich's daughter, of whom so far only a few words have been said, is the heroine of our story. At the time of which we are writing she was seventeen and in the full bloom of her beauty. Her father loved her to distraction but treated her in his characteristically arbitrary fashion, at one moment doing his best to gratify her slightest whim, at another frightening her by his harsh discipline and even cruelty. Convinced of her affection, he could never win her confidence. She was too uncertain what his response would be, ever to share her thoughts and feelings with her father. She had no friends and had grown up in solitude. The neighbours' wives and daughters seldom visited Kiril Petrovich, whose amusements and conversation usually called for the company of men rather than the presence of ladies. Our beautiful young heroine rarely appeared among the guests making merry in her father's house. She had the run of the extensive library, consisting mostly of the works of the French writers of the eighteenth century. Her father never read anything except the *Perfect Cook* and could not guide her in her choice of books, and Masha, after dipping into volumes of various kinds, naturally gave her preference to romances. In this manner she was completing the education that had begun under the tuition of Mademoiselle Michaud. Kiril Petrovich had reposed great trust in that lady and had shown her much good will, until he had been obliged to send her in secret to another estate when the consequences of their friendship became too apparent. Mademoiselle Michaud had left rather a pleasant memory behind her. She was a good-hearted girl and had never abused her influence on Kiril Petrovich, unlike some of the other favourites who constantly superseded one another in his affections. Kiril Petrovich himself seemed to be fonder of her than of the others, and a dark-eyed, roguish little boy of nine, whose features bore a resemblance to Mademoiselle Michaud's southern looks, was being brought up by him and was recognized as his son, in spite of the fact that a considerable number of little boys who were as like Kiril Petrovich as one drop of water is to another ran about barefoot outside his windows, and were regarded as serf-children. Kiril Petrovich had sent to Moscow for a French tutor for his little Sasha, and the tutor arrived at Pokrovskoe during the events we are now describing.

Kiril Petrovich was agreeably taken with his pleasant appearance and simple manner. He presented his testimonials and a letter from one of Troyekurov's relatives in whose house he had been tutor for four years. Kiril Petrovich examined all these, and the only point that was not satisfactory was the Frenchman's youth – not because he considered this amiable defect to be incompatible with patience and experience, so necessary in the wretched calling of a tutor, but for reasons of his own, which he decided to put before the young man at once. For this purpose he sent for Masha (Kiril Petrovich did not speak French, and she acted as interpreter for him).

'Come here, Masha. Tell this *monsoo* that, so be it, I engage him, but only on condition that he does not venture to run after my servant-girls, or I'll give it him, the puppy.... Translate that to him, Masha.'

Masha blushed, and turning to the tutor told him in French that her father counted on his virtue and decorous behaviour.

The Frenchman bowed, and answered that he hoped to earn their respect even if they refused him their favour.

Masha translated his reply word for word.

'Very well, very well!' said Kiril Petrovich. 'He needn't trouble about either respect or favour. His business is to look after Sasha and teach him grammar and geography.... Translate that to him.'

Masha softened her father's discourtesy in her translation, and Kiril Petrovich dismissed his Frenchman to the wing where a room had been allotted to him.

Masha had not given a thought to the young Frenchman.
Brought up with aristocratic prejudices, a tutor to her mind
was only a sort of servant or workman, and servants or
workmen were not men in her eyes. She did not even remark
the impression she had produced on Monsieur Desforges, or
his confusion, his agitation, the tremor in his voice. For
several days she came across him fairly often but without
taking any particular notice of him. An unexpected incident
put him in quite a new light.

A number of bear-cubs were generally kept in the courtyard,
providing Kiril Petrovich with one of his chief forms of
amusement. While they were young they were fetched every
day to the parlour, where Kiril Petrovich played with them
for hours on end, setting them on cats and puppies. When
they grew up they were put on a chain, to await being baited
in real earnest. Sometimes a bear would be brought out in
front of the manor-house windows, and an empty wine-barrel
studded with nails was rolled towards it. The bear would sniff
it, then touch it cautiously and get its paws pricked. Angrily
it would give the cask a more violent push, and so be hurt
still more. Then the beast would work itself up into a perfect
frenzy and fling itself upon the barrel, growling furiously,
until they removed from the poor animal the object of its
hopeless rage. On other occasions a couple of bears were
harnessed to a cart and visitors, willing or unwilling, seated
in it and sent off at a gallop whither chance would take them.
But the trick Kiril Petrovich loved best was as follows:

A hungry bear would be shut up in an empty room, tied by a
rope to a ring in the wall. The rope was almost the length of
the room, so that only the far corner was out of reach of the
terrible creature. An unsuspecting caller was taken to the door
of the room and, as if by accident, pushed in along with the
bear; the door was locked and the luckless victim left alone
with the shaggy recluse. The poor visitor, with the skirts of
his coat in shreds and a torn arm, soon discovered the safe
corner, but sometimes had to stand for three whole hours,
pressed against the wall while the savage beast, a couple of

steps away, reared up, stood growling on its hind legs and jerked at the rope in an effort to get at him. Such were the noble amusements of a Russian country gentleman!

A few days after the tutor's arrival Troyekurov thought of him and decided he should have a taste of the bear's room. For this purpose the young man was summoned one morning and conducted along several dark passages; suddenly a side door opened – two servants pushed the Frenchman through the door and locked it after him. Recovering from his surprise, the tutor saw a bear chained to the wall. The brute began to snort, sniffing from a distance at his visitor, and then suddenly, rearing up on its hind legs, made for him. . . . The Frenchman was not scared; he did not retreat but waited for the attack. The bear drew near; Desforges took a small pistol from his pocket, thrust it into the ravening beast's ear, and fired. The bear rolled over. Everyone came running back, the door was opened, and Kiril Petrovich entered, wide-eyed at the outcome of his jest.

Kiril Petrovich was determined to get to the bottom of the affair. Who had warned Desforges of the practical joke that was to be played on him, or how was it he had a loaded pistol in his pocket? He sent for Masha. Masha hurried in and translated her father's questions to the Frenchman.

'I did not know anything about the bear,' replied Desforges, 'but I always carry a pistol about with me because I do not intend to put up with insults for which, on account of my calling, I cannot demand satisfaction.'

Masha stared at him in amazement and translated his words to Kiril Petrovich. Kiril Petrovich made no answer. He gave orders for the bear to be removed and skinned. Then, turning to his men, he said:

'What a brave fellow! Nothing of the coward about him – by heaven, no!'

From that day he took a fancy to Desforges and never again thought of putting him to the test.

But this incident produced a still greater impression upon Maria Kirilovna. Her imagination had been struck by the sight of the dead bear and Desforges standing calmly beside its body and as calmly talking to her. She saw that courage and a proud sense of personal dignity did not belong exclusively to one class, and from that day she began to show a regard for the young tutor which grew more and more marked as time went on. A certain intimacy sprang up between them. Masha had a lovely voice and great musical ability; Desforges suggested giving her lessons. After this it will not be difficult for the reader to guess that, without acknowledging it to herself, Masha fell in love with him.

9

VISITORS began to arrive on the eve of the patronal festival; some were accommodated in the manor-house, others put in the wings. Still others were quartered at the steward's, at the priest's and with the more well-to-do of the peasants. The stables were full of the visitors' horses, the coach-houses and barns were blocked with carriages of all sorts. At nine o'clock the bells began to ring for Mass, and everybody set out for the new stone church that Kiril Petrovich had built and which every year he improved and made more beautiful. Such a number of distinguished worshippers had come to Mass that there was no room for the peasants who had to stand in the porch or in the open air inside the fence. The Mass had not begun: they were waiting for Kiril Petrovich. He arrived in a carriage drawn by six horses, and solemnly walked to his place accompanied by Maria Kirilovna. The eyes of both men and women were turned on her – the first admiring her beauty, the second scrutinizing her attire. The service began. Singers from his household formed the choir and Kiril Petrovich joined in with them. He prayed, keeping his eyes from straying to right or to left, and with proud humility bowed to the ground when the deacon entreated in a loud voice 'for the founder of this temple'.

The Mass ended. Kiril Petrovich was the first to kiss the cross.[1] All the others flocked after him; the neighbours went up to him to pay their respects, the ladies surrounded Masha. As he was leaving the church Kiril Petrovich invited everybody to dine, and stepping into his carriage drove home. They all followed.

The rooms filled with guests: new-comers arrived every

1. At the end of the Liturgy in the Orthodox Church all the members of the congregation go up to kiss the crucifix which the priest holds out to them.

moment and with difficulty threaded their way to their host. The ladies, in pearls and diamonds and costly old-fashioned gowns that had seen better days, sat sedately in a semicircle. The men crowded round the caviar and vodka, raising their voices in animated discussion. Eighty places were being set in the dining-hall; the servants bustled about arranging bottles and decanters and straightening the table-cloths. At last the butler announced that dinner was served. Kiril Petrovich led the way to the table and sat down. After him the married ladies took their places with an air of dignity, observing a sort of order of precedence as they did so. The young ladies clung together like a timid herd of gazelles, choosing places next to one another. The men settled opposite. The tutor sat at the end of the table next to little Sasha.

The servants attended to the guests in the order of their rank; where they were uncertain they acted according to the principles of Lavater[1] and hardly ever made a mistake. The clatter of plates and jingle of spoons mingled with the noise of conversation. Kiril Petrovich looked gaily round the table, thoroughly enjoying his part as hospitable host. At that moment a carriage drawn by six horses drove into the court-yard.

'Who is that?' Troyekurov asked.

'Anton Pafnutyevich,' several voices answered.

The doors opened and Anton Pafnutyevich Spitsyn, a stout man of about fifty years of age with a round, pock-marked face adorned by a triple chin, rolled into the dining-room, bowing, smiling and apologetic.

'A cover here!' cried Kiril Petrovich. 'Welcome, Anton Pafnutyevich. Sit down and tell us what this means: you weren't at my Mass and you are late for dinner. It isn't like you: you are a pious man and you relish good fare.'

'I am sorry,' Anton Pafnutyevich answered, tucking a corner of his napkin into the buttonhole of his pea-green

---

1. Lavater, born in Zurich in 1741, is remembered mainly for an exhaustive work on the art of judging character and disposition from the features of the face or the form of the body generally.

coat. 'I am sorry, my dear fellow – I left home early but I had not gone half a dozen miles before the iron rim of one of my front wheels split in two, so what was I to do? Fortunately we were not far from a village but by the time we had crawled there and found a blacksmith, and patched things up somehow, three hours had gone—there was nothing for it, I would not venture the shortest way through the Kistenyovka forest, so I drove round.'

'O-ho!' Kiril Petrovich interrupted him. 'You are not over brave, I see! What are you afraid of?'

'What am I afraid of, Kiril Petrovich, sir? Why, Dubrovsky, of course. One might fall into his clutches at any moment. He knows what he's about, and no one is safe with him; and me he would skin twice over.'

'Why such a distinction?'

'Why, sir, because of his father, Andrei Gavrilovich, to be sure. Wasn't it I who to please you – that is, in all conscience and justice – testified that the Dubrovskys had no right to Kistenyovka but held the property solely by virtue of your kindness? And did not the deceased (God rest his soul) swear to get even with me in his own way, and might not the son keep his father's word? Up to now God has had pity on me – they have only broken into a barn of mine – but one of these days they may get at the house.'

'Where they will have a fine time of it,' remarked Kiril Petrovich. 'I expect the little red cash-box is crammed to overflowing.'

'Not a bit, my dear Kiril Petrovich. It was full once, but now it is quite empty.'

'Don't talk nonsense. We know you. You are not one for spending money. At home you live in squalor, you never entertain, and you fleece your peasants. You are hoarding it up all right.'

'You are pleased to joke, Kiril Petrovich,' murmured Anton Pafnutyevich with a smile, 'but I swear to you that we are destitute,' and he swallowed a slice of rich pie to take away the taste of his host's contemptuous teasing.

Kiril Petrovich left him and turned to the new police-captain, who had come to his house for the first time and was sitting at the other end of the table next to the tutor.

'Well, sir, and will you be long catching Dubrovsky?'

The police-captain shrank back, bowed, smiled, stammered, and brought out at last:

'We shall do our best, your excellency.'

'Hm! Do your best! You have been doing your best for a long time but nothing has come of it yet. And indeed, why catch him? Dubrovsky's robberies are a perfect godsend to police-captains, what with investigations, travelling expenses and the money that goes into their pockets. Why bring down such a benefactor? Is not that the way of it, police-captain?'

'Absolutely, your excellency,' the police-captain answered, utterly confused.

The company roared with laughter.

'I like this young fellow for his candour,' said Kiril Petrovich. 'I see I shall have to tackle the business myself without waiting for any help from the local authorities. But it is a pity about the old police-captain. If they hadn't burnt him to death there would have been less trouble about in the district. But what news of Dubrovsky? Where was he seen last?'

'At my house, Kiril Petrovich,' a deep feminine voice replied. 'He had dinner with me last Tuesday.'

All eyes were turned on Anna Savishna Globov, a rather homely widow who was universally loved for her kindly, cheerful disposition. Everyone prepared to listen to her story with great interest.

'I must tell you that three weeks ago I sent my steward to the post with a letter for my Vanyusha. I do not spoil my son, and indeed I haven't the means to do so even if I wanted to, but of course, as you know very well, an officer in the Guards has to keep up appearances and I share my income with Vanyusha as best I can. Well, I sent him two thousand roubles; and although the thought of Dubrovsky more than once came into my head I said to myself, The town is not far off, only five miles, and we might just get through, God willing. And behold – in the evening my steward comes home looking quite pale and with his clothes all torn, and on foot. I gasped, I did. "What is the matter? What has happened to you?" I cried. Said he: "Anna Savishna, ma'am, highwaymen robbed me and very near killed me. Dubrovsky himself was there and he was for hanging me, but then he took pity and let me go. But he robbed me of everything – took the horse and cart too." My heart sank. King of Heaven, what will become of my Vanyusha? There was nothing to be done. I wrote another letter to him, telling him what had happened, and sent him my blessing without enclosing a penny.

'A week or two passed. Suddenly one day a carriage drove into my courtyard. Some general I did not know asked to see me; I said he was welcome. A dark-complexioned man of about thirty-five came in. He had black hair, a moustache and a beard, and was the very image of Kulnev.[1] He introduced himself as a friend and colleague of my late husband: he was passing by, he said, and could not resist paying a visit to his old comrade's widow, knowing that I lived here. I invited him in to our simple meal, we talked of this and that and, finally, of Dubrovsky. I told him of my trouble. "That is strange," he said. "I have heard that Dubrovsky does not attack all and sundry but only people who are known to be rich, and even then he leaves them something and doesn't strip them completely. And as for murdering people, no one has accused him of that yet: I wonder if there isn't some trickery here. Will you oblige me by sending for your steward?" I sent for the steward. The man came. The moment he saw the general he opened his mouth, dumbfounded. "Tell me, my good fellow, about Dubrovsky robbing you and wanting to hang you." My steward began to tremble, and he fell at the general's feet. "I did wrong, sir . . . the devil led me astray . . . I lied." – "If that is so," replied the general, "have the goodness to relate to your mistress just what happened, and I will listen." My steward tried in vain to collect his wits.

1. A successful Russian general in the struggle against Napoleon (Russo-Swedish war, 1808–9).

"Come now," the general went on, "tell us where you met Dubrovsky." – "By the two pine-trees, sir, by the two pine-trees." – "And what did he say to you?" – "He asked me whose servant I was, and where I was going, and on what errand." – "Well, and after that?" – "After that he asked me for the letter and the money, and I gave them to him." – "And what did he do?" – "He gave me the money back and the letter, and said, 'Go in peace, take it to the post.'" – "Well?" – "Sir, I did wrong!" – "I will settle with you, my lad!" said the general fiercely. "And you, madam, have this rascal's box searched and then hand him over to me: I will teach him a lesson. Let me tell you that Dubrovsky was himself an officer in the Guards and he would not offend against a comrade." I guessed who his excellency was but there was no sense in saying anything to him. The coachman tied my steward to the box of his carriage; the money was found; the general had dinner with me and departed immediately after, taking the steward with him. The steward was discovered in the forest next day, tied to an oak-tree and properly fleeced.'

The company listened in silence to Anna Savishna's story, the young ladies with particular attention. Many of them secretly wished Dubrovsky well, seeing in him a romantic hero – Maria Kirilovna especially, who was an ardent day-dreamer, gorged with the mysterious horrors of Mrs Rad-cliffe.[1]

'And you think, Anna Savishna, it was Dubrovsky himself came to see you?' Kiril Petrovich asked. 'You are very much mistaken. I do not know who your visitor may have been but he certainly was not Dubrovsky.'

'How do you mean, not Dubrovsky? Who else would stop travellers on the high road and search them?'

'I can't tell you that, but I feel sure it was not Dubrovsky. I remember him as a child. I don't know if his hair has turned black – as a boy he had fair, curly hair; but I do know that

1. Mrs Ann Ward Radcliffe, English romantic novelist of the late eighteenth century. Her favourite 'props' were ruined castles, secret passages, and dark and desperate villains.

Dubrovsky is five years older than my Masha, and that makes him not thirty-five but about three and twenty.'

'Quite so, your excellency,' observed the police-captain. 'I have in my pocket a description of Vladimir Dubrovsky. It says definitely that he is in his twenty-third year.'

'Ah!' said Kiril Petrovich. 'By the way, read it and we will listen. It will not be a bad thing for us to know what he looks like: we may come across him, and if so he won't escape in a hurry.'

The police-captain took out of his pocket a rather dirty sheet of paper, unfolded it solemnly and began to read in sing-song tones:

'Description of Dubrovsky, based upon the depositions of his former serfs:

'Twenty-two years of age, of medium height, clear complexion, does not wear a beard, hazel-brown eyes, light brown hair, straight nose. Special peculiarities: none.'

'And that is all?' Kiril Petrovich said.

'That is all,' replied the police-captain, folding the paper.

'I congratulate you, police-captain. A very valuable document! With that description you will have no difficulty in finding Dubrovsky. As though most people weren't of medium height with brown hair, a straight nose and brown eyes! I would wager you could talk to Dubrovsky himself for three hours at a stretch and never guess in whose company you were. A smart lot you officials are, I must say!'

Meekly putting the sheet of paper back into his pocket, the police-captain busied himself in silence with his roast goose and cabbage. Meanwhile the servants had gone the round of the table more than once, filling up the wine-glasses. Several bottles of Caucasian and Crimean wine were uncorked with a loud pop and favourably received under the name of champagne. Cheeks began to glow and conversation grew louder, gayer and more inconsequent.

'No,' continued Kiril Petrovich, 'we shall never see another police-captain like our old Taras Alexeyevich! He knew what was what, he was no wool-gatherer. A pity they burnt the fellow to death. Not a single man of their band would have escaped him otherwise. He would have caught the whole lot of 'em – not even Dubrovsky himself would have slipped his clutches. Taras Alexeyevich would have taken a bribe from him right enough but he would not have let him go all the same. That was his way. There is nothing for it: it seems I shall have to see about the matter myself and go for the brigands with my own men. I'll begin by sending a score of them to scour the wood. My people are not cowards: any of them will tackle a bear single-handed – and they are not likely to turn tail at the sight of brigands.'

'How is your bear, Kiril Petrovich?' asked Anton Pafnutyevich, reminded of his shaggy acquaintance and of certain practical jokes of which he had once been the victim.

'Misha the bear has departed this life,' answered Kiril Petrovich. 'He died an honourable death at the hand of an enemy. There is his conqueror!' and Kiril Petrovich pointed to Desforges. 'You ought to get a portrait of my Frenchman. He has avenged your ... if I may say so ... do you remember?'

'I should think I do!' said Anton Pafnutyevich, scratching his head. 'I remember only too well. So Misha is dead – I am sorry to hear it, I really am! What an amazing creature he was! So intelligent! You will not find another bear like him. And why did monsieur kill him?'

Kiril Petrovich began with great satisfaction to relate the exploit of his Frenchman, for he had the happy faculty of priding himself on all that in any way belonged to him. The guests listened attentively to the story of the bear's death, glancing in amazement at Desforges who, unaware that his bravery was the subject of the conversation, sat quietly in his place, occasionally admonishing his restive pupil.

The dinner, which had lasted some three hours, came to an end. The host put his napkin on the table and everybody rose and went to the drawing-room, where coffee and cards awaited them, and a continuation of the drinking so excellently begun in the dining-room.

10

TOWARDS seven o'clock in the evening some of the guests were ready to go home, but Kiril Petrovich, exhilarated by punch, ordered the gates to be closed and forbade anyone to leave before morning. Soon the strains of a band swelled out, the doors into the big drawing-room were thrown open, and dancing began. The host and his cronies sat in a corner drinking glass after glass, watching the young people enjoy themselves. The elderly ladies played cards. There was a shortage of men as generally happens unless some cavalry brigade is quartered in the neighbourhood, and all the men who could dance were enlisted as partners. The tutor particularly distinguished himself: he danced more than anyone, all the young ladies desiring him for their partner and finding him very easy to waltz with. He danced several times with Maria Kirilovna, and the other girls observed them with knowing smiles. At last, around midnight, the host, who was tired, stopped the dancing, ordered supper to be served and then betook himself to bed.

With Kiril Petrovich out of the way the company felt more at ease and livelier; the gentlemen ventured to sit near the ladies; the young girls laughed and whispered with their partners; the ladies talked loudly across the table. The older men drank and argued with boisterous laughter – in short the supper-party was extremely gay and left many a pleasant memory behind it.

One man only took no part in the general enjoyment. Anton Pafnutyevich sat gloomy and silent, eating absent-mindedly and apparently feeling exceedingly ill at ease. The conversation about the brigands had disturbed his imagination. We shall soon see that he had good reason to fear them.

In calling God to witness that the little red cash-box was empty Anton Pafnutyevich had committed no sin, told no lie:

the red cash-box really was empty. The money that had once been kept in it had been transferred to a leather pouch which he wore round his neck under his shirt. It was only this precaution that appeased to some extent his continual fear and distrust of every one. Obliged to spend the night in a strange house, he was afraid of being put in some distant room where thieves would have no difficulty in breaking in. He looked round for a reliable companion and at last selected Desforges. His strong build and, still more, the courage he had shown in the encounter with the bear, whom poor Anton Pafnutyevich could never think of without a shudder, decided his choice. When they got up from the table Anton Pafnutyevich hung round the young Frenchman and, clearing his throat and giving a preliminary cough, finally addressed him directly.

'Hm! Hm! Could I spend the night in your room, monsieur, because you see . . .'

'*Que désire monsieur?*' asked Desforges with a polite bow.

'Oh, how unfortunate, monsieur, that you have not yet learnt Russian. *Je veux, moi chez vous coucher*, do you understand?'

'*Monsieur, très volontiers,*' replied Desforges. '*Veuillez donner des ordres en conséquence.*'

Very much pleased with his knowledge of the French language, Anton Pafnutyevich went at once to make the necessary arrangements.

The guests wished each other good night and retired to the rooms appointed to them, while Anton Pafnutyevich accompanied the tutor to the far wing. The night was dark. The tutor lighted the way with a lantern. Anton Pafnutyevich followed with a fair amount of confidence, occasionally touching the pouch hidden in his breast to make sure that his money was still there.

When they came to their apartment the tutor lit a candle and they both began to undress, Anton Pafnutyevich as he did so walking about and examining the doors and windows, and shaking his head at the unsatisfactory state of things revealed by his inspection. The doors had no lock but only a latch, and there were no double frames to the windows.[1] He tried to complain of all this to Desforges but his knowledge of French was too limited for so complicated an explanation. The Frenchman did not understand him, and Anton Pafnutyevich was obliged to stop grumbling. Their beds were opposite each other. They both lay down, and Desforges blew out the candle.

'*Pourquoi vous touchez, pourquoi vous touchez?*' cried Anton Pafnutyevich, managing with a great effort to conjugate the Russian infinitive '*tooshit*', to blow out, as if it were a French verb. 'I cannot *dormir* in the dark.'

But to Desforges the exclamations were meaningless, and he wished Anton Pafnutyevich good night.

'Wretched infidel!' muttered Spitsyn, wrapping himself up in the bedclothes. 'The idea of blowing out the candle! So much the worse for him, though. I cannot sleep without a light. *Monsieur, monsieur!*' he went on, '*je veux avec vous parler.*'

But the Frenchman made no answer, and soon began to snore.

'Snoring brute of a Frenchman,' mumbled Anton Pafnutyevich to himself, 'and I can't even think of going to sleep. Thieves might walk in at any moment, or climb in through the window, and a cannon would not wake that brute. *Monsieur, monsieur!* – the devil take you!'

Anton Pafnutyevich lapsed into silence. Fatigue and the wine he had drunk gradually overcame his fears. He dozed off and soon sank into profound slumber.

A strange awakening was in store for him. He felt in his sleep that someone was tugging gently at the collar of his shirt. Anton Pafnutyevich opened his eyes, and by the pale light of an autumn morning saw Desforges standing over him. The Frenchman held a pistol in one hand, and with the other was unfastening the precious leather pouch.

'*Qu'est ce que c'est, monsieur, qu'est ce que c'est?*' he brought out in a trembling voice.

'Sssh! Be quiet!' the tutor replied in the purest Russian. 'Be quiet, or you are lost. I am Dubrovsky.'

1. The Russians put in a second set of windows to their houses in winter.

II

WE will now ask the reader's permission to explain these last incidents of our story by referring to circumstances that preceded them which we have not yet had time to relate.

In the house of the post-master, whom we have mentioned once before, a traveller sat in a corner with a mild and patient air that showed him to be a man of plebeian origin or a foreigner – that is to say, a man who had no rights at post-stations. His trap stood in the courtyard, waiting for the wheels to be greased. In it lay a small portmanteau, its meagre dimensions a proof of his lack of means. The traveller ordered neither tea nor coffee but sat looking out of the window and whistling, to the great annoyance of the post-master's wife sitting behind the partition.

'A regular affliction, that whistler!' she said in an under-tone. 'Whistling away like that! Plague take him, the accursed infidel!'

'Why, what does it matter?' said the post-master. 'Let him whistle to himself.'

'What does it matter?' his wife retorted angrily. 'Surely you know the saying?'

'What saying? That whistling drives the money away? Nonsense, my dear! Whistling or not, it makes no difference to us, we never have any money anyway.'

'Do send him off, Sidorych. Why do you keep him? Give him the horses and let him go to the devil.'

'He can wait, my dear. I have only three troikas ready, the fourth is resting. Important travellers may turn up any minute: I don't want to risk my neck for a Frenchman. Listen, I thought so! There's someone galloping up now! Pretty smartly, too. I wonder if it's some general?'

A carriage stopped at the steps. The servant jumped down from the box, opened the carriage door, and a moment later a young man in a military cloak and a white cap came into the post-master's house. The servant followed, carrying a box which he put in the window.

'Horses!' said the officer peremptorily.

'At once, sir!' the post-master answered. 'May I have your road-pass, please.'

'I have no road-pass. I am not taking the main road. . . . And surely you recognize me?'

The station-master fussed about and rushed off to hurry the drivers. The young man started pacing up and down the room. Then he went behind the partition and inquired of the post-master's wife in a low voice who the other traveller was.

'Heaven only knows,' she answered. 'Some Frenchman or other. He's been here five hours waiting for horses and whistling the whole time. Fair sick of him I am, confound him!'

The young man addressed the traveller in French.

'Where are you going?' he asked him.

'To the next town,' replied the Frenchman, 'and from there to a landed gentleman who has engaged me by letter as a tutor. I thought I would be there today but the post-master has evidently decided otherwise. In this country it is not easy to get horses, *monsieur l'officier*.'

'And with which of the local gentlemen have you found employment?' the officer asked.

'With Monsieur Troyekurov,' the Frenchman answered.

'Troyekurov? Who is this Troyekurov?'

'*Ma foi, monsieur,* I have not heard much good of him. They say he is a proud, headstrong man, cruel to his dependants; that nobody can get on with him, that everyone trembles at the mention of his name; and that he does not stand upon ceremony with tutors and has already flogged two of them to death.'

'Good heavens! And you venture to enter the service of such a monster?'

'What can I do, *monsieur l'officier*? He offers me good wages, three thousand roubles a year and all found. I may be more fortunate than the others. My mother is no longer young – I shall send her half my salary to live on, and out of the rest I shall be able to save enough in five years to provide a small capital which will make me independent for the rest of my life. Then, *bonsoir*, I return to Paris and set up in business on my own.'

'Does anyone in Troyekurov's house know you?' the officer asked.

'No one,' answered the tutor. 'He heard of me through a friend of his in Moscow, whose cook, my fellow-countryman, recommended me. I must tell you that I was trained to be a pastry-cook, not a teacher, but they say in your country being a teacher is far more lucrative.'

The officer reflected.

'Look here,' he said, interrupting the Frenchman. 'What would you say if, instead of this future that awaits you, you were offered ten thousand roubles in cash on condition that you went back to Paris at once?'

The Frenchman stared at the officer in amazement, and shook his head with a smile.

'The horses are ready,' the post-master said, coming in.

The servant corroborated this.

'Just coming,' said the officer. 'Leave the room for a moment.' The post-master and the servant withdrew. 'I am not joking,' he continued in French. 'I can give you ten thousand roubles; all I want is your absence and your papers.'

So saying, he opened his box and took out several bundles of notes.

The Frenchman stared with wide-open eyes. He did not know what to make of it.

'My absence ... my papers,' he repeated in astonishment. 'Here are my papers ... but surely you must be joking? What do you want with my papers?'

'That is nothing to do with you. I ask, do you consent or not?'

The Frenchman, still unable to believe his own ears, handed his papers to the young officer, who quickly looked them over.

'Your passport ... good; a letter of recommendation ... let's look at it; your birth certificate ... excellent. Well, here is the money, go back now. Good-bye.'

The Frenchman stood, rooted to the ground. The officer turned round to him.

'I nearly forgot the most important thing of all. Give me your word of honour that all this will remain between ourselves ... your word of honour.'

'My word of honour,' the Frenchman answered. 'But my papers? What shall I do without them?'

'In the first town you come to say you were robbed by Dubrovsky. They will believe you and give you the necessary certificate. God grant you a speedy return to Paris, and may you find your mother in good health.'

Dubrovsky left the room, seated himself in the carriage and drove off at a gallop.

The post-master was looking out of the window, and when the carriage had gone he turned to his wife, exclaiming:

'My dear! Do you know? Why, that was Dubrovsky!'

His wife rushed to the window but it was too late. Dubrovsky was already a long way off. She began scolding her husband:

'How could you, Sidorych! Why didn't you tell me sooner – I might at least have caught a glimpse of Dubrovsky, but now goodness knows how long it might be before he comes this way again. A shameless creature, you are, and that's a fact.'

The Frenchman stood as though rooted to the spot. The pact with the officer, the money – it was all like a dream. But the bundle of bank notes was there in his pocket, eloquently confirming the reality of the wonderful adventure.

He decided to hire horses to take him to the town. The driver went at a snail's pace and it was night when they arrived.

Before they reached the town-gates, where in place of a watch-man there was a tumbledown sentry-box, the Frenchman told the driver to stop, got out of the carriage and proceeded on foot, explaining by signs to the driver that he might keep the vehicle and the portmanteau by way of a gratuity. The driver was as dumbfounded by his generosity as the Frenchman himself had been by Dubrovsky's proposal. But, concluding that the foreign gentleman had taken leave of his senses, he thanked him with a low bow and, deeming it wiser not to go into the town, made his way to a certain place of entertainment he knew of, the owner of which was a friend of his. There he spent the night, and next morning set off home with his three horses but no trap and no portmanteau, his face swollen and his eyes red.

Dubrovsky, with the Frenchman's papers, boldly presented himself, as we have already seen, to Troyekurov, and settled down in his house. Whatever his secret intentions were (we shall learn about them later), there was nothing reprehensible about his conduct. True, he did not occupy himself overmuch with little Sasha's education, letting the boy do what he liked in play-time. Nor was he very exacting in the matter of lessons, which were only set to the child for form's sake. On the other hand, however, he paid great attention to the musical studies of his fair pupil, and frequently sat for hours beside her at the piano. Every one liked the young tutor: Kiril Petrovich for his spontaneous daring in the hunting field, Masha for his unbounded devotion and slavish attentiveness, Sasha for his leniency with his pranks, the servants for his kindness and a liberality which seemed out of keeping with his position. He himself appeared to be fond of the whole family and already regarded himself as a member of it.

Nearly a month had elapsed from the time of his entering the teaching profession to the date of the memorable patronal festival, and nobody suspected that the modest young Frenchman was the terrible brigand whose name inspired all the landed proprietors of the neighbourhood with terror. During all that time Dubrovsky had not left Pokrovskoe but rumours of his robberies never ceased to spread, thanks to the country people's fertile imagination; although it may have been, too, that his band continued with their exploits in the absence of their chief.

Passing the night in the same room with a man whom he could only regard as a personal enemy and one of the principal authors of his misfortune, Dubrovsky could not resist the temptation. He knew of the precious wallet and decided to gain possession of it. We have seen how greatly he surprised poor Anton Pafnutyevich by his sudden transformation from tutor to brigand.

12

At nine o'clock in the morning the visitors who had spent the night at Pokrovskoe repaired one after the other to the parlour, where a samovar was already boiling. Maria Kirilovna sat before the samovar in a morning gown, and Kiril Petrovich in a frieze coat and slippers was drinking his tea out of a big cup that looked like a slop-basin. Anton Pafnutyevich was the last to come in. He looked so pale and distressed that every one was struck by his appearance, and Kiril Petrovich inquired after his health. Spitsyn gave a random answer and glanced in terror at the tutor, who sat at the table with the others as if nothing had happened. A few minutes later a servant entered and told Spitsyn that his carriage was ready. Anton Pafnutyevich hastened to take leave of the company and drove away at once. Neither guests nor host could understand what had happened to him, and Kiril Petrovich came to the conclusion that he must have overeaten. After the morning tea and a farewell breakfast the other guests began to depart, and soon Pokrovskoe was deserted and things resumed their normal course.

Several days passed and nothing worthy of note happened. Life at Pokrovskoe was uneventful. Kiril Petrovich rode out hunting every day, while reading, walks and music lessons occupied Maria Kirilovna's time – especially music lessons. She was beginning to understand her own heart and acknowledged to herself with involuntary vexation that it was not indifferent to the young Frenchman's fine qualities. For his part he never overstepped the bounds of respect and strict propriety, and thereby assuaged her pride and timid doubts. With more and more confidence she gave herself up to the pleasant habit of being with him. She felt restless without him and when he was present she constantly turned to him, wanting to know his opinion on every subject and agreeing with him in everything. Perhaps she was not in love as yet; but at the first casual obstacle or unexpected reverse of fortune the flame of passion was bound to flare up in her heart.

Going into the large drawing-room one day, where the tutor was waiting for her, Maria Kirilovna was surprised to observe a look of confusion on his pale face. She opened the piano and sang a few notes; but Dubrovsky excused himself, saying that he had a headache and could not continue the lesson. Closing the book of music, he handed her a note. Maria Kirilovna took it before she had time to think, and then instantly repented; but Dubrovsky was no longer there. Maria Kirilovna went to her room and unfolding the note read as follows:

Come to the arbour by the brook at seven o'clock this evening: I must speak to you.

Her curiosity was thoroughly aroused. For some time she had been expecting a declaration, which she both longed for and dreaded. It would have been agreeable to hear a confirmation of what she divined; but she felt that it would be unseemly for her to listen to an avowal from a man who, owing to his station in life, ought not to aspire ever to obtain her hand in marriage. She decided to keep the tryst but could not make up her mind on one point: should the tutor's declaration be received with aristocratic indignation, with friendly admonition, with good-humoured banter, or with silent sympathy. Meanwhile she kept looking at the time. It grew dark; candles were brought in. Kiril Petrovich sat down to play boston with some of the neighbours who had called. The clock in the dining-room struck a quarter to seven, and Maria Kirilovna walked quietly out on to the steps, looked about her, and ran into the garden.

The night was dark, the sky covered with clouds, and it was impossible to see anything at a distance of two paces, but Maria Kirilovna went forward in the darkness along the familiar paths and in a minute she reached the arbour. There she paused in order to draw breath and present herself before

Desforges with an air of calm indifference. But Desforges already stood before her.

'Thank you for not having refused my request,' he said in a low, sad voice. 'I should have been in despair if you had not come.'

Maria Kirilovna answered him with a phrase she had prepared beforehand:

'I hope you will not cause me to repent of my kindness.'

He said nothing, and seemed to be mustering his courage.

'Circumstances require . . . I have to leave you,' he said at last. 'Soon maybe you will hear . . . but I must explain to you myself before we part.'

Maria Kirilovna did not answer. She thought his words were a prelude to the declaration she had been expecting.

'I am not what you suppose,' he went on, bowing his head. 'I am not the Frenchman Desforges – I am Dubrovsky.'

Maria Kirilovna uttered a cry.

'Do not be alarmed, for God's sake! You need not be afraid of my name. Yes, I am that unhappy person whom your father, after depriving him of his last crust of bread, drove out of his paternal home to plunder and rob on the highways. But you need have no fear of me, either on your own account or on his. It is all over . . . I have forgiven him; listen, you have saved him. His was the first blood I meant to shed. I was prowling round his house, deciding where the fire was to break out, from where I should enter his bedroom, and how I should cut him off from all means of escape. At that moment you passed by me like a heavenly vision and my heart was conquered. I realized that the house in which you dwelt was sacred to me, that not a single being related to you by ties of blood could lie under my curse. I renounced vengeance as madness. For days on end I wandered round the gardens of Pokrovskoe in the hope of catching a glimpse of your white dress in the distance. I followed you in your careless walks, stealing from bush to bush, happy in the thought that there could be no danger for you where I was secretly present. At last an opportunity occurred . . . I established myself in your house. These three weeks were days of happiness for me: the memory of them will be the joy of my melancholy existence. . . . This morning I received news which makes it impossible for me to stay here any longer. . . . I am leaving you today – at this very moment. . . . But before going I had to open my heart to you so that you should not hold me up to execration or despise me. Think of Dubrovsky sometimes. Believe that he was born for another fate, that his soul was capable of loving you, that never . . .'

Just then there was a loud whistle, and Dubrovsky fell silent. He seized her hand and pressed it to his burning lips. The whistle was repeated.

'Farewell,' said Dubrovsky. 'They are calling me. A moment's delay may be fatal.'

He walked away. . . . Maria Kirilovna stood motionless. Dubrovsky came back and took her hand again.

'If ever,' he said in a tender, moving voice – 'if ever some misfortune befalls you and there is none to protect and help you, will you promise to have recourse to me, demanding that I do all in my power to save you? Will you promise not to spurn my devotion?'

Maria Kirilovna wept silently. The whistle sounded for the third time.

'You will destroy me!' cried Dubrovsky. 'I will not leave you until you give me an answer: do you promise or not?'

'I promise!' the poor girl whispered.

Greatly agitated by her tryst with Dubrovsky, Maria Kirilovna started back indoors. There seemed to be a great many people in the courtyard; a troika stood at the steps, all the servants were running about, the house was in commotion. From some distance she heard Kiril Petrovich's voice and hurried to reach her room, afraid lest her absence be noticed. In the large drawing-room she ran into Kiril Petrovich. His guests were pressing round our old acquaintance, the police-officer, bombarding him with questions. The police-captain, in travelling attire and armed to the teeth, answered them with a mysterious and preoccupied air.

'Where have you been, Masha?' asked Kiril Petrovich. 'Have you seen Monsieur Desforges?'

Masha just managed to answer in the negative.

'Would you believe it?' Kiril Petrovich went on. 'The police-captain has come to arrest him, and assures me that he is Dubrovsky.'

'The description tallies exactly, your excellency,' said the police-captain respectfully.

'Oh, my dear man, go to – you know where – with your description,' Kiril Petrovich interrupted. 'I won't give you my Frenchman till I've seen into the matter myself. One can't take Anton Pafnutyevich's word for it – a coward, and a man like that! He must have dreamt that the tutor wanted to rob him. Why didn't he tell me about it the next morning? He never said a word.'

'The Frenchman threatened him, your excellency,' replied the police-captain, 'and made him swear to keep quiet.'

'Rubbish!' Kiril Petrovich decided. 'I'll have the whole matter cleared up immediately. Well, where is the tutor?' he asked of a servant who had come into the room.

'He is nowhere to be found, sir,' the man answered.

'Then search for him!' shouted Troyekurov, beginning to feel doubtful. 'Show me that description you are so proud of,' he said to the police-captain, who instantly handed him the paper.

'Hm! Hm! Twenty-three years of age, and so on. It's all very well, but it does not prove anything. Well, where is the tutor?'

'He is not to be found, sir,' was the answer again.

Kiril Petrovich began to be uneasy; Maria Kirilovna was more dead than alive.

'You are pale, Masha,' her father remarked to her. 'Have they frightened you?'

'No, papa,' Masha replied; 'I have a headache.'

'Go along to your room, Masha, and don't you worry.'

Masha kissed his hand and hastened to her room. There she threw herself on her bed and broke into hysterical sobs.

The maids ran in, undressed her with difficulty, and with difficulty succeeded in soothing her by means of cold water and all kinds of smelling-salts. They put her to bed and she fell asleep.

The Frenchman, meanwhile, was nowhere to be found. Kiril Petrovich paced up and down the room, loudly whistling 'Thunder of victory, resound!'. The visitors whispered among themselves; the police-captain had evidently been fooled; the Frenchman had disappeared. He had probably managed to escape, having been forewarned. But by whom, and how? That remained a mystery.

It was eleven o'clock, but no one thought of sleep. At last Kiril Petrovich said angrily to the police-captain:

'Well, what about it? You can't stay here till daylight, you know: my house is not an inn. You aren't quick enough to catch Dubrovsky, my good man – if he really is Dubrovsky. Go home, and try to be a bit smarter in future. And it's time for you to be off, too,' he went on, turning to his visitors. 'Order your carriages; I want to go to bed.'

Thus ungraciously did Troyekurov take leave of his guests.

13

Some time passed without anything of interest happening. But at the beginning of the following summer many changes occurred in Kiril Petrovich's family life.

About twenty miles away there was a rich estate belonging to Prince Vereisky. For many years the prince had lived in foreign parts while a retired major managed his property for him; and there was no contact between Pokrovskoe and Arbatovo. But at the end of May the prince returned from abroad and went to live in his country-seat which until then he had never seen. Accustomed to a continual round of pleasure, he could not endure solitude, and on the third day after his arrival he set out to dine with Troyekurov, whom he had known years before.

The prince was some fifty years of age but he looked much older. Excesses of every kind had undermined his health and left their indelible stamp on him. He was perpetually in need of distraction, and perpetually bored. In spite of that, he had an attractive and distinguished appearance, and long years in society had given him a certain courtesy of manner, especially with women. Kiril Petrovich was exceedingly gratified by his visit, regarding it as a mark of respect from a man who knew the world. In accordance with his usual custom he began to entertain the prince by conducting him over his establishment and taking him to the kennels. But the prince felt almost stifled by the smell of the dogs and hurried out, pressing a scented handkerchief to his nose. The old-fashioned garden with its clipped lime-trees, square pond and formal avenues did not please him: he liked English parks and so-called nature, but he praised everything and was apparently delighted. A servant came to announce that dinner was served. They went in. The prince was limping slightly, tired with the walk and already regretting having come.

But Maria Kirilovna met them in the large drawing-room, and the old rake was struck by her beauty. Troyekurov placed his visitor beside her. Excited by her company, the prince was gay and succeeded several times in attracting her attention by his interesting stories. After dinner Kiril Petrovich proposed a ride on horseback but the prince excused himself, pointing to his velvet boots and joking about his gout. He suggested going for a drive so that he should not be separated from his charming companion. The carriage was ordered. The two old men and the beautiful girl stepped in and drove off. The conversation never flagged. Maria Kirilovna was listening with pleasure to the flattering compliments and witty remarks of the man of the world beside her, when suddenly Vereisky turned to Kiril Petrovich and asked what were those charred ruins, and did they belong to him? Kiril Petrovich frowned: the memories that the burned-out farmstead roused were distasteful to him. He answered that the land was his now but that formerly it had belonged to Dubrovsky.

'To Dubrovsky?' Vereisky echoed. 'What, to the famous brigand?'

'To his father,' replied Troyekurov; 'and his father was a bit of a brigand too.'

'And what has become of our Rinaldo?[1] Have they caught him? Is he alive?'

'Alive and still at large, and so long as we have thieves and villains for police-captains he is not likely to be caught. By the way, prince, didn't Dubrovsky pay you a visit at Arbatovo?'

'Yes, I believe last year he burnt something down or broke into some building or other. Don't you think, mademoiselle, it would be interesting to make a closer acquaintance with this romantic hero?'

'Interesting, indeed!' said Troyekurov. 'She knows him already. For three whole weeks he taught her music, but thank Heavens he did not take anything for his lessons.'

And Kiril Petrovich began telling the story of the so-called

1. Hero of Christiane Vulpius' 'Robin Hood' novel *Rinaldo Rinaldini*.

French tutor. Maria Kirilovna was on tenterhooks. Vereisky listened with deep interest and found it all very odd, and changed the subject. When they returned from the drive he ordered his carriage and, though Kiril Petrovich begged him to stay the night, departed immediately after tea. Before leaving, however, he invited Kiril Petrovich to pay him a visit with Maria Kirilovna, and the conceited Troyekurov promised to do so; for, taking into consideration the princely title, the two decorations and the three thousand serfs belonging to his ancestral estate, he regarded Prince Vereisky as in a sense his equal.

14

Two days after this visit Kiril Petrovich and his daughter set out to visit Prince Vereisky. As they approached Arbatovo he could not sufficiently admire the clean, gay huts of the peasants and the stone manor-house built after the style of an English castle. In front of the house stretched an oval meadow with lush green grass on which Swiss cows with tinkling bells round their necks were grazing. The house stood in the middle of a spacious park. Vereisky met his visitors on the steps and gave his arm to the beautiful young girl. They went into a magnificent reception-room where a table had been laid for three. The prince led his guests to the window, and a delightful view opened before them. The Volga flowed past outside; loaded barges under full sail floated by, and little fishing-boats, so aptly called smacks, flashed here and there. Beyond the river stretched hills and fields, and several small villages enlivened the landscape. Then the three proceeded to inspect the picture-gallery of paintings which the prince had purchased abroad. He explained to Maria Kirilovna the subject of each picture, told her about the painters and pointed out the merits and defects of their work. He spoke of pictures, not in the stock-language of the pedantic connoisseur, but with feeling and imagination. Maria Kirilovna enjoyed listening to him. They went into dinner. Troyekurov did full justice to his Amphitryon's wines and to the art of his cook, and Maria Kirilovna felt neither shy nor constrained in talking to a man whom she was seeing for the second time in her life. After dinner the prince proposed to his guests that they should go into the garden. They drank coffee in the arbour on the bank of a broad lake dotted with islands. Suddenly they heard the music of wind instruments, and a row-boat with six oars drifted up to the arbour. They rowed on the lake, round the islands, visiting some of them; on one they found a marble statue, on another a lonely grotto, on a third a monument with a mysterious inscription which aroused the young girl's curiosity, which the prince's courteous but reticent explanations did not altogether satisfy. The time slipped past imperceptibly. It began to grow dusk. The prince hurried his guests home because of the dew and the evening chill; the samovar was waiting for them. The prince asked Maria Kirilovna to play the part of hostess in an old bachelor's house. She poured out the tea, listening to the amiable raconteur's inexhaustible stories. Suddenly there was a report, and a rocket blazed in the sky. . . . The prince gave Maria Kirilovna a shawl and invited her and Troyekurov on to the balcony. In front of the house many-coloured lights flared up into the darkness, whirled round, rose in sheaves, cascaded in fountains, fell in showers of rain and stars, died down and flared up again. Maria Kirilovna was carried away like a child. Vereisky was delighted with her happiness, and Troyekurov was vastly pleased with him, for he regarded *tous ces frais* as signs of respect for himself and a desire to please him.

Supper was in no way inferior to the dinner in excellence. The guests retired to the bedrooms prepared for them, and next morning parted from their agreeable host, promising to see each other again in the near future.

15

MARIA KIRILOVNA was sitting in her room, embroidering at her frame before the open window. She did not mix up her silks like Konrad's mistress, who in her amorous distraction embroidered a rose in green silk.[1] Her needle faultlessly reproduced on the canvas the design she was copying; but for all that her thoughts were not on her work – they were far away.

Suddenly a hand was thrust gently in at the window, someone put a letter on the embroidery frame and disappeared before Maria Kirilovna had recovered from her surprise. At the same moment a servant came in to call her to Kiril Petrovich. Tremblingly she hid the letter under her fichu and hastened to her father's study.

Kiril Petrovich was not alone. Prince Vereisky was there with him. When Maria Kirilovna appeared he got up and bowed to her in silence, with a confusion most unusual for him.

'Come here, Masha,' said Kiril Petrovich. 'I have a piece of news to tell you which I hope will please you very much. Here is a suitor for you: the prince seeks your hand in marriage.'

Masha was aghast; a deathly pallor overspread her face. She was silent. The prince went up to her and, looking deeply moved, took her hand and asked if she would consent to make him a happy man. Masha remained silent.

'Consent? Of course she consents,' said Kiril Petrovich. 'But you know, prince, a girl finds it hard to express herself. Well, children, kiss one another and be happy.'

Masha stood motionless. The old prince kissed her hand.

1. A reference to a poem by the Polish poet Mickiewicz in which the hero's beloved, musing sadly on his absence, abstractedly embroidered a rose in green silk and its leaves in red.

Suddenly tears ran down her pale face. The prince frowned slightly.

'Off with you, off with you now,' Kiril Petrovich said. 'Dry your tears and come back to us gay as a lark. They all weep at their betrothal,' he continued, turning to Vereisky; 'it's customary, you know. Now, prince, let us talk business – that is, about the dowry.'

Maria Kirilovna eagerly took advantage of the permission to escape. Running to her room, she locked the door and gave way to her tears, imagining herself as the old prince's wife. He had suddenly become repugnant and hateful to her. . . . The idea of marriage terrified her like the executioner's block, like the grave! . . . 'No! No!' she repeated in despair. 'I'd rather go into a convent, I'd rather marry Dubrovsky. . . .' She remembered the letter and took it out, intent, guessing that it was from him. It was indeed written by him, and contained only the following words:

This evening, at ten o'clock, in the same place.

The moon was shining; the country night was still; a little breeze rose from time to time, and a gentle rustle ran through the garden.

Like an airy shadow the beautiful girl approached the trysting-place. She could not see anyone. Suddenly, emerging from behind the arbour, Dubrovsky stood before her.

'I know everything,' he said in a low, sad voice. 'Remember your promise.'

'You offer me your protection?' replied Masha. 'But – do not be angry – the idea frightens me. How could you help me?'

'I could save you from that odious man.'

'For God's sake do not lay hands on him, do not venture to lay hands on him, if you love me! I do not want to be the cause of anything horrible. . . .'

'I will not touch him: your wish is sacred for me. He owes his life to you. Never shall a crime be committed in your name. You must be unstained even where my misdeeds are concerned. But how can I save you from a cruel father?'

'There is still hope: I may move his heart with my tears, my despair. He is obstinate, but he loves me dearly.'

'Do not put your trust in vain hopes: he will see in your tears simply the timidity and aversion common to all young girls when they are marrying not for love but for sensible motives. What if he takes it into his head to arrange for your happiness in spite of yourself? What if you are led to the altar by force and your destiny placed for ever in the hands of that valetudinarian?'

'Then – then there will be nothing else to do. Come for me – I will be your wife.'

Dubrovsky trembled; his pale face flushed crimson and then grew paler than before. He paused for a while, with bowed head

'Muster all your courage, implore your father, throw yourself at his feet. Picture to him all the horror of the future that he is preparing for you, your youth fading away at the side of a feeble old rake. Tell him that riches will not procure for you even a single moment of happiness: luxury only comforts the poor, and even then but for a brief season while they are unused to it. Keep on entreating him and do not be afraid of his anger or his threats so long as there is a shadow of hope. For God's sake do not give up! But if you have no other resource left make up your mind to speak deliberately. Tell him that if he remains relentless you ... you will find a terrible protector. ...'

Dubrovsky buried his face in his hands; he seemed to be choking. Masha wept.

'My wretched, wretched fate!' he said with a bitter sigh. 'I was ready to give my life for you; to see you from a distance, to touch your hand was ecstasy for me. And now when there opens up before me the possibility of pressing you to my throbbing heart and saying "My angel, let us die together!" – unhappy creature that I am, I must guard against such bliss, I must put it from me with all the strength I have. I dare not fall at your feet and thank heaven for incredible, unmerited happiness! Oh, how I ought to hate him who ... but I feel that now there is no place in my heart for hatred.'

He put his arm gently round her slim waist and gently drew her to his heart. Trustfully she rested her head on the young brigand's shoulder. Both were silent. . . . Time flew.

'I must be going,' Masha said at last.

Dubrovsky seemed to wake from a dream. He took her hand and placed a ring on her finger.

'If you decide you want my help,' he said, 'drop the ring into the hollow of this oak: I shall know what to do.'

Dubrovsky kissed her hand and disappeared among the trees.

16

PRINCE VEREISKY'S suit was now no secret to the neighbourhood. Kiril Petrovich received congratulations, and preparations started for the wedding. Masha postponed from day to day the decisive explanation with her father. Meanwhile her manner towards her elderly suitor was cold and constrained. The prince did not worry about that. He troubled not at all about her love, satisfied with her mute consent.

But time was passing. Masha at last decided to act, and wrote a letter to Prince Vereisky. She tried to rouse a nobility of feeling in his heart, candidly confessing that she had not the slightest affection for him and begging him to renounce her hand and even to protect her from her father's power. She slipped the missive into the prince's hand. The latter read it when he was alone, and was not in the least moved by his betrothed's outspokenness. On the contrary, he perceived the necessity of hastening the wedding, and for this purpose deemed it advisable to show the letter to his future father-in-law.

Kiril Petrovich was furious; the prince had the greatest difficulty in persuading him to keep his knowledge of the letter secret from Masha. Kiril Petrovich agreed not to speak about the matter to her, but he decided to waste no time, and fixed the wedding for the following day. The prince found this very sensible; he went to his betrothed and told her that her letter had grieved him very much but that he hoped in time to gain her affection; that the thought of losing her was too painful for him to bear, and that he had not the strength to agree to his own death sentence. Then he kissed her hand respectfully and went away, not having said a word to her about Kiril Petrovich's decision.

But he had hardly left the house before her father came in and peremptorily ordered her to be ready the next day. Maria

Kirilovna, already upset by her interview with Prince Vereisky, burst into tears and threw herself at her father's feet.

'Papa!' she cried piteously. 'Papa, don't kill me. I do not love the prince, I do not want to be his wife!'

'What is the meaning of this?' said Kiril Petrovich fiercely. 'You have said nothing all this time, and been quite agreeable, and now, when everything is settled, you take it into your head to turn capricious and want to go back on it! Enough of your silly nonsense, please: you will gain nothing from me by it.'

'Do not kill me!' repeated poor Masha. 'Why are you sending me away from you and giving me to a man I do not love? Are you tired of me? I want to stay with you as before. Papa, you will be miserable without me, and more miserable still when you know that I am unhappy. Don't force me, papa: I don't want to be married.'

Kiril Petrovich was moved, but he concealed his emotion and pushing her away from him said sternly:

'That is all nonsense, do you hear? I know better than you what is necessary for your happiness. Tears will not help you: your wedding will take place the day after tomorrow.'

'The day after tomorrow!' cried Masha. 'Merciful heavens! No, no, impossible, it cannot be! Papa, listen: if you are resolved on my destruction I will find a protector you do not dream of. You shall see, you will be horrified at what you have driven me to!'

'What? What?' said Troyekurov. 'Threats! Threats to me? Insolent girl! You'll see: I shall do something with you you little imagine. You dare threaten me with your protector! We'll see who is going to be the protector.'

'Vladimir Dubrovsky,' Masha answered in despair.

Kiril Petrovich thought she had gone out of her mind, and stared at her in amazement.

'Very well,' he said after a pause. 'Look to whom you please to save you, but in the meantime you stay in this room. You shall not leave it till your wedding.'

With these words Kiril Petrovich went out and locked the door behind him.

For a long time the poor girl wept, imagining all that awaited her; but the stormy scene had relieved her heart and she could reflect more calmly on her fate and on what she must now do. The principal thing was to escape from the hateful marriage; the lot of a brigand's wife seemed paradise by comparison with the fate that was being prepared for her. She looked at Dubrovsky's ring. She longed fervently to see him alone and talk things over once more before the decisive moment. She had a presentiment that in the evening she would find him in the garden by the arbour; she decided to go and wait for him there as soon as it grew dusk. Darkness fell. Masha got ready; but the door was locked. From the other side her maid told her that Kiril Petrovich had given orders that she was not to be let out. She was under arrest. Deeply hurt, she sat down by the window and without undressing remained there till the small hours of the morning, gazing fixedly at the dark sky. Towards dawn she dozed off; but her light sleep was disturbed by sad visions and she was soon awakened by the rays of the rising sun.

17

SHE awoke, and with her first thought all the horror of her position flashed into her mind. She rang the bell. The maid entered and in answer to her questions replied that Kiril Petrovich had gone out the evening before and returned very late; that he had given strict orders that she was not to be allowed to leave her room and to see that no one spoke to her; that otherwise there were no signs of any particular preparations for the wedding, except that the priest had been told not to leave the village on any pretext whatsoever. After telling her this news the girl left Maria Kirilovna and locked the door again.

Her words hardened the young prisoner's heart. Her head was on fire, her blood in a turmoil. She decided to let Dubrovsky know everything, and began casting about for some means of getting the ring into the hollow of the oak-tree. At that moment a pebble struck her window, the glass rattled, and looking out into the courtyard she saw little Sasha signalling to her. She knew that he was attached to her, and rejoiced to see him.

'Good morning, Sasha. Why did you call me?'

'I came to see if you wanted anything. Papa is angry and has forbidden any one to do what you tell them; but you can tell me to do anything you like, and I will do it for you.'

'Thank you, Sasha, dear. Listen, you know the old hollow oak-tree by the arbour?'

'Yes, I know.'

'Well, if you love me, run there as quickly as you can and put this ring in the hollow; but mind nobody sees you.'

With this she threw the ring to him and shut the window.

The boy picked up the ring and ran off as fast as his legs could carry him, and three minutes later had reached the oak. He stopped, out of breath, looked all round, and dropped the

ring in the hollow. Having successfully accomplished his
mission, he was keen to let Masha know at once, when
suddenly a ragged red-haired boy darted out from behind the
arbour, dashed towards the oak and thrust his hand in the
hole. Sasha flew at him quicker than a squirrel and seized him
with both hands.

'What are you doing here?' he said fiercely.

'What's that to do with you?' the boy answered, trying to
wrench himself free.

'Leave that ring alone, ginger,' cried Sasha, 'or I'll give
you a good hiding.'

For answer the boy struck him in the face with his fist, but
Sasha held on, shouting at the top of his voice:

'Thieves! Thieves! Help!'

The boy fought to free himself. He looked a couple of
years older than Sasha and much stronger; but Sasha was
the more agile. They struggled for some minutes, until at
last the red-haired boy had the better of it. He knocked Sasha
down and grasped him by the throat. But at that moment a
strong hand seized him by his bristly red hair and Stepan, the
gardener, lifted him half a yard from the ground.

'Ah, you red-haired little brute,' said the gardener. 'How
dare you strike the young gentleman?'

Sasha had had time to jump up and recover.

'You got me under the arms,' he said, 'otherwise you'd
never have forced me down. Give me back the ring at once
and clear out.'

'Not likely,' replied the red-haired boy, and suddenly
twisting round he freed his bristly head from Stepan's grasp.

He started to run off but Sasha caught up with him and
pushed him in the back. The boy fell headlong. The gardener
grabbed him again and tied his arms with his belt.

'Give me the ring!' Sasha cried.

'Wait a moment, young master,' Stepan said. 'We'll take
him to the steward – he'll deal with him.'

The gardener led the captive into the courtyard and Sasha
followed, glancing uneasily at his knickers which were torn

and stained with grass. Suddenly all three found themselves face to face with Kiril Petrovich, on his way to inspect the stables.

'What's this?' he asked Stepan.

In a few words Stepan described all that had happened.

Kiril Petrovich listened carefully.

'Now, you rascal,' he said, turning to Sasha, 'what did you fight him for?'

'He stole the ring from the hollow tree, papa. Make him give me back the ring.'

'What ring? What hollow tree?'

'The one Masha . . . the ring . . .'

Sasha stammered and became confused. Kiril Petrovich frowned and said, shaking his head:

'Masha is mixed up in this. Make a clean breast of it or I'll give you such a birching that you won't know where you are.'

'Really and truly, papa, I . . . papa . . . Masha did not ask me anything, papa.'

'Stepan, go and cut me a good birch switch.'

'Wait a minute, papa, I will tell you everything. I was running about in the courtyard today and Masha opened her window, and I ran up and she dropped a ring not on purpose, and I went and hid it in the hollow tree and . . . and . . . this red-haired boy tried to steal the ring.'

'Dropped it not on purpose . . . you tried to hide it . . . Stepan, fetch me that switch.'

'Papa, wait, I'll tell you all about it. Masha told me to run to the oak-tree and put the ring in the hollow; so I ran and put the ring there but this horrid boy . . .'

Kiril Petrovich turned to the 'horrid boy' and asked him sternly:

'Who do you belong to?'

'I am a house-serf of Mr Dubrovsky's.'

Kiril Petrovich's face darkened.

'It seems, then, that you do not acknowledge me as master – very well. And what were you doing in my garden?'

'Stealing raspberries,' the boy answered carelessly.

'Aha, like master, like man, I see! And do raspberries grow on my oak-trees? Have you ever heard so?'

The boy did not answer.

'Papa, make him give back the ring,' Sasha said.

'Silence!' commanded Kiril Petrovich. 'Do not forget, I intend to deal with you presently. Go to your room. And you, squint-eye, you seem a sharp lad: if you come out with the truth I won't whip you but give you five kopecks to buy sweets with. Hand back the ring and be off.' (The boy opened his fist to show that there was nothing in his hand.) 'Or else I'll do something to you that you little expect. Well?'

The lad made no answer and stood with his head down, pretending to look half-witted.

'Very well!' said Kiril Petrovich. 'Lock him up somewhere, and see that he does not escape, or I'll flay the lot of you.'

Stepan took the boy to the pigeon-loft and locking him in told the old poultry woman, Agatha, to keep watch on him.

'There is no doubt whatever: she has kept up with that accursed Dubrovsky. Can she really have appealed to him for help?' thought Kiril Petrovich, pacing up and down the room and angrily whistling 'Thunder of victory, resound!' 'Perhaps I am hot on his track and he won't evade me. We will take advantage of this opportunity. ... Hark! a bell! What a good thing, it's the police-captain. Hey, fetch the lad here that we caught.'

Meanwhile a trap had driven into the courtyard and our old acquaintance, the police-captain, entered the room, covered with dust.

'Famous news!' said Kiril Petrovich. 'I have caught Dubrovsky!'

'Thank Heavens, your excellency!' said the police-captain, beaming with delight. 'Where is he?'

'That is, not Dubrovsky himself but one of his band. They're bringing him in now. He will help us to catch his chieftain. Here he is.'

The police-captain, expecting some fierce-looking brigand,

was surprised to see a somewhat puny boy of thirteen. He turned incredulously to Kiril Petrovich, waiting for an explanation. Kiril Petrovich then related the events of the morning, without, however, mentioning Masha's name.

The police-captain listened to him attentively, glancing from time to time at the little rascal pretending to be an idiot and apparently paying not the slightest heed to what was happening around him.

'Allow me to have a word with you alone, your excellency,' the police-captain said at last.

Kiril Petrovich led him into the next room, shutting the door after him.

Half an hour later they returned to the hall where the little prisoner was waiting for his fate to be decided.

'The gentleman wanted to have you locked up in prison and whipped, and then sent to the convict settlement,' the police-captain told him, 'but I pleaded for you and persuaded him to let you off. Untie him!'

The boy was untied.

'Thank the gentleman,' said the police-captain.

The lad went up to Kiril Petrovich and kissed his hand.

'Run away home,' Kiril Petrovich told him; 'and don't steal raspberries off oak-trees any more.'

The boy went, sprang cheerfully down the front steps and without looking round dashed off across the fields to Kistenyovka. Reaching the village, he stopped at a tumble-down cottage, the first in a row, and tapped at the window. The pane was lifted and an old woman looked out.

'Granny, some bread!' said the boy. 'I've had nothing to eat all day, I'm starving.'

'Ah, it's you, Mitya. But where have you been all this time, you little imp?'

'I'll tell you afterwards, granny. For mercy's sake, give me some bread.'

'Come indoors then.'

'I haven't time, granny: I must hurry somewhere else first. Give me some bread, for Heaven's sake!'

'What a fidgety creature the boy is!' grumbled the old woman. 'Well, here's a slice for you,' and she pushed a hunk of black bread through the open window.

The boy bit into it greedily and continued his course, eating as he went.

It was beginning to grow dusk. Mitya made his way between barns and kitchen-gardens to the Kistenyovka wood. When he reached the two pine-trees that stood like sentinels at the edge of the wood he stopped, looked round on every side, gave a sharp, shrill whistle, and then listened. He heard a faint, prolonged whistle in reply; someone stepped out of the wood and walked towards him.

18

KIRIL PETROVICH strode up and down the large drawing-room, whistling his favourite tune louder than ever. The whole house was in a commotion; men-servants ran to and fro, maids bustled backwards and forwards. In the coach-house the carriage was being got ready. A crowd of people waited in the courtyard. In Maria Kirilovna's room, before a looking-glass, a lady surrounded by maid-servants was dressing the pale and listless bride; her head drooped languidly beneath the weight of her diamonds; she started slightly when someone carelessly pricked her with a pin, but remained silent, gazing into the mirror with unseeing eyes.

'Will you be long?' Kiril Petrovich's voice asked at the door.

'Ready!' replied the lady. 'Maria Kirilovna, stand up and look at yourself – is everything all right?'

Maria Kirilovna stood up but made no answer. The door was opened.

'The bride is ready,' said the lady to Kiril Petrovich. 'Tell them to bring round the carriage.'

'God be with you!' Kiril Petrovich responded. 'Come here, Masha,' he said in a voice full of feeling, and picking up the icon from the table, 'I give you my bless – '

The poor girl fell at his feet and broke into sobs.

'Papa ... papa ...' she said through her tears, and her voice failed her.

Kiril Petrovich hastened to give her his blessing. She was lifted from the floor and almost carried to the coach. Her matron of honour and a maid-servant got in with her. They drove off to the church, where the bridegroom awaited them. He came out to meet the bride and was struck by her pallor and strange expression. Together they entered the cold empty church, and the doors were locked after them. The priest emerged from behind the ikonostasis and immediately began the ceremony. Maria Kirilovna saw nothing and heard nothing: since early morning she had had but one thought – she was waiting for Dubrovsky. Not for an instant did hope desert her. But when the priest turned to her with the customary question she shuddered and went faint with horror, but still she hung back, still she was expectant. Without waiting to hear her answer the priest pronounced the irrevocable words.

The ceremony was over. She felt the cold kiss of the husband she did not love; she heard the obsequious congratulations of those present; and yet she could not believe that her life was fettered for ever, that Dubrovsky had not come to her rescue. The prince turned to her with tender words – she did not understand them. They left the church; in the porch was a crowd of peasants from Pokrovskoe. She scanned them with a swift glance and relapsed into her former apathy. The newly-married couple stepped into a carriage and drove off to Arbatoe, whither Kiril Petrovich had gone earlier in order to meet them there. Alone with his young wife the prince was not at all disconcerted by her cold manner. He did not worry her with mawkish protestations and ridiculous ecstasies; his remarks were commonplace and required no answer. They drove in this way for about seven miles; the horses cantered along the uneven country roads and the carriage scarcely jolted on its English springs. Suddenly there were shouts of pursuit. The carriage stopped and a posse of armed men surrounded it. A man wearing a half-mask opened the door on the side where the young princess was sitting and said to her:

'You are free! Alight.'

'What does this mean?' the prince shouted. 'Who are you?'

'It is Dubrovsky,' replied the princess.

The prince, keeping his presence of mind, drew a travelling pistol from his side-pocket and fired at the masked brigand. The princess shrieked and covered her face with both hands, horror-stricken. Dubrovsky was wounded in the shoulder; blood was flowing. Not losing a moment, the prince drew another pistol. But he was not given time to use it: the carriage doors were opened and several strong arms dragged him out and snatched the pistol away. Knives glittered over him.

'Do not touch him!' Dubrovsky cried, and his awesome confederates fell back.

'You are free!' Dubrovsky continued, turning to the white-faced princess.

'No!' she answered. 'It is too late! I am married – I am Prince Vereisky's wife.'

'What are you saying?' Dubrovsky cried in despair. 'No, you are not his wife! You were forced to, you could never have given your consent. . . .'

'I did; I made the marriage vow,' she answered firmly. 'The prince is my husband. Tell your men to let him go, and leave me with him. I did not play false, I waited for you up to the last moment . . . but now, I tell you, now it is too late. Let us go.'

But Dubrovsky could no longer hear her: the pain of his wound and the violence of his emotions overcame him. He fell against the wheel of the carriage; the brigands moved forward and stood round him. He managed to say a few words to them; they lifted him into the saddle. Two of them held him up, a third took the horse by the bridle and the company went off by a side-track, leaving the carriage in the middle of the road, the servants bound, the horses unharnessed, but without carrying anything away with them or shedding one drop of blood in revenge for the blood of their chief.

19

In a narrow clearing in the deep heart of the forest was a small fort consisting of a rampart and a ditch running round some huts and shelters. A number of men immediately recognizable as bandits by their various garments and the fact that all were armed were eating their dinner, sitting bareheaded round a large cauldron. A sentry sat cross-legged on the rampart beside a small cannon. He was sewing a patch on part of his attire, plying the needle with an art that indicated the experienced tailor, and at the same time keeping a sharp look-out in every direction.

Though the drinking-cup had been passed round several times a strange hush reigned among the gathering. The bandits finished their dinner; one after another they got to their feet and silently offered their thanksgiving. Some dispersed to their huts, others wandered off into the forest or lay down for a brief nap as Russians do.

The sentry finished his sewing, gave his patched-up garment a shake, admired his handiwork, stuck the needle in his sleeve, sat astride the cannon and sang at the top of his voice the melancholy old song:

> 'Rustle not, Mother-forest, with all your green leaves,
> And stay not a young lad from thinking his thoughts.'

At that moment the door of one of the huts opened and an old woman in a white cap, neatly and primly dressed, appeared on the threshold.

'That's enough, Styopka,' she said crossly. 'The master is having a rest, and you keep on yelling like this! You people have no conscience, no pity.'

'I'm sorry, Yegorovna,' Styopka answered. 'All right, I'll be quiet. Let him sleep and get better.'

The old woman withdrew into the hut and Styopka began pacing up and down the rampart.

Inside the hut from which the old woman had emerged the wounded Dubrovsky lay on a camp-bed behind a partition. His pistols were on a table in front of him and his sword hung near his head. The floor and the walls of the mud-hut were covered with rich rugs. In a corner was a lady's silver toilet-set and a cheval-glass. Dubrovsky held an open book in his hand but his eyes were closed and the old woman, who kept peeping at him from the other side of the partition, could not tell whether he was asleep or merely lost in thought.

Suddenly Dubrovsky started. There was a commotion in the stronghold and Styopka thrust his head in at the window.

'Vladimir Andreyevich, sir!' he shouted. 'Our men are signalling – they are on our track!'

Dubrovsky leaped from his bed, seized his weapons and came out from the hut. The brigands were crowding noisily together in the enclosure but when they saw him there was a deep silence.

'Are you all here?' Dubrovsky asked.

'All except the patrols,' was the reply.

'To your stations!' cried Dubrovsky, and the brigands took up each his appointed place.

At that moment three of the scouts ran up to the gate of the fort. Dubrovsky went over to them.

'What is it?' he asked.

'Soldiers in the forest, they are surrounding us.'

Dubrovsky ordered the gates to be locked and went to examine the cannon. Voices were heard in the forest, drawing nearer and nearer. The brigands waited in silence. Suddenly three or four soldiers appeared out of the forest and immediately drew back again, firing their muskets as a signal to their comrades.

'Prepare for battle!' cried Dubrovsky, and there was a movement among the bandits. Then all was still again.

They could hear the noise of the approaching column; see the glint of weapons among the trees. Some hundred and fifty soldiers poured out of the forest and rushed with a shout towards the rampart. Dubrovsky lit the fuse; the shot was successful – one soldier had his head blown off and two others were wounded. The troops were thrown into confusion but the officer dashed forward, the soldiers followed him and jumped down into the ditch. The brigands fired down at them with muskets and pistols, and then with axes in their hands prepared to defend the rampart against the infuriated soldiers who were now climbing it, leaving a score of their fellows wounded in the ditch below. A hand-to-hand struggle followed. The soldiers were already on the rampart and the brigands losing ground but Dubrovsky advanced towards the officer in command of the attacking party, put his pistol to the man's breast and fired. The officer crashed backwards to the ground. Some soldiers lifted him into their arms and hastened to carry him into the wood; the others, having lost their leader, stopped fighting. Encouraged by their momentary hesitation, the brigands pressed them back into the ditch. The attackers began to run; with fierce yells the brigands started in pursuit. The victory was decisive. Feeling sure that the enemy was completely routed, Dubrovsky called his men off and, giving orders to pick up the wounded, shut himself in his fortress, after having doubled the number of sentries and forbidden anyone to leave the place.

These last events drew the attention of the Government to Dubrovsky's daring robberies. Information was obtained of his whereabouts and a detachment of soldiers sent to capture him dead or alive. Several of his band were caught and from them it was learned that Dubrovsky was no longer with them. A few days after the battle he had called together all his confederates and declared that he was leaving them for ever, and advised them to change their way of living.

'You have become rich under my command. Each of you has a pass with which he can safely make his way to some distant province and there spend the rest of his life in honest labour and prosperity. But you are all rascals and probably will not wish to give up your trade.'

After this speech he left them, taking with him only one man. No one knew what became of him. At first the truth of this testimony was doubted – the brigands' devotion to their leader was well known and it was thought that they were trying to shield him; but subsequently it found confirmation. The dreadful raids, the incendiarism and the robberies ceased. The roads became safe once more. According to other sources it appeared that Dubrovsky had fled to some foreign country.[1]

1. Pushkin did not finish *Dubrovsky,* which was first published posthumously in 1841. His MSS. notes contain the following synopsis for the continuation of the novel:

> Maria Kirilovna's life
> Death of Prince Vereisky
>   The Widow
> The Englishman [Dubrovsky returns to Maria Kirilovna in the guise of an Englishman]
>   The Meeting [between Dubrovsky and Maria Kirilovna]
>   The Gamblers
> The Chief of Police
>   *Dénouement*

Another plan reads:

> Moscow, the Surgeon, Solitude
>   The Tavern, Denunciation
> Suspicion, the Chief of Police.

1832–3

The Queen of Spades

THE QUEEN OF SPADES BETOKENS
THE EVIL EYE
Modern Guide to Fortune-Telling

I

When bleak was the weather
They would meet together
For cards — God forgive them!
Some would win, others lost,
And they chalked up the cost
In bleak autumn weather
When they met together.

THERE was a card party in the rooms of Narumov, an officer of the Horse Guards. The long winter night had passed unnoticed and it was after four in the morning when the company sat down to supper. Those who had won enjoyed their food; the others sat absent-mindedly in front of empty plates. But when the champagne appeared conversation became more lively and general.

'How did you fare, Surin?' Narumov asked.

'Oh I lost, as usual. I must confess, I have no luck: I stick to *mirandole*, never get excited, never lose my head, and yet I never win.'

'Do you mean to tell me you were not once tempted to back the red the whole evening? Your self-control amazes me.'

'But look at Hermann,' exclaimed one of the party, pointing to a young officer of the Engineers. 'Never held a card in his hands, never made a bet in his life, and yet he sits up till five in the morning watching us play.'

'Cards interest me very much,' said Hermann, 'but I am not in a position to risk the necessary in the hope of acquiring the superfluous.'

'Hermann is a German: he's careful, that's what that is!' remarked Tomsky. 'But if there is one person I can't understand it is my grandmother, Countess Anna Fedotovna.'

'Why is that?' the guests cried.

'I cannot conceive how it is that my grandmother does not play.'

'But surely there is nothing surprising in an old lady in the eighties not wanting to gamble?' said Narumov.

'Then you don't know about her?'

'No, nothing, absolutely nothing!'

'Well, listen then. I must tell you that some sixty years ago my grandmother went to Paris and was quite the rage there. People would run after her to catch a glimpse of *la Vénus moscovite*; Richelieu was at her beck and call, and grandmamma maintains that he very nearly blew his brains out because of her cruelty to him. In those days ladies used to play faro. One evening at the Court she lost a very considerable sum to the Duke of Orleans. When she got home she told my grandfather of her loss while removing the beauty spots from her face and untying her farthingale, and commanded him to pay her debt. My grandfather, so far as I remember, acted as a sort of major-domo to my grandmother. He feared her like fire; however, when he heard of such a frightful gambling loss he almost went out of his mind, fetched the bills they owed and pointed out to her that in six months they had spent half a million roubles and that in Paris they had neither their Moscow nor their Saratov estates upon which to draw, and flatly refused to pay. Grandmamma gave him a box on the ear and retired to bed without him as a sign of her displeasure. The following morning she sent for her husband, hoping that the simple punishment had had its effect, but she found him as obdurate as ever. For the first time in her life she went so far as to reason with him and explain, thinking to rouse his conscience and arguing with condescension, that there were debts and debts, and that a prince was different from a coachbuilder. But it was not a bit of good – grandfather just would not hear of it. "Once and for all, no!" Grandmamma did not know what to do. Among her close acquaintances was a very remarkable man. You have heard of Count Saint-Germain, about whom so many marvellous stories are told. You know that he posed as the Wandering Jew and claimed to have discovered the elixir of life and the philosopher's stone, and so on. People laughed at him as a charlatan, and Casanova in his *Memoirs* says that he was a spy. Be that as it may, Saint-Germain, in spite of the mystery that surrounded him, had a most dignified appearance and was a very amiable person in society. Grandmamma is still to this day quite devoted to his memory and gets angry if anyone speaks of him with disrespect. Grandmamma knew that Saint-Germain had plenty of money at his disposal. She decided to appeal to him, and wrote a note asking him to come and see her immediately. The eccentric old man came at once and found her in terrible distress. She described in the blackest colours her husband's inhumanity, and ended by declaring that she laid all her hopes on his friendship and kindness. Saint-Germain pondered. "I could oblige you with the sum you want," he said, "but I know that you would not be easy until you had repaid me, and I should not like to involve you in fresh trouble. There is another way out – you could win it back."

'"But, my dear count," answered grandmamma, "I tell you I have no money at all."

'"That does not matter," Saint-Germain replied. "Listen now to what I am going to tell you."

'And he revealed to her a secret which all of us would give a great deal to know. . . .'

The young gamblers redoubled their attention. Tomsky lit his pipe, puffed away for a moment and continued:

'That very evening grandmamma appeared at Versailles, at the *jeu de la reine*. The Duke of Orleans kept the bank. Grandmamma lightly excused herself for not having brought the money to pay off her debt, inventing some little story by way of explanation, and began to play against him. She selected three cards and played them one after the other: all three won, and grandmamma retrieved her loss completely.'

'Luck!' said one of the party.

'A fairy tale!' remarked Hermann.

'Marked cards, perhaps,' put in a third.

'I don't think so,' replied Tomsky impressively.

'What!' said Narumov. 'You have a grandmother who knows how to hit upon three lucky cards in succession, and you haven't learnt her secret yet?'

'That's the deuce of it!' Tomsky replied. 'She had four sons, one of whom was my father; all four were desperate gamblers, and yet she did not reveal her secret to a single one of them, though it would not have been a bad thing for them, or for me either. But listen to what my uncle, Count Ivan Ilyich, used to say, assuring me on his word of honour that it was true. Tchaplitsky – you know him, he died a pauper after squandering millions – as a young man once lost three hundred thousand roubles, to Zorich, if I remember rightly. He was in despair. Grandmamma was always very severe on the follies of young men, but somehow she took pity on Tchaplitsky. She gave him three cards, which he was to play one after the other, at the same time exacting from him a promise that he would never afterwards touch a card so long as he lived. Tchaplitsky went to Zorich's; they sat down to play. Tchaplitsky staked fifty thousand on his first card and won; doubled his stake and won; did the same again, won back his loss and ended up in pocket. . . .

'But, I say, it's time to go to bed: it is a quarter to six already.'

And indeed dawn was breaking. The young men emptied their glasses and went home.

2

'Il paraît que monsieur est décidément pour les suivantes.'
'Que voulez-vous, madame? Elles sont plus fraîches.'

FROM A SOCIETY CONVERSATION[1]

THE old Countess X was seated before the looking-glass in her dressing-room. Three maids were standing round her. One held a pot of rouge, another a box of hairpins, and the third a tall cap with flame-coloured ribbons. The countess had not the slightest pretensions to beauty – it had faded long ago – but she still preserved all the habits of her youth, followed strictly the fashion of the seventies, and gave as much time and care to her toilette as she had sixty years before. A young girl whom she had brought up sat at an embroidery frame by the window.

'Good morning, *grand'maman*!' said a young officer, coming into the room. *'Bonjour, Mademoiselle Lise. Grand'maman*, I have a favour to ask of you.'

'What is it, Paul?'

'I want you to let me introduce to you a friend of mine and bring him to your ball on Friday.'

'Bring him straight to the ball and introduce him to me then. Were you at the princess's last night?'

'Of course I was! It was most enjoyable: we danced until five in the morning. Mademoiselle Yeletsky looked enchanting!'

'Come, my dear! What is there enchanting about her? She isn't a patch on her grandmother, Princess Daria Petrovna.

1. The conversation occurred between the poet Denis Davuidov and Mme Maria Naryshkin, Alexander I's favourite, and had been related to Pushkin years previously by Davuidov.
cf. Davuidov's letter to Pushkin of 4 April 1834.

By the way, I expect Princess Daria Petrovna must have aged considerably?'

'How do you mean, aged?' Tomsky replied absent-mindedly. 'She's been dead for the last seven years.'

The girl at the window raised her head and made a sign to the young man. He remembered that they concealed the deaths of her contemporaries from the old countess, and bit his lip. But the countess heard the news with the utmost indifference.

'Dead! I didn't know,' she said. 'We were maids of honour together, and as we were being presented the Empress . . .'

And for the hundredth time the countess repeated the story to her grandson.

'Well, Paul,' she said at the end; 'now help me to my feet. *Lise*, where is my snuff-box?'

And the countess went with her maids behind the screen to finish dressing. Tomsky was left *à deux* with the young girl.

'Who is it you want to introduce?' Lizaveta Ivanovna asked softly.

'Narumov. Do you know him?'

'No. Is he in the army?'

'Yes.'

'In the Engineers?'

'No, Horse Guards. What made you think he was in the Engineers?'

The girl laughed and made no answer.

'Paul!' the countess called from behind the screen. 'Send me a new novel to read, only pray not one of those modern ones.'

'How do you mean, *grand'maman*?'

'I want a book in which the hero does not strangle either his father or his mother, and where there are no drowned corpses. I have a horror of drowned persons.'

'There aren't any novels of that sort nowadays. Wouldn't you like something in Russian?'

'Are there any Russian novels? . . . Send me something, my dear fellow, please send me something!'

'Excuse me, *grand'maman*: I must hurry. . . . Good-bye, Lizaveta Ivanovna! I wonder, what made you think Narumov was in the Engineers?'

And Tomsky departed from the dressing-room.

Lizaveta Ivanovna was left alone. She abandoned her work and began to look out of the window. Soon, round the corner of a house on the other side of the street, a young officer appeared. Colour flooded her cheeks; she took up her work again, bending her head over her embroidery-frame. At that moment the countess came in, having finished dressing.

'Order the carriage, *Lise*,' she said, 'and let us go for a drive.'

Lizaveta Ivanovna rose from her embroidery-frame and began putting away her work.

'What is the matter with you, my child, are you deaf?' the countess cried. 'Be quick and order the carriage.'

'I will go at once,' the young girl answered quietly, and ran into the ante-room.

A servant came in and handed the countess a parcel of books from Prince Paul Alexandrovich.

'Good! Tell him I am much obliged,' said the countess. '*Lise, Lise*, where are you off to?'

'To dress.'

'There is plenty of time, my dear. Sit down here. Open the first volume and read to me.'

The girl took the book and read a few lines.

'Louder!' said the countess. 'What is the matter with you, my dear? Have you lost your voice, or what? Wait a minute. . . . Give me that footstool. A little closer. That will do!'

Lizaveta Ivanovna read two more pages. The countess yawned.

'Throw that book away,' she said. 'What nonsense it is! Send it back to Prince Paul with my thanks. . . . What about the carriage?'

'The carriage is ready,' said Lizaveta Ivanovna, glancing out into the street.

'How is it you are not dressed?' the countess said. 'You always keep people waiting. It really is intolerable!'

Liza ran to her room. Hardly two minutes passed before the countess started ringing with all her might. Three maids rushed in at one door and a footman at the other.

'Why is it you don't come when you are called?' the countess said to them. 'Tell Lizaveta Ivanovna I am waiting.'

Lizaveta Ivanovna returned, wearing a hat and a pelisse.

'At last, my dear!' said the countess. 'Why the finery? What is it for? . . . For whose benefit? . . . And what is the weather like? Windy, isn't it?'

'No, your ladyship,' the footman answered, 'there is no wind at all.'

'You say anything that comes into your head! Open the window. Just as I thought: there is a wind, and a very cold one too! Dismiss the carriage. *Lise*, my child, we won't go out – you need not have dressed up after all.'

'And this is my life!' Lizaveta Ivanovna thought to herself.

Indeed, Lizaveta Ivanovna was a most unfortunate creature. 'Another's bread is bitter to the taste,' says Dante, 'and his staircase hard to climb';[1] and who should know the bitterness of dependence better than a poor orphan brought up by an old lady of quality? The countess was certainly not bad-hearted but she had all the caprices of a woman spoiled by society, she was stingy and coldly selfish, like all old people who have done with love and are out of touch with life around them. She took part in all the vanities of the fashionable world, dragged herself to balls, where she sat in a corner, rouged and attired after some bygone mode, like a misshapen but indispensable ornament of the ball-room. On their arrival the guests all went up to her and bowed low, as though in accordance with an old-established rite, and after that no one took any more notice of her. She received the whole town

1. *La Divina Commedia, Il Paradiso,* canto xvii:
    Tu proverai sí come sa di sale
      lo pane altrui, e com'è duro calle
      lo scendere e 'l salir per l'altrui scale.

at her house, observing the strictest etiquette and not recognizing the faces of any of her guests. Her numerous servants,
grown fat and grey in her entrance hall and the maids'
quarters, did what they liked and vied with each other in
robbing the decrepit old woman. Lizaveta Ivanovna was the
household martyr. She poured out tea and was reprimanded
for using too much sugar; she read novels aloud to the
countess and was blamed for all the author's mistakes; she
accompanied the countess on her drives and was answerable
for the weather and the state of the roads. She was supposed
to receive a salary, which was never paid in full and yet she
was expected to be as well dressed as everyone else – that is,
as very few indeed. In society she played the most pitiable
role. Everybody knew her and nobody gave her any thought.
At balls she danced only when someone was short of a
partner, and the ladies would take her by the arm each time
they wanted to go to the cloak-room to rearrange some detail
of their toilette. She was sensitive and felt her position keenly,
and looked about impatiently for a deliverer to come; but
the young men, calculating in their empty-headed frivolity,
honoured her with scant attention though Lizaveta Ivanovna
was a hundred times more charming than the cold, brazen-
faced heiresses they ran after. Many a time she crept away
from the tedious, glittering drawing-room to go and weep in
her humble little attic with its wall-paper screen, chest of
drawers, small looking-glass and painted wooden bedstead,
and where a tallow-candle burned dimly in a brass candle-
stick.

One morning, two days after the card party described at the
beginning of this story and a week before the scene we have
just witnessed – one morning Lizaveta Ivanovna, sitting at
her embroidery-frame by the window, happened to glance out
into the street and see a young Engineers officer standing
stock-still gazing at her window. She lowered her head and
went on with her work. Five minutes afterwards she looked
out again – the young officer was still on the same spot. Not
being in the habit of coquetting with passing officers, she

looked out no more and went on sewing for a couple of hours without raising her head. Luncheon was announced. She got up to put away her embroidery-frame and, glancing casually into the street, saw the officer again. This seemed to her somewhat strange. After luncheon she went to the window with a certain feeling of uneasiness, but the officer was no longer there, and she forgot about him. . . .

A day or so later, just as she was stepping into the carriage with the countess, she saw him again. He was standing right by the front door, his face hidden by his beaver collar; his dark eyes sparkled beneath his fur cap. Lizaveta Ivanovna felt alarmed, though she did not know why, and seated herself in the carriage, inexplicably agitated.

On returning home she ran to the window – the officer was standing in his accustomed place, his eyes fixed on her. She drew back, consumed with curiosity and excited by a feeling quite new to her.

Since then not a day had passed without the young man appearing at a certain hour beneath the windows of their house, and between him and her a sort of mute acquaintance was established. Sitting at her work she would sense his approach, and lifting her head she looked at him longer and longer every day. The young man seemed to be grateful to her for looking out: with the keen eyes of youth she saw the quick flush of his pale cheeks every time their glances met. By the end of a week she had smiled at him. . . .

When Tomsky asked the countess's permission to introduce a friend of his the poor girl's heart beat violently. But hearing that Narumov was in the Horse Guards, not the Engineers, she regretted the indiscreet question by which she had betrayed her secret to the irresponsible Tomsky.

*

Hermann was the son of a German who had settled in Russia and who left him some small capital sum. Being firmly convinced that it was essential for him to make certain of his independence, Hermann did not touch even the interest on his income but lived on his pay, denying himself the slightest extravagance. But since he was reserved and ambitious his companions rarely had any opportunity for making fun of his extreme parsimony. He had strong passions and an ardent imagination, but strength of character preserved him from the customary mistakes of youth. Thus, for instance, though a gambler at heart he never touched cards, having decided that his means did not allow him (as he put it) 'to risk the necessary in the hope of acquiring the superfluous'. And yet he spent night after night at the card tables, watching with feverish anxiety the vicissitudes of the game.

The story of the three cards had made a powerful impression upon his imagination and it haunted his mind all night. 'Supposing,' he thought to himself the following evening as he wandered about Petersburg, 'supposing the old countess were to reveal her secret to me? Or tell me the three winning cards! Why shouldn't I try my luck? . . . Get introduced to her, win her favour – become her lover, perhaps. But all that would take time, and she is eighty-seven. She might be dead next week, or the day after tomorrow even! . . . And the story itself? Is it likely? No, economy, moderation and hard work are my three winning cards. With them I can treble my capital – increase it sevenfold and obtain for myself leisure and independence!' Musing thus, he found himself in one of the main streets of Petersburg, in front of a house of old-fashioned architecture. The street was lined with carriages which followed one another up to the lighted porch. Out of the carriages stepped now the shapely little foot of a young beauty, now a military boot with clinking spur, or a diplomat's striped stockings and buckled shoes. Fur coats and cloaks passed in rapid procession before the majestic-looking concierge. Hermann stopped.

'Whose house is that?' he asked a watchman in his box at the corner.

'The Countess X's,' the man told him. It was Tomsky's grandmother.

Hermann started. The strange story of the three cards came

into his mind again. He began walking up and down past the house, thinking of its owner and her wonderful secret. It was late when he returned to his humble lodgings; he could not get to sleep for a long time, and when sleep did come he dreamed of cards, a green baize table, stacks of bank-notes and piles of gold. He played card after card, resolutely turning down the corners, winning all the time. He raked in the gold and stuffed his pockets with bank-notes. Waking late in the morning, he sighed over the loss of his fantastic wealth, and then, sallying forth to wander about the town again, once more found himself outside the countess's house. It was as though some supernatural force drew him there. He stopped and looked up at the windows. In one of them he saw a dark head bent over a book or some needlework. The head was raised. Hermann caught sight of a rosy face and a pair of black eyes. That moment decided his fate.

3

Vous m'écrivez, mon ange, des lettres de quatre pages plus vite que je ne puis les lire.

FROM A CORRESPONDENCE[1]

LIZAVETA IVANOVNA had scarcely taken off her hat and mantle before the countess sent for her and again ordered the carriage. They went out to take their seats. Just as the two footmen were lifting the old lady and helping her through the carriage door Lizaveta Ivanovna saw her Engineers officer standing by the wheel. He seized her hand; before she had recovered from her alarm the young man had disappeared, leaving a letter between her fingers. She hid it in her glove, and for the rest of the drive neither saw nor heard anything. It was the countess's habit when they were out in the carriage to ask a constant stream of questions: 'Who was that we met?' – 'What bridge is this?' – 'What does that signboard say?' This time Lizaveta Ivanovna returned such random and irrelevant answers that the countess grew angry with her.

'What is the matter with you, my dear? Have you taken leave of your senses? Don't you hear me or understand what I say? . . . I speak distinctly enough, thank heaven, and am not in my dotage yet!'

Lizaveta Ivanovna paid no attention to her. When they returned home she ran up to her room and drew the letter out of her glove: it was unsealed. She read it. The letter contained a declaration of love: it was tender, respectful and had been copied word for word from a German novel. But Lizaveta Ivanovna did not know any German and she was delighted with it.

1. In 1829 Pushkin planned a romance in the form of letters, on the lines of the old sentimental novel (cf. Richardson), and wrote passages of it during the thirties. The heroine's name was Liza, the hero's – Hermann. This work eventually developed into *The Queen of Spades*.

For all that, the letter troubled her greatly. For the first time in her life she was embarking upon secret and intimate relations with a young man. His boldness appalled her. She reproached herself for her imprudent behaviour, and did not know what to do: ought she to give up sitting at the window and by a show of indifference damp the young man's inclination to pursue her further? Should she return his letter to him? Or answer it coldly and firmly? There was nobody to whom she could turn for advice: she had neither female friend nor preceptor. Lizaveta Ivanovna decided to reply to the letter.

She sat down at her little writing-table, took pen and paper – and began to ponder. Several times she made a start and then tore the paper across: what she had written seemed to her either too indulgent or too harsh. At last she succeeded in composing a few lines with which she felt satisfied. 'I am sure', she wrote, 'that your intentions are honourable and that you had no wish to hurt me by any thoughtless conduct; but our acquaintance ought not to have begun in this manner. I return you your letter, and hope that in future I shall have no cause to complain of being shown a lack of respect which is undeserved.'

Next day, as soon as she saw Hermann approaching, Lizaveta Ivanovna got up from her embroidery-frame, went into the drawing-room, opened the little ventilating window and threw the letter into the street, trusting to the young officer's alertness. Hermann ran forward, picked the letter up and went into a confectioner's shop. Breaking the seal, he found his own letter and Lizaveta Ivanovna's reply. It was just what he had expected and he returned home engrossed in his plot.

Three days after this a sharp-eyed young person brought Lizaveta Ivanovna a note from a milliner's establishment. Lizaveta Ivanovna opened it uneasily, fearing it was a demand for money, and suddenly recognized Hermann's handwriting.

'You have made a mistake, my dear,' she said. 'This note is not for me.'

'Oh yes it is for you!' retorted the girl boldly, not troubling to conceal a knowing smile. 'Please read it.'

Lizaveta Ivanovna glanced at the letter. In it Hermann wanted her to meet him.

'Impossible!' she cried, alarmed at the request, at its coming so soon, and at the means employed to transmit it. 'I am sure this was not addressed to me.' And she tore the letter into fragments.

'If the letter was not for you, why did you tear it up?' said the girl. 'I would have returned it to the sender.'

'Be good enough, my dear,' said Lizaveta Ivanovna, flushing crimson at her remark, 'not to bring me any more letters. And tell the person who sent you that he ought to be ashamed ...'

But Hermann did not give in. Every day Lizaveta Ivanovna received a letter from him by one means or another. They were no longer translated from the German. Hermann wrote them inspired by passion and in a style which was his own: they reflected both his inexorable desire and the disorder of an unbridled imagination. Lizaveta Ivanovna no longer thought of returning them: she drank them in eagerly and took to answering – and the notes she sent grew longer and more affectionate every hour. At last she threw out of the window to him the following letter:

There is a ball tonight at the Embassy. The countess will be there. We shall stay until about two o'clock. Here is an opportunity for you to see me alone. As soon as the countess is away the servants are sure to go to their quarters, leaving the concierge in the hall but he usually retires to his lodge. Come at half past eleven. Walk straight up the stairs. If you meet anyone in the ante-room, ask if the countess is at home. They will say 'No', but there will be no help for it – you will have to go away. But probably you will not meet anyone. The maids all sit together in the one room. Turn to the left out of the ante-room and keep straight on until you reach the countess's bedroom. In the bedroom, behind a screen, you will find two small doors: the one on the right leads into the study where the countess never goes; and the other on the left opens into a passage with a narrow winding staircase up to my room.

Hermann waited for the appointed hour like a tiger trembling for its prey. By ten o'clock in the evening he was already standing outside the countess's house. It was a frightful night: the wind howled, wet snow fell in big flakes; the street lamps burned dimly; the streets were deserted. From time to time a sledge drawn by a sorry-looking hack passed by, the driver on the watch for a belated fare. Hermann stood there without his great-coat, feeling neither the wind nor the snow. At last the countess's carriage was brought round. Hermann saw the old woman wrapped in sables being lifted into the vehicle by two footmen; then Liza in a light cloak, with natural flowers in her hair, flitted by. The carriage doors banged. The vehicle rolled heavily over the wet snow. The concierge closed the street-door. The lights in the windows went out. Hermann started to walk to and fro outside the deserted house; he went up to a street-lamp and glanced at his watch: it was twenty minutes past eleven. He stood still by the lamp-post, his eyes fixed on the hand of the watch. Precisely at half past eleven Hermann walked up the steps of the house and entered the brightly lit vestibule. The concierge was not there. Hermann ran up the stairs, opened the door of the ante-room and saw a footman asleep in a soiled, old-fashioned arm-chair by the side of a lamp. With a light, firm tread Hermann passed quickly by him. The ball-room and drawing-room were in darkness but the lamp in the ante-room shed a dim light into them. Hermann entered the bedroom. Ancient icons filled the icon-stand before which burned a golden lamp. Arm-chairs upholstered in faded damask and sofas with down cushions, the tassels of which had lost their gilt, were ranged with depressing symmetry round the walls hung with Chinese wall-paper. On one of the walls were two portraits painted in Paris by Madame Lebrun: the first of a stout, red-faced man of some forty years of age, in a light-green uniform with a star on his breast; the other – a beautiful young woman with an aquiline nose and a rose in the powdered hair drawn back over her temples. Every corner was crowded with porcelain shepherdesses, clocks made by the celebrated Leroy, little boxes, roulettes, fans and all the thousand and one playthings invented for ladies of fashion at the end of the last century together with Montgolfier's balloon and Mesmer's magnetism. Hermann stepped behind the screen. A small iron bedstead stood there; to the right was the door into the study – to the left, the other door into the passage. Hermann opened it and saw the narrow winding staircase leading to poor little Liza's room. But he turned about and went into the dark study.

The time passed slowly. Everything was quiet. The drawing-room clock struck twelve; the clocks in the other rooms chimed twelve, one after the other, and all was still again. Hermann stood leaning against the cold stove. He was quite calm: his heart beat evenly, like that of a man resolved upon a dangerous but inevitable undertaking. The clocks struck one, and then two, and he heard the distant rumble of a carriage. In spite of himself he was overcome with agitation. The carriage drove up to the house and stopped. He heard the clatter of the carriage-steps being lowered. In the house all was commotion. Servants ran to and fro, there was a confusion of voices, and lights appeared everywhere. Three ancient lady's maids bustled into the bedroom, followed by the countess who, half dead with fatigue, sank into a Voltaire arm-chair. Hermann watched through a crack in the door. Lizaveta Ivanovna passed close by him and he heard her footsteps hurrying up the stairs to her room. For a moment something akin to remorse assailed him but he quickly hardened his heart again.

The countess began undressing before the looking-glass. Her maids took off the cap trimmed with roses and lifted the powdered wig from her grey, closely-cropped head. Pins showered about her. The silver-trimmed yellow dress fell at her puffy feet. Hermann witnessed the hideous mysteries of her toilet; at last the countess put on bed jacket and night-cap, and in this attire, more suited to her age, she seemed less horrible and ugly.

Like most old people the countess suffered from sleeplessness. Having undressed, she sat down in a big arm-chair by the window and dismissed her maids. They took away the candles, leaving only the lamp before the icons to light the room. The countess sat there, her skin sallow with age, her flabby lips twitching, her body swaying to and fro. Her dim eyes were completely vacant and looking at her one might have imagined that the dreadful old woman was rocking her body not from choice but owing to some secret galvanic mechanism.

Suddenly an inexplicable change came over the death-like face. The lips ceased to move, the eyes brightened: before the countess stood a strange young man.

'Do not be alarmed, for heaven's sake, do not be alarmed!' he said in a low, clear voice. 'I have no intention of doing you any harm, I have come to beg a favour of you.'

The old woman stared at him in silence, as if she had not heard. Hermann thought she must be deaf and bending down to her ear he repeated what he had just said. The old woman remained silent as before.

'You can ensure the happiness of my whole life,' Hermann went on, 'and at no cost to yourself. I know that you can name three cards in succession . . .'

Hermann stopped. The countess appeared to have grasped what he wanted and to be seeking words to frame her answer.

'It was a joke,' she said at last. 'I swear to you it was a joke.'

'No, madam,' Hermann retorted angrily. 'Remember Tchaplitsky, and how you enabled him to win back his loss.'

The countess was plainly perturbed. Her face expressed profound agitation; but soon she relapsed into her former impassivity.

'Can you not tell me those three winning cards?' Hermann went on.

The countess said nothing. Hermann continued:

'For whom would you keep your secret? For your grandsons? They are rich enough already: they don't appreciate the value of money. Your three cards would not help a spend-thrift. A man who does not take care of his inheritance will die a beggar though all the demons of the world were at his command. I am not a spendthrift: I know the value of money. Your three cards would not be wasted on me. Well? . . .'

He paused, feverishly waiting for her reply. She was silent. Hermann fell on his knees.

'If your heart has ever known what it is to love, if you can remember the ecstasies of love, if you have ever smiled tenderly at the cry of your new-born son, if any human feeling has ever stirred in your breast, I appeal to you as wife, beloved one, mother – I implore you by all that is holy in life not to reject my prayer: tell me your secret. Of what use is it to you? Perhaps it is bound up with some terrible sin, with the loss of eternal salvation, with some bargain with the devil . . . Reflect – you are old: you have not much longer to live, and I am ready to take your sin upon my soul. Only tell me your secret. Remember that a man's happiness is in your hands; that not only I, but my children and my children's children will bless your memory and hold it sacred. . . .'

The old woman answered not a word.

Hermann rose to his feet.

'You old hag!' he said, grinding his teeth. 'Then I will make you speak. . . .'

With these words he drew a pistol from his pocket. At the sight of the pistol the countess for the second time showed signs of agitation. Her head shook and she raised a hand as though to protect herself from the shot. . . . Then she fell back . . . and was still.

'Come, an end to this childish nonsense!' said Hermann, seizing her by the arm. 'I ask you for the last time – will you tell me those three cards? Yes or no?'

The countess made no answer. Hermann saw that she was dead.

4

7 mai 18—
Homme sans mœurs et sans religion!
FROM A CORRESPONDENCE

LIZAVETA IVANOVNA was sitting in her room, still in her ball dress, lost in thought. On returning home she had made haste to dismiss the sleepy maid who reluctantly offered to help her, saying that she would undress herself, and with trembling heart had gone to her own room, expecting to find Hermann and hoping that she would not find him. A glance convinced her he was not there, and she thanked fate for having prevented their meeting. She sat down without undressing and began to recall the circumstances that had led her so far in so short a time. It was not three weeks since she had first caught sight of the young man from the window – and yet she was carrying on a correspondence with him, and he had already succeeded in inducing her to agree to a nocturnal tryst! She knew his name only because he had signed some of his letters; she had never spoken to him, did not know the sound of his voice, had never heard him mentioned ... until that evening. Strange to say, that very evening at the ball, Tomsky, piqued with the young Princess Pauline for flirting with somebody else instead of with him as she usually did, decided to revenge himself by a show of indifference. He asked Lizaveta Ivanovna to be his partner and danced the interminable mazurka with her. And all the time he kept teasing her about her partiality for officers of the Engineers, assuring her that he knew far more than she could suppose, and some of his sallies so found their mark that several times Lizaveta Ivanovna thought he must know her secret.

'Who told you all this?' she asked, laughing.

'A friend of someone you know,' Tomsky answered, 'a very remarkable person.'

'And who is this remarkable man?'

'His name is Hermann.'

Lizaveta Ivanovna said nothing; but her hands and feet turned to ice.

'This Hermann', continued Tomsky, 'is a truly romantic figure: he has the profile of a Napoleon and the soul of a Mephistopheles. I think there must be at least three crimes on his conscience. How pale you look!'

'I have a bad headache . . . Well, and what did this Hermann – or whatever his name is – tell you?'

'Hermann is very annoyed with his friend: he says that in his place he would act quite differently. . . . I suspect in fact that Hermann has designs upon you himself; at any rate he listens to his friend's ecstatic exclamations with anything but indifference.'

'But where has he seen me?'

'In church, perhaps, or when you were out walking. . . . heaven only knows! – in your own room maybe, while you were asleep, for there is nothing he –'

Three ladies coming up to invite Tomsky to choose between *'oubli ou regret?'* interrupted the conversation which had become so painfully interesting to Lizaveta Ivanovna.

The lady chosen by Tomsky was the Princess Pauline herself. She succeeded in effecting a reconciliation with him while they danced an extra turn and spun round once more before she was conducted to her chair. When he returned to his place neither Hermann nor Lizaveta Ivanovna was in Tomsky's thoughts. Lizaveta Ivanovna longed to resume the interrupted conversation but the mazurka came to an end and shortly afterwards the old countess took her departure.

Tomsky's words were nothing more than the usual small-talk of the ball-room; but they sank deep into the girl's romantic heart. The portrait sketched by Tomsky resembled the picture she had herself drawn, and thanks to the novels of the day the commonplace figure both terrified and fascinated her. She sat there with her bare arms crossed and with her head, still adorned with flowers, sunk upon her naked bosom.

. . . Suddenly the door opened and Hermann came in. . . . She shuddered.

'Where were you?' she asked in a frightened whisper.

'In the old countess's bedroom,' Hermann answered. 'I have just left her. The countess is dead.'

'Merciful heavens! . . . what are you saying?'

'And I think', added Hermann, 'that I am the cause of her death.'

Lizaveta darted a glance at him, and heard Tomsky's words echo in her soul: '. . . there must be at least three crimes on his conscience'. Hermann sat down in the window beside her and related all that had happened.

Lizaveta Ivanovna listened to him aghast. So all those passionate letters, those ardent pleas, the bold, determined pursuit had not been inspired by love! Money! – that was what his soul craved! It was not she who could satisfy his desires and make him happy! Poor child, she had been nothing but the blind tool of a thief, of the murderer of her aged benefactress! . . . She wept bitterly in a vain agony of repentance. Hermann watched in silence: he too was suffering torment; but neither the poor girl's tears nor her indescribable charm in her grief touched his hardened soul. He felt no pricking of conscience at the thought of the dead old woman. One thing only horrified him: the irreparable loss of the secret which was to have brought him wealth.

'You are a monster!' said Lizaveta Ivanovna at last.

'I did not mean her to die,' Hermann answered. 'My pistol was not loaded.'

Both were silent.

Morning came. Lizaveta Ivanovna blew out the candle which had burned down. A pale light illumined the room. She wiped her tear-stained eyes and looked up at Hermann: he was sitting on the window-sill with his arms folded, a menacing frown on his face. In this attitude he bore a remarkable likeness to the portrait of Napoleon. The likeness struck even Lizaveta Ivanovna.

'How shall I get you out of the house?' she said at last. 'I had thought of taking you down the secret staircase but that means going through the bedroom, and I am afraid.'

'Tell me how to find this secret staircase – I will go alone.'

Lizaveta rose, took a key from the chest of drawers and gave it to Hermann with precise instructions. Hermann pressed her cold, unresponsive hand, kissed her bowed head and left her.

He walked down the winding stairway and entered the countess's bedroom again. The dead woman sat as though turned to stone. Her face wore a look of profound tranquillity. Hermann stood in front of her and gazed long and earnestly at her, as though trying to convince himself of the terrible truth. Then he went into the study, felt behind the tapestry for the door and began to descend the dark stairway, excited by strange emotions. 'Maybe some sixty years ago, at this very hour,' he thought, 'some happy youth – long since turned to dust – was stealing up this staircase into that very bedroom, in an embroidered tunic, his hair dressed *à l'oiseau royal*, pressing his three-cornered hat to his breast; and today the heart of his aged mistress has ceased to beat. . . .'

At the bottom of the stairs Hermann saw a door which he opened with the same key, and found himself in a passage leading to the street.

5

That night the dead Baroness von W. appeared before me. She was all in white and said: 'How do you do, Mr Councillor?'

SWEDENBORG

THREE days after that fatal night, at nine o'clock in the morning, Hermann repaired to the Convent of * * * *, where the last respects were to be paid to the mortal remains of the dead countess. Though he felt no remorse he could not altogether stifle the voice of conscience which kept repeating to him: 'You are the old woman's murderer!' Having very little religious faith, he was exceedingly superstitious. Believing that the dead countess might exercise a malignant influence on his life, he decided to go to her funeral to beg and obtain her forgiveness.

The church was full. Hermann had difficulty in making his way through the crowd. The coffin rested on a rich catafalque beneath a canopy of velvet. The dead woman lay with her hands crossed on her breast, in a lace cap and a white satin robe. Around the bier stood the members of her household: servants in black clothes, with armorial ribbons on their shoulders and lighted candles in their hands; relatives in deep mourning – children, grandchildren and great-grandchildren. No one wept: tears would have been *une affectation*. The countess was so old that her death could not have taken anybody by surprise, and her family had long ceased to think of her as one of the living. A famous preacher delivered the funeral oration. In simple and touching phrases he described the peaceful passing of the saintly woman whose long life had been a quiet, touching preparation for a Christian end. 'The angel of death', he declared, 'found her vigilant in devout meditation, awaiting the midnight coming of the bridegroom.' The service was concluded in melancholy decorum. First the relations went forward to bid farewell of the corpse. They were followed by a long procession of all those who had come to render their last homage to one who had for so many years been a partici-pator in their frivolous amusements. After them came the members of the countess's household. The last of these was an old woman-retainer the same age as the deceased. Two young girls supported her by the arms. She had not strength to prostrate herself – and she was the only one to shed tears as she kissed her mistress's cold hand. Hermann decided to approach the coffin after her. He knelt down on the cold stone strewed with branches of spruce-fir, and remained in that position for some minutes; at last he rose to his feet and, pale as the deceased herself, walked up the steps of the catafalque and bent over the corpse. . . . At that moment it seemed to him that the dead woman darted a mocking look at him and winked her eye. Hermann drew back, missed his footing and crashed headlong to the floor. They picked him up. At the same time Lizaveta Ivanovna was carried out of the church in a swoon. This incident momentarily upset the solemnity of the mournful rite. There was a dull murmur among the congrega-tion, and a tall thin man in the uniform of a court-chamberlain, a close relative of the deceased, whispered in the ear of an Englishman who was standing near him that the young officer was the natural son of the countess, to which the Englishman coldly replied, 'Oh?'

The whole of that day Hermann was strangely troubled. Repairing to a quiet little tavern to dine, he drank a great deal of wine, contrary to his habit, in the hope of stifling his inner agitation. But the wine only served to excite his imagination. Returning home, he threw himself on his bed without un-dressing, and fell heavily asleep.

It was night when he woke and the moon was shining into his room. He glanced at the time: it was a quarter to three. Sleep had left him; he sat on the bed and began thinking of the old countess's funeral.

Just then someone in the street looked in at him through

the window and immediately walked on. Hermann paid no attention. A moment later he heard the door of his ante-room open. Hermann thought it was his orderly, drunk as usual, returning from some nocturnal excursion, but presently he heard an unfamiliar footstep: someone was softly shuffling along the floor in slippers. The door opened and a woman in white came in. Hermann mistook her for his old nurse and wondered what could have brought her at such an hour. But the woman in white glided across the room and stood before him – and Hermann recognized the countess!

'I have come to you against my will,' she said in a firm voice: 'but I am commanded to grant your request. The three, the seven and the ace will win for you if you play them in succession, provided that you do not stake more than one card in twenty-four hours and never play again as long as you live. I forgive you my death, on condition that you marry my ward, Lizaveta Ivanovna.'

With these words she turned softly, rustled to the door in her slippers, and disappeared. Hermann heard the street-door click and again saw someone peeping in at him through the window.

It was a long time before he could pull himself together and go into the next room. His orderly was asleep on the floor: Hermann had difficulty in waking him. The man was drunk as usual: there was no getting any sense out of him. The street-door was locked. Hermann returned to his room and, lighting a candle, wrote down all the details of his vision.

6

'Attendez!'
'*How dare you say* "Attendez!" *to me?*'
'*Your Excellency, I said* "Attendez", *sir.*'

Two *idées fixes* cannot co-exist in the moral world any more than two physical bodies can occupy one and the same space. 'The three, the seven, the ace' soon drove all thought of the dead woman from Hermann's mind. 'Three, seven, ace' were perpetually in his head and on his lips. If he saw a young girl he would say, 'How graceful she is! A regular three of hearts!' Asked the time, he would reply, 'Five minutes to seven.' Every stout man reminded him of the ace. 'Three, seven, ace' haunted his dreams, assuming all sorts of shapes. The three blossomed before him like a luxuriant flower, the seven took the form of a Gothic portal, and aces became gigantic spiders. His whole attention was focused on one thought: how to make use of the secret which had cost him so dear. He began to consider resigning his commission in order to go and travel abroad. In the public gambling-houses in Paris he would compel fortune to give him his magical treasure. Chance spared him the trouble.

A circle of wealthy gamblers existed in Moscow, presided over by the celebrated Tchekalinsky, who had spent his life at the card-table and amassed millions, accepting promissory notes when he won and paying his losses in ready money. His long experience inspired the confidence of his fellow-players, while his open house, his famous chef and his gay and friendly manner secured for him the general respect of the public. He came to Petersburg. The young men of the capital flocked to his rooms, forsaking balls for cards and preferring the excitement of gambling to the seductions of flirting. Narumov brought Hermann to him.

They passed through a succession of magnificent rooms full of attentive servants. The place was crowded. Several generals and privy councillors were playing whist; young men smoking long pipes lounged about on sofas upholstered in damask. In the drawing-room some twenty gamblers jostled round a long table at which the master of the house was keeping bank. Tchekalinsky was a man of about sixty years of age and most dignified appearance; he had silvery-grey hair, a full, florid face with a kindly expression, and sparkling eyes which were always smiling. Narumov introduced Hermann. Shaking hands cordially, Tchekalinsky requested him not to stand on ceremony, and went on dealing.

The game continued for some while. On the table lay more than thirty cards. Tchekalinsky paused after each round to give the players time to arrange their cards and note their losses, listened courteously to their observations and more courteously still straightened the corner of a card that some careless hand had turned down. At last the game finished. Tchekalinsky shuffled the cards and prepared to deal again.

'Will you allow me to take a card?' said Hermann, stretching out his hand from behind a stout gentleman who was punting.

Tchekalinsky smiled and bowed graciously, in silent token of consent. Narumov laughingly congratulated Hermann on breaking his long abstention from cards and wished him a lucky start.

'There!' said Hermann, chalking some figures on the back of his card.

'How much?' asked the banker, screwing up his eyes. 'Excuse me, I cannot see.'

'Forty-seven thousand,' Hermann answered.

At these words every head was turned in a flash, and all eyes were fixed on Hermann.

'He has taken leave of his senses!' thought Narumov.

'Allow me to point out to you', said Tchekalinsky with his unfailing smile, 'that you are playing rather high: nobody here has ever staked more than two hundred and seventy-five at a time.'

'Well?' returned Hermann. 'Do you accept my card or not?'

Tchekalinsky bowed with the same air of humble acquiescence.

'I only wanted to observe', he said, 'that, being honoured with the confidence of my friends, I can only play against ready money. For my own part, of course, I am perfectly sure that your word is sufficient but for the sake of the rules of the game and our accounts I must request you to place the money on your card.'

Hermann took a bank-note from his pocket and handed it to Tchekalinsky, who after a cursory glance placed it on Hermann's card. He began to deal. On the right a nine turned up, and on the left a three.

'I win!' said Hermann, pointing to his card.

There was a murmur of astonishment among the company. Tchekalinsky frowned, but the smile quickly reappeared on his face.

'Would you like me to settle now?' he asked Hermann.

'If you please.'

Tchekalinsky took a number of bank-notes out of his pocket and paid there and then. Hermann picked up his money and left the table. Narumov could not believe his eyes. Hermann drank a glass of lemonade and departed home.

The following evening he appeared at Tchekalinsky's again. The host was dealing. Hermann walked up to the table; the players immediately made room for him. Tchekalinsky bowed graciously. Hermann waited for the next deal, took a card and placed on it his original forty-seven thousand together with his winnings of the day before. Tchekalinsky began to deal. A knave turned up on the right, a seven on the left.

Hermann showed his seven.

There was a general exclamation. Tchekalinsky was obviously disconcerted. He counted out ninety-four thousand and handed them to Hermann, who pocketed them in the coolest manner and instantly withdrew.

The next evening Hermann again made his appearance at

the table. Every one was expecting him; the generals and privy councillors left their whist to watch such extraordinary play. The young officers leaped up from their sofas and all the waiters collected in the drawing-room. Every one pressed round Hermann. The other players left off punting, impatient to see what would happen. Hermann stood at the table, prepared to play alone against Tchekalinsky, who was pale but still smiling. Each broke the seal of a pack of cards. Tchekalinsky shuffled. Hermann took a card and covered it with a pile of bank-notes. It was like a duel. Deep silence reigned in the room.

Tchekalinsky began dealing; his hands trembled. A queen fell on the right, an ace on the left.

'Ace wins!' said Hermann, and showed his card.

'Your queen has lost,' said Tchekalinsky gently.

Hermann started: indeed, instead of an ace there lay before him the queen of spades. He could not believe his eyes or think how he could have made such a mistake.

At that moment it seemed to him that the queen of spades opened and closed her eye, and mocked him with a smile. He was struck by the extraordinary resemblance. . . .

'The old woman!' he cried in terror.

Tchekalinsky gathered up his winnings. Hermann stood rooted to the spot. When he left the table every one began talking at once.

'A fine game, that!' said the players.

Tchekalinsky shuffled the cards afresh and the game resumed as usual.

CONCLUSION

HERMANN went out of his mind. He is now in room number 17 of the Obuhov Hospital. He returns no answer to questions put to him but mutters over and over again, with incredible rapidity: 'Three, seven, ace! Three, seven, queen!'

Lizaveta Ivanovna has married a very pleasant young man; he is in the civil service somewhere and has a good income. He is the son of the old countess's former steward. Lizaveta Ivanovna in her turn is bringing up a poor relative.

And Tomsky, who has been promoted to the rank of captain, has married the Princess Pauline.

October–November 1833

The Captain's Daughter

LOOK AFTER YOUR HONOUR
FROM YOUR YOUTH UP

Maxim

I

SERGEANT OF THE GUARDS

> *'He could enter the Guards a captain tomorrow.'*
> *– 'Why should he? Let him serve in the line.'*
> *'Well said! Let him ruff it awhile and win his spurs!*
> *. . . . . .*
> *'But who is his father?'*
> KNIAZHNIN[1]

As a young man my father, Andrei Petrovich Griniov, served under Count Münnich,[2] and retired with the rank of major, in the year 17—.[3] After that, he lived on his estate in the province of Simbirsk, where he married Maid Avdotia Vassilievna U—, the daughter of an impecunious nobleman of the district. There were nine of us children. All my brothers and sisters died in infancy. As for me, I was entered as a sergeant in the Semeonovsky regiment, thanks to the favour of Prince B—, a major in the Guards and near relative of ours. I was considered to be on leave of absence until I had finished my studies. In those days children were brought up very differently from today. At the age of five I was entrusted to Savelich, our groom, who for his sobriety was promoted to the

1. Kniazhnin (1742–91), dramatist.
2. Von Münnich (1683–1767), a Dane who entered the service of Peter the Great.
3. Pushkin's manuscript has the date 1762, which he deleted when the book was published, probably in order not to offend the censors. Griniov's father must have retired from the army after the *coup d'état* of Catherine II, being unwilling to serve the new ruler. (This would explain his ill humour when he reads in the *Court Calendar* of the dignities conferred on his former comrades who had shown more enthusiasm than he at the accession of the Empress.)

dignity of being my personal attendant. Under his supervision by the age of twelve I had learned to read and write Russian, and had a good eye for a greyhound. At this time my father engaged a Frenchman for me, a Monsieur Beaupré, whom he sent for from Moscow together with our yearly supply of wine and olive oil. Savelich was not at all pleased at his coming.

'By God's grace,' he would growl to himself, 'so far's I see, the child be clean and tidy and well fed. What be the good of wasting money getting a "Mossieu" – as if we hadn't servants enough of our own kith 'n kin?'

Beaupré in his native land had been a barber, then a soldier in Prussia, after which he had come to Russia 'to be an *outchitel*' – a teacher – without having much understanding of the meaning of the word. He was a good fellow, but flighty and rakish to a degree. His chief weakness was a passion for the fair sex; his attentions were often rewarded by cuffs that made him sigh for days. In addition, he was not (as he phrased it) an enemy of the bottle, which is to say (in Russian) that he was fond of swigging a drop too much. But since in our house wine was only served at dinner, and then only one glass each with the tutor generally missed out, my Beaupré very quickly accustomed himself to Russian home-made brandy, which he even came to prefer to the wines of his own country as being incomparably better for the digestion. We made friends at once, and although it had been arranged that he was to teach me French, German and all other subjects he very soon preferred to pick up some Russian from me and, after that, we each followed our own pursuits. We got on capitally together. I certainly wished for no other mentor. But fate soon parted us, and this is how it happened.

One fine day Palashka, the laundrymaid, a stout, pock-marked wench, and the one-eyed dairymaid, Akulka, mutually decided to throw themselves at the same moment at my mother's feet, confessing to wicked weakness and complaining tearfully of 'Mossieu', who had taken advantage of their inexperience. My mother did not treat such matters lightly. She went to my father, whose justice was swift. He immediately

sent for that scoundrel of a Frenchman. He was told that
'Mossieu' was giving me my lesson. My father came to my
room. At that particular moment Beaupré was sleeping the
sleep of innocence on my bed. I was busy with my own affairs.
I ought to mention that a map of the world had been obtained
for me from Moscow. It hung on the wall but was never used
and for long I had been tempted by the size and quality of the
paper it was printed on. Now I had decided to make a kite with
it and, taking advantage of Beaupré's slumbers, I had set to
work. My father came in just as I was trying to fit a bast tail
to the Cape of Good Hope. At the sight of my geography
exercises my father pulled my ear sharply, then ran over to
Beaupré, roused him without ceremony and started heaping
reproaches on him. In consternation Beaupré tried to get to
his feet but could not: the unhappy Frenchman was dead
drunk. In for a penny, in for a pound. My father lifted him
from the bed by his collar, kicked him out of the room and
sent him away that same day, to Savelich's indescribable
delight. Thus ended my education.

I lived the life of any other young boy of the gentry,
chasing pigeons and playing leap-frog with the servants'
children. Meanwhile I had turned sixteen. Then there came a
change in my life.

One autumn day my mother was making jam with honey in
the parlour, while I licked my lips as I watched the bubbling
froth. My father sat by the window reading the *Court Calendar,*
which he received every year. The book always had a powerful effect on him: he never read it without agitation, and
perusal of it invariably stirred his bile. My mother, who knew
all his ways by heart, always tried to stuff the wretched book
as far out of sight as possible, and often the *Court Calendar* did
not catch his eye for months on end, so that when by accident
he did come across it it would be hours before he would let it
out of his hands. As I have said, my father was reading the
Court Calendar, every now and then shrugging his shoulders
and muttering to himself: 'Lieutenant-general! ... He used
to be a sergeant in my Company! ... Knight of both Russian

Orders![1] ... And how long is it since together we ...?'
Finally, my father flung the *Calendar* down upon the sofa and
sank into a reverie which boded nothing good.

Suddenly he turned to my mother: 'Avdotia Vassilievna,
how old is Petrusha now?'

'Why, he'll be seventeen next birthday,' replied my mother.
'Petrusha was born the same year Aunty Nastasia Gerassi-
movna went blind in one eye, and when ...'

'Very well,' my father interrupted, 'it's time that he entered
the Service. He has been running about the servants' quarters
and climbing the dove-cotes long enough.'

The thought of soon being parted from me so overwhelmed
my mother that she dropped the spoon into the stewpan, and
the tears streamed down her face. My delight, however, could
hardly be described. The idea of military service was connected in my mind with thoughts of freedom and the pleasures
of life in Petersburg. I imagined myself an officer in the
Guards, which to my way of thinking was the height of
human bliss.

My father cared neither for going back on his decisions nor
for putting off their execution. The day for my departure was
fixed. On the night before, my father announced his intention
of giving me a letter for my future commanding officer, and
demanded pen and paper.

'Don't forget, Andrei Petrovich,' said my mother, 'to give
my kind regards, too, to Prince B—, and to say that I hope he
will take our Petrusha under his protection.'

'What fiddlesticks!' replied my father with a frown. 'Why
should I be writing to Prince B—?'

'But you said just now you were going to write to Petrusha's
commanding officer.'

'Well, what of it?'

'But Petrusha's commanding officer *is* Prince B—. Petrusha's
entered for the Semeonovsky regiment.'

'Entered! What do I care about that? Petrusha is not going

1. The Order of St Andrei founded by Peter the Great in 1689, and the
Order of Alexander Nevsky founded by Catherine in 1725.

to Petersburg. What would he learn, serving in Petersburg? To be a spendthrift and a rake? No, let him serve in the line, let him learn to carry a pack on his back, and know the smell of powder – let him be a soldier and not a fop in the Guards. Where is his passport? Bring it here.'

My mother got out my passport, which she kept in her little chest along with my christening robe, and with a trembling hand passed it to my father. My father read it through attentively, put it on the table in front of him and began his letter.

I was consumed by curiosity. Where were they sending me if not to Petersburg? My eyes never left my father's pen, which progressed slowly enough. At last he finished, sealed the letter up with the passport, took off his spectacles and, calling me to him, said: 'Here is a letter to Andrei Karlovich R—, an old comrade and friend of mine. You are going to Orenburg to serve under him.'

And so all my brilliant hopes were dashed to the ground! Instead of a gay life in Petersburg boredom awaited me in some forsaken hole at the other end of the world. Army service which a moment ago I had thought of with such enthusiasm now appeared to me a dreadful misfortune. But it was no use protesting! The next morning a travelling-chaise was driven up to the steps. My trunk, a canteen with tea things and some little packets of white bread and pasties, the last tokens of the spoiling I had at home, were packed into it. My parents gave me their blessing. My father said to me: 'Good-bye, Piotr. Carry out faithfully your oath of allegiance. Obey your superiors; do not try to curry favour with them; do not put yourself forward, but never shirk a duty, and remember the maxim: "Look after your clothes while they are new, and your honour from your youth up."' My mother enjoined me with tears to take care of my health, and bade Savelich look after the child. They helped me on with my coat of hare-skin and over it a cloak of fox fur. I took my seat in the chaise with Savelich and set off, weeping bitterly.

In the evening I arrived in Simbirsk, where I was to spend

the next day in order to purchase things that I needed, an errand which Savelich was entrusted with. I put up at an inn. In the morning Savelich sallied out early to the shops. Tired of looking from my window on to a muddy alley-way, I wandered through the other rooms of the inn. Going into the billiard-room, I saw a tall gentleman of about five and thirty, with long black moustaches and in his dressing-gown, a billiard cue in one hand and a pipe between his teeth. He was playing with the marker, who tossed off a glass of vodka every time he won and when he lost had to crawl on all fours under the table. I stopped to watch their play. The longer they went on the more frequent were the excursions on all fours, until at last the marker remained under the table altogether. The gentleman pronounced several vigorous epithets over him, by way of a funeral oration, and invited me to have a game. I refused, saying that I did not know how to play. This seemed to strike him as strange. He looked at me with something like pity. However, we got into conversation. I learned that his name was Ivan Ivanovich Zurin, that he was a captain in the regiment of — Hussars, stationed at Simbirsk to receive recruits, and was staying in the inn. Zurin invited me to take pot luck and dine with him, as between soldiers. I accepted with pleasure. We sat down to table. Zurin drank a great deal and filled my glass to the brim, saying that I must get used to army ways. He recounted guard-room stories which had me almost rolling on the floor with laughter, and we rose from the table fast friends. Then he offered to teach me to play billiards. 'It's indispensable for us army men,' he said. 'On the march, for instance, you arrive in some trumpery little town. What are you going to do with yourself? One can't always be thrashing Jews. So there's nothing for it but to go to the inn and start playing billiards: but for that you must know how to play!' I was quite convinced and set about learning with diligence. Zurin was loud in his encouragement, marvelled at my rapid progress and after a few lessons suggested that we play for money, at two kopecks a hundred, not for the sake of gain but merely to avoid playing for nothing, which, he said, was a most detestable practice. I agreed to this too. Zurin called for some punch, and persuaded me to try it, repeating that one must accustom oneself to army life, for what would army life be without punch! I obeyed. Meanwhile, we continued our game. The more often I sipped from my glass the more reckless I became. The balls kept flying over the cushion; I got excited, railed at the marker, who was scoring heaven knows how, from hour to hour I raised the stake – in short, I behaved like a boy having his first taste of freedom. Meanwhile, time passed imperceptibly. Zurin looked at his watch, put down his cue and remarked that I had lost a hundred roubles. That disconcerted me somewhat. Savelich held my money. I began to apologize. Zurin interrupted me: 'I beg of you, do not worry yourself. I can wait, and meantime let us go and see Arinushka.'

Well, I ended the day as wildly as I had begun. We took supper at Arinushka's. Zurin kept filling my glass, repeating that I must get used to the ways of the army. When I rose from the table I could hardly stand. At midnight Zurin drove me back to the inn.

Savelich met us at the steps. He uttered a groan when he saw the unmistakable signs of my zeal for the Service.

'What happened to you, master?' he said in a woeful voice. 'Where did you go to get yourself into such a state? Merciful heavens! Never has such a dreadful thing happened to you before!'

'Be quiet, you old dotard!' I mumbled in an unsteady voice. 'It's you who must be drunk. Get off to bed . . . and put me to bed.'

Next morning I woke with a splitting head and a confused recollection of the day before. My reflections were interrupted by Savelich coming in with a cup of tea. 'You're beginning early, Piotr Andreich – ' he said to me, shaking his head, 'you're beginning early to go out on the spree. Who do you take after? It's my belief neither your dad nor your grandad were drinkers. And of course there be no need to speak of your mamma: she hasn't touched a drop of anything stronger than *kvass* since the day she was born. Who is at the bottom of all this? It's that cursed "Mossieu". He was for ever running round to Antipievna's: "Madame, shu voo pree, vodque." That's what comes of *shu voo pree!* There be no doubt about it, he taught you some pretty ways, the son of a dog! And we had to engage that heathen tutor for you, as if the master had not servants enough of his own!'

I felt ashamed of myself. I turned my back and said to him: 'Go away, Savelich. I don't want any tea.' But it was not easy to stop Savelich once he began sermonizing. 'You see now, Piotr Andreich, what happens when you go drinking. A bad head and no appetite. A man who drinks is good for nothing. ... Some cucumber and honey mixture now, or, best thing of all for getting rid of a sick headache, half a glass of liqueur. What do you say?'

At that moment a lad came in and handed me a note from Zurin. I opened it and read the following lines:

Dear Piotr Andreyevich,
Be so good as to send me by this lad of mine the hundred roubles which I won from you yesterday. I am in urgent need of money.
Always at your service,
Ivan Zurin

There was no help for it. I assumed an air of indifference and, turning towards Savelich, who had charge of my money, my clothes and all my affairs, told him to give the boy a hundred roubles.

'What? Why?' asked Savelich, aghast.

'I owe them to him,' I replied as coolly as possible.

'Owe them?' echoed Savelich, more and more aghast. 'And when was it, sir, you found time to incur a debt to him? There be something fishy about this business. Do what you like, sir, but I am not going to pay out the money.'

I reflected that if at this critical moment I did not gain the upper hand of the obstinate old man it would be difficult later on to free myself from his tutelage, so, looking at him haughtily, I said:

'I am your lord and master, while you are only my servant. The money is mine. I lost it at play because such was my fancy. I advise you not to argue but to do as you are told.'

Savelich was so struck by my words that he clasped his hands in the air and stood dumbfounded.

'What are you standing there for?' I shouted at him angrily.

Savelich began to weep.

'Good master, Piotr Andreich,' he said in a trembling voice, 'don't bring me to the grave with a broken heart. Light of my eyes, listen to me – listen to an old man. Write to that brigand that it was all a joke, that we have not got such money. A hundred roubles! Merciful heavens! Tell him your parents absolutely forbade you to gamble for anything except nuts . . .'

'That will do!' I interrupted him severely. 'Bring me the money or I'll throw you out by the scruff of your neck.'

Savelich looked at me with profound sadness and went to fetch the money. I was sorry for the poor old man, but I wanted to assert my independence and show that I was no longer a child. The money was paid to Zurin. Savelich made haste to get me out of the confounded inn. He came to tell me that the horses were ready. With an uneasy conscience and full of silent remorse I left Simbirsk without taking leave of my teacher and not expecting ever to see him again.

2

THE GUIDE

O distant land, now land of mine,
'Tis not my wish that I am come,
'Tis not my good horse brings me here
But lusty youth and nimble wit,
Audacity and tavern wine.

AN OLD SONG

MY reflections as we journeyed were not particularly agreeable. The sum I had lost, according to the value of money at that time, was considerable. I could not help confessing in my innermost heart that I had behaved foolishly at the Simbirsk inn, and I felt in the wrong with Savelich. All this made me wretched. The old man sat morosely on the box, his back turned away from me, and was silent except for an occasional sigh. I was extremely anxious to make my peace with him but not sure how to begin. At last I said:

'Come now, Savelich! That's enough, let us be friends, I was to blame. I can see myself that I was wrong. I behaved foolishly yesterday, and hurt your feelings unjustly. I promise to be more sensible in future, and listen to you. So don't be angry – let us make it up!'

'Alas, alas, Piotr Andreich, master!' he replied with a deep sigh. 'I be angry with myself: 'twas all my fault. How could I have gone and left you alone in the inn! But there 'tis – the devil tempted me: I took it into my head to drop in on the wife of the *diatchok*,[1] an old crony of mine. That is the way of it: drop in on an old crony and you might be in prison, the time you stay. Was there ever such a calamity! How shall I

1. The *diatchok* reads the Psalms and chants the responses in the Eastern Orthodox Church.

be able to show myself in the sight of the master and mistress? What will they say when they hear that their child is a drunkard and a gambler?'

In order to comfort poor Savelich I gave him my word that in future I would not spend a single kopeck without his consent. Gradually he calmed down, although from time to time he still muttered to himself, shaking his head: 'A hundred roubles! Oh, a mere trifle!'

I was approaching my destination. Around me stretched desolate wastes, intersected by hills and ravines, and everything covered with snow. The sun was setting. The sledge was travelling along a narrow roadway, or, to be more precise, a track made by the sledges of the peasants. Suddenly the driver began looking over to the side, and finally, taking off his cap, he turned to me and said:

'Will you not have me go back, sir?'

'What for?'

'The weather is uncertain: the wind is getting up a bit. See how it's lifting the newly-fallen snow.'

'What does that matter?'

'But look over there.' (The driver pointed with his whip to the east.)

'I don't see anything save white steppe and clear sky.'

'But over there, away in the distance: that tiny cloud.'

I did indeed see a small white cloud on the edge of the horizon which I had taken at first for a faraway hillock. The driver explained that the little cloud presaged a snowstorm.

I had heard of the snowstorms in those parts and knew that often entire convoys of sledges got buried by them. Savelich was of the driver's opinion and advised a return. But the wind not appearing to be at all strong, I hoped to reach the next post-station in time, and gave the order to drive faster.

The driver put the horses at a gallop but still kept looking towards the east. The beasts sped along steadily together. The wind meanwhile was getting up. The little cloudlet was transformed into a great white cloud, which climbed heavily and grew until it overran the whole sky. Fine snow began to fall, and then suddenly came down in great flakes. The wind howled, and the storm burst upon us. In a trice the sombre heavens were merged in a sea of snow. Everything was lost to sight.

'Well, sir,' cried the driver, 'the misfortune's come: it's a snowstorm!'

I looked through the curtain of the sledge: all was darkness and hurricane. The wind howled with such savage violence that it seemed to be alive. Savelich and I were covered with snow. The horses slowed to a walking pace and soon stopped altogether.

'Why don't you go on!' I called to the driver impatiently.

'What good to go on?' he replied, jumping down from the box. 'As it is we don't know where we've got ourselves to: no track, and a fog of snow all round.'

I began to rail at him. Savelich took his part.

'Why couldn't you have listened?' he said irritably. 'You would have been back at the inn by now, drinking cup after cup of tea, and slept in comfort until the morning. The storm would have died down and we should be on our way again. And where's our hurry? 'Tisn't as if we were going to a wedding!'

Savelich was right. There was nothing to be done. The snow continued to fall thick and fast. It piled high around the sledge. The horses stood still, their heads down, and every now and again they gave a shiver. For want of something to do the driver walked round them, adjusting the harness. Savelich grumbled. I looked about me, hoping to discover some sign of habitation or a road, but could make out nothing save the dense swirl of the storm. Suddenly I caught sight of something black.

'Hey, driver!' I shouted. 'Look – what's that black thing over there?'

The driver stared into the distance.

'Heaven only knows, sir,' he said, climbing back on to his seat. 'It's no sort of a cart, it can't be a tree. And yet it seems to be moving: must be a wolf or a man.'

I told him to make for the unknown object which immediately started to advance in our direction. A couple of minutes later we came up with a man.

'Hey, my good man!' the driver shouted to him. 'Do you know where the road is?'

'The road – this is the road: I am standing on firm ground,' replied the wayfarer, 'but what use is that?'

'Listen, my good fellow,' I said to him. 'Do you know these parts? Can you guide me to a night's lodging?'

'I know the country well enough,' he replied. 'I should think I have trodden every inch of it, yes and covered it on horseback too. But you see what the weather is: we should get lost straight away. Better stop here, and wait till it's over. Maybe the storm will abate, and the sky clear: then we can find our bearings by the stars.'

His composure put heart into me. I had already made up my mind to trust Providence and spend the night out in the steppes, when suddenly the man climbed nimbly on to the box and said to the driver:

'Come, thanks be to God, there is a dwelling not far off: turn right and let us go there.'

'But why should I go right?' asked the driver in annoyance. 'Where do you see a road? Of course the horses are not yours, or their collars, so whip up, then, and away – is that it?'

The driver seemed to me to be right.

'Yes, indeed,' said I, 'what makes you think we are close to a house?'

'Why, because a gust of wind blew from that direction,' replied the traveller, 'and I smelt smoke, which proves there's a hamlet nearby.'

His shrewdness and keen sense of smell amazed me. I told the driver to push on. The horses advanced with difficulty in the deep snow. The sledge moved slowly, now clambering up a snowdrift, now tumbling into a hollow and leaning over first to one side, then to the other. It was like the pitching of a boat in a rough sea. Savelich groaned as he kept lurching into my side every minute. I let down the matting which served as a *portière,* wrapped my cloak round me and dozed off, lulled by the singing of the storm and the swaying of our slow progress.

I had a dream which I have never forgotten, and in which to this day I see something prophetic when considered in connexion with the strange vicissitudes of my life. The reader will forgive me, for he probably knows from experience how natural it is for man to indulge in superstition, however great his contempt for vain imaginings may be.

I found myself in that condition of mind and feeling when reality gives place to reverie and merges into the shadowy visions of the first stages of sleep. It seemed to me that the storm was still raging, and we were still wandering in the wilderness of snow. . . . Suddenly I saw a gateway and drove into the courtyard of our estate. My first thought was one of apprehension lest my father should be angry because of my involuntary return home, and regard it as intentional disobedience. With a feeling of uneasiness I sprang out of the sledge and saw my mother coming down the steps to meet me, a look of deep sorrow upon her face. 'Hush, quietly,' she says to me, 'your father is ill and dying, and wants to say good-bye to you.' Terror-stricken, I follow her into the bedroom. The room is feebly lit; people with sad faces are standing round the bed. I creep up to the bed; my mother lifts the curtains a little, and says: 'Andrei Petrovich, Petrusha has arrived; he came back when he heard you were ill: give him your blessing.' I knelt down and fixed my eyes on the sick man. But what's this? . . . Instead of my father, a peasant with a black beard is lying on the bed, looking at me merrily. I turn to my mother in perplexity, and say: 'What does it mean? This is not my father. And why must I ask this peasant's blessing?' – 'Never mind, Petrusha,' replied my mother. 'He is taking your father's place for the wedding; kiss his hand and let him give you his blessing. . . .' I refused. Whereupon the peasant jumped out of the bed, seized an axe from behind his back and began flourishing it about. I wanted to run away . . . and could not. The room was full of dead bodies; I kept stumbling against them, and my feet slipped in the pools of blood. . . . The dreadful peasant called to me in a kindly voice: 'Don't be afraid,' he cried. 'Come and let me bless you. . . .' Horror and bewilderment possessed me. . . . And at that moment I awoke. The horses had stopped. Savelich was holding me by the arm, and saying:

'Get out, master, we have arrived.'

'Where have we arrived?' I asked, rubbing my eyes.

'At an inn. By God's help we ran right up against the fence. Make haste, master, and come and warm yourself.'

I stepped out of the sledge. The storm still continued, though with less violence. It was pitch dark. The landlord greeted us at the gate, holding a lantern under the skirt of his coat, and conducted me into a room that was small but tolerably clean, and lighted by a pine-torch. A gun and a tall Cossack cap hung on the wall.

The landlord, a Cossack from Yaïk, appeared to be a man of about sixty, active and well preserved. Savelich followed me with the box of tea-things, and demanded a fire to make tea, which had never seemed to me more welcome. Our host departed to set to work.

'But where is our guide?' I asked Savelich.

'Here, your Honour,' replied a voice from above.

I looked up and on the shelf over the stove saw a black beard and two flashing eyes.

'Well, friend, are you frozen?'

'I should think I am frozen with nothing but a thin jerkin on! I did have a sheepskin coat but I confess I left it in pawn yesterday with the owner of a tavern: the frost did not seem to be so bad.'

At this point the landlord came in with a boiling samovar: I offered our guide a cup of tea. The peasant let himself down from the shelf. His appearance struck me as remarkable. He was about forty years old, of medium height, thin and broad-shouldered. His black beard was streaked with grey; his big sparkling eyes were never still. His face had a rather pleasant but sly expression. His hair was cropped round after the

Cossack manner. He wore a tattered jerkin over wide Turkish trousers. I handed him a cup of tea. He tasted it and made a wry face. 'Be so kind, your Honour . . . tell them to bring me a glass of vodka: tea is not the drink for us Cossacks.' I willingly did as he asked. The landlord took a square bottle and a glass out of the dresser, went up to the man and, looking him in the face, said: 'Well, well, you round here again! Where have you sprung from?' My guide winked significantly and replied with this adage: 'I was flying about the kitchen-garden, picking up hempseed. The old woman threw a stone at me, but it missed. And how are your fellows getting on?'

'Nothing much to say of them,' replied the landlord, continuing the conversation in allegorical terms. 'They were just going to ring the bells for vespers, but the parson's wife forbade them: with the priest away on a visit, the devils make merry in the parish.'

'Hold your tongue, man,' retorted my vagabond. 'If it rains there will be mushrooms; if there are mushrooms there will be a basket to put them in; but now' (and he winked his eye again) 'hide the axe behind your back: the forester's making his rounds. Your Honour, here's to your health!'

With these words he took his glass, crossed himself and emptied it at a gulp, then bowed to me and returned to his shelf.

I could understand nothing of this thieves' slang at the time but afterwards I guessed that they were talking of matters concerning the Yaïk Cossacks, who had only recently been put down after the 1772 rebellion. Savelich listened with a look of deep displeasure. He took stock suspiciously now of the landlord now of the guide. The inn, or shelter for travellers, as the local people called it, stood isolated in the middle of the steppe, a long way from any village, and looked uncommonly like a place of rendezvous for brigands. But there was no help for it. To continue our journey was out of the question. I was much amused by Savelich's anxiety. Meanwhile I got ready to pass the night, and stretched out on the bench. Savelich decided to sleep on the stove; the landlord lay down on the floor. Soon the hut was full of snoring, and I dropped off sound as a log.

I awoke somewhat late next morning, and saw that the storm had died away. The sun was shining. The snow lay in a dazzling sheet over the boundless steppe. The horses were harnessed. I paid the landlord, who charged us such a modest sum that even Savelich did not argue with him and start his usual haggling, and quite forgot his suspicions of the night before. Calling our guide, I thanked him for his help, and told Savelich to give him half a rouble. Savelich scowled. 'Half a rouble for a tip!' he exclaimed. 'And what for? Because you were good enough to give him a lift to the inn? As you please, sir; but we have no half roubles to spare. If we tip everybody we shall soon go hungry ourselves.' I could not quarrel with Savelich. I had promised that he should have the entire control of our money. But I felt vexed not to be able to show my gratitude to the man who had saved me if not from disaster at least from a most disagreeable situation.

'Very well,' I said to him coldly. 'If you do not want to give him half a rouble, get out some of my clothes for him. He is not wearing enough. Give him my hare-skin coat.'

'Mercy on us, my good master, Piotr Andreich!' cried Savelich. 'Why give him your hare-skin coat? He'll sell it for drink at the first pot-house he comes to, the dog!'

'That is no concern of yours, old fellow,' put in my tramp, 'whether I sell it for drink or not. His Honour is making me a present of one of his own coats. It is your master's pleasure to do so, and your duty as a servant not to argue but obey.'

'Have you no fear of God, brigand!' replied Savelich in an angry voice. 'You can see the child has not yet reached the age of wisdom, and you are only too glad to take advantage of his inexperience. What do you want with my master's coat? You could not squeeze your hulking shoulders into it, however you try.'

'No palavering now, please,' I said to the old man. 'Bring the coat at once.'

'Gracious heavens!' groaned my Savelich. 'Why the

hare-skin coat is almost brand new! It would be different if it were for someone deserving, but to give it to a scamp of a drunkard!'

However, the hare-skin coat appeared. The peasant immediately began to try it on. The coat, which I had slightly outgrown, was certainly a little tight for him. All the same, he managed to get into it somehow, after bursting the seams. Savelich nearly howled when he heard the stitches cracking. The tramp was exceedingly pleased with my present. He accompanied me to the sledge, and said with a low bow: 'Thank you, your Honour. May the Lord reward you for your goodness. I shall never forget your kindness so long as I live.' He went his way, and I continued on mine, taking no notice of Savelich, and I soon forgot the snowstorm of the day before, my guide and the hare-skin coat.

Arriving in Orenburg, I presented myself at once to the general. I saw a tall man though already bent by age, with long, completely white hair. His old faded uniform recalled the soldier of Anna Ivanovna's reign, and he spoke with a strong German accent. I handed him my father's letter. At the mention of his name the general glanced at me quickly. '*Mein Gott!*' he said. 'It doess not seem so long ago since Andrei Petrovich vass your age. And now see what a fine big son he hass! Ach, how time flies!' He broke the seal of the letter and began reading it in an undertone, interposing his own remarks: '"Esteemed Sir, Andrei Karlovich, I hope that your Excellency . . ." Here iss zeremony for you! Pshaw, I vonder he iss not ashamed! Of course disscipline before everyt'ing, but iss diss der way to write to an old Kamerad? ". . . your Excellency hass not forgotten . . ." H'm . . . "and when the late Field-Marshal Munnich . . . in the campaign . . . and also the . . . little Caroline . . ." Ach, ach, der Bruder! So he still remembers our old pranks, then? "Now to business . . . I am sending my rascal to you . . ." H'm . . . "Handle him with mitts of porcupine . . ." What are mitts of porcupine? Dat must be a Russian saying. . . . What does *to handle with mitts of porcupine* mean?' he repeated, turning to me.

'It means', I answered him, looking as innocent as possible, 'to treat kindly, not to be too strict, to give plenty of freedom – *to handle with mitts of porcupine.*'

'H'm, I see ... "and not to give him too much rope – " No, mitts of porcupine must mean somet'ing different. ... "Enclosed you vill find his passport." Where is it though? Oh yes ... "Take his name off the register of the Semeonovsky regiment ..." Very goot, very goot: everyt'ing shall be attended to ... "You vill allow me wit'out zeremony to embrace you and ... as an old Kamerad and friend ..." Ah, at last he has got round to it! ... and so on, and so on. Vell, my boy,' he said, when he had finished reading the letter and put aside my passport, 'everyt'ing shall be arranged; you vill be transferred mit' der rank of officer to the — regiment, and, not to lose time, you shall leaf tomorrow for der Bielogorsky fortress, where you vill serve under Captain Mironov, a goot and upright man. T'ere you vill see real service, und be taught what iss disscipline. Der is not'ing for you to do in Orenburg; dissipation iss bad for a young man. Und today I invite you to dine mit' me.'

'From bad to worse!' I thought to myself. 'What is the good of my having been a sergeant in the Guards almost before I was born! Where has it brought me? To the — regiment and a fortress buried in the steppes by the Kirghiz-Kaissak border. ...'

I had dinner with Andrei Karlovich, in company with his old aide-de-camp. A rigorous German economy reigned at his table, and I believe that fear of an additional guest to share his frugal bachelor meal was partly the cause of my hurried despatch to the garrison. Next day I took leave of the general and set off to my destination.

3

THE FORTRESS

In this fortress we live,
Bread and water our fare,
But when the fierce en'my
Comes to savour our ware —
A fine feast we'll prepare,
With grape-shot our cannon
We'll load.

SOLDIERS' SONG

They are old-fashioned people, my dear sir.

THE MINOR[1]

THE Bielogorsky fortress lay forty versts[2] from Orenburg. The road followed the steep bank of the Yaïk. The river was not yet frozen, and its leaden waves looked black and mournful between the white, monotonous, snow-covered banks. Away on the other side the Kirghiz steppes stretched into the distance. I was absorbed in reflections, for the most part of a melancholy nature. Garrison life held little attraction for me. I tried to picture Captain Mironov, my future chief, and imagined him a stern, bad-tempered old man, ignorant of everything but the Service, and ready to put me under arrest on a diet of bread and water for the merest trifle. Meanwhile, it was beginning to grow dark. We were driving fairly quickly.

'Is it far to the fortress?' I asked the driver. 'No, not far,' he replied. 'You can see it over yonder.' I looked round on every side, expecting to catch sight of menacing battlements, towers and a moat, but saw nothing save a little hamlet sur-

1. Comedy of manners by Fonvizin (1745–92).
2. A little over twenty-five miles.

rounded by a picket-fence of stakes. On one side of it stood three or four haystacks half buried under the snow; on the other a tumble-down windmill with wings of bast which hung idle. 'But where is the fortress?' I asked in surprise. 'Why, there it is,' replied the driver, pointing to the hamlet, and as he spoke we drove into it. At the gate I saw an old cannon made of cast iron; the streets were narrow and crooked; the cottages small and for the most part with thatched roofs. I told the driver to take me to the commandant, and a minute later the sledge stopped before a small wooden house built on rising ground near the church, which was likewise of wood.

No one came out to meet me. I walked into the lobby and opened the door into the next room. An old soldier was sitting on the table, sewing a blue patch on the sleeve of a green uniform. I told him to announce me. 'Go in, my dear,' he replied. 'They're at home.' I went into a neat little room, furnished in the old-fashioned style. In one corner stood a dresser with plates and dishes; on the wall hung an officer's diploma, glazed and framed; coloured woodcuts, representing *The Taking of Küstrin*, *The Taking of Ochakov*, *Choosing a Bride*, and *The Cat's Funeral*, made bright splashes on either side of it. An old woman wearing a quilted jacket with a kerchief on her head was sitting by the window. She was winding a hank of yarn which a one-eyed old man in an officer's uniform held for her between outstretched hands. 'What is your pleasure, good sir?' she asked me, continuing with her work. I answered that I had come to serve in the army, and to present myself, as duty bid, to the Captain, and I was about to address the one-eyed old man by that title, supposing him to be the commandant, when the lady of the house interrupted the speech I had prepared. 'Ivan Kuzmich is not at home,' said she. 'He has gone to see Father Gerassim. But it makes no difference, good sir, I am his wife. You are very welcome. Please sit down and make yourself comfortable.' She called to the maid and told her to summon the sergeant. The old man kept looking at me inquisitively with his one eye. 'May I be so bold as to ask in what regiment you have been serving?' I satisfied his curiosity.

'And may I ask', he continued, 'why you have exchanged the Guards for garrison service?' I replied that such was the wish of my superiors. 'For conduct unbecoming an officer of the Guards, I presume?' persisted my indefatigable interrogator. 'That's enough of your chatter,' the captain's lady interrupted him. 'You can see the young man is tired after his journey: he doesn't want to be bothered with you. ... Hold your hands straighter now. ... As for you, my good sir,' she went on, turning to me, 'don't take it to heart that you have been packed off to these wilds. You are not the first, and you will not be the last. You will like it well enough when you get used to it. Shvabrin – Alexei Ivanich – was transferred to us five years ago for killing a man. Heaven alone knows what possessed him: would you believe it, he went out of town with a certain lieutenant. They had taken their swords with them, and they started prodding each other, and Alexei Ivanich ran the lieutenant through, and before two witnesses too! Well, there it is – one never knows what one may do.'

At this point the sergeant came in, a well-built young Cossack.

'Maximich!' the captain's lady said to him. 'Find a lodging for this officer, and mind it is clean.'

'Yes, ma'am, Vassilissa Yegorovna,' replied the sergeant. 'Could not his Honour lodge at Ivan Polezhayev's?'

'Certainly not, Maximich,' said the captain's wife. 'Polezhayev's is crowded enough as it is. Besides, he is a friend, and always remembers that we are his superiors. Take the gentleman – what is your name, sir?'

'Piotr Andreich.'

'Take Piotr Andreich to Semeon Kuzov's. He let his horse into my kitchen-garden, the rascal. Well, Maximich, is everything going all right?'

'Everything in order, praise God,' the Cossack answered. 'Only Corporal Prohorov had a set-to in the bath-house with Ustinia Negulina over a bucket of hot water.'

'Ivan Ignatyich!' said the captain's wife to the one-eyed old man. 'See into this business between Prohorov and Ustinia and find out which of them was in the wrong. And then punish the pair of them. Well, Maximich, you can go now. Piotr Andreich, Maximich will accompany you to your quarters.'

I bowed and took my departure. The Cossack brought me to a cottage situated on the steep bank of the river at the extreme end of the village. One half of the cottage was occupied by the family of Semeon Kuzov, the other half was allotted to me. It consisted of one fairly well kept room divided in two by a partition. Savelich began unpacking while I looked out of the narrow window. The melancholy steppe stretched before me. On one side I got a glimpse of a few cottages; two or three hens strutted about the street. An old woman, standing on the steps with a trough in her hands, was calling some pigs, who answered her with friendly grunting. And this was the place in which I was condemned to spend my youth! I was suddenly overwhelmed with misery. I came away from the window and went to bed without eating any supper in spite of the entreaties of Savelich, who kept repeating in tones of distress: 'Lord in heaven! Isn't he going to eat anything? What will the mistress say if the child falls ill?'

Next morning I had just begun to dress when the door opened and a young officer, short, swarthy and remarkably ugly but with an extraordinarily animated face, walked in. 'Excuse me,' he began in French, 'for coming in without ceremony to make your acquaintance. I heard yesterday of your arrival; the desire at last to see a human face was too strong to be resisted. You will understand when you have lived here for a while.' I guessed that this was the officer who had been dismissed from the Guards on account of the duel. We quickly made each other's acquaintance. Shvabrin was certainly no fool. His conversation was witty and entertaining. He gave me the most spirited description of the commandant's family, their friends and the place to which fate had brought me. I was helpless with laughter, when the old soldier whom I had seen mending his uniform in the captain's lobby came in with an invitation from Vassilissa Yegorovna to dine with them. Shvabrin offered to go with me.

As we approached the commandant's house we saw in the square a score or so of old soldiers with long plaits of hair and three-cornered hats. They were drawn up to attention. The commandant, a tall, vigorous old man wearing a night-cap and nankeen dressing-gown stood facing them. When he saw us he came up, said a few affable words to me, and went back to drilling his men. We would have stopped to watch but he asked us to go on to his house, promising to join us without delay. 'There is nothing for you to look at here,' he added.

Vassilissa Yegorovna gave us a cordial, homely welcome, treating me as though she had known me all my life. The old pensioner and Palashka were laying the table. 'But what keeps my Ivan Kuzmich so long at his drilling today?' said the commandant's wife. 'Palashka, call your master in to dinner. And where is Masha?' At that moment a girl of about eighteen entered the room, with a round rosy face and light flaxen hair combed back smoothly behind her ears, which were hot and burning with shyness. I was not particularly taken with her at first glance. I regarded her with prejudiced eyes: Shvabrin had described Masha, the captain's daughter, as a perfect little idiot. Maria Ivanovna [Masha] sat down in a corner and began sewing. Meanwhile, cabbage soup was brought in. Not seeing her husband, Vassilissa Yegorovna sent Palashka a second time to call him. 'Tell your master that our guests are waiting, and the soup will get cold. Thank heaven, there is always time for drilling: he can shout himself hoarse later on.' The captain soon made his appearance, accompanied by the one-eyed little old man.

'What has come over you, my dear?' his wife said to him. 'Dinner has been ready an eternity, but there was no getting you in.'

'But I was busy drilling my men, Vassilissa Yegorovna, let me tell you,' replied Ivan Kuzmich.

'Come, come!' his wife retorted. 'It is all talk about your instructing the men. They are no good in the Service, and you don't know anything about it either. You would do far better to sit at home and say your prayers. My dear guests, please come to table.'

We sat down to dinner. Vassilissa Yegorovna was never silent for a moment and bombarded me with questions. Who were my parents? Were they alive? Where did they live and how much were they worth? When she heard that my father had three hundred serfs – 'Just fancy!' she exclaimed. 'Can there be such rich people in the world? And we, my dear, have only our one maid, Palashka, but we manage pretty well, thank heaven. Our only trouble is, Masha ought to be getting married, but what has she got for a dowry? A fine comb, a fibre glove[1] and three kopecks (God forgive me!) for a visit to the bath-house! Well and good if a decent lad turns up; if not, she will have to die an old maid.' I glanced at Maria Ivanovna; she had flushed crimson and tears were dropping into her plate. I felt sorry for her and hastened to change the conversation.

'I have heard rumours', I remarked, rather inappropriately, 'that the Bashkirs are assembling to attack your fortress.'

'And from whom did you hear that, my good sir?' asked Ivan Kuzmich.

'They told me so in Orenburg,' I replied.

'All nonsense!' said the commandant. 'It's a long time since there was talk of that. The Bashkirs have been scared off, and the Kirghiz, too, have learnt a lesson. They'll fight shy of us all right; but if they should poke their noses in I'll give them a dressing-down that will keep them quiet for the next ten years.'

'And are you not afraid', I continued, turning to the captain's wife, 'to remain in a fortress exposed to such dangers?'

'It's all a question of habit, my dear,' she replied. 'Twenty years ago when we were transferred from the regiment to this place – merciful heavens, how terrified I was of those accursed infidels! The moment I caught sight of their caps of lynx fur, and heard their yelping – would you believe it, my heart stood still. But now I have grown so accustomed to it that I would

1. Used for scrubbing the skin.

not stir an inch if I were told that the villains were prowling round the fortress.'

'Vassilissa Yegorovna is a most courageous lady,' remarked Shvabrin pompously. 'Ivan Kuzmich can bear witness to that.'

'Yes, she is not one of the timid sort, let me tell you!' declared Ivan Kuzmich.

'And what about Maria Ivanovna?' I asked. 'Is she as brave as you are?'

'Masha brave?' replied her mother. 'No, Masha is a coward. She can't bear even now to hear a rifle-shot: it makes her tremble all over. And a couple of years ago when Ivan Kuzmich took it into his head to fire our cannon on my name-day, she nearly died of fright, poor child. Since then we have not fired the cursed cannon again.'

We rose from the table. The captain and his wife went to lie down, while I returned with Shvabrin to his quarters, where we spent the rest of the day together.

4

THE DUEL

Very well, then, take up your position,
And you shall see me run your person through!

KNIAZHNIN

SEVERAL weeks had passed and my life in the Bielogorsky fortress had grown not merely endurable but positively pleasant. In the commandant's house I was received as one of the family. Both husband and wife were most worthy people. Ivan Kuzmich, who was the son of a soldier and had risen to the rank of officer, was a simple, uneducated man, but exceedingly upright and kind. His wife ruled him, which suited his easy-going disposition. Vassilissa Yegorovna considered even Service matters her own concern, and managed the fortress as she did her own home. Maria Ivanovna soon lost her shyness with me. We got to know each other. I found her to be a girl of feeling and good sense. Imperceptibly I grew attached to this kind family, and even to Ivan Ignatyich, the one-eyed lieutenant of the garrison, for whom Shvabrin had invented an improper relationship with Vassilissa Yegorovna, though there was not a shadow of probability for this accusation; but Shvabrin did not trouble himself about that.

I received my commission. My military duties were no burden to me. In our fortress, which God protected, we had neither parades, drills nor sentry duty. Occasionally, when he had a mind to, the commandant instructed the garrison but had not yet succeeded in teaching all of them to know their left hand from their right, although many, so as to make no mistake, crossed themselves at each about-turn. Shvabrin had several French books in his possession. I began reading them

213

and developed a taste for literature. In the mornings I read, did some translating and sometimes even composed verses. I generally dined at the commandant's and usually spent the rest of the day there, and sometimes of an evening Father Gerassim would come with his wife, Akulina Pamfilovna, the biggest gossip of the whole neighbourhood. Of course I saw Alexei Ivanich Shvabrin daily but his conversation became more and more distasteful to me as time went on. I very much disliked his constant jesting about the commandant's family, and especially his derisive remarks concerning Maria Ivanovna. There was no other society in the garrison, but then I wished for no other.

In spite of the predictions, the Bashkirs did not rise. Peace reigned around our fortress. But the peace was suddenly disturbed by internal dissension.

I have already mentioned that I was dabbling in literature. For those days my attempts were fairly passable, and some years later Alexander Petrovich Sumarokov[1] praised them highly. One day I succeeded in writing a song which met with my satisfaction. We know that sometimes on the pretext of seeking advice authors try to find an appreciative listener. And so, having copied out my little verses, I bore them off to Shvabrin, who was the only person in the whole fortress capable of doing justice to a poet's work. After a few preliminary remarks I took my manuscript from my pocket and read to him the following lines:

> *I banish thoughts of love, and try*
> *My fair one to forget;*
> *And to be free again I fly*
> *From Masha with regret.*

> *But wheresoever I may go,*
> *Those eyes I still do see.*
> *My troubled soul no peace may know,*
> *There is no rest for me.*

1. A. P. Sumarokov (1718–77), poet and dramatist, regarded as the founder of the modern Russian theatre.

O when thou dost learn my torment,
Pity, Masha, O pity me!
My cruel fate is plain to see –
I am prisoner held by thee.

'What do you think of it?' I asked Shvabrin, expecting the praise which I considered my right. But to my extreme annoyance Shvabrin, usually an indulgent critic, roundly condemned my song.

'Why so?' I asked, concealing my vexation.

'Because', he replied, 'they are the sort of lines my teacher, Vassily Kirillich Tredyakovsky[1] would write – they put me very much in mind of his love couplets.'

He took my notebook from me and began mercilessly criticizing every verse and every word of the poem, jeering at me in the most sarcastic manner. This was more than I could endure and, snatching the manuscript from his hands, I declared I would never show him my verses again so long as I lived, at which threat Shvabrin laughed again.

'We shall see', he said, 'whether you will keep your word. A poet needs an audience in the same way as Ivan Kuzmich needs his vodka before dinner. And who is this Masha to whom you declare your tender passion and love-sick plight? Can it be Maria Ivanovna by any chance?'

'It's none of your business whoever she is,' I replied frowning. 'I want neither your opinion nor your conjectures.'

'Oho, the sensitive poet, the discreet lover!' Shvabrin went on, irritating me more and more. 'But take a friend's advice: if you want to succeed, you must not put all your faith in songs.'

'What do you mean, sir? Kindly explain yourself.'

'With pleasure. I mean that if you want Masha Mironov to come to your room at dusk, a pair of ear-rings would be a better offering than your tender verses.'

1. V. K. Tredyakovsky (1703–69) owes his place in Russian literature to his work as a critic. Peter the Great is reported to have said of him: 'A busy worker, but master of nothing.'

My blood boiled.

'And why have you such an opinion of her?' I asked, hardly able to restrain my indignation.

'Because', he replied with a devilish smile, 'I know by experience her morals and habits.'

'It's a lie, you scoundrel!' I cried in fury. 'It's a most shameless lie!'

Shvabrin changed colour.

'You shall pay for this,' he said, gripping my arm. 'You shall give me satisfaction.'

'Certainly – whenever you like!' I replied, delighted. There and then I could have torn him to pieces.

I hastened off to Ivan Ignatyich, whom I found with a needle in his hand: the commandant's wife had set him to thread mushrooms to dry for the winter. 'Ah, Piotr Andreich, come straight in!' he said, on seeing me. 'What good fortune brings you here? What might you be wanting, if I may inquire?' I explained briefly that I had quarrelled with Alexei Ivanich and had come to ask him – Ivan Ignatyich – to be my second. Ivan Ignatyich listened attentively, staring at me with his solitary eye.

'You mean to say', he answered, 'that you intend to kill Alexei Ivanich and would like me to witness it? Is that so, may I ask?'

'Exactly.'

'In heaven's name, Piotr Andreich, whatever are you thinking of? You have had words with Alexei Ivanich? What does that matter? Calling names is of no consequence. He insults you, and you give him a piece of your mind; he punches you on the nose, and you reply with a box on the ear – and on the other – and again – and each of you goes his own way; and later on we reconcile the pair of you. But to kill a man, would that be right, tell me that. If you kill him, well and good – so much the worse for him – I have no particular love for Alexei Ivanich myself. But supposing he makes holes through you? How are things then? Who would look a fool then, will you tell me?'

The sensible old man's arguments had no effect. I stuck to my intention.

'As you please,' said Ivan Ignatyich. 'Do as you think best. But why should I be present? What is the point? Two men fighting each other – what is the wonderful spectacle there, may I ask? Praise God, I have fought against the Swedes and the Turks, and seen fighting enough.'

I tried to explain as best I could the duties of a second but Ivan Ignatyich simply could not understand me at all.

'Have your own way,' he said, 'but if I am to be mixed up in this business it shall only be to go and report to Ivan Kuzmich, in accordance with duty, that a crime contrary to the interests of the State is being hatched in the fortress, and to ask if his Honour will take the necessary measures ...'

I was alarmed and implored Ivan Ignatyich to say nothing to the commandant: I had great difficulty in persuading him. He gave me his word, and I abandoned the idea of asking for his help.

I spent the evening as usual at the commandant's, and did my best to appear cheerful and indifferent so as not to excite suspicion and in order to avoid troublesome questions; but I confess I could not boast the cool composure which people in my position generally profess to feel. That evening I inclined to be tender and emotional. Maria Ivanovna attracted me more than ever. The thought that I might be seeing her for the last time imparted to her in my eyes something very touching. Shvabrin likewise made his appearance at the commandant's. I took him aside and told him of my conversation with Ivan Ignatyich. 'What do we want with seconds?' he said to me dryly. 'We can do without them.' We arranged to fight behind the corn-stacks near the fortress, and to meet there the following morning between six and seven. We appeared to be talking so amicably together that Ivan Ignatyich, delighted, let the cat out of the bag. 'That's what you ought to have done a long time ago,' he said to me contentedly. 'A bad peace is better than a good quarrel, and a damaged name better than a damaged skin.'

'What's that, what's that, Ivan Ignatyich?' asked the commandant's wife, who was telling fortunes with playing cards over in the corner. 'I did not catch what you said.'

Ivan Ignatyich, seeing my look of annoyance and remembering his promise, got flustered, not knowing what to answer. Shvabrin hastened to his assistance.

'Ivan Ignatyich', said he, 'approves of our reconciliation.'

'And with whom have you been quarrelling, my dear?'

'Piotr Andreich and I have fallen out rather seriously.'

'What about?'

'The merest trifle, Vassilissa Yegorovna – a song.'

'What a thing to quarrel about – a song! . . . However did it happen?'

'It happened like this: Piotr Andreich recently composed a song and today when he began to sing it to me, I broke into my favourite ditty:

> *Captain's daughter, O captain's daughter,*
> *Walk not abroad at the midnight hour.*

Words followed. Piotr Andreich was angry at first but then he reflected that everyone is free to sing what he likes. And that was the end of the matter.'

Shvabrin's effrontery very nearly made me boil over with fury, but nobody except myself understood his coarse insinuations – or, at any rate, nobody took any notice of them. From songs the conversation turned upon poets, and the commandant observed that they were a rakish lot and terrible drunkards, and advised me, as a friend, to give up writing verses, for such an occupation did not accord with the interests of the Service, and led to no good.

Shvabrin's presence was unendurable. I soon said good night to the commandant and his family, and back at home examined my sword, tested the point of it and went to bed, telling Savelich to wake me just after six.

The next morning, at the appointed hour, I stood behind the corn-stacks awaiting my opponent. He soon made his appearance. 'We may be disturbed,' he said. 'We must be quick.' We took off our uniforms and, wearing our sleeveless under-jackets only, drew our swords. At that moment Ivan Ignatyich with five soldiers of the garrison suddenly appeared from behind the stacks. He summoned us to the commandant. Resentfully we obeyed; the soldiers surrounded us and we followed behind Ivan Ignatyich, who led the way in triumph, striding along with an air of astonishing importance.

We reached the commandant's house. Ivan Ignatyich opened the door, announcing triumphantly: 'Here they are!' Vassilissa Yegorovna came towards us. 'How now, my good sirs! What do you mean by this? What has come over you? Whatever next? Plotting to commit murder here in our fortress! Ivan Kuzmich, put them under arrest at once! Piotr Andreich, Alexei Ivanich – give up your swords this instant! Give them up, give them up! Palashka, take these swords to the store-room. Piotr Andreich, I did not expect this of you: are you not ashamed of yourself? It is all very well for Alexei Ivanich – he was turned out of the Guards for killing a man, he does not believe in God even; but imagine you doing a thing like this! Do you wish to imitate him?'

Ivan Kuzmich, in full agreement with his wife, kept saying: 'Yes, you know, Vassilissa Yegorovna is quite right. Duelling is explicitly forbidden by the regulations.' Meanwhile, Palashka took our swords and carried them away to the store-room. I could not help laughing. Shvabrin preserved his gravity. 'With all my respect for you,' he said to Vassilissa Yegorovna coolly, 'I cannot help remarking that you give yourself unnecessary trouble in constituting yourself our judge. Leave it to Ivan Kuzmich – it is his business.' – 'Ah, my dear sir!' retorted the commandant's lady. 'Are not husband and wife one spirit and one flesh? Ivan Kuzmich, what are you waiting for? Place them under arrest at once, in solitary confinement, and on bread and water, until they come to their senses. And let Father Gerassim impose a public penance on them, that they may beg God's forgiveness and confess their sins before everyone.'

Ivan Kuzmich did not know what to do. Maria Ivanovna was exceedingly pale. Little by little the storm subsided; the commandant's wife calmed down and made us embrace each other. Palashka brought us back our swords. We left the house seemingly reconciled. Ivan Ignatyich accompanied us. 'Aren't you ashamed', I said to him angrily, 'to go and report us to the commandant when you had given me your word not to?' – 'God is my witness, I never mentioned a thing to Ivan Kuzmich,' he replied. 'Vassilissa Yegorovna wormed it all out of me. It was she arranged it without the commandant's knowledge. Anyhow, let us thank heaven that it has all ended in the way it has!' With these words he turned home and Shvabrin and I were left alone. 'We cannot let it rest at this,' I said to him. 'Of course not,' replied Shvabrin, 'you shall answer me with your blood for your insolence; but I expect we shall be watched. We shall have to dissemble for a few days. Goodbye.' And we parted as though nothing had happened.

Returning to the commandant's house, I sat down as usual near Maria Ivanovna. Ivan Kuzmich was not at home. Vassilissa Yegorovna was busy with household matters. We talked together in an undertone. Maria Ivanovna reproached me tenderly for the anxiety I had caused them all by my quarrel with Shvabrin.

'I fainted away', she said, 'when we were told that you intended to fight with swords. How strange men are! Because of a single word which they would probably have forgotten a week later they are ready to murder one another and sacrifice not only their lives but their consciences and the happiness of those . . . But I am sure it was not you who began the quarrel. No doubt Alexei Ivanich was to blame.'

'And what makes you think so, Maria Ivanovna?'

'Oh, I don't know . . . he is so sarcastic. I don't like Alexei Ivanich. I loathe him, and yet, strange to say, I wouldn't for anything have him dislike me so much. That would worry me dreadfully.'

'And what do you think, Maria Ivanovna? Does he like you, or not?'

Maria Ivanovna stammered and blushed.

'I think . . .' she said, 'I believe he does like me.'

'Why do you think so now?'

'Because he asked for my hand in marriage.'

'Marriage! Asked for your hand in marriage? When was that?'

'Last year. About two months before you came.'

'And you refused?'

'As you can see. Of course, Alexei Ivanich is clever and rich and comes of good family. But when I think that at the wedding I should have to kiss him in public . . . no, nothing would induce me to!'

Maria Ivanovna's words opened my eyes and explained a great many things. I now understood the persistent slander with which Shvabrin pursued her. He had no doubt observed our mutual attraction and was doing his utmost to alienate us from each other. The words which had given rise to our quarrel seemed to me all the more vile when, instead of coarse and ill-mannered mockery, I saw in them premeditated calumny. My desire to punish the insolent traducer became still more violent, and I waited impatiently for a favourable opportunity.

I had not long to wait. The following day as I sat composing an elegy, and biting my pen as I searched for a rhyme, Shvabrin tapped at my window. I abandoned my pen, picked up my sword and went out to join him. 'Why put it off?' said Shvabrin. 'Nobody is watching us. Let us go down to the river. We shall not be disturbed there.' We set off in silence. Descending by a steep path, we stopped at the river-bank and bared our swords. Shvabrin was the more expert but I was stronger and more daring, and Monsieur Beaupré, who had once upon a time been a soldier, had given me a few lessons in fencing, which I turned to good account. Shvabrin had not expected to find in me such a dangerous opponent. For a long time neither of us was able to inflict any injury upon the other; at last, observing that Shvabrin was weakening, I began to press him vigorously and almost forced him into the river. Suddenly I heard someone shouting my name. I glanced round and saw Savelich running down the steep path towards me. . . . At that same moment I felt a sharp stab in the breast, under my right shoulder. I fell and lost consciousness.

5

LOVE

Ah, you young maiden, O maiden fair!
You must not marry while still so young.
Ask your father, then ask your mother,
Father and mother and all your kin.
Cull wisdom, my beauty, and common sense,
And so these twain shall thy dowry be.

FOLK SONG

Find a better one, and you'll forget me.
But if she be worse – you'll think of me.

FOLK SONG

WHEN I regained consciousness I could not at first understand where I was and what had happened to me. I was lying in bed in a strange room, feeling very weak. Savelich was standing before me with a candle in his hand. Someone was carefully unwinding the bandages round my chest and shoulder. Gradually my head cleared. I remembered the duel and guessed that I had been wounded. At that moment the door creaked. 'Well, how is he?' whispered a voice which sent a thrill through me. 'Still the same,' Savelich answered with a sigh. 'Still unconscious: this makes the fifth day.' I tried to turn my head but could not. 'Where am I? Who is here?' I said with an effort. Maria Ivanovna came up to the bed and bent over me. 'Well, how do you feel?' she asked. 'All right,' I answered in a weak voice. 'Is that you, Maria Ivanovna? Tell me . . .' I had not the strength to go on, and broke off. Savelich uttered a cry. His face lit up with joy. 'He has come round, he has come round!' he kept on repeating. 'Thank God! Well, Piotr Andreich, dear, you have given me a fright. It was no joke –

five whole days . . .' Maria Ivanovna interrupted him. 'Do not talk too much to him, Savelich,' she said. 'He is still weak.' She went out and quietly closed the door. My thoughts were in a turmoil. And so I was in the commandant's house: Maria Ivanovna had been in to see me. I wanted to ask Savelich a question or two but the old man shook his head and stopped his ears. I closed my eyes in vexation and soon dropped asleep.

When I woke up I called Savelich, but instead of him there was Maria Ivanovna: her angelic voice greeted me. I cannot describe the blissful feeling which enveloped me at that moment. I seized her hand and pressed it to me, bathing it with tears of emotion. Masha did not withdraw her hand . . . and suddenly her lips touched my cheek and I felt their hot, fresh kiss. A flame ran through me. 'Dear, good Maria Ivanovna,' I said to her, 'be my wife, consent to make my happy.' She recovered herself. 'Calm yourself, for heaven's sake,' she said, withdrawing her hand. 'You are not out of danger yet: your wound may open again. Take care of yourself, if only for my sake.' With these words she went out, leaving me in an ecstasy of bliss. Happiness restored me. She would be mine! She loved me! The thought filled my whole being.

From that moment I grew better every hour. The regimental barber attended to my wound, for there was no other doctor in the fortress, and fortunately he did not try to be too clever. Youth and nature accelerated my recovery. The whole family fussed over me. Maria Ivanovna never left my side. Naturally, at the first opportunity I returned to my interrupted declaration of love, and Maria Ivanovna heard me out with more patience. Without any affectation she confessed her fondness for me, and said that her parents would certainly be glad of her happiness. 'But think it over well,' she added. 'Won't your parents raise objections?'

I pondered. I was not at all uneasy on the score of my mother's affection, but knowing my father's disposition and way of thinking I felt that my love would not move him very much and that he would look upon it as a young man's fancy. I candidly admitted this to Maria Ivanovna but decided to write to my father as eloquently as possible, imploring his paternal blessing. I showed the letter to Maria Ivanovna, who found it so convincing and touching that she never doubted its success and abandoned herself to the feelings of her tender heart with all the trustfulness of youth and love.

I made it up with Shvabrin in the first days of my convalescence. In reprimanding me for the duel Ivan Kuzmich had said to me: 'See now, Piotr Andreich, I ought really to put you under arrest, but you have been punished enough already. Alexei Ivanich, though, is shut up in the granary, and Vassilissa Yegorovna has got his sword under lock and key. Let him have plenty of time to think things over and repent.' I was far too happy to cherish any hostile feeling in my heart. I interceded for Shvabrin and the good commandant with his wife's consent agreed to release him. Shvabrin came to see me; he expressed deep regret for what had happened, confessed that he had been thoroughly in the wrong, and begged me to forget the past. Not being by nature of a rancorous disposition, I readily forgave him both our quarrel and the wound which I had received at his hands. I ascribed his slandering to the chagrin of injured vanity and rejected love, and I generously pardoned my unhappy rival.

I was soon fully recovered and able to return to my lodgings. I waited impatiently for the answer to my letter, not daring to hope, and trying to stifle melancholy forebodings. I had not yet spoken to Vassilissa Yegorovna and her husband of my intentions; but my proposal was not likely to surprise them. Neither Maria Ivanovna nor I made any attempt to conceal our feelings from them, and we were certain of their consent beforehand.

At last one morning Savelich came into my room, holding a letter. I seized it with trembling fingers. The address was written in my father's hand. This detail prepared me for something momentous, for as a rule it was my mother who wrote to me, my father merely adding a few lines at the end as a postscript. It was several minutes before I broke the seal – I kept reading over again and again the solemn superscription:

> To my Son, Piotr Andreyevich Griniov,
> Bielogorsky Fortress,
> Province of Orenburg.

I tried to guess from the handwriting in what mood the letter had been written. At last I brought myself to open it, and saw from the very first lines that all was lost. The letter ran as follows:

My son Piotr,

Your letter, in which you ask for our parental blessing and consent to your marriage with the Mironov girl, reached us on the fifteen of this month, and not only have I no intention of giving you either my blessing or my consent but I propose to arrive and teach you the lesson you deserve for your pranks, notwithstanding your officer's rank; for you have shown that you are not yet worthy to carry the sword which has been entrusted to you for the defence of your country, and not to fight duels with other scapegraces like yourself. I shall write at once to Andrei Karlovich, asking him to transfer you from the Bielogorsky fortress to some post further away, where you can get over your foolishness. When your mother heard of your duel, and that you had been wounded, she was taken ill with grief and is now confined to her bed. What will become of you? I pray God that you may return to the right path, although I dare not hope in His great mercy.

Your father,

A.G.

The perusal of this letter stirred various feelings in me. The harsh expressions, of which my father had not been sparing, wounded me deeply. The contemptuous way in which he referred to Maria Ivanovna seemed to me as indecorous as it was unjust. The thought of being transferred from the Bielogorsky fortress appalled me; but I was upset most of all by the news of my mother's illness. I felt indignant with Savelich, having no doubt that it was he who had informed my parents of the duel. Striding up and down my narrow room, I stopped in front of him and said with a threatening look:

'It seems you are not satisfied that, thanks to you, I should be wounded and for a whole month lie at death's door: you want to kill my mother as well.'

Savelich was thunderstruck.

'For mercy's sake, sir, what are you saying?' he almost sobbed. 'Me the cause of your getting wounded? God is my witness I was running to shield you with my own breast from Alexei Ivanich's sword! 'Twas old age – devil take it – hampered me. And what have I done to your mamma?'

'What have you done?' replied I. 'Who asked you to write and inform against me? Have you been set to spy on me then?'

'Me write and inform against you?' Savelich answered with tears in his eyes. 'Heavens above! Here, then, read what the master writes to me: you will see how I informed against you.'

And he pulled a letter out of his pocket and read the following:

You ought to be ashamed of yourself, you knave, for not having written to me about my son, Piotr Andreyevich – in spite of my strict injunctions to you to do so – and leaving it to strangers to notify me of his pranks. Is this the way you perform your duty and carry out your master's will? I will send you to tend pigs, you mongrel, for concealing the truth and conniving with the young man. As soon as you receive this I command you to write back to me without delay about the present state of his health, which, so I am told, is improved; also the exact place of his wound, and whether he has been well attended to.

It was obvious that Savelich was innocent, and that I had outraged him unfairly with my reproaches and suspicions. I begged his pardon but the old man was inconsolable.

'That I should have lived to come to this!' he kept repeating. 'These are the thanks I get from my masters! Me an old mongrel, and a swineherd, and the cause of your wound into the bargain! No, my good Piotr Andreich, not me but that accursed Frenchman is to blame: 'twas him taught you to thrust at people with those turn-spits, and to stamp your feet, as though thrusting 'n stamping could save one from an evil man! Much need there was to hire that Frenchman and spend money for naught!'

But who, then, had taken upon himself to inform my father of my conduct? The general? But he did not appear to show overmuch interest in me, and Ivan Kuzmich had not thought it necessary to report my duel to him. I was lost in conjectures. My suspicions settled upon Shvabrin. He alone could benefit by informing against me and thus causing me, perhaps, to be removed from the fortress and parted from the commandant's family. I went off to tell it all to Maria Ivanovna. She met me on the steps. 'What has happened to you?' she said when she saw me. 'How pale you are!' – 'All is lost,' I answered, and gave her my father's letter. She now in her turn grew pale. After reading the letter she restored it to me with trembling hand and said in a trembling voice: 'Evidently it was not my destiny. ... Your parents do not want me in their family. The Lord's will be done! God knows better than we do what is good for us. It can't be helped, Piotr Andreich; you at least be happy!' – 'This shall not be!' I cried, seizing hold of her hand. 'You love me: I am ready to face anything. Let us go and throw ourselves at your parents' feet: they are simple people, not hard-hearted and proud. ... They will give us their blessing; we will marry ... and then, in time, I am sure we shall succeed in bringing my father round – my mother will be on our side. He will forgive me ...' – 'No, Piotr Andreich,' replied Masha. 'I will not marry you without your parents' blessing. Without their blessing there can be no happiness for you. Let us submit to God's will. If you find the one who is destined for you, if you come to love another woman – God be with you, Piotr Andreich, I shall pray for you both. ...' She burst into tears and left me. I wanted to follow her indoors but I felt that I was not in a condition to control myself, and returned home to my quarters.

I was sitting plunged in profound reverie when Savelich broke in on my reflections. 'Here, sir,' he said, handing me a sheet of paper covered with writing, 'see if I am an informer against my master, and if I try to make mischief between father and son.' I took the paper from his hands: it was Savelich's answer to the letter he had received. Here it is, word for word:

Dear Sir, Andrei Petrovich, our gracious Father,

I received your gracious letter in which you are pleased to be angry with me, your servant, saying that I ought to be ashamed not to obey my master's orders; but I am not an old mongrel but your faithful servant, I obey my master's orders, and I have always served you zealously until now I am a white-haired old man. I did not write to you anything about Piotr Andreich's wound so as not to alarm you without a reason, and I hear that the mistress, our good lady Avdotia Vassilievna, as it is has taken to her bed with fright, and I am going to pray God to make her better. And Piotr Andreich was wounded below the right shoulder, in the breast, just below the bone, one vershock and a half[1] deep, and he was put to bed in the commandant's house, where we carried him from the river-bank, and it was the barber of these parts, Stepan Paramonov, attended him, and now Piotr Andreich, God be praised, is well and there is nothing but good news to write about him. His superiors, I hear, are satisfied with him; while Vassilissa Yegorovna treats him as though he were her own son. And as to the little accident that befell him, one cannot blame the lad: even the best of horses may stumble. And you are pleased to write that you will send me to herd pigs, and let your master's will be done in this too. Whereupon I humbly salute you.

> *Your faithful serf,*
> *Arhip Savelich.*

I could not help smiling more than once as I read the good old man's epistle. I did not feel ready to answer my father, and Savelich's letter seemed sufficient to relieve my mother's anxiety.

From that time my position changed. Maria Ivanovna scarcely spoke to me and tried her utmost to avoid me. The commandant's house had become hateful to me. Gradually I accustomed myself to sitting at home alone. Vassilissa

1. A little over 2½ inches.

Yegorovna upbraided me for it at first but, seeing my obstinacy, left me in peace. Ivan Kuzmich I only saw when my duties required it. I seldom met Shvabrin, and then with reluctance, all the more so as I noticed his veiled hostility towards me, which confirmed my suspicions. Life grew to be intolerable. I sank into despondent brooding, which was nourished by isolation and idleness. My love waxed more ardent in solitude and oppressed me more and more. I lost the taste for reading and composition. My spirits drooped. I was afraid I should either go out of my mind or take to wild living. Then unexpected events, which exercised an important influence upon my whole life, suddenly gave all my being a powerful and salutary shock.

6

THE PUGACHEV REBELLION

And now you young men do you listen
To what we, the old 'uns, will tell you.
SONG

BEFORE I proceed to describe the strange events of which I was a witness I must say a few words concerning the position in the province of Orenburg at the end of the year 1773.

This vast and wealthy province was inhabited by a number of half-savage tribes who had but recently acknowledged the sovereignty of the Russian Tsars. Their continual revolts, the fact that they were unused to laws and a civilized life, their irresponsibility and cruelty demanded constant vigilance on the part of the Government in order to keep them in subjection. Fortresses had been erected in opportune places, and were garrisoned for the most part by Cossacks who had occupied the banks of the Yaïk for generations. But these Yaïk Cossacks whose duty it was to preserve peace and watch over the safety of the country-side had themselves for some time past been a source of trouble and danger to the Government. In the year 1772 an insurrection broke out in their capital city. It was caused by the severe measures adopted by Major-general Traubenberg to bring the Cossack troops to a due state of obedience. The result was the barbarous murder of Traubenberg, a revolutionary change in the Administration, and, finally, the suppression of the outbreak by means of cannon and cruel punishments.

This had happened a little while before my arrival in the Bielogorsky fortress. All was now quiet, or seemed so; the authorities believed too easily in the feigned repentance of the wily rebels, who nursed their rancour in secret and waited for a favourable opportunity to make fresh trouble.

To return to my story.

One evening (it was at the beginning of October 1773) I was sitting at home alone, listening to the moaning of the autumn wind and gazing out of the window at the black clouds that raced past the moon. Someone came to fetch me to the commandant's. I went at once. There I found Shvabrin, Ivan Ignatyich and the Cossack sergeant. Neither Vassilissa Yegorovna nor Maria Ivanovna was in the room. The commandant greeted me with a preoccupied air. He closed the door, made us all be seated except the sergeant who was standing by the door, drew a paper out of his pocket and said to us: 'Gentlemen, important news! Listen to what the general writes.' Then he put on his spectacles and read the following:

To the Commandant of the Bielogorsky Fortress,
  Captain Mironov.

CONFIDENTIAL

I hereby inform you that the fugitive Don Cossack and Old Believer, Emelian Pugachev, has had the unpardonable insolence to assume the name of the deceased Emperor Peter III, has assembled a band of evilly disposed persons, has caused disturbances in the Yaïk settlements and has already taken and sacked several fortresses, pillaging and murdering on every side. Wherefore, upon receipt of these presents, you, Captain, will take the necessary measures for repulsing the said villain and pretender, and, if possible, for his total annihilation, should he attack the fortress entrusted to your care.

'Take the necessary measures!' said the commandant, removing his spectacles and folding up the paper. 'Easy enough to say, you know! The villain is evidently powerful; and we have only a hundred and thirty men all told, not counting the Cossacks on whom there is no relying – no offence meant, Maximich.' (The sergeant smiled.) 'However, we must do the best we can, gentlemen! Carry out your responsibilities scrupulously, arrange for sentry duty and night patrols. In case of attack, shut the gates and assemble the men. You, Maximich, keep a sharp eye on your Cossacks. The cannon must be seen to and cleaned thoroughly. And, above all things, keep all this secret, so that no one in the fortress knows about it beforehand.'

Having given these orders, Ivan Kuzmich dismissed us. Shvabrin and I walked away together, talking of what we had just heard.

'What will be the end of it, do you think?' I asked him.

'Heaven only knows,' he replied. 'We shall see. So far, I don't believe it will be much. But if . . .'

He became thoughtful and began absent-mindedly whistling a French tune.

In spite of all our precautions the news of Pugachev's appearance soon spread through the fortress. Although Ivan Kuzmich entertained the greatest respect for his wife he would not for anything in the world have disclosed to her a secret entrusted to him in connexion with the Service. Upon receipt of the general's letter he rather skilfully got Vassilissa Yegorovna out of the way by telling her that Father Gerassim had apparently heard some startling news from Orenburg, which he was guarding jealously. Vassilissa Yegorovna immediately decided to go and call on the priest's wife and, on Ivan Kuzmich's advice, took Masha with her, lest the girl should feel lonely left by herself.

Ivan Kuzmich, thus in complete command of the house, had at once sent for us, having locked Palashka in the store-room so that she should not overhear us.

Vassilissa Yegorovna returned home without having gained any information from the priest's wife, and learned that in her absence Ivan Kuzmich had held a council and that Palashka had been put under lock and key. She guessed that her husband had deceived her, and proceeded to assail him with questions. But Ivan Kuzmich was prepared for the attack. Not in the least disconcerted, he made firm answer to his inquisitive consort. 'You see, my dear, the good women hereabouts have taken it into their heads to heat their ovens with straw, and since this may cause a fire I have given strict orders that in future they are not to use straw but brushwood and other dead wood instead.'

'Then why did you have to lock Palashka up?' asked the commandant's wife. 'What had the poor girl done that she should have to sit in the store-room till our return?'

Ivan Kuzmich was not ready for this question: he became confused and mumbled something incoherent. Vassilissa Yegorovna perceived her husband's trick but, knowing that she would extract nothing from him, abstained from further questioning and turned the conversation on the salted cucumbers which the priest's wife prepared in some special way. All that night Vassilissa Yegorovna could not sleep a wink for trying to guess what could be in her husband's mind that she was not allowed to know.

The next day, returning from morning service, she saw Ivan Ignatyich pulling out of the cannon bits of rag, small stones, wood shavings, knuckle-bones and rubbish of every sort that the children had stuffed into it. 'What can these martial preparations mean?' wondered the commandant's wife. 'Are they expecting another Kirghiz raid? But surely Kuzmich would not conceal such trifles from me?' She hailed Ivan Ignatyich, determined to discover from him the secret that tormented her feminine curiosity.

Vassilissa Yegorovna began by making a few observations to him concerning household matters, like a magistrate who starts his cross-examination with irrelevant questions in order to put the accused off his guard. Then, after a few moments' silence, she heaved a deep sigh and said, shaking her head: 'Oh dear, oh dear, just think what news! What will come of it?'

'Don't you worry, ma'am,' Ivan Ignatyich answered. 'The Lord is merciful: we have soldiers enough, plenty of powder, and I have cleaned out the cannon. We may yet send Pugachev packing. Those God helps nobody can't harm.'

'And what sort of a man is this Pugachev?' asked the commandant's wife.

Ivan Ignatyich saw that he had said too much and bit his tongue. But it was too late. Vassilissa Yegorovna forced him to make a clean breast of everything, promising not to breathe a word to a soul.

Vassilissa Yegorovna kept her promise and did not utter a syllable except to the priest's wife, and that only because her cow was still grazing in the steppe and might be seized by the rebels.

Soon everyone was talking about Pugachev. The rumours differed. The commandant dispatched Maximich to glean all he could in the neighbouring villages and fortresses. The sergeant returned after a couple of days' absence and reported that in the steppe, some sixty versts from the fortress, he had seen a quantity of lights and the Bashkirs had told him an unheard-of host was approaching. For the rest, he could not say anything positive because he had feared to venture farther afield.

We now began to notice an unwonted ferment among the Cossacks of the fortress: in all the streets they stood about in little groups, whispering together and dispersing whenever they caught sight of a dragoon or a garrison soldier. Spies were sent among them. Yulaï, a Kalmyck converted to the Christian faith, brought important information to the commandant. The sergeant's report, according to Yulaï, was a false one: on his return the treacherous Cossack had announced to his comrades that he had been among the rebels, had presented himself to their leader, who gave him his hand to kiss and held a long conversation with him. The commandant had the sergeant arrested at once, and put Yulaï in his place. This change was received with manifest dissatisfaction by the Cossacks. They murmured loudly, and Ivan Ignatyich, who had to carry out the commandant's instructions, with his own ears heard them say: 'Just you wait, you garrison rat!' The commandant had intended interrogating his prisoner that same day, but Maximich had escaped, no doubt with the help of his comrades.

Another circumstance served to increase the commandant's

anxiety. A Bashkir was caught carrying seditious papers. On this occasion the commandant again decided to call his officers together and again wanted to send Vassilissa Yegorovna away on some plausible pretext. But since Ivan Kuzmich was a most straightforward and truthful man he could think of no other device than the one he had employed formerly.

'I say, Vassilissa Yegorovna,' he began, clearing his throat. 'Father Gerassim, I hear, has received from town . . .'

'Enough of your stories, Ivan Kuzmich,' his wife interrupted him. 'I expect you want to call a council to talk about Emelian Pugachev without me there; but you can't bamboozle me.'

Ivan Kuzmich stared at her.

'Well, my dear,' he said, 'if you know all about it already there is no point in your leaving: we will do our talking with you in the room.'

'That's better, man,' she answered. 'You are no hand at deception. So send for the officers.'

We assembled again. Ivan Kuzmich, in the presence of his wife, read to us Pugachev's manifesto, drawn up by some half-literate Cossack. The outlaw announced his intention of marching against our fortress without delay; invited the Cossacks and the soldiers to join him, and the commanders he exhorted not to resist him, threatening to put them to death if they did so. The manifesto was couched in crude but vigorous language, and must have made a dangerous impression on the minds of simple people.

'The blackguard!' cried the commandant's wife. 'To think of his daring to make suggestions to us! We are to go out and meet him and lay our flags at his feet! Ah, the dog! Perhaps he does not know that we've been forty years in the Service, and have seen a thing or two? Surely no commanders have listened to the brigand?'

'I should not have thought so,' replied Ivan Kuzmich. 'But it appears the scoundrel has already taken a good many fortresses.'

'He must be really strong then,' remarked Shvabrin.

'We shall soon find out just how strong he is,' said the commandant. 'Vassilissa Yegorovna, give me the key of the storehouse. Ivan Ignatyich, you fetch the Bashkir, and tell Yulaï to bring the whip.'

'Wait, Ivan Kuzmich,' said the commandant's wife, getting up. 'Let me take Masha somewhere out of the house: otherwise she will hear the screams and be terrified. And, to tell the truth, I don't care for torture myself either. So good-bye for the moment.'

Torture in the old days formed so integral a part of judicial procedure that the humane edict[1] abolishing it for long remained a dead letter. It was thought that the criminal's own confession was necessary in order to find him guilty – an idea not only without foundation but even wholly contrary to judicial good sense; for if the accused person's denial of the charge is not accepted as proof of his innocence, the confession that has been wrung from him ought still less to be regarded as proof of his guilt. Even now I sometimes hear old judges regretting the abolition of the barbarous custom. But in those days no one, judge or accused, doubted the necessity of torture. And so the commandant's order did not surprise or alarm any of us. Ivan Ignatyich went to fetch the Bashkir, who was locked up in Vassilissa Yegorovna's storehouse, and a few minutes later the prisoner was led into the lobby. The commandant commanded him to be brought into the room.

The Bashkir crossed the threshold with difficulty (his feet were in fetters) and, taking off his tall cap, remained standing near the door. I glanced at him and shuddered. Never shall I forget that man. He appeared to be over seventy. He had neither nose nor ears. His head was shaven; instead of a beard a few grey hairs sprouted on his chin; he was short, thin and bent; but his narrow little eyes still had a gleam of fire in them. 'Aha!' said the commandant, recognizing by

---

1. Early in her reign (1762–96) Catherine II set up a Commission to draft a new legal Code. One of the 500 or so Articles in the book which she herself wrote for the guidance of this Commission rejects the use of torture.

these dreadful marks one of the rebels punished in 1741. 'I see you are an old wolf – you have been caught in our traps before. It seems this is not the first time you have rebelled, to judge by the way they've planed your noddle. Come nearer – tell me, who sent you here in secret?'

The old Bashkir was silent and gazed at the commandant with a completely stolid air. 'Why don't you speak?' continued Ivan Kuzmich. 'Or don't you understand Russian? Yulaï, ask him in your language who sent him to our fortress?'

Yulaï repeated Ivan Kuzmich's question in Tartar. But the Bashkir looked at him with the same expression and made no answer.

'Very well,' said the commandant. 'I shall make you speak. Take off that ridiculous striped garment of his, my lads, and streak his back. Mind you do it thoroughly, Yulaï!'

Two old pensioners began undressing the Bashkir. The unfortunate man's face expressed anxiety. He looked about him like a little wild animal caught by children. But when one of the pensioners seized his hands to twine them round his neck, and raised the old man upon his shoulders, and Yulaï grasped the whip and began to flourish it, the Bashkir uttered a feeble, imploring groan and, nodding his head, opened his mouth, in which, instead of a tongue, moved a short stump.

When I reflect that this happened in my lifetime, and that now I have lived to see the gentle reign of the Emperor Alexander, I cannot but marvel at the rapid progress of civilization and the spread of humane principles. Young man, if these lines of mine ever fall into your hands, remember that the best and most enduring of transformations are those which proceed from an improvement in morals and customs, and not from any violent upheaval.

We were all horror-stricken.

'Well,' said the commandant, 'it is evident we shall get nothing out of him. Yulaï, take the Bashkir back to the storehouse. Gentlemen, we have a few more things to talk over!'

We were beginning to discuss our situation when suddenly

Vassilissa Yegorovna rushed into the room, out of breath and beside herself with alarm.

'What is the matter with you?' the commandant asked in surprise.

'My dear, dreadful news!' exclaimed Vassilissa Yegorovna. 'The Nizhneozerny fortress was captured this morning. Father Gerassim's servant has just returned from there. He saw it being taken. The commandant and all the officers were hanged one after the other. All the soldiers were made prisoner. The villains may be here at any moment.'

This unexpected news was a great shock to me. I knew the commandant of the Nizhneozerny fortress, a modest, quiet young man: some two months before, he had put up at Ivan Kuzmich's on his way from Orenburg with his young wife. The Nizhneozerny fortress lay twenty-five versts or so from our fortress. Pugachev might attack us at any moment. I saw a vivid picture of the fate in store for Maria Ivanovna, and my heart sank within me.

'Listen, Ivan Kuzmich,' I said to the commandant. 'Our duty is to defend the fortress to our last breath: there can be no question about that. But we must think of the safety of the women. Send them to Orenburg, if the road is still open, or to some safer fortress farther away out of these villains' reach.'

Ivan Kuzmich turned to his wife and said:

'I say, my dear, hadn't I better send you and Masha away until we have settled with the rebels?'

'What nonsense!' she replied. 'No fortress is safe from bullets. What's wrong with the Bielogorsky? We have lived in it these two and twenty years, thanks be to God. We have seen the Bashkirs and the Kirghiz: God willing, we shall hold out against Pugachev too!'

'Well, my dear,' rejoined Ivan Kuzmich, 'stay if you like, since you have confidence in our fortress. But what are we to do about Masha? All well and good if we ward them off, or last out until reinforcements come – but what if the villains take the fortress?'

'Why, in that case . . .'

Vassilissa Yegorovna hesitated and paused, looking deeply agitated.

'No, Vassilissa Yegorovna,' continued the commandant, observing that his words had produced an effect perhaps for the first time in his life. 'It is not right for Masha to stay here. Let us send her to Orenburg, to her godmother's: there are soldiers and cannon in plenty there, and the walls are of stone. And I should advise you to go with her: you may be an old woman but think what would happen to you if they take the fortress.'

'Very well,' said the commandant's wife, 'so be it, we will send Masha away. But don't you dream of asking me – I won't leave. I wouldn't think of parting from you in my old age, to go and seek a lonely grave in a strange place. We have lived together, and together we will die.'

'There is something in that,' said the commandant. 'Well, we must not waste time. Go and get Masha ready for the journey. We will send her off before daybreak tomorrow, and she shall have an escort, too, although we have no men to spare. But where is Masha?'

'At Akulina Pamfilovna's,' replied the commandant's wife. 'She fainted away when she heard about Nizhneozerny being taken. I am afraid of her falling ill. Heavens above, to have come to this at our age!'

Vassilissa Yegorovna went to see about her daughter's departure. The discussion continued, but I took no further part in it and did not listen. Maria Ivanovna came in to supper, pale and tear-stained. We ate in silence and rose from the table sooner than usual. Then, after saying good-bye to the family, we returned to our respective quarters. But I purposely left my sword behind and went back for it: I had a feeling that I should find Maria Ivanovna alone. Sure enough, she met me at the door and handed me my sword. 'Farewell, Piotr Andreich,' she said with tears. 'I am being sent to Orenburg. Keep safe and sound, and be happy. Perhaps God will grant that we meet again, but if not . . .' And she broke into sobs. I clasped her in my arms. 'Farewell, my angel,' I said. 'Farewell, my dear one, my heart's desire! Whatever may happen to me, rest assured that my last thought and my last prayer will be for you!' Masha sobbed with her head pressed against my breast. I kissed her fervently and hastened out of the room.

7

THE ASSAULT

O my poor head, O my head, my head,
That has served my Tsar and country well!
That has served for three and thirty years
Yet won for thyself no joy or gold,
Neither word of praise nor rank on high!
Two upright posts are all that be thine,
With beech-wood cross-beam, and noose of silk.

FOLK SONG

THAT night I did not sleep, nor did I undress, I intended to go at dawn to the fortress gate from which Maria Ivanovna would leave, and there say good-bye to her for the last time. I was conscious of a great change in myself: my agitation of mind was far less burdensome to me than my recent low spirits. The grief of parting was mingled with vague but delicious hope, with an eager expectation of danger and sentiments of noble ambition. The night sped by unnoticed. I was on the point of going out when my door opened and the corporal came in to tell me that our Cossacks had left during the night, taking Yulaï with them by force, and that strange men were reconnoitring round the fortress. The thought that Maria Ivanovna would not be able to get away filled me with alarm: I gave the corporal a few hasty instructions and rushed off to the commandant's.

Day had already begun to dawn. I was flying down the street when I heard someone calling me. I stopped.

'Where are you going?' said Ivan Ignatyich, catching up with me. 'Ivan Kuzmich is on the rampart and has sent me for you. Pugachev has come.'

'Has Maria Ivanovna left?' I asked with sinking heart.

'She was not in time,' answered Ivan Ignatyich. 'The road to Orenburg is cut off; the fortress is surrounded. It's a bad look out, Piotr Andreich!'

We made our way to the rampart, a natural rise in the ground reinforced by a palisade. All the inhabitants of the fortress were crowding there already. The garrison was under arms. The cannon had been dragged up the day before. The commandant was walking up and down in front of his scanty detachment. The approach of danger had inspired the old warrior with unusual vigour. In the steppe, not very far from the fortress, some twenty men were riding to and fro. They seemed to be Cossacks but there were Bashkirs among them too, easily recognizable by their caps of lynx fur and their quivers. The commandant went round his little company, saying to the soldiers: 'Well, children, let us stand firm today for our good Empress and prove to all the world that we are brave and loyal men!' The soldiers expressed their zeal with loud shouts. Shvabrin was standing next to me, looking intently at the enemy. Noticing the movement in the fortress, the horsemen riding about the steppe gathered in a little knot and began conferring among themselves. The commandant told Ivan Ignatyich to aim the cannon at the group, and himself applied the match. The cannon-ball whistled over their heads without doing any damage. The horsemen dispersed, instantly galloping out of sight, and the steppe was empty.

At that moment Vassilissa Yegorovna appeared on the rampart, followed by Masha who would not leave her side.

'Well, what's happening?' asked the commandant's wife. 'How goes the battle? Where is the enemy?'

'The enemy is not far off,' replied Ivan Kuzmich. 'God willing, all will go well. Well, Masha, are you afraid?'

'No, papa,' Maria Ivanovna answered. 'I am more frightened at home by myself.'

She looked at me and made an effort to smile. I instinctively clasped the hilt of my sword, remembering that the day before I had received it from her hands, as it were to defend my beloved. My heart glowed. I imagined myself her chevalier. I thirsted to prove that I was worthy of her trust, and longed impatiently for the decisive hour.

All of a sudden some fresh bodies of mounted men appeared from behind a hill half a verst from the fortress, and soon the steppe was covered with a multitude of men armed with lances and bows and arrows. A man in a red kaftan, holding a drawn sword in his hand, was riding among them mounted on a white horse: it was Pugachev himself. He stopped; the others gathered round him and, obviously at his command, four men galloped at full tilt right up to the fortress. We recognized them for our treacherous Cossacks. One of them held a sheet of paper above his cap, while another had Yulaï's head stuck on the point of his spear which he shook off and threw to us over the palisade. The poor Kalmyck's head fell at the commandant's feet. The traitors shouted:

'Do not fire! Come out and pay homage to the Tsar! The Tsar is here!'

'I'll teach you!' Ivan Kuzmich shouted. 'Ready, lads – fire!'

Our soldiers fired a volley. The Cossack who held the letter reeled from his horse; the others galloped back. I glanced at Maria Ivanovna. Horrified by the sight of Yulaï's bloodstained head and deafened by the volley, she seemed dazed. The commandant called the corporal and bade him take the paper from the dead man's hand. The corporal went out into the plain and returned, leading the dead Cossack's horse by the bridle. He handed the letter to the commandant. Ivan Kuzmich read it to himself and then tore it in pieces. Meanwhile, we could see the rebels making ready for action. Some bullets began to whistle about our ears and several arrows fell close to us, sticking in the ground and in the palisade. 'Vassilissa Yegorovna,' said the commandant, 'this is no place for women. Take Masha away. You see, the girl is more dead than alive.'

Vassilissa Yegorovna, who had gone quiet when the bullets began to fly, cast a glance at the steppe where there was much movement to be seen. Then she turned to her husband and

said: 'Ivan Kuzmich, life and death are in God's hands: give
Masha your blessing. Masha, go to your father.'

Masha, pale and trembling, went up to Ivan Kuzmich,
knelt down before him and bowed herself to the ground.
The old commandant made the sign of the cross over her
three times. Then he raised her and, kissing her, said in a
changed voice:

'Well, Masha, may you be happy. Pray to God. He will not
forsake you. If you meet a good man, may God give you love
and concord. Live together as your mother and I have lived.
Well now, adieu, Masha. Vassilissa Yegorovna, take her
away quickly.'

Masha flung her arms round his neck and sobbed aloud.

'Let us kiss each other too, you and I,' said the commandant's wife. 'Good-bye, my Ivan Kuzmich. Forgive me
if I have ever vexed you in any way.'

'Good-bye, good-bye, my dear,' said the commandant,
embracing his old wife. 'There now, that will do! Make haste
and go home; and if you have time dress Masha in peasant
clothes.'

The commandant's wife and daughter moved away. I
followed Maria Ivanovna with my eyes: she looked round and
nodded to me. Ivan Kuzmich now turned to us again, and
directed all his attention to the enemy. The rebels gathered
round their leader and suddenly began dismounting from
their horses. 'Now, stand firm,' said the commandant. 'They
are about to attack . . .' At that moment there were frightful
yells and cries: the rebels dashed full tilt towards the fortress.
Our cannon was charged with grape-shot. The commandant
let the attackers come quite close, and then suddenly fired
again. The shot fell right in the middle of the crowd. The
rebels recoiled on either side and drew back. Their leader
alone remained. . . . He brandished his sword and seemed to
be exhorting them heatedly. . . . The shouting and yelling
which had ceased for a moment were immediately renewed.
'Well, lads,' said the commandant, 'now open the gates, and
beat the drum. Forward, lads, for a sortie, follow me!'

The commandant, Ivan Ignatyich and I were over the rampart in a trice; but the scared garrison did not stir. 'Why do you hold back, children?' Ivan Kuzmich shouted. 'If we must die, we must – it's all in the day's work!' At that moment the rebels rushed upon us and broke into the fortress. The drum fell silent; our soldiers flung down their muskets; I was knocked over but picked myself up and entered the fortress along with the rebels. The commandant, wounded in the head, was standing surrounded by the villains who demanded the keys. I was about to rush to his assistance but several burly Cossacks seized and bound me with their sword-belts, exclaiming: 'You see, it will be all up with you presently, you enemies of the Tsar!' They dragged us along the streets; the townspeople came out of their houses offering the bread and salt of submission. The church bells rang. Suddenly a cry was raised among the crowd that the Tsar was awaiting the prisoners in the market-square and receiving the oath of allegiance. The throng surged to the market-place; we were hustled there too.

Pugachev was sitting in an arm-chair on the steps of the commandant's house. He was wearing a red Cossack coat trimmed with gold lace. A tall sable cap with golden tassels was set low over his flashing eyes. His face seemed familiar to me. The Cossack elders surrounded him. Father Gerassim, pale and trembling, was standing by the steps with the cross in his hands, and seemed to be silently imploring mercy for those shortly to lose their lives. In the square gallows were hastily being erected. When we approached, the Bashkirs forced the crowd back and brought us before Pugachev. The bells stopped ringing; there was a profound silence. 'Which is the commandant?' asked the Pretender. Our Cossack sergeant stepped forward out of the crowd and pointed to Ivan Kuzmich. Pugachev looked at the old man menacingly and said to him: 'How dared you resist me, your Sovereign?' The commandant, spent from his wound, summoned his last remaining strength and replied in a firm voice: 'You are not my Sovereign: you are a thief and a pretender, do you hear!'

Pugachev frowned darkly and waved a white handkerchief. Several Cossacks seized the old Captain and dragged him to the gallows. Astride upon the cross-beam sat the mutilated Bashkir whom we had questioned the day before. He was holding a rope in his hand and a minute later I saw poor Ivan Kuzmich hoisted into the air. Then Ivan Ignatyich was brought before Pugachev. 'Take the oath of allegiance to the Tsar Peter III,' Pugachev said to him. 'You are not our Tsar,' Ivan Ignatyich answered, repeating his captain's words. 'You, my dear man, are a thief and a pretender!' Pugachev waved his handkerchief again and the good lieutenant swung by the side of his old chief.

It was my turn next. I looked boldly at Pugachev, preparing to echo the answer of my noble comrades, when to my utter astonishment I saw Shvabrin among the rebel elders. He had his hair cropped in circular fashion like a Cossack, and was wearing a Cossack coat. He went up to Pugachev and whispered something in his ear. 'Hang him!' said Pugachev, without even looking at me. The noose was thrown round my neck. I began to pray silently, sincerely repenting before God of all my sins and begging Him to save all those dear to my heart. I was dragged under the gallows. 'Never you fear – don't be afraid,' my executioners repeated to me, perhaps really wishing to give me courage. Suddenly I heard a shout: 'Stop, you wretches, wait! ...' The hangmen paused. I looked and saw Savelich on his knees at Pugachev's feet. 'Dear father,' the poor old man was saying, 'what good would the death of this gentle-born child do you? Let him go: they will give you a good ransom for him; and as an example and a warning to others hang me, if you like – an old one!' Pugachev made a sign and I was immediately unbound and set free. 'Our father pardons you,' they said to me. I cannot say that at that moment I rejoiced at my deliverance, nor would I say that I regretted it. My feelings were too confused. I was brought before the Pretender again and made to kneel down. Pugachev stretched out his sinewy hand to me. 'Kiss his hand, kiss his hand,' said people around me. But I would have preferred the most cruel punishment to such vile humiliation. 'Piotr Andreich, my dear master,' whispered Savelich, standing behind me and pushing me forward, 'don't be obstinate! What does it matter? Spit and kiss the brig – I mean, kiss his hand.' I did not stir. Pugachev let his hand drop, saying with a smile: 'His lordship seems bewildered with joy. Lift him up!' They pulled me to my feet and released me. I stood watching the terrible comedy.

The townspeople began swearing allegiance. They came up one after another, kissed the cross and then bowed to the Pretender. The garrison soldiers were there too. The regimental tailor, armed with his blunt scissors, cut off their plaits. Shaking themselves, they approached to kiss Pugachev's hand: he gave them his pardon and enlisted them among his followers. All this went on for about three hours. At last Pugachev got up from his arm-chair and descended the steps, accompanied by his elders. A white horse, richly harnessed, was led forward. Two Cossacks took him by the arms and assisted him into the saddle. He announced to Father Gerassim that he would have dinner at his house. At that moment a woman's scream was heard. Some of the brigands had dragged Vassilissa Yegorovna, dishevelled and stripped naked, on to the steps. One of them had already arrayed himself in her mantle. Others were carrying off feather-beds, chests, crockery, linen and chattels of every sort. 'Good friends, spare my life! Kind sirs, take me to Ivan Kuzmich.' Suddenly she looked up at the gallows and recognized her husband. 'Villains!' she cried in a frenzy of rage. 'What have you done to him? Ivan Kuzmich, light of my eyes, brave soldier heart! You came to no harm from Prussian bayonets or Turkish bullets: 'tis not on the field of honour you have fallen – you have perished at the hands of a runaway galley-slave!' – 'Silence the old witch!' said Pugachev. A young Cossack hit her on the head with his sword and she fell dead on the steps. Pugachev rode away. The crowd rushed after him.

8

AN UNINVITED GUEST

An uninvited guest is worse than a Tartar.
PROVERB

THE market-square was deserted. I was still standing there, unable to collect my thoughts, bewildered as I was by so many terrible emotions.

Uncertainty as to Maria Ivanovna's fate tortured me most of all. Where was she? What had happened to her? Had she had time to hide? Was her place of refuge safe? ... Full of anxiety, I entered the commandant's house. ... It was quite empty: chairs, tables and coffers had been smashed, the crockery broken and everything dragged hither and thither. I ran up the short staircase that led to the top floor, and for the first time in my life entered Maria Ivanovna's room. I saw her bed all pulled to pieces by the brigands; the clothes-press had been broken and ransacked; the little lamp was still burning before the empty ikon-case. The tiny looking-glass that hung between the windows was intact, too. ... Where was the mistress of this humble virginal cell? A terrible thought flashed through my mind: I imagined her in the hands of the brigands. ... My heart sank. ... I wept bitterly, and called aloud my beloved's name. ... At that moment I heard a slight noise, and Palasha, pale and trembling, appeared from behind the clothes-press.

'Ah, Piotr Andreich!' she cried, clasping her hands. 'What a day! What horrors!'

'And Maria Ivanovna?' I asked impatiently. 'What has become of Maria Ivanovna?'

'The young lady is alive,' Palasha answered. 'She is hiding at Akulina Pamfilovna's house.'

'At the priest's!' I cried in horror. 'Merciful God, Pugachev is there!'

I dashed out of the room, and in the twinkling of an eye was in the street and running headlong to the priest's house, not seeing or feeling anything. Shouts, bursts of laughter and songs resounded from within. ... Pugachev was feasting with his companions. Palasha had followed me. I sent her to call Akulina Pamfilovna without attracting attention. A minute later the priest's wife came out to me in the lobby, with an empty bottle in her hands.

'For God's sake, where is Maria Ivanovna?' I asked in indescribable agitation.

'She is laying on my bed there, behind the partition, the poor dear,' replied the priest's wife. 'We very nearly had trouble, Piotr Andreich, but thank God all passed off well: the bandit had just sat down to dinner when the poor child came to and uttered a groan. ... I was half dead with fright. He heard her. "Who is that groaning there, granny?" I made a deep bow to the thief. "It's my niece, sire, she was taken ill and this is the second week she's abed." – "And is your niece young?" – "She is, sire." – "Well, show me this niece of yours, granny." My heart trembled and fluttered but there was no help for it. "Certainly, sire: only the girl cannot get up and come into your presence." – "Never mind, granny, I will go and have a look at her myself." And the wretch did go behind the partition. And what do you think – he actually drew back the bed-curtain and glanced at her with those hawk's eyes – and nought happened. ... God saved us! But, believe me, the priest and I were all ready for a martyr's death. Fortunately my little dear did not know who he was. Lord God, what things we have lived to see! There's no denying it! Poor Ivan Kuzmich! Who would have thought it! ... And Vassilissa Yegorovna? And Ivan Ignatyich? What did they hang him for? ... How was it they spared you? And what do you think of Shvabrin? You know, he cropped his hair like a Cossack and now he's sitting in there feasting with them? He knows how many beans make five all right! And when I spoke of my sick niece his eyes, would you believe it, went through me like a knife; but he did not betray us, and that's something to be thankful for.'

At that moment there were drunken shouts from the company and Father Gerassim's voice calling. The guests were clamouring for wine and the priest was summoning his wife. Akulina Pamfilovna bustled away.

'You go back home, Piotr Andreich,' she said. 'I cannot stop now: the brigands are drinking themselves under the table. It would be the end of you if they got hold of you now. What is to be, will be: let us hope God will not forsake us!'

The priest's wife left me. Somewhat reassured, I returned to my lodgings. As I crossed the market-place I saw several Bashkirs crowding round the gallows and dragging the boots off the hanged men's feet. I had difficulty in suppressing my indignation but I knew that it would have been useless to intervene. The brigands were running all over the fortress, plundering the officers' quarters. The shouts of the drunken rebels resounded on every side. I reached my lodgings. Savelich met me on the threshold.

'Praise be!' he exclaimed when he saw me. 'I was beginning to think the villains had seized you again. Well, Piotr Andreich, my dear, would you believe it, the rogues have robbed us of everything: clothes, linen, belongings, crockery – nothing be left. But what does it matter? Thank God they spared your life! But did you recognize their leader, sir?'

'No, I didn't. Who is he, then?'

'What, sir? Have you forgotten that drunken scoundrel who screwed your hare-skin jacket out of you at the inn? Your brand new hare-skin jacket, and the rascal went and split all the seams struggling into it?'

I was dumbfounded. In truth, the Pretender bore a striking resemblance to my guide. I felt certain Pugachev and he were one and the same person and now understood why he had spared my life. I could not help marvelling at the concatenation of circumstances: a child's pelisse given to a roving vagrant had saved me from the noose, and a tosspot who had roamed from inn to inn was besieging fortresses and shaking the realm!

'Would you not like something to eat?' asked Savelich, whom nothing could break of his habits. 'There is nought in the house but I will ferret about and prepare a bite for you.'

Left alone, I began to reflect. What was I to do? To remain in the fortress that was in the hands of the brigand, or to follow after his band, was unworthy of an officer. Duty demanded that I should go where my services might still be of use to my country in the present critical circumstances. But love prompted me strongly to stay near Maria Ivanovna and be her defender and protector. Although I foresaw a speedy and certain change in the situation I could not help shuddering at the thought of the danger she was in.

My reflections were interrupted by the arrival of a Cossack who ran up to tell me that 'the great Tsar required me to appear before him'.

'Where is he?' I said, making ready to obey.

'In the commandant's house,' replied the Cossack. 'After dinner our master went to the bath-house, and now he is resting. Ah, your Honour, everything shows him to be a person of quality: at dinner he was pleased to eat up two roast sucking-pigs, and he likes the bath-house so hot that even Tarass Kurochkin could not bear it – he had to give the bath-broom to Fomka Bikbayev, and only came to himself through having cold water poured over him. There's no denying it: all his ways are so grand. . . . And they say in the bath-house he showed them the marks of Imperial dignity on his breasts: the two-headed eagle on one, the size of a penny, and on the other his own likeness.'

I did not consider it necessary to dispute the Cossack's opinion and set off with him for the commandant's house, trying to picture beforehand my meeting with Pugachev, and wondering how it would end. The reader will easily imagine that I did not feel altogether comfortable.

It was growing dusk when I reached the commandant's

house. The gallows with their victims loomed black and terrible in the dark. Poor Vassilissa Yegorovna's body still lay sprawled at the bottom of the steps, where two Cossacks were mounting guard. The Cossack who had fetched me went in to announce my arrival and, returning at once, conducted me into the room where, the evening before, I had taken such tender farewell of Maria Ivanovna.

An extraordinary spectacle met my eyes. Pugachev and a dozen Cossack chiefs, wearing coloured shirts and their caps on their heads, were sitting round the table which was covered with a cloth and littered with bottles and glasses. Their faces were flushed with drink and their eyes glittered. Neither of the freshly recruited traitors, Shvabrin and our sergeant, was among them. 'Ah, your Honour!' said Pugachev, catching sight of me. 'Welcome and honour and a place for you – come and sit down.' The company made room for me. I sat down in silence at the end of the table. My neighbour, a handsome, well-proportioned young Cossack, poured me out a glass of vodka, which I did not touch. I began to examine the assembly with curiosity. Pugachev occupied the seat of honour, his elbows leaning on the table and his black beard resting on his broad fist. His features, which were regular and pleasant enough, betrayed no sign of violence. He frequently turned to speak to a man of some fifty years of age, addressing him sometimes as Count, sometimes as Timofeich, and occasionally as . . . dear uncle. All those present treated one another as comrades and showed no particular deference to their leader. They talked of the morning's attack, of the success of the rising, and of plans for the future. Everyone bragged, offered his opinion and freely joined issue with Pugachev. And at this strange council of war it was decided to march on Orenburg: a bold move which was very nearly crowned with disastrous success! The march was announced for the following day. 'Now, my boys,' said Pugachev, 'before we go to bed let us have my favourite song. Tchumakov, strike up!' In a high-pitched voice my neighbour began a dismal Volga-boatman's song, and all joined in:

Murmur not, mother-forest of rustling green leaves,
Hinder not a right brave lad from thinking his thoughts,
For tomorrow, good lad that I am, I must go
Before the most dread judge, our great sovereign Tsar,
And the Tsar, our great lord, will put question to me:
'Tell me now, good lad, tell me now, you peasant's son,
'With whom you went stealing, and with whom you have robbed.
'Was it a great number of companions you had?'
– 'I will tell thee the whole truth, and never a lie,
'My companions were four, and the first, the dark night,
'My second true comrade was my cutlass of steel;
'My trusty steed was my third, and the fourth my stout bow.
'For my messengers arrows I had, sharp and swift.'
Then up will speak my hope, the Tsar; true-believer:
'Well done, my lad, brave peasant's son! Right well you know
'How to plunder and steal and yet make bold answer.
'So therefore, my lad, I will make you a present –
'Of a lofty mansion in the midst of the plain,
'Of two upright posts, yea, and a cross-beam above.'

It is impossible to describe the impression produced upon me by this folk-song about the gallows sung by men themselves destined for the gallows. Their forbidding faces, their tuneful voices, the mournful expression they imparted to words expressive enough in themselves – shook my being with a kind of mystic awe and dread.

The guests tossed off a last glass, rose from the table and took leave of Pugachev. I made to follow them but Pugachev said to me: 'Sit still, I want to talk to you.' We were left alone.

For some minutes we both sat silent. Pugachev was watching me intently, occasionally screwing up his left eye with an extraordinary look of craftiness and mockery. At last he burst into laughter of such unaffected gaiety that, looking at him, without knowing why I began to laugh too.

'Well, your Honour?' he said to me. 'Confess now, you had a fright when my lads put the rope round your neck? I'll warrant you you were scared out of your wits ... And you would certainly have swung had it not been for your servant. I recognized the old greybeard at once. Well, would you have thought, your Honour, that the man who led you to the inn was the great Tsar in person?' (He now assumed an air of mystery and importance.) 'You are guilty of a serious offence against me,' he continued, 'but I have spared you for your kindness, for the help you were to me when I was obliged to hide from my enemies. But that is nothing to what I shall do for you! I shall shower favours on you when I enter into possession of my kingdom! Do you promise to serve me zealously?'

The rascal's question and his impudence struck me as so amusing that I could not help smiling.

'What are you smiling at?' he asked with a frown. 'Perhaps you do not believe that I am the Tsar? Answer me plainly.'

I was disconcerted. Acknowledge the vagrant as Tsar, I could not: to do so seemed to me unpardonable cowardice. To call him an impostor to his face meant exposing myself to certain death, and that which I had been ready to do beneath the gallows, in sight of everyone and in the first blaze of indignation, now seemed to me useless bravado. I hesitated. Pugachev darkly awaited my reply. At last (and to this day I recall that moment with self-satisfaction) the sentiment of duty triumphed over human weakness. I answered Pagachev:

'Listen, I will tell you the whole truth. Judge for yourself – how can I acknowledge you as Tsar? You are an intelligent man: you would see that I was using cunning.'

'Who am I, then, in your opinion?'

'Heaven only knows; but whoever you are, you are playing a dangerous game.'

Pugachev gave me a swift glance.

'So you do not believe', he said, 'that I am the Tsar Peter III? Very well. But is there no such thing as success for the bold? Didn't Grishka Otrepyev[1] sit on the throne once upon a time? Think what you please about me, but do not go

1. Grishka Otrepyev became the first False-Dmitri who seized the Russian throne in June 1605 and held it for almost a year.

from me. What does the rest matter to you? One master is as good as another. Serve me loyally and truly, and I will make you a field-marshal and a prince too. What do you say?'

'No,' I answered firmly. 'I am noble by birth; I swore allegiance to my Sovereign Lady the Empress: I cannot serve you. If you really wish me well, then let me go to Orenburg.'

Pugachev reflected.

'And if I let you go,' he said, 'will you at any rate promise not to fight against me?'

'How can I promise you that?' I answered. 'You know yourself that I am not free to do as I like: if I am ordered to march against you, I shall march, there is no help for it. You yourself are now the one to be obeyed: you demand obedience from your followers. What would you call it if I refused to serve when my services were needed? My life is in your hands: if you set me free, you will have my thanks; if you put me to death – God will be your judge; but I have told you the truth.'

My sincerity impressed Pugachev.

'So be it,' he said, slapping me on the shoulder. 'I don't do things by halves. Go wherever you like and do what you think best. Tomorrow come and say good-bye to me, and now be off to bed. I am growing sleepy myself.'

I left Pugachev and went out into the street. The night was still and frosty. The moon and the stars shone brightly, lighting up the market-place and the gallows. In the fortress all was dark and quiet. Only in the tavern was there a light and the noise of late revellers. I looked up at the priest's house. The shutters and gates were closed. All seemed quiet within.

I reached my lodgings and found Savelich anxious over my absence. The news that I was free filled him with unutterable joy.

'Thanks be to Thee, O Almighty God!' he said, crossing himself. 'We will leave the fortress before daybreak and follow our noses. I have prepared some supper for you. A bit to eat, my dear, and then sleep peacefully till morning.'

I followed his advice and having eaten my supper with great relish fell asleep on the bare floor, exhausted both in mind and body.

9

THE PARTING

O sweet was it, my dear heart,
To meet and learn to love thee;
But O now that we must part –
Torn is my soul within me.

KHERASKOV[1]

EARLY next morning I was awakened by the drum. I went
to the place of assembly. Pugachev's followers were already
forming into ranks round the gallows, where the victims of the
day before were still hanging. The Cossacks were on horseback, the soldiers had shouldered their muskets. Banners were
flying. Several cannon, among which I recognized ours, were
mounted on their field-carriages. All the local inhabitants
were there, too, waiting for the Pretender. A Cossack stood at
the steps of the commandant's house, holding a magnificent
white Kirghiz horse by the bridle. I searched about with my
eyes for Vassilissa Yegorovna's body. It had been moved a
little to one side and covered with matting. At last Pugachev
appeared in the doorway. The people took off their caps.
Pugachev paused on the steps and greeted them all. One of
the Cossack elders gave him a bag filled with copper coins
which he began throwing to the crowd by the handful. With
eager cries the people rushed to pick them up, and some got
hurt in the scramble. Pugachev was surrounded by his chief
confederates. Among them was Shvabrin. Our eyes met. In
mine he could read contempt, and he turned away with an
expression of genuine animosity and affected mockery. Catching sight of me in the crowd, Pugachev nodded and beckoned

1. M. M. Kheraskov (1733-1807) was rector of Moscow University
from 1778 to 1802. He wrote odes, dramas, long epic poems, and exercised
a great influence upon the youth of his day.

256

to me. 'Listen,' he said. 'Set off at once for Orenburg and tell the Governor and all his generals from me that I am to be expected within a week. Advise them to welcome me with filial love and obedience; otherwise they shall not escape a cruel death. A pleasant journey, your Honour!' Then he turned to the people and said, pointing to Shvabrin. 'Here, children, is your new commandant. Obey him in everything: he is to be answerable to me for you and the fortress.' I heard these words with dread: Shvabrin in command of the fortress – Maria Ivanovna would be in his power! O God, what would become of her! Pugachev descended the steps. His horse was brought to him. He vaulted nimbly into the saddle without waiting for the Cossacks who were ready to help him mount.

At that moment I saw my Savelich step out of the crowd, go up to Pugachev and hand him a sheet of paper. I could not imagine what would be the outcome of this.

'What is it?' Pugachev asked importantly.

'Read and you will see,' Savelich answered.

Pugachev took the paper and examined it significantly for several moments.

'Why do you write in such a scrawl?' he said at last. 'Our august eyes cannot decipher a word. Where is my chief secretary?'

A young lad in the uniform of a corporal quickly ran up to Pugachev. 'Read it aloud,' said the Pretender, giving him the paper. I was extremely curious to know what Savelich could have written to Pugachev. The chief secretary began to spell out as follows:

'Two dressing-gowns, one calico and one striped silk – value six roubles.'

'What does this mean?' asked Pugachev, with a frown.

'Tell him to read on,' Savelich replied placidly.

The chief secretary continued:

'One uniform coat of fine green cloth – seven roubles. White cloth breeches – five roubles. Twelve cambric shirts with frills – ten roubles. A chest containing a tea-service – two and a half roubles . . .'

T – Q.S. – I

'What tomfoolery is this?' Pugachev interrupted. 'What are these tea-sets and breeches with ruffles to do with me?'

Savelich cleared his throat and began explaining.

'Well, you see, sir, this be an inventory of my master's goods stolen by the bandits . . .'

'What bandits?' demanded Pugachev threateningly.

'Beg pardon, a slip of the tongue,' Savelich answered. 'Not bandits if you like, but your fine lads who ransacked and stole everything. Do not be angry: even the best of horses may stumble. So tell him to read to the end.'

'Read on,' said Pugachev.

The secretary continued:

'One chintz counterpane, another of taffety quilted with cotton wool – four roubles. A crimson rateen pelisse lined with fox fur – forty roubles. Likewise a hare-skin jacket given to your Grace at the inn – fifteen roubles.'

'What next!' shouted Pugachev, his eyes blazing.

I confess I felt extremely alarmed for my poor Savelich. He was about to launch into more explanations but Pugachev interrupted him. 'How dare you come pestering me with such trash!' he cried, snatching the paper out of the secretary's hands and flinging it in Savelich's face. 'Stupid old fool! Been plundered! Too bad! Why, you old dotard, to the end of your life you ought to pray for me and my stout fellows, and thank your stars that you and your master are not swinging from the gallows here, along with others who did not know their duty to me . . . Hare-skin jacket, indeed! I'll give you hare-skin jacket! Why, I'll have you flayed alive and a jacket made of your skin!'

'As you please,' replied Savelich, 'but I am a bondman, and have to answer for my master's property.'

Pugachev was evidently in a magnanimous mood. He turned away and rode off without saying another word. Shvabrin and the Cossack elders followed him. The gang of brigands marched out of the fortress in orderly fashion. The towns-people set off to accompany Pugachev. Savelich and I were left alone in the market-place. He was holding in his hands the inventory of my chattels and looking at it with a profoundly disconsolate air.

Seeing me on such good terms with Pugachev, he had thought to take advantage of it, but his sage intention had not met with success. I tried to scold him for his misplaced zeal, but could not help laughing. 'It's all very well to laugh, sir,' replied Savelich, 'but when we have to equip ourselves entirely afresh – we shall see then if there is anything to laugh at.'

I hastened to the priest's house to see Maria Ivanovna. Akulina Pamfilovna met me with sad news. In the night Maria Ivanovna had been taken with a high fever. She lay unconscious and in delirium. The priest's wife led me to her room. I crept up to the bed. The change in her face startled me. She did not know me. For a long time I stood by her bedside, not listening to Father Gerassim and his kindly wife, who were, I think, trying to comfort me. Sombre thoughts agitated me. The condition of the poor defenceless orphan left alone among vindictive rebels, and my own helplessness, terrified me. But it was Shvabrin – above all, it was Shvabrin tortured my imagination. Invested with power by the usurper, put in charge of the fortress where the unhappy girl – the innocent object of his hatred – remained, he was capable of anything. What was I to do? How could I help her? How could I rescue her from the villain's hands? There was only one thing left me: I decided to set out immediately for Orenburg and do my utmost to expedite the deliverance of the Bielogorsky fortress. I said good-bye to the priest and to Akulina Pamfilovna, begging her to look after Masha whom I already regarded as my wife. I took the poor girl's hand and kissed it, bedewing it with my tears. 'Adieu,' said the priest's wife, accompanying me to the door. 'Adieu, Piotr Andreich. Perhaps we shall meet again in happier times. Don't forget us, and write to us often. Poor Maria Ivanovna has nobody except you now, to comfort and protect her.'

Coming out into the market-place, I stopped for a moment to look up at the gallows, bowed my head, and then left the fortress by the Orenburg road, accompanied by Savelich, who never let me out of his sight.

I was walking on, occupied with my thoughts, when suddenly I heard the clatter of a horse's hoofs behind me. Turning round, I saw a Cossack galloping from the fortress; he was leading a Bashkir horse by the bridle and signalling to me from a distance. I stopped and soon recognized our sergeant. Overtaking me, he dismounted and said, handing me the reins of the other horse:

'Your Honour, our good Father presents you with a horse and a pelisse from his own shoulders.' (A sheepskin pelisse was tied to the saddle.) 'And he also sends you' – Maximich hesitated – 'fifty kopecks in money ... but I have lost it on the way: be merciful and forgive me.'

Savelich eyed him askance and growled:

'Lost it on the way! And what is that chinking in your breast pocket there, you shameless rascal?'

'What is that chinking in my pocket?' replied the sergeant, not in the least abashed. 'Why, mercy on you, my good man, 'tis the horse's snaffle, not the fifty kopecks!'

'Very well,' I said, interrupting the argument. 'Give my thanks to him who sent you; and on your way back try to pick up the last half-rouble and keep it for vodka.'

'Thank you kindly, your Honour,' he answered, turning his horse. 'I shall pray for you as long as I live.'

With these words he galloped back, holding one hand to his breast pocket, and a minute later was lost to sight.

I put on the sheepskin and mounted the horse, taking Savelich up behind me. 'So you see now, sir,' said the old man, 'I did not present the petition to the rascal in vain: the thief's conscience pricked him. True, this raw-boned Bashkir nag and this sheepskin pelisse are not worth the half of what they stole from us, the rascals, and what you chose to give him yourself, but they will come in useful all the same: and from a vicious dog it's something to get even a tuft of hair.'

10

THE SIEGE

His tent he pitched in hill and meadow,
From eagle-heights gazed on the city,
Behind his camp he made an earth-work
To hide his thunderbolts which by night
He darkly brought to the city wall.

KHERASKOV

As we approached Orenburg we saw a crowd of convicts with shaven heads and faces disfigured by the hangman's pincers. They were at work on the fortifications, under the supervision of the soldiers of the garrison. Some were wheeling away the rubbish which filled the moat, others with spades were digging up the ground; on the ramparts masons were carrying bricks and repairing the town walls. At the gates we were stopped by the sentinels who demanded our passports. As soon as the sergeant heard that I came from the Bielogorsky fortress he took me straight to the general's house.

I found the general in the garden. He was examining the apple-trees, which the breath of autumn had stripped of their leaves, and, with the help of an old gardener, was carefully covering them with warm straw. His face wore a look of serenity, health and good nature. He was pleased to see me and began questioning me about the terrible happenings I had witnessed. I told him everything. The old man listened attentively as he pruned off the dry twigs. 'Poor Mironov!' he said, when I had finished my sad story. 'I feel very sorry for him: he vass a fine soldier; and Mme Mironov vass an excellent woman – and what a hand at pickling mushrooms! And what hass become of Masha, der Captain's daughter?' I replied that she was still in the fortress in the care of the priest's wife. 'Aïe, aïe, aïe!' exclaimed the general. 'Dat iss bad, ver[y] bad. Dere iss no placing any reliance on the disscipline o[f] brigands. What will become of der poor girl?' I answered tha[t] the Bielogorsky fortress was not far distant, and that hi[s] Excellency would probably not delay in sending troops t[o] rescue its poor inhabitants. The general shook his head doubt[t]fully. 'Ve shall see, ve shall see,' he said. 'Dere vill be tim[e] enough to talk about that. May I haf der pleasure of you[r] company for tea? A council of war iss to be held at my hous[e] today. You can gif us trustvorthy informations concernin[g] diss rascally Pugachev und hiss army. Und, meanwhile, tak[e] some rest.'

I went to the quarters allotted to me, where Savelich ha[d] already installed himself, and sat down to wait impatiently fo[r] the appointed hour. The reader may well imagine that I di[d] not fail to appear at the council which would have such a[n] influence on my future. At the time arranged I was at th[e] general's.

I found there one of the town officials, the director of th[e] custom-house, if I remember rightly, a stout, red-faced ol[d] man in a brocade coat. He inquired after the fate of Iva[n] Kuzmich, with whom he was connected, and frequentl[y] interrupted me with further questions and moral observations which, if they did not prove him to be a man well versed in th[e] military art, at least showed that he possessed sagacity an[d] common sense. Meanwhile, other guests who had bee[n] invited arrived. When all were seated and the cups of tea ha[d] been handed round, the general very clearly and in detai[l] explained the situation. 'Now, gentlemen,' he continued, 'v[e] must decide how ve are to act against the rebels: must ve tak[e] offensive or defensive action? Each course hass its advantage[s] und disadvantages. Der offensive offers more hope of ex[-] terminating der enemy in der shortest possible time; defensiv[e] action iss safer and less dangerous. ... Und so let us put de[r] question to der vote in der prescribed manner – dat iss, begin[-] ning mit der youngest in rank. Mr Ensign,' he said, addressin[g] himself to me, 'be so kind as to oblige us mit your opinion.'

I rose and after giving a brief description of Pugachev and his gang of followers declared firmly that the impostor was not in a position to stand up to regular troops.

My opinion was received by the civilian officials with obvious disfavour. They saw in it the rashness and temerity of youth. There was a murmur and I distinctly heard the word 'greenhorn' uttered by someone in an undertone. The general turned to me and said with a smile: 'Mr Ensign, der first votes in councils of war are generally in favour of offensive measures: diss iss as it should be. Now let us continue and hear vat ot'ers haf to say. Mr Collegiate Councillor, gif us your views.'

The little old man in the brocade coat hastily emptied his third cup of tea, considerably diluted with rum, and said in answer to the general:

'I think, your Excellency, that we ought to act neither offensively nor defensively.'

'How so, sir?' exclaimed the general in surprise. 'Tactics present no ot'er alternative: ve must eit'er take der offensive or be on der defensive. . . .'

'Your Excellency, proceed by bribery.'

'Ha, ha, ha! Your suggestion iss a very sensible one. Military tactics admit of procedure by bribery, und ve vill make use of your advice. Ve might offer seventy . . . or perhaps even an hundred . . . for der rascal's head . . . to be paid out of the secret purpose funds. . . .'

'And then,' interrupted the Chief Customs Officer, 'may I be a Kirghiz ram and not a collegiate councillor if those thieves do not surrender their leader to us, bound hand and foot.'

'Ve vill consider t'at furt'er, and discuss it again,' replied the general. 'But in any case ve must take military precautions. Gentlemen, please gif your votes in the usual manner.'

The opinions of all were opposed to mine. The civilian officials expatiated upon the unreliability of the troops, the uncertainty of success, the necessity of being cautious, and the like. All thought it wiser to remain behind strong walls of stone defended by cannon, rather than to try the fortune of arms in open country. At last the general, having heard all their opinions, shook the ashes from his pipe and made the following speech:

'Gentleman, I must state dat for my part I entirely agree mit der Ensign, for his view iss based upon sound rules of tactics, which nearly always prefers offensive to defensive action.'

At this point he paused and began to fill his pipe. My vanity felt very gratified. I cast a proud glance at the officials, who were whispering to one another with an air of vexation and anxiety.

'But, gentlemen,' continued the general, giving vent to a deep sigh and at the same time emitting a thick puff of tobacco smoke, 'I dare not take upon myself so great a responsibility when der security of der provinces entrusted to me by Her Imperial Majesty, my Most Gracious Sovereign, is at stake. Therefore I adopt der view of der majority dat it is viser und safer to stay wit'in der city walls und repulse der enemy's attacks by artillery und (if possible) by sorties.'

The officials in their turn now glanced mockingly at me. The council dispersed. I could not help regretting the weakness of the estimable soldier who had decided, against his own convictions, to follow the advice of ignorant and inexperienced persons.

Some days after this memorable council we learned that Pugachev, true to his promise, was approaching Orenburg. From the top of the town ramparts I saw the rebel army. It seemed to me that their numbers had increased tenfold since the last attack which I had witnessed. They now had artillery, taken by Pugachev from the small fortresses he had captured. Remembering the council's decision, I foresaw a prolonged confinement within the walls of Orenburg and nearly wept with vexation.

I will not describe the siege of Orenburg which belongs to history and is not a subject for family memoirs. I will merely observe that, owing to the carelessness of the local authorities, this siege was a frightful one for the inhabitants, who had to endure famine and every possible privation. It is not difficult to imagine that life in Orenburg was well nigh unbearable. All waited despondently for their fate to be decided: all groaned over the dearness of everything – prices, indeed, were exorbitant. The inhabitants became accustomed to cannon-balls falling in their back-yards: even Pugachev's assaults no longer produced any excitement. I was dying of ennui. Time wore on. I received no letter from the Bielogorsky fortress. All the roads were cut off. Separation from Maria Ivanovna was growing intolerable. Uncertainty as to her fate tortured me. My one distraction was in making a sortie outside the city. Thanks to Pugachev I had a good horse, with whom I shared my scanty pittance, and I rode out every day to exchange shots with the partisans. As a rule the advantage in these skirmishes was on the side of the villains, who had plenty to eat and drink and were well mounted. The emaciated cavalry of the town could not get the better of them. Sometimes our famished infantry also went afield; but the thick snow prevented their operations from being successful against horsemen scattered all over the plain. The artillery thundered in vain from the top of the rampart, and in the open country stuck in the snow because the horses were too wasted to drag it out. Such was the nature of our military operations! But this was what the civilian officials of Orenburg called being cautious and sensible!

One day when we had somehow succeeded in scattering and driving off a sizeable body of the enemy, I came up with a Cossack who had lagged behind his companions. I was just about to thrust at him with my Turkish sabre when he suddenly took off his cap and cried: 'Piotr Andreich! How is God treating you?'

I looked at him and recognized our Cossack sergeant. I cannot express how delighted I was to see him.

'How are you, Maximich?' I said to him. 'Is it long since you left the Bielogorsky fortress?'

'No, sir: I went back there only yesterday. I have a letter for you, Piotr Andreich.'

'Where is it?' I cried, beside myself with impatience.

'Here,' replied Maximich, thrusting his hand between his shirt and his skin. 'I promised Palasha to get it to you somehow.'

He then gave me a folded paper and galloped away. I opened it and, deeply agitated, read the following lines:

It has pleased God to deprive me suddenly of both father and mother; I have no friends or relatives in this world. I appeal to you, knowing that you have always wished me well and that you are ever ready to help others. I pray that somehow or other this letter may reach you! Maximich has promised to take it to you. Palasha has also heard from Maximich that he often sees you from a distance in the sorties; and that you do not take the least care of yourself or think of those who pray for you with tears. I was ill for a long time and, when I recovered, Alexei Ivanovich Shvabrin, who commands here in place of my late father, compelled Father Gerassim to deliver me up to him, threatening him with Pugachev. Alexei Ivanovich is trying to make me marry him. He says that he saved my life because he did not betray Akulina Pamfilovna when she told the rebels that I was her niece. But I would rather die than become the wife of a man like Alexei Ivanovich. He treats me very cruelly, and threatens that if I do not change my mind and marry him he will take me to the brigand's camp, and there, he says, I shall suffer the same fate as Lizaveta Kharlova.[1] I have asked Alexei Ivanovich to give me time to think. He has consented to wait for three more days and if I don't marry him in three days' time I am to look for no mercy. Dear Piotr Andreich, you are my only protector: save a poor helpless girl! Implore and persuade the General and all the commanders to make haste and send a relief party, and come yourself if you can. Poor orphan that I am, I remain your dutiful

Maria Mironov

The reading of this letter almost drove me off my head. I galloped back to town, spurring my poor horse mercilessly. On the way I turned over in my mind one plan after another for rescuing the poor girl, but could not think of anything

1. A commandant's daughter whom Pugachev took for a mistress. Jealous of her influence, his Cossack companions later murdered her.

satisfactory. On reaching the town I rode straight to the general's, and rushed headlong into his house.

The general was walking up and down the room, smoking his meerschaum pipe. At the sight of me he stood still. He must have been struck by my appearance: he inquired with concern the reason for my precipitate arrival.

'Your Excellency,' I said to him, 'I come to you as I would to my own father. For God's sake do not refuse me: the happiness of my whole life is at stake.'

'What iss it, my dear?' asked the astonished old man. 'What can I do for you? Speak.'

'Your Excellency, give me a company of soldiers and half a hundred Cossacks, and let me go and clear the Bielogorsky fortress.'

The general looked at me earnestly, probably thinking that I had taken leave of my senses (and for the matter of that he was not far wrong).

'How do you mean – clear der Bielogorsky fortress?' he brought out at last.

'I will vouch for success,' I said eagerly. 'Only let me go.'

'No, young man,' said he, shaking his head. 'At so great a distance der enemy would find it easy to cut off your communications mit der main strategic point, and gain a complete victory over you ... Once der communication cut. ...'

I was afraid when I perceived that he was about to enter upon a military dissertation, and made haste to interrupt him. 'Captain Mironov's daughter', I said, 'has written me a letter begging for help: Shvabrin wants to force her to marry him.'

'Really? Oh, dat Shvabrin is a t'orough rogue, and if he falls into my hands I vill haf him court-martialled wit'in tventy-four hours and ve vill shoot him on der fortress parapet! But meanwhile ve must haf patience. ...'

'Have patience!' I cried, beside myself. 'But meanwhile he will marry Maria Ivanovna! ...'

'Oh, that vill be no great misfortune,' the general retorted. 'Better for her to be Shvabrin's wife for der time being: he can offer her protection for der present, and afterwards, ven ve haf shot him, God villing dere vill be no lack of suitors for her. Pretty little widows do not remain single long. ... I mean, a young widow vill find a husband sooner dan a girl vould.'

'I would rather die', I cried in a rage, 'than give her up to Shvabrin.'

'Oho, I see!' said the old man. 'Now I onderstand: you are evidently in lof mit Maria Ivanovna, and dat alters der case entirely! Poor boy! But, for all dat, I cannot possibly gif you a detachment of soldiers und half a hundred Cossacks. Such an expedition would be the height of folly: I cannot take der responsibility for it.'

I bowed my head: despair possessed me. Suddenly an idea flashed through my mind: what it was, the reader will discover in the following chapter, as the old-fashioned novelists say.

II

THE REBELS' CAMP

The lion had eaten his fill,
No longer ferocious was he,
So it was kindly he asked me
'O what brings you here to my lair?'

A. SUMAROKOV

I LEFT the general and hastened to my lodgings. Savelich met me with his usual admonitions. 'Why ever do you want to go measuring swords with those drunken brigands, sir? It isn't the correct thing for a gentleman. Luck turns: you may lose your life for nothing. Well and good if you were fighting Turks or Swedes – but these wretches are not even fit to be spoken of.'

I interrupted his speech by asking: 'How much money have we, all told?' – 'Enough for your needs,' he replied with a satisfied air. 'The thieves poked and rummaged but I still managed to hide it from them.' And with these words he took from his pocket a long knitted purse full of silver.

'Well, Savelich,' I said to him, 'give me half now, and keep the rest for yourself. I am going to the Bielogorsky fortress.'

'Piotr Andreich, good master!' said my dear old Savelich in a shaking voice. 'Do not tempt God. How can you travel at a time like this with the brigands all over the place? Have pity on your parents, if you have no pity for yourself. Where do you want to go? And why? Wait a little while: troops will soon be here and make short work of the rascals. Then you can go anywhere you like.'

But my resolution was not to be shaken.

'It is too late to argue,' I said to the old man. 'I must go, I cannot do otherwise than go. Do not take it to heart, Savelich: God willing, we will meet again! Mind now, have no scruples about spending the money, and don't stint yourself. Buy everything you need, even if you have to pay three times its value. I make you a present of this money. If I am not back in three days . . .'

'What are you talking about, sir?' Savelich interrupted me. 'Do you think I would let you go alone? Don't dream of asking that. Since you have made up your mind to go, I shall accompany you, on foot if necessary – I will not let you go alone. The idea of my sitting down behind a stone wall without you! I haven't taken leave of my senses yet. Say what you will, sir, but I am coming with you.'

I knew it was useless to argue with Savelich, and I allowed him to prepare for the journey. Half an hour later I mounted my good horse, and Savelich a lean and limping nag which one of the townspeople had given to him for nothing, not having the means to feed it any longer. We rode to the town gates; the sentries let us pass, and we left Orenburg.

It was growing dusk. My route led past the village of Berda, occupied by Pugachev's troops. The straight road was blocked with snow; but all over the steppe could be seen the marks of horses' hoofs, printed afresh each day. I rode at a quick trot. Savelich could barely follow me at a distance, and kept shouting: 'Not so fast, sir, for heaven's sake, not so fast! My sorry jade cannot keep up with your long-legged devil. What's the use of hurrying? Well and good if we were on our way to a banquet, but, you mind, we be more likely going to our deaths. . . . Piotr Andreich! . . . Piotr Andreich, my dear! . . . Heavens above, my master's child will perish!'

Soon the lights of Berda began to twinkle. We rode up to the ravines which formed the natural defences of the village. Savelich never let me alone, giving me no respite from his plaintive entreaties. I was hoping to skirt the place without being observed when suddenly I perceived in the twilight, straight in front of me, five or six peasants armed with clubs: it was the advance-guard of Pugachev's camp. They challenged us. Not knowing the password, I wanted to ride past them without saying anything; but they immediately surrounded me, and one of them seized my horse by the bridle. I pulled out my sword and struck the peasant on the head: his cap saved him but he staggered and let the bridle fall from his hands. The others were disconcerted and took to their heels. I grasped the opportunity, set spurs to my horse and galloped on.

The darkness of the approaching night might have saved me from further danger but, turning round, all at once I saw that Savelich was not with me. The poor old man on his lame horse had not been able to get clear of the brigands. What was I to do? After waiting for him a few minutes, and feeling convinced that he had been arrested, I turned my horse back and went to his rescue.

Approaching the ravine, I heard in the distance a noise, shouts and my Savelich's voice. I rode faster and soon found myself once more in the midst of the peasant guard who had stopped me a few minutes before. Savelich was with them. They had dragged the old man off his nag and were preparing to bind him. They threw themselves on me with a shout, and in a twinkling I was unseated. One of them, apparently their leader, informed us that he was taking us at once to the Tsar. 'And it is for our Father-Tsar to decide', he added, 'whether you shall be hanged immediately or wait till God's daylight.' I offered no resistance; Savelich followed my example, and the sentries led us away in triumph.

We crossed the ravine and entered the village. Lights were burning in all the windows. Noise and shouting resounded from every side. In the streets I met a large number of people; but in the dark no one noticed us or recognized me for an officer from Orenburg. They took us straight to a cottage which stood at the corner where two streets intersected. There were several wine-barrels and two pieces of artillery at the gate. 'Here is the place,' said one of the peasants. 'We will announce you at once.' He went into the cottage. I glanced at Savelich: the old man was making the sign of the cross and repeating a prayer to himself. I waited for a long time. At last the peasant returned and said to me: 'Come inside; our Father says he will see the officer.'

I entered the cottage, or the palace as the peasants called it. It was lighted by two tallow candles, and the walls were hung with gold paper; otherwise, the benches, the table, the ewer suspended by a piece of string, the towel hanging on a nail, the oven-fork in the corner and the broad hearth loaded with pots – all were just as in any other cottage. Pugachev, wearing a red coat and a tall cap, was sitting in the place of honour under the icons, his arms importantly akimbo. Several of his principal associates were standing by him with expressions of feigned servility. It was obvious that news of the arrival of an officer from Orenburg had aroused great curiosity among the rebels, and they had prepared to receive me with as much pomp as possible. Pugachev recognized me at first glance. His assumed air of importance suddenly vanished. 'Ah, your Honour!' he said genially. 'How are you? What fair wind brings you here?' I replied that I was travelling on a personal matter and that his men had detained me. 'And what is this personal matter?' he asked. I did not know how to answer. Supposing that I was unwilling to explain in the presence of witnesses, Pugachev turned to his comrades and bade them leave the room. All obeyed except two, who did not stir. 'Speak boldly before them,' Pugachev said to me. 'I do not hide anything from them.' I threw a sidelong glance at the impostor's confidants. One of them, a puny, bent old man with a stubbly grey beard, had nothing remarkable about him except a blue ribbon worn across the shoulder over his grey tunic. But never in my life shall I forget his companion. He was tall, stout and broad-shouldered, and seemed to me to be about forty-five years of age. A thick red beard, glittering grey eyes, a nose without nostrils and reddish scars on his forehead and cheeks lent an indescribable expression to his broad, pock-marked face. He was wearing a red shirt, a Kirghiz robe and Cossack trousers. The first (as I learned later) was the deserter, Corporal Bieloborodov; the second, Afanassy Sokolov, nicknamed

Hlopusha, a convict who had escaped three times from the mines of Siberia. In spite of the unusual feelings which agitated me, the company in which I so unexpectedly found myself profoundly stirred my imagination. But Pugachev brought me back to myself by repeating: 'Speak, on what business did you leave Orenburg?'

A strange thought came into my head: it seemed that Providence, by bringing me for the second time to Pugachev, was giving me an opportunity to carry out my intention. I decided to take advantage of it and, without any further reflection, answered Pugachev:

'I was going to the Bielogorsky fortress to rescue an orphan who is being ill-treated there.'

Pugachev's eyes blazed.

'Which of my people dares to ill-treat an orphan?' he cried. He may be more cunning than the devil but he won't escape my justice. Tell me, who is the offender?'

'Shvabrin is the offender,' I replied. 'He keeps under lock and key the girl whom you saw lying ill at the priest's house, and he wants to marry her by force.'

'I'll teach Shvabrin!' said Pugachev threateningly. 'He shall learn what it is to take the law into his own hands where I am concerned, and ill-treat people. I will have him hanged.'

'Allow me to put in a word,' said Hlopusha in a hoarse voice. 'You were in overmuch of a hurry to make Shvabrin commandant of the fortress, and now you are in a hurry to hang him. You have already given offence to the Cossacks by setting a gentleman over them: do not now alarm the gentry by hanging them at the first denunciation.'

'They are neither to be pitied nor favoured!' said the little old man with the blue ribbon. 'No harm in hanging Shvabrin; neither would it be amiss to interrogate this officer in due and proper form. Why has he come here? If he does not acknowledge you as Tsar he has no cause to seek justice from you; and if he does acknowledge you – then why to this day did he remain in Orenburg along with your enemies? Will you not let me take him to the office and there warm him up a little?

My opinion is that his Grace has been sent to us by the Oren
burg commanders.'

The old villain's logic struck me as convincing enough.
shiver ran down my spine when I thought in whose hands
was. Pugachev noticed my agitation. 'Well, your Honour?
he said to me with a wink. 'I fancy my field-marshal is talkin
sense. What do you think?'

Pugachev's raillery restored my courage. I answered calml
that I was in his power and that he was free to deal with me i
whatever way he pleased.

'Good,' said Pugachev. 'Now tell me, how are things goin
with you in the town?'

'Thanks be to God,' I replied, 'all is well!'

'All well?' Pugachev repeated. 'With the population dyin
of hunger?'

The Pretender spoke the truth; but in accordance with m
duty as an officer loyal to my oath I began assuring him tha
these were baseless rumours and that Orenburg had a suffic
ency of every kind of provision.

'You see,' the little old man chimed in, 'he is deceiving yo
to your face. All the refugees are unanimous that famine an
plague are rife in Orenburg, that people eat carrion and thin
it a treat; and yet his Grace would have you believe there
plenty of everything. If you want to hang Shvabrin, then han
this young fellow on the same gallows, that neither may b
envious of the other.'

The accursed old man's words seemed to shake Pugachev
Fortunately Hlopusha began contradicting his comrade. 'Stop
Naumich,' he said to him. 'You always want to be stranglin
and cutting throats. What sort of a hero are you? To look
you is to wonder what keeps your soul in your body. You hav
one foot in the grave yourself, and you want everyone else t
perish. Isn't there enough blood on your conscience?'

'A fine saint you are, aren't you?' retorted Bieloborodov
'Whence this compassion?'

'Of course I've done wrong too,' replied Hlopusha, 'an
this arm' (he clenched his bony fist and pushing back h

leeve disclosed a hairy arm) 'has been guilty of shedding Christian blood. But I killed my enemy, not my guests: I killed at the cross-roads upon the open highway, or in a dark wood – not at home sitting before the fire. I killed with club and axe – not with womanish slander.'

The old man turned away and muttered the words: 'Slit nostrils! . . .'

'What are you muttering, you old greybeard?' cried Hlopusha. 'I'll give you "slit nostrils". You wait, your time will come: if God wills, you too will sniff the hangman's pincers. . . . And meanwhile, take care I don't pluck out your curvy beard!'

'Gentlemen *yenerals*!' said Pugachev loftily, 'that's enough of your quarrelling. It would be no matter if all the Orenburg pack were dangling from the same cross-beam; but it does matter if our dogs are at one another's throats. So make it up and be friends again.'

Hlopusha and Bieloborodov said not a word and looked at each other darkly. I felt the necessity of changing the conversation which might end very badly for me, and, turning to Pugachev, I said to him with a cheerful air:

'Oh, I had almost forgotten to thank you for the horse and sheepskin pelisse. Had it not been for you, I should never have reached the town and should have frozen to death on the road.'

My ruse succeeded. Pugachev recovered his good humour.

'One good turn deserves another,' he said with a wink and a sidelong glance. 'And now tell me, why are you concerned about the girl Shvabrin is ill-treating? Could she have kindled a flame in the young man's heart, eh?'

'She is my betrothed,' I answered, observing the favourable change in the weather and not deeming it necessary to conceal the truth.

'Your betrothed!' exclaimed Pugachev. 'Why did you not say so before? Why, we'll have you married and make merry at your wedding!' Then, turning to Bieloborodov, 'Listen, field-marshal! His Lordship and I are old friends, so let us sit

down to supper. We will sleep on it, and see in the mornin
what we are to do with him.'

I would gladly have declined the proposed honour but ther
was no help for it. Two young girls, daughters of the Cossac
to whom the hut belonged, spread the table with a whit
cloth, brought in bread, fish-soup and several bottles of vodk
and beer, and for the second time I found myself at table wit
Pugachev and his terrible companions.

The orgy of which I was an involuntary witness lasted fa
into the night. At last drink overcame the company. Pugache
dozed in his chair; his friends rose and made signs to me t
leave him. I went out with them. At Hlopusha's orders th
watchman took me to the cottage that served as an office
where I found Savelich and where we were locked up togethe
The old man was so bemused by all that was happening tha
he did not ask a single question. He lay down in the dark, an
continued to sigh and groan for a long time; at last he bega
to snore, and I abandoned myself to reflections that did nc
allow me a wink of sleep the whole night.

In the morning Pugachev sent for me. I went to him. A
chaise drawn by three Tartar horses was standing at the gate
A crowd waited in the street. I met Pugachev in the lobby. H
was dressed for a journey in a fur cloak and a Kirghiz cap. Hi
companions of the night before surrounded him with an air c
servility contrasting strongly with all I had witnessed th
previous evening. Pugachev greeted me cheerfully, and tol
me to step into the chaise with him.

We took our seats. 'To the Bielogorsky fortress!' sai
Pugachev to the broad-shouldered Tartar who drove th
troika standing. My heart beat violently. The horses s
off, the hand-bell pealed, the sledge was away like a
arrow. . . .

'Stop! Stop!' cried a voice which I knew only too well, an
I saw Savelich running towards us. Pugachev ordered th
driver to halt.

'Piotr Andreich, dear!' shouted Savelich. 'Do not abando
me in my old age among those rasc . . .'

'Ah, old greybeard!' Pugachev said to him. 'So God has brought us together again. Well, sit yourself on the box.'

'Thank you, sire, thank you, good father!' said Savelich, taking his place. 'May God let you live to be a hundred for your kindness to an old man. I will pray for you all the days of my life, and never breathe another word about that hare-skin jacket.'

This allusion to the hare-skin jacket might have made Pugachev seriously angry. Fortunately, the Pretender either had not heard or took no notice of the inopportune remark. The horses set off at a gallop; the people in the streets stood still and bowed to the waist. Pugachev nodded right and left. A minute later we left the village and whirled along the smooth surface of the road.

It is not difficult to imagine what my feelings were at that moment. In a few hours I was to see her whom I had already considered lost to me. I pictured to myself the moment of our reunion. . . . I was thinking, too, of the man who held my fate in his hands and by a strange concourse of circumstances had become mysteriously connected with me. I remembered the impetuous cruelty and bloodthirsty habits of this man who had come forward to rescue my beloved. Pugachev did not know that she was Captain Mironov's daughter; Shvabrin, infuriated, might tell him everything; Pugachev might find out the truth in some other way. . . . Then what would happen to Maria Ivanovna? A shiver ran down my back and my hair stood on end.

Suddenly Pugachev interrupted my reflections, turning to me with the question:

'What are you so thoughtful about, your Honour?'

'How can I help being thoughtful?' I answered. 'Only yesterday I was fighting against you, and now today I am riding side by side with you in the same sledge, and the happiness of my whole life depends upon you.'

'Well, what about it?' asked Pugachev. 'Are you afraid?'

I replied that, since he had spared me once, I was trusting not only to his mercy but to his help, too.

'And you are right, upon my soul, you are right!' cried th
Pretender. 'You saw that my men were looking askance a
you: and the old man insisted again this morning that you wer
a spy and ought to be tortured and hanged; but I would no
agree,' he added, lowering his voice so that Savelich and th
Tartar should not hear, 'because I remembered your glass o
vodka and the hare-skin jacket. You can see that I am not th
bloodthirsty creature your brethren make out.'

I thought of the taking of the Bielogorsky fortress but di
not deem it necessary to join issue with him, and made n
answer.

'What do they say of me in Orenburg?' Pugachev asked
after a short silence.

'They say that it's no easy matter to get the upper hand o
you. There's no denying it – you have made an impression.'

The Pretender's face depicted satisfied vanity.

'Yes!' he said cheerfully. 'I'm a dab at fighting. Do yo
Orenburg people know about the battle of Yuzeyeva? Fort
yenerals killed, four armies taken captive! What do you think
would the King of Prussia be a match for me?'

The brigand's boasting seemed comical.

'What do you think yourself?' I asked him. 'Could yo
beat Frederick?'

'Why not? I beat your *yenerals* and they have often beate
him. So far I have been fortunate in war. With time you'll se
even better things, when I march on Moscow.'

'Are you thinking of marching on Moscow?'

The Pretender pondered for a moment and then said in
low voice:

'Only God knows. My hands are tied: I cannot do as I like
My followers are too independent. They are robbers an
highwaymen. I have to keep a sharp look-out: at the firs
reverse they will save their own necks at the expense of m
head.'

'That's just it!' I said to Pugachev. 'Would it not be bette
to abandon them first, in good time, and throw yourself on th
Empress's mercy?'

Pugachev smiled bitterly.

'No,' he replied. 'It is too late for me to repent now. There will be no mercy for me. I will go on as I have begun. Who knows? I may succeed after all! Grisha Otrepyev did reign over Moscow, you remember.'

'And do you know what his end was? They threw him out of a window, tore his body limb from limb, burned it and fired a cannon with his ashes!'

'Listen,' Pugachev said, with a kind of wild inspiration. 'I will tell you a story which was told to me in my childhood by an old Kalmyck woman. The eagle asked the raven one day: "Tell me, raven-bird, how is it that you live in the wide world for three hundred years, and I, all in all, for thirty-three?" – "Because, dear eagle," the raven replied, "you drink fresh blood, while I feed on carrion." The eagle pondered and thought: "I will try living on the food he does." Very well. The eagle and the raven flew off together. Suddenly they caught sight of a dead horse, alighted and perched on it. The raven began to pick the flesh and found it very tasty. The eagle took one peck, then another, waved his wing and said to the raven: "No, brother raven, rather than live on carrion for three hundred years better one long drink of fresh blood – and leave the rest to God!" What do you think of the Kalmyck tale?'

'Very ingenious,' I replied. 'But to live by murder and robbery is to my mind just the same as pecking carrion.'

Pugachev looked at me in astonishment and made no answer. We both sank into silence, each absorbed in his own reflections. The Tartar broke into plaintive song. Savelich, dozing, swayed from side to side on the box. The sledge glided along the smooth winter road. ... All of a sudden I caught sight of the little village on the steep bank of the Yaïk, with its palisade and belfry – and in another quarter of an hour we drove into the Bielogorsky fortress.

12

THE ORPHAN

Just as our little young apple-tree
Neither branches has, nor leafy top,
So our fair young bride to care for her
Neither father has, nor mother dear —
No one to bless her, no one at all.
WEDDING SONG

THE sledge drew up in front of the commandant's house. The
people had recognized the sound of Pugachev's bell, and ran
after us in a crowd. Shvabrin met the Pretender on the steps.
He was dressed like a Cossack and had grown a beard. The
traitor helped Pugachev to alight from the sledge, expressing
in obsequious terms his delight and devotion. He was disconcerted when he saw me but, quickly recovering himself,
held out his hand, saying: 'You one of us now? And high
time too!' I turned away from him and made no answer.

My heart ached when we found ourselves in the long familiar room, where the certificate of the late commandant still
hung on the wall as a sad epitaph of bygone days. Pugachev
seated himself on the same sofa on which Ivan Kuzmich used
to doze, lulled to sleep by his wife's scolding. Shvabrin himself brought him some vodka. The Pretender drank off a glass
and said, pointing to me: 'Serve some to his Honour, too.'
Shvabrin came up to me with the tray but I turned away a
second time. He did not seem to me to be his usual self. With
his customary quickwittedness he guessed, of course, that
Pugachev was displeased with him. He was frightened and
cast distrustful glances in my direction. Pugachev inquired
about the state of the fortress, what reports there were of the
enemy's troops, and other like matters, then suddenly asked

him point-blank: 'Tell me, my friend, who is this young girl you keep locked up here? Show her to me.'

Shvabrin went deathly pale. 'Sire,' he said in a trembling voice. 'Sire, she is not locked up ... she is ill ... she is upstairs, in bed.'

'Then take me to her,' said the Pretender, getting up.

It was impossible to refuse. Shvabrin led Pugachev to Maria Ivanovna's room. I followed.

Shvabrin stopped on the stairs.

'Sire!' he said. 'You are master and may demand of me whatever you please, but I do not allow a stranger to enter my wife's bedroom.'

I shuddered.

'So you are married!' I said to Shvabrin, preparing to tear him to pieces.

'Silence!' Pugachev interrupted me. 'This is my affair. And you,' he continued, turning to Shvabrin, 'keep your airs and graces to yourself, and don't try to be clever: your wife or not, I take to her whomsoever I choose. Your Honour, follow me.'

At the door of the room Shvabrin stopped again and said in a faltering voice:

'Sire, I warn you, she is delirious and has been raving incessantly for the last three days.'

'Open the door!' said Pugachev.

Shvabrin began searching in his pockets and then said that he had not brought the key with him. Pugachev kicked the door with his foot, the lock gave way, the door opened and we went in.

I looked – and was aghast. Maria Ivanovna, pale and thin and with dishevelled hair, was sitting on the floor, wearing a peasant dress which was all torn. A pitcher of water covered with a piece of bread stood before her. When she saw me she started and cried out. What I felt then I cannot describe.

Pugachev looked at Shvabrin and said with a biting smile:

'A nice hospital you have here!' Then he went up to Maria

Ivanovna and said: 'Tell me, my dear, what is your husband punishing you for? What wrong have you done him?'

'My husband!' she echoed. 'He is not my husband. I will never be his wife! I would rather die, and I shall die if I am not set free.'

Pugachev cast a threatening glance at Shvabrin.

'And you dared to deceive me!' he said to him. 'Do you know, you scoundrel, what you deserve?'

Shvabrin dropped on his knees. . . . At that moment contempt outweighed in me all feelings of hatred and anger. I looked with disgust at the sight of a nobleman grovelling at the feet of a fugitive Cossack. Pugachev softened.

'I will spare you this time,' he said to Shvabrin. 'But bear in mind that the next time you are at fault this wrong, too, will be remembered against you.' Then he turned to Maria Ivanovna and said kindly: 'Go, my pretty maid. I give you your liberty. I am the Tsar.'

Maria Ivanovna looked up at him quickly and realized that before her stood the murderer of her parents. She buried her face in her hands and fainted away. I rushed to her, but at that moment my old acquaintance Palasha pushed her way very boldly into the room and began attending to her mistress. Pugachev walked out and the three of us went downstairs to the parlour.

'Well, your Honour,' Pugachev said, laughing. 'We have delivered the fair maiden! What do you say to sending for the priest and having him marry you to his niece? I'll give her away if you like, and Shvabrin shall be best man. Then we will eat, drink and make merry on our own.'

The very thing that I was afraid of happened. Shvabrin lost control of himself when he heard Pugachev's suggestion.

'Sire!' he cried in a frenzy. 'I am in the wrong: I lied to you; but Griniov, too, is deceiving you. This girl is not the priest's niece: she is the daughter of Captain Mironov who was hanged when the fortress was taken.'

Pugachev fixed me with his fiery eye.

'What does this mean?' he asked, taken aback.

'Shvabrin is right,' I answered firmly.

'You did not tell me,' remarked Pugachev, and his face clouded.

'But just consider,' I answered him. 'How could I have said, in your men's presence, that Mironov's daughter was alive? They would have torn her to pieces. Nothing would have saved her!'

'That's true enough,' Pugachev said, laughing. 'My toss-pots would not have spared the poor girl. The priest's old goodwife did well to mislead them.'

'Listen,' I said, seeing him so kindly disposed. 'I do not know what to call you, and I do not want to know. . . . But God is my witness that I would gladly repay you with my life for what you have done for me. Only do not demand of me anything which would be against my honour and my Christian conscience. You are my benefactor. Finish as you have begun: let me go away with that poor orphan whither God may lead us. And wherever you may be, and whatever happens to you, we will pray every day of our lives for the salvation of your sinful soul. . . .'

Pugachev's grim heart seemed touched.

'So be it!' he said. 'Whether it be punishing or pardoning, I don't believe in half measures. Take your sweetheart, go with her wherever you will, and God grant you love and concord!'

Then he turned to Shvabrin and told him to give me a safe-conduct for all outposts and fortresses subject to his rule. Shvabrin, utterly crushed, stood like one transfixed. Pugachev went to look at the fortress. Shvabrin accompanied him, while I remained behind on the pretext of making ready for the journey.

I ran upstairs. The door was locked. I knocked. 'Who is there?' asked Palasha. I called out my name. Maria Ivanovna's sweet voice came from behind the door. 'Wait a moment, Piotr Andreich. I am changing my dress. Go to Akulina Pamfilovna's: I shall be there directly.'

I obeyed and went to Father Gerassim's house. Both he and

his wife ran out to meet me. Savelich had already told them I had come.

'Good day to you, Piotr Andreich,' said the priest's wife. 'God has brought us together again. How are you? Not a day has passed without our talking of you. Maria Ivanovna, poor little dear, has been through a dreadful time without you! . . . But tell me, my friend, how come you to hit it off with that Pugachev? How is it he hasn't murdered you? Excellent! We must thank the villain for that, at all events.'

'That will do, my dear,' Father Gerassim interrupted her. 'Don't always go babbling about what you know. There is no salvation in too much talking. Come in now, Piotr Andreich, come in, please. It is a long, long time since we saw you.'

The priest's wife set before me what food there was in the house, chattering away incessantly as she did so. She told me how Shvabrin had forced them to give up Maria Ivanovna; how Maria Ivanovna wept and did not want to be parted from them; how Maria Ivanovna had always kept in touch with her through Palashka (a spirited girl who had the sergeant himself dancing to her tune); how she had advised Maria Ivanovna to write to me, and so on. I in my turn briefly related my story. The priest and his wife crossed themselves when they learned that Pugachev knew of their deception. 'The power of the Holy Cross be with us!' said Akulina Pamfilovna. 'May God avert the storm! Fancy that Shvabrin betraying us – the serpent!' At that moment the door opened and Maria Ivanovna came in, a smile on her pale face. She had doffed her peasant clothes and was dressed as before, with a becoming simplicity.

I clasped her hand and for some time could not utter a word. The hearts of both of us were too full for speech. Our hosts felt that we did not need their presence, and left us. We were alone. Everything else was forgotten. We talked and talked and could not say enough to each other. Maria Ivanovna related to me all that had happened to her after the fortress was taken; she described all the horror of her position and all that she had had to endure at the hands of the infamous Shvabrin. We recalled the happy days of the past. . . . We were both weeping. . . . At last I began to unfold my plans. For her to remain in a fortress subject to Pugachev and ruled by Shvabrin was impossible. Neither could I think of taking her to Orenburg, then undergoing all the miseries of a siege. She had no one belonging to her in the whole world. I suggested that she should go to my parents in their village. She hesitated at first, being alarmed by my father's unfriendly disposition towards her, which she knew of. But on that score I made her mind easy. I knew that my father would be happy and consider it his duty to welcome the daughter of a gallant soldier who had died in the service of his country. 'Dear Maria Ivanovna,' I said to her at last, 'I look upon you as my wife. Miraculous circumstances have united us for ever: nothing on earth can part us.' Maria Ivanovna listened to me simply, without any pretended bashfulness or feigned reluctance. She felt that her fate was linked with mine. But she repeated that she would only marry me if my parents consented. I did not gainsay her. We kissed each other fervently, sincerely – and in this manner all was settled between us.

An hour later, Maximich brought me my safe-conduct, signed with Pugachev's scrawl, and said that he wanted to see me. I found him ready to take to the road. I cannot describe what I felt on parting company with this terrible man, this monster of evil to all but me. Why not confess the truth? At that moment a strong instinctive sense of liking drew me to him. I longed to tear him away from the criminals whose leader he was, and to save his head before it was too late. But Shvabrin and the people who crowded round us prevented me from giving expression to all that was in my heart.

We parted friends. Catching sight of Akulina Pamfilovna in the press, Pugachev shook his finger at her and winked meaningfully. Then he seated himself in his sledge, told the driver to return to Berda, and as the horses moved off he leaned his head out once more and shouted to me: 'Adieu, your Honour! We may yet meet again.' We did indeed meet again, but in what circumstances! . . .

Pugachev was gone. I stood for a long time gazing at the

white steppe over which his troika went gliding rapidly away. The crowd dispersed. Shvabrin disappeared. I returned to the priest's house. Everything was ready for our departure. I did not wish to delay any longer. All our belongings had been packed in the commandant's old travelling carriage. The horses were harnessed in a twinkling. Maria Ivanovna went to say farewell to the graves of her parents, who were buried behind the church. I wanted to accompany her but she begged to go alone. After a few minutes she came back, weeping silently. The carriage was brought up. Father Gerassim and his wife came out on to the steps. The three of us – Maria Ivanovna, Palasha and I – seated ourselves inside, while Savelich perched himself on the box. 'Good-bye, Maria Ivanovna, my little one! Good-bye, Piotr Andreich, brave knight!' the priest's kind wife said to us. 'A safe journey, and may God grant the two of you happiness!' We set off. I saw Shvabrin standing at the little window of the commandant's house. His face wore an expression of black animosity. I had no wish to exult over a defeated enemy and turned my eyes in another direction. At last we passed out of the gates, and left the fortress of Bielogorsk for ever.

13

THE ARREST

'Sire, be not angry, for duty bids
Me send you to gaol this very day.'
– 'As you please, I am ready, although I
Could hope you would first let me have my say.'

                                        KNIAZHNIN

UNITED so unexpectedly with the dear girl about whom only
that morning I had been so terribly anxious, I could scarcely
believe the evidence of my senses, and fancied that all that had
happened to me was an empty dream. Maria Ivanovna gazed
abstractedly now at me now at the road, and it seemed as if she
was not yet fully recovered. We were both silent. Our hearts
were spent. We did not notice the passing of time, and a couple
of hours later suddenly found ourselves at the neighbouring
fortress which was also in Pugachev's hands. Here we changed
horses. By the rapidity with which they were harnessed, and
by the marked obligingness of the bearded Cossack, promoted
by Pugachev to the dignity of commandant, I perceived that,
thanks to our driver's loquacity, I was being taken for one of
their master's favourites.

We continued our journey. Dusk was falling. We approached a small town where, according to the bearded commandant, there was a strong detachment of Pugachev's sup-
porters on their way to join him. We were stopped by the
sentries. To the challenge: 'Who goes there?' our driver replied in a loud voice: 'The Tsar's friend with his lady.'
Suddenly a troop of hussars surrounded us, uttering the most
fearful curses. 'Come out, you friend of the devil!' said their
heavily-moustached sergeant to me. 'We'll make it hot for you
presently, and that good lady of yours too!'

I stepped out of the sledge and demanded to be taken to their commanding officer. Seeing my uniform, the soldiers ceased their imprecations. The sergeant conducted me to the major. Savelich did not leave my side, muttering to himself: 'There's "Tsar's friend" for you! Out of the frying-pan into the fire. . . . Lord Almighty, what will be the end of it all?' The sledge followed slowly behind us.

After five minutes' walk we came to a small, brilliantly lighted house. The sergeant left me with the sentries and went in to announce me. He returned at once, saying that his high Honour had not time to see me but that I was to be gaoled and my lady brought to him.

'What is the meaning of this?' I exclaimed in a rage. 'Has he gone out of his mind?'

'I do not know, your Honour,' replied the sergeant. 'Only his high Honour said that your Honour was to be taken to gaol and her Honour brought to his high Honour!'

I dashed up the steps. The sentries made no attempt to detain me and I ran straight into the room where half a dozen hussar officers were playing cards. The major was dealing. What was my amazement when I glanced at him and recognized Ivan Ivanovich Zurin, who had rooked me at the Simbirsk inn!

'Is it possible?' I cried. 'Ivan Ivanich! Can it be you?'

'Zounds! Piotr Andreich! What chance brings you here? Where have you come from? Capital, my friend! Would you care for a hand?'

'I thank you. But I would rather you gave orders to have lodgings found for me.'

'What do you want with lodgings? Stay with me.'

'I cannot: I am not alone.'

'Well, bring your comrade along too.'

'I am not with a comrade, I am . . . with a lady.'

'A lady! Where did you pick her up? Aha, brother mine!'

And with these words Zurin whistled so expressively that all the others burst out laughing and I felt completely disconcerted.

'Well,' Zurin went on, 'so be it. You shall have quarters. But it's a pity. . . . We could have junketed a bit, the way we did before. . . . Hey, boy! Why don't they bring along Pugachev's sweetheart? Or doesn't she want to come? Tell her she need not be afraid, the gentleman is very kind and will do her no harm – and then give her a good slap to hurry her up.'

'What are you talking about?' I said to Zurin. 'Pugachev's sweetheart? It is the late Captain Mironov's daughter. I rescued her and now I am taking her to my father's, where I shall leave her.'

'What! So it was you, then, who was announced to me just now? Upon my word, what does all this mean?'

'I will tell you afterwards. But now for heaven's sake re-assure the poor girl whom your hussars have frightened out of her wits.'

Zurin immediately issued the necessary orders. He went out into the street himself to apologize to Maria Ivanovna for the involuntary misunderstanding, and told the sergeant to give her the best lodging in the town. I was to spend the night with him.

We had supper and when we were left alone together I related my adventures. Zurin listened with deep attention. When I had finished he shook his head and said: 'That is all very well, brother: except for one thing – why the devil do you want to get married? As an officer and a man of honour, I would not mislead you: believe me, marriage is all nonsense. Why saddle yourself with a wife and spend your life dandling brats? A pox on the idea! Do as I tell you: get rid of the Captain's daughter. I have cleared the road to Simbirsk and it is safe now. Send the girl on by herself to your parents tomorrow, and you stay with me in my detachment. There is no need for you to return to Orenburg. If you should fall into the rebels' hands again you might not escape so easily yet another time. Thus this love-foolishness of yours will die a natural death and all will be well.'

Although I did not altogether agree with him, yet I felt that duty and honour demanded my presence in the army of the Empress. I resolved to follow Zurin's advice and send Maria Ivanovna to my home village while I remained in his detachment.

Savelich came in to help me undress; I told him that he must be ready next day to continue the journey with Maria Ivanovna. He was for objecting at first. 'What are you thinking of, sir? How can I leave you? Who will look after you? What will your parents say?'

Knowing Savelich's obstinacy, I resolved to win him by wheedling and coaxing.

'Dear Savelich!' I said. 'Do not refuse me: be my good friend. I shall not need you here, and I should not feel easy if Maria Ivanovna were to journey without you. By serving her you will be serving me, for I am determined to marry her so soon as circumstances will allow.'

At this Savelich threw up his hands in a gesture of indescribable astonishment.

'To marry!' he repeated. 'The child wants to marry? But what will your father say? What will your mother think?'

'They will give their consent. I am sure they will give their consent when they know Maria Ivanovna,' I answered. 'I rely on you, too. Father and Mother have great confidence in you: you will intercede for us, won't you?'

The old man was touched.

'Ah, Piotr Andreich, dear,' he answered, 'though it is early days for you to be thinking of getting married, Maria Ivanovna is such a good young lady that it would be a sin to miss the opportunity. Have it your own way! I will accompany her, the angel, and tell your parents faithfully that such a bride does not need a dowry.'

I thanked Savelich and lay down to sleep in the same room with Zurin. My mind was in a turmoil, and I chattered away without intermission. At first Zurin answered me readily enough, but gradually his words became fewer and more disconnected; at last, instead of a reply to one of my questions, I heard a snore and the whistle of his breathing. I stopped talking and soon followed his example.

Next morning I betook myself to Maria Ivanovna and told her of my plans. She recognized their good sense and agreed with me at once. Zurin's detachment was to leave the town that same day. There was no time to lose. I said good-bye to Maria Ivanovna there and then, putting her in Savelich's care and giving her a letter to my parents. Maria Ivanovna burst into tears. 'Farewell, Piotr Andreich,' she said in a low voice. 'Whether we shall meet again, only God knows; but I will never forget you as long as I live: till my dying day you alone shall remain in my heart.' I could not answer her. Other people were there. I did not want to abandon myself before them to the feelings that agitated me. At last she drove away. I returned to Zurin, depressed and silent. He tried to cheer me; I sought distraction: we spent a noisy, riotous day, and in the evening set out on our march.

It was now near the end of February. The winter, which had rendered military operations difficult, was drawing to its close, and our generals were preparing for concerted action. Pugachev was still camped outside the walls of Orenburg. Meanwhile, our different detachments were joining forces and approaching the brigand's nest from all sides. Rebellious villages were restored to obedience at the sight of our troops; brigand bands fled from us, and everything indicated a speedy and successful termination of the campaign.

Soon Prince Golitsyn defeated Pugachev at the gates of the fortress of Tatishcheva, routed his hordes, relieved Orenburg and dealt, so it seemed, the final and decisive blow to the rebellion. At this time Zurin was sent against a party of rebellious Bashkirs, who dispersed before we could catch sight of them. Spring found us in a little Tartar village. Rivers were in flood and roads impassable. We comforted ourselves in our inaction with the thought that this petty and tedious war with brigands and savages would soon be over.

But Pugachev had not been captured. He appeared in the foundry districts of Siberia, where he gathered together a fresh collection of followers and recommenced his malefactions. Again rumours of his successes spread abroad. We

heard of the destruction of the Siberian fortresses. Soon news
that Kazan had been captured and that the Pretender was
marching on Moscow alarmed our leaders who had been
slumbering carefree in the fond hope that the despised rebel
was powerless to do anything. Zurin received orders to cross
the Volga.[1]

I shall not describe our campaign and the end of the war.
I will only say that misery was widespread. Law and order
came to a standstill; the gentry hid in the forests. Bands of
brigands roamed the countryside, robbing and plundering.
Commanders of isolated detachments punished and pardoned
as they pleased; the whole of the immense region where the
conflagration raged was in a parlous condition. . . . Heaven
send that we may never see such another senseless and merciless rebellion *à la russe*!

Pugachev was in flight, pursued by Ivan Ivanovich Mikhelson.[2] Soon we learned of his complete defeat. At last Zurin
received news of the capture of the impostor, and, at the same
time, orders to halt. The war was over. I could go to my
parents at last! The thought of embracing them, and of seeing
Maria Ivanovna, of whom I had heard nothing, filled me with
transports of delight. I danced about like a child. Zurin
laughed and said with a shrug of his shoulders: 'No, no good
will come of it! If you marry, you will be done for, and to no
advantage!'

But withal a strange feeling poisoned my joy: the thought
of the miscreant smeared with the blood of so many innocent
victims, and of the punishment which awaited him, troubled
me in spite of myself. 'Why did he not fall on a bayonet? Or
get hit by grape-shot?' I thought to myself miserably. 'That
would have been the best thing for him to do.' And how could

---

1. The paragraph that follows replaces in the printed version the long
episode contained in Pushkin's manuscript, and which is included here
at the end of the book.

2. I. I. Mikhelson (1740–1807) was one of Catherine II's greatest war
leaders. He drove Pugachev south from Kazan, and finally routed him on
24 August 1774.

I feel otherwise? I could not think of Pugachev without remembering how he had spared me at one of the most terrible moments of my life, and how he had rescued my betrothed from the hands of the infamous Shvabrin.

Zurin granted me leave of absence. In a few days I should be with my family again, and see my Maria Ivanovna. . . . Suddenly an unexpected storm burst upon me.

On the day fixed for my departure, at the very moment when I was preparing to set off, Zurin came into my room, holding a paper in his hand and looking exceedingly concerned. My heart sank. I was frightened without knowing why. He sent away my orderly and said he had something to tell me. 'What is it?' I asked anxiously. 'Something slightly disagreeable,' he answered, handing me the paper. 'See what I have just received.' I began reading it: it was a secret order to all commanders of isolated detachments to arrest me wherever I might be found and to send me at once under escort to Kazan, to appear before the Commission of Inquiry into the Pugachev Rising.

The paper almost dropped out of my hands. 'There is nothing for it,' Zurin said. 'My duty is to obey orders. Probably reports of your friendly journeys with Pugachev have somehow reached the authorities. I hope the affair will have no serious consequences, and that you will exonerate yourself before the Commission. Keep up your spirits and set off at once.'

My conscience was clear; I had no fear of the tribunal; but the thought of putting off, it might be for several months, the sweet moment of reunion appalled me. The wagon was ready. Zurin bade me a friendly good-bye. I took my place in the vehicle. Two hussars with drawn swords seated themselves beside me and we drove off along the high road.

14

THE TRIBUNAL

Popular rumour
Is like a sea-wave.
PROVERB

I WAS certain it was all due to my absence from Orenburg without permission. I could easily justify myself: sallying out against the enemy had never been prohibited – indeed, it had been actively encouraged. I might be accused of undue rashness, but not of disobedience. My friendly relations with Pugachev, however, could be attested by a multitude of witnesses and must have seemed, to say the least, highly suspect. Throughout our journey I kept thinking of the interrogation which awaited me and pondering the answers I should make, and resolved to tell the plain truth at the trial, believing that this was the simplest and, at the same time, the surest way of justifying myself.

I arrived in Kazan – the town had been sacked and burnt down. Where formerly houses had stood, the streets were now littered with heaps of charred wood and blackened walls without roofs or windows. Such were the traces left by Pugachev! I was brought to the fortress which had escaped the ravages of the fire. The hussars handed me over to the officer of the guard. He summoned the blacksmith. Shackles were put on my feet and riveted together. Then I was taken to the prison and left alone in a dark and narrow cell with blank walls and a tiny iron-barred window.

Such a beginning boded nothing good. For all that, I did not lose either hope or courage. I had recourse to the consolation of all those in affliction, and, having tasted for the first time the sweetness of prayer poured out from a pure but tortured heart, fell into a quiet sleep, regardless of what might lie in store.

The next morning the gaoler woke me with the announcement that I was to appear before the Commission. Two soldiers took me across the yard to the commandant's house: they stopped in the lobby and sent me into the inner room by myself.

I walked into a good-sized room. Two men were sitting at a table covered with papers: an elderly general who looked cold and forbidding, and a young captain of the Guards of some eight and twenty years, with a most pleasant appearance and a free and easy manner. At a separate table near a little window sat a secretary with a pen behind his ear, bending over a sheet of paper in readiness to take down my depositions. The interrogation began. I was asked my name and rank. The general inquired whether I was the son of Andrei Petrovich Griniov. When I said I was, he remarked severely: 'A pity so estimable a man should have such an unworthy son!' I replied calmly that whatever the accusations against me might be, I hoped to refute them by a candid avowal of the truth. My assurance did not please him. 'You have your wits about you, fellow,' he said to me, frowning, 'but we have seen cleverer men than you!'

Then the young man asked me in what circumstances and at what time I had entered Pugachev's service, and on what missions I had been employed.

I replied indignantly that, as an officer and a gentleman, I could never have entered Pugachev's service and could not possibly have accepted any mission from him.

'How comes it, then,' continued my interrogator, 'that this gentleman and officer was the only one spared by the Pretender, while all his comrades were cruelly done to death? How comes it that this same officer and gentleman feasted with the rebels, as their friend, and accepted presents from the brigand chief – a sheepskin coat, a horse and fifty kopecks in money? How did such a strange friendship spring up, and what could it be founded upon, if not upon treason, or, at any rate, upon base and criminal cowardice?'

I was deeply offended by the words of the officer of the

Guards and heatedly began my defence. I told them how I had first met Pugachev in the steppe in the snowstorm, how he had recognized me when the Bielogorsky fortress was taken, and spared my life. I admitted that I had not scrupled to accept the sheepskin coat and the horse from the Pretender, but said that I had defended the fortress of Bielogorsky against him to the last extremity. In conclusion I referred them to my General who could bear witness to my zealous service during the calamitous siege of Orenburg.

The stern old man picked up an unsealed letter from the table and began reading it aloud:

In reply to your Excellency's inquiry concerning Ensign Griniov, said to be involved in the present insurrection and to have entered into communication with the scoundrel, contrary to the regulations of the Service and to our oath of allegiance – I have the honour to report as follows: the said Ensign Griniov formed part of the garrison at Orenburg from the beginning of October 1773 to the twenty-fourth of February of the present year, on which date he quitted the town and since that time has not made his appearance again under my command. But we have heard from some turncoats that he was in Pugachev's camp and that he accompanied him to the Bielogorsky fortress, where he had formerly been garrisoned. With respect to his conduct, I can only . . .

Here the general interrupted his reading and said to me harshly:

'What can you say for yourself now?'

I wanted to go on as I had begun, and explain my connexion with Maria Ivanovna as frankly as all the rest, but suddenly I felt an overwhelming repulsion. It occurred to me that if I mentioned her the Commission would summon her to appear before them, and the idea of implicating her name with the vile denunciations of the miscreants, and of herself being confronted with them, so appalled me that I hesitated and became confused.

My judges, who seemed at first to have listened to my

answers with a certain amount of good will, were once more prejudiced against me when they saw my embarrassment. The officer of the Guards demanded that I should be faced with my principal accuser. The general ordered 'yesterday's villain' to be brought in. I turned to the door with interest, waiting for the appearance of my accuser. A few minutes later there was the clanking of chains, the door opened and – Shvabrin walked in. I was astounded at the change in him. He was terribly thin and pale. His hair, but a short time ago as black as pitch, was now quite white; his long beard was unkempt. He repeated his accusations in a feeble but determined voice. According to him I had been sent by Pugachev to Orenburg as a spy; under the pretence of sallies I used to ride out every day in order to transmit written news of all that was happening in the town; at last I had openly joined Pugachev, had accompanied him from fortress to fortress, doing my utmost to bring about the downfall of my fellow-traitors so as to occupy their posts and get the rewards handed out by the Pretender. I listened to him in silence and was pleased with but one thing: Maria Ivanovna's name was not mentioned by the villain, either because his vanity could not bear the thought of one who had scorned him, or because there lingered in his heart a spark of the same feeling which had compelled me to keep silent. In any case, the name of the daughter of the commandant of Bielogorsk was not mentioned in the presence of the Commission. I became still more confirmed in my resolution not to bring it up, and when the judges asked me what I had to say in answer to Shvabrin's accusations I replied that I adhered to my original statement and had nothing to add in justification of myself. The general ordered us to be led away. We quitted the room together. I glanced calmly at Shvabrin but did not say a word. He gave me a spiteful smile and, lifting his chains, hurried past me. I was escorted back to my cell and was not called for any further interrogation.

I was not witness of all that now remains for me to impart to the reader; but I have heard it related so often that the most minute details are engraved in my memory, and I feel as though I have been invisibly present.

Maria Ivanovna was received by my parents with that genuine kindness which distinguished people of the older generation. They regarded it as a blessing of Providence that the opportunity was afforded them of sheltering and consoling a poor orphan. Soon she had won their sincere attachment, for it was impossible to know and not love her. My love no longer appeared mere folly to my father, and my mother's one desire was that her Piotr should marry the Captain's nice little daughter.

The news of my arrest was a shock to my family. Maria Ivanovna had related my strange acquaintance with Pugachev so simply that, far from being uneasy about it, they had often laughed heartily over the whole story. My father refused to believe that I could have been implicated in an infamous rebellion, the aim of which was the overthrow of the throne and the extermination of the gentry. He questioned Savelich closely. The old man made no secret of the fact that I had been Pugachev's guest, and had indeed found favour with the villain; but he swore that he had never heard a word of any treason. My dear parents were reassured and waited impatiently for agreeable news. Maria Ivanovna was in a great state of agitation but she held her peace, being in the highest degree modest and prudent.

Several weeks passed. . . . Then my father suddenly received a letter from our relative in Petersburg, Prince B——. The prince wrote about me. After the usual opening compliments he went on to say that the suspicions about my participation in the rebel's designs had unfortunately proved to be only too well founded; and that capital punishment would have been meted out to me as an example to others had not the Empress, in consideration of my father's faithful service and advanced age, decided to spare the criminal son and commuted the shameful death penalty to exile for life in a remote part of Siberia.

This unexpected blow very nearly killed my father. He lost

his customary self-control, and his grief (as a rule mute) over-flowed in bitter complaints. 'What!' he would repeat, beside himself. 'My son an accomplice of Pugachev's! Merciful heavens, that I should live to see this! The Empress spares his life! Does that make it any better for me? It is not the death penalty that is terrible: my great-great-grandfather's father died on the scaffold for what to him was a matter of conscience. My father paid the price with Volynsky and Hrushchev.[1] But for a gentleman to betray his oath of allegiance and associate with brigands, murderers and runaway serfs! ... Shame and disgrace upon our name! ...' Frightened by his despair, my mother did not dare to weep in his presence and tried to cheer him by talking of the uncertainty of rumour and the small faith to be attached to people's opinions. My father was inconsolable.

Maria Ivanovna suffered more than anybody. She was firmly convinced that I could have cleared myself had I chosen to do so, and, guessing the truth, considered herself the cause of my misfortune. She hid from everyone her tears and misery, and yet was continually thinking of ways and means to save me.

One evening my father was sitting on the sofa turning over the leaves of the *Court Calendar* but his thoughts were far away and the reading did not have its usual effect upon him. He was whistling an old march. My mother sat in silence, knitting a woollen waistcoat, and from time to time a tear dropped on her work. All at once Maria Ivanovna, who was in the room with them, busy with her needlework, declared that it was absolutely necessary for her to go to Petersburg, and begged of my parents to furnish her with the means of doing so. My mother was very much upset. 'Why must you go to Petersburg?' she said. 'Can it be, Maria Ivanovna, that you, too, want to forsake us?' Maria Ivanovna replied that her whole future depended upon this journey, that she was going to seek

1. A. P. Volynsky (1689–1740) and his accomplices, one of whom was A. F. Hrushchev (1691–1740), were executed in June 1740, having been accused by Biren, the unscrupulous German favourite of the Empress Anna, of endeavouring to put Peter the Great's daughter Elizabeth on the throne.

influence and help from important people, as the daughter of a man who had suffered for his loyalty.

My father bent his head: every word that reminded him of his son's alleged crime was painful to him and seemed like a bitter reproach. 'Go, my dear,' he said to her with a sigh. 'We do not want to stand in the way of your happiness. God give you an honest man for a husband, and not a dishonoured traitor.' He got up and walked out of the room.

Left alone with my mother, Maria Ivanovna in part explained her plan. My mother embraced her with tears and prayed for the success of her undertaking. Preparations were made for the journey, and a few days later Maria Ivanovna set out on her road with the faithful Palasha and the faithful Savelich, who in his enforced separation from me comforted himself with the thought that at least he was serving my betrothed.

Maria Ivanovna arrived at Sofia[1] without mishap, and hearing that the Court was then at Tsarkoe Selo decided to stop there. At the posting-station she was assigned a tiny recess behind a partition. The station-master's wife immediately got into conversation with her, said that she was niece to one of the stokers at the Palace, and initiated her into all the mysteries of Court life. She told her at what hour the Empress usually woke in the morning, took coffee, went out for walks; what great lords were then with her; what she had deigned to say at table the day before; whom she had received in the evening. In short, Anna Vlassyevna's conversation was as good as several pages of historical memoirs and would have been a precious gift to posterity. Maria Ivanovna listened to her attentively. They went into the park together. Anna Vlassyevna related the history of every avenue and every ornamental bridge, and they returned to the post-house after a long walk, much pleased with each other.

Early next morning Maria Ivanovna woke, dressed and quietly betook herself to the park. It was a lovely morning,

1. Sofia forms part of Tsarkoe Selo – taking its name from the Cathedral of St Sofia which was built by Catherine II after the plan of St Sofia in Constantinople.

the sun shone on the tops of the linden-trees, already turning yellow from the chill breath of autumn. The broad still lake glittered in the sunlight. The swans, but newly awake, came sailing majestically out from under the bushes overhanging the banks. Maria Ivanovna walked towards a beautiful lawn where a monument had just been erected to commemorate Count Piotr Alexandrovich Rumyantsev's recent victories.[1] Suddenly a little white dog of English breed ran barking towards her. Maria Ivanovna was frightened and stood still. At that moment she heard a pleasant female voice call out: 'Do not be afraid, he won't bite.' And Maria Ivanovna saw a lady sitting on a bench opposite the monument. Maria Ivanovna sat down at the other end of the bench. The lady looked at her intently. Maria Ivanovna, in her turn, by a succession of stolen glances contrived to examine her from head to foot. She was wearing a white morning gown, a night-cap and a mantle. She seemed to be about forty. Her plump, rosy face expressed calm dignity, while her blue eyes and slight smile had an indescribable charm. The lady was the first to break the silence.

'You are a stranger here, are you not?' she said.

'Yes, ma'am: I arrived from the country only yesterday.'

'You came with your parents?'

'No, ma'am, I came alone.'

'Alone! But you are so young.'

'I have neither father nor mother.'

'You are here on some business, of course?'

'Yes, ma'am. I have come to present a petition to the Empress.'

'You are an orphan: I suppose you are complaining of some wrong or injustice?'

'No, ma'am. I have come to ask for mercy, not justice.'

'May I ask who you are?'

'I am Captain Mironov's daughter.'

1. Rumyantsev (1725–93) fought and defeated the Turks, for which Catherine II made him a field-marshal and had obelisks erected in his honour at Tsarkoe Selo and in Petersburg.

'Captain Mironov! The same who was commandant of one of the Orenburg fortresses?'

'Yes, ma'am.'

The lady was evidently touched.

'Forgive me', she said, still more kindly, 'for interfering in your affairs, but I am frequently at Court: tell me the nature of your petition and perhaps I may be able to help you.'

Maria Ivanovna rose and thanked her respectfully. Everything about this unknown lady instinctively attracted and inspired her confidence. Maria Ivanovna took a folded paper out of her pocket and gave it to the lady, who began reading it to herself.

At first she read with an attentive and benevolent air; but suddenly her expression changed, and Maria Ivanovna, who was watching her every movement, was frightened at the stern look on her face, so soft and pleasant a moment before.

'You are interceding for Griniov?' said the lady coldly. 'The Empress cannot pardon him. He joined the usurper, not out of ignorance and credulity but as a depraved and dangerous ne'er-do-well.'

'Oh, it isn't true!' Maria Ivanovna cried.

'What do you mean, not true?' retorted the lady, flushing red.

'It isn't true, I swear to God it isn't! I know all about it, I will tell you everything. It was solely for my sake that he exposed himself to all the misfortunes that have overtaken him. And if he did not clear himself before the tribunal, it was only because he did not want to implicate me.'

And she related with great warmth all that is already known to the reader.

The lady listened attentively.

'Where are you staying?' she asked at the end, and hearing that it was at Anna Vlassyevna's added with a smile: 'Ah, I know. Good-bye, do not tell anyone of our meeting. I hope you will not have to wait long for an answer to your letter.'

With these words she rose and proceeded down a covered avenue, while Maria Ivanovna returned to Anna Vlassyevna's full of a joyous hope.

The post-mistress scolded her for going out so early: the autumn air, she said, was not good for a young girl's health. She brought in the samovar, and over a cup of tea was about to embark again on her interminable stories of the Court when suddenly a Palace landau stopped at the door and a footman came into the room, saying that the Empress was pleased to summon to her presence Captain Mironov's daughter.

Anna Vlassyevna was amazed, and started to bustle about. 'Dear me!' she cried. 'The Empress summons you to Court. How did she get to hear of you? And how are you going to appear before Her Majesty, my dear? I'll warrant you know nothing of Court manners. . . . Hadn't I better accompany you? I could warn you about one or two things at any rate. And how can you go in your travelling-dress? Should we not send to the midwife for her yellow gown with the hoop petticoat?'

The footman announced that it was the Empress's pleasure that Maria Ivanovna should go alone and in the clothes she was wearing. There was nothing for it: Maria Ivanovna took her seat in the carriage and was driven off to the Palace, with parting admonitions and blessings from Anna Vlassyevna.

Maria Ivanovna felt that our fate was about to be decided: her heart beat violently. In a few moments the carriage drew up at the Palace. Maria Ivanovna walked up the steps with limbs that trembled. The doors were flung wide open before her. She passed through a succession of deserted, magnificent rooms, preceded by the footman. At last, coming to a closed door, he said that he would go in and announce her, and she was left alone.

The thought of seeing the Empress face to face was so terrifying that her legs could scarcely support her. In another minute the door opened and she was ushered into the Empress's dressing-room.

The Empress was seated at her toilet-table, surrounded by several ladies of her suite who respectfully made way for Maria Ivanovna. The Empress turned round to her with a gracious look and Maria Ivanovna recognized the lady to whom she had talked so frankly not so many minutes before. Calling Maria Ivanovna to her side, the Empress said with a smile: 'I am glad to have been able to keep my word and grant your petition. Your affairs are attended to. I am convinced that your betrothed is innocent. Here is a letter which you will give to your future father-in-law.'

Maria Ivanovna took the letter with a trembling hand and fell, weeping, at the feet of the Empress, who raised her up and kissed her. 'I know you are not rich,' she said, 'but I am in debt to Captain Mironov's daughter. Do not worry about the future. I will provide for you.'

After having made much of her, the Empress dismissed the poor orphan. Maria Ivanovna was driven back in the same royal carriage. Anna Vlassyevna, who had been impatiently awaiting her return, bombarded her with questions, which Maria Ivanovna answered somewhat vaguely. Anna Vlassyevna was disappointed at her poor memory but ascribed it to provincial shyness, and magnanimously excused her. That same day Maria Ivanovna went back to the country, without even bestowing a glance on Petersburg. . . .

*

The memoirs of Piotr Andreich Griniov end at this point. Family history tells us that he was released from his imprisonment towards the close of the year 1774 at the express order of the Empress; that he was present at the execution of Pugachev, who recognized him in the crowd and nodded his head to him which a moment later was shown lifeless and bleeding to the people. Shortly afterwards, Piotr Andreich and Maria Ivanovna were married. Their descendants still flourish in the province of Simbirsk. Some thirty versts from — there is a village belonging to ten owners. In one of the manor-houses a letter written by Catherine II may be seen in a frame under glass. It is addressed to Piotr Andreich's father and affirms the innocence of his son, and praises the intelligence and heart of Captain Mironov's daughter.

Piotr Andreich Griniov's manuscript was given to me by one of his grandchildren who had heard that I was engaged upon a work dealing with the period described by his grandfather. With the relatives' consent I have decided to publish it separately, after finding a suitable epigraph for each chapter and taking the liberty of changing some of the proper names.

THE EDITOR

19 October 1836.

ADDITION TO CHAPTER 13[1]

ZURIN received orders to cross the Volga and hasten to Simbirsk, where the flames of insurrection were already burning. The thought that I might be able to go home, embrace my parents and see Maria Ivanovna filled me with delight. I danced about like a child, and kept repeating as I hugged Zurin: 'To Simbirsk! To Simbirsk!' Zurin sighed and said, with a shrug of his shoulders: 'No, no good will come of it. If you marry, you will be done for, and to no advantage!...'

We were approaching the banks of the Volga. Our regiment entered the village of X. and stopped there for the night. The next morning we were to cross the river. The village elder told me that all the villages on the other side had risen, and that Pugachev's bands were prowling about everywhere.

This news filled me with profound alarm.

I was seized with impatience which allowed me no rest. My father's estate was on the other side of the river, thirty versts away. I asked if there was anyone who would row me across. All the peasants were fishermen; there were plenty of boats. I went to Zurin and told him of my intention. 'Be careful,' he said. 'It is dangerous to go alone. Wait till morning. We will be the first to cross and will pay a visit to your parents with fifty hussars in case of emergency.'

I insisted on having my way. The boat was ready. I stepped into it with two boatmen. They pushed off and plied their oars.

The sky was clear. The moon shone brightly. The air was still. The Volga flowed smooth and calm. Swaying rhythmically, the boat glided over the crest of the dark waves. Half an hour passed. I was absorbed in reverie. We reached the middle of the river.... Suddenly the boatmen started whispering together. 'What is it?' I asked, returning to reality. 'Heaven

1. This fragment of a preliminary version of the novel was found among Pushkin's MSS. and published in *Russian Archives* in 1880.

only knows: we can't tell,' the boatmen answered, both staring to one side. I looked in the same direction and saw in the dark something floating down stream. The mysterious object was approaching us. I told the oarsmen to stop and wait. 'What can it be?' they wondered. 'It's not a sail, and it's not a mast.' The moon hid behind a cloud. The floating phantom became still blacker. It was now quite close to me and yet I could not make out what it was. Suddenly the moon reappeared from behind the cloud and lit up a terrible sight. A gallows fixed to a raft was floating towards us. Three bodies were hanging from the cross-piece. A morbid curiosity possessed me. I wanted to look into the hanged men's faces. I told the oarsmen to grab the raft with a boat-hook, and my boat bumped against the floating gallows. I jumped on to the raft and found myself between the dreadful posts. The full moon illumined the mutilated faces of the unfortunate creatures. One of them was an old Tchuvash,[1] the second a Russian peasant, a strapping lad of about twenty. Lifting my eyes to look at the third, I was shocked and could not refrain from crying out: it was our Vanka,[2] our poor Vanka, who in his foolishness went over to Pugachev. A black board had been nailed over their heads on which was written in big white letters: 'Thieves and rebels'. The boatmen waited for me unconcerned, keeping hold of the raft with the boat-hook. I got back into the boat. The raft floated on down the river. For a long time the gallows towered black in the dim light. At last it disappeared and our craft reached the tall, steep bank.

I paid the boatmen handsomely. One of them took me to the elder of the village by the ferry-stage. I went into the hut with him. On hearing that I wanted horses he was about to treat me in a somewhat unmannerly fashion but my guide whispered some words in his ear and the incivility immediately gave place to an eager obligingness. In a moment a troika was ready, and seating myself I bade the driver take me to our village.

1. The Tchuvashes are a Mongolian tribe which settled in Russia.
2. A character who disappeared from Pushkin's final draft of the book.

We galloped along the high road past sleeping villages. I feared only one thing – being stopped on the way. My nocturnal encounter on the Volga might prove the presence of rebels but it was likewise evidence of strong counter-action on the part of the government. To provide against all emergencies I carried in my pocket both the safe-conduct given to me by Pugachev and Colonel Zurin's travel-pass. But we did not meet anyone and towards morning I caught sight of the river and the grove of pines behind which lay our village. The driver whipped up the horses and a quarter of an hour later we drove into X. The manor-house was at the other end of the village. The horses were flying along. Suddenly, in the middle of the village street, the driver began pulling up. 'What is it?' I asked impatiently. 'A barrier, sir,' the driver answered, with difficulty bringing the quivering horses to a standstill. Indeed, I could see a *cheval de frise* and a sentry armed with a club. The man came up to me and, taking off his hat, requested my passport. 'What does this mean?' I asked him. 'Why is this barricade here? Who are you guarding?' – 'But, my good sir, we are in rebellion,' he answered, scratching himself. 'And where are your masters?' I asked, with a sinking heart. 'Where are our masters?' the peasant repeated. 'Master and mistress are in the granary.' – 'What do you mean – in the granary?' – 'Why, Andriushka our scribe put them in the stocks, you see, and wants to take them to our Sovereign Tsar!' – 'Heavens above! Lift the bar, you blockhead. What are you waiting for?'

The man took his time. I jumped out of the troika, boxed his ears (I am sorry to say) and pushed the barrier aside myself. The peasant watched me in stupid amazement. Getting back into the carriage, I told the driver to drive to the house as fast as possible. The granary was in the courtyard. Two peasants armed with clubs were standing by the locked doors. The troika drew up just in front of them. I leaped out and rushed at them. 'Open the doors!' I commanded. I must have looked formidable for, throwing down their clubs, they ran away. I tried to wrench the padlock off and break in; but the doors were of oak and the huge padlock impregnable. At that moment a young peasant emerged from the servants' quarters and asked me arrogantly how I dared make such a disturbance. 'Where is Andriushka, the scribe?' I shouted. 'Call him to me.'

'My name is Andrei Afanassyevich, not Andriushka,' he replied haughtily, his arms akimbo. 'What do you want?'

Instead of answering, I seized him by the collar and dragging him to the granary doors told him to open them. The scribe was for resisting; but a 'paternal' cuff had due effect on him, too. He pulled out the key and opened the granary. I dashed over the threshold and in a dark corner feebly lit by a narrow skylight saw my mother and father. Their hands were bound, their feet in stocks. I flew to embrace them and could not utter a word. They both looked at me in amazement: I was so altered by three years of military life that they could not recognize me.

Suddenly I heard a dear familiar voice. 'Piotr Andreich, is that you?' I looked round and saw Maria Ivanovna in another corner, also bound hand and foot. I was transfixed. My father looked at me in silence, not daring to believe his eyes. Joy shone on his face. 'Welcome, welcome, Piotr, my dear!' he said, pressing me to his heart. 'Thank God you have come in time!' My mother drew a breath and melted into tears. 'Petrusha, my dear boy! How has the Lord brought you here? Are you well?'

I made haste to cut their bonds with my sword and to free them from confinement; but when I went to the door I found that it had been locked again. 'Andriushka!' I shouted. 'Open!' – 'Oh, to be sure!' he answered from behind the door. 'You may as well be shut up, too! That will teach you to brawl and drag the Tsar's officials by the collar!'

I began to look round the granary to see if there was any way of getting out. 'Do not give yourself the pains,' my father said to me. 'I am not one to have a granary with holes for thieves to creep in and out of.' My mother, who had rejoiced a moment before at my coming, now fell into despair at the thought that I, too, would have to perish with the rest of the family. But I felt easier now that I was with them and Maria Ivanovna. I had a sword and two pistols: I could withstand a siege. Zurin was due to arrive in the evening and would set us free. I told all this to my parents and succeeded in calming my mother and Maria Ivanovna. They gave themselves up completely to the happiness of our reunion, and several hours passed unnoticed in the uninterrupted exchange of tender words and conversation.

'Well, Piotr,' said my father, 'you have committed your share of follies and I was thoroughly angry with you at the time. But it is no use harping on the past. I hope that you have sown your wild oats now and are reformed. I know that you have performed your duties as befits the honour of an officer. I thank you, you have comforted me in my old age. If I owe my deliverance to you, life will be doubly agreeable.' With tears in my eyes I kissed his hand and looked at Maria Ivanovna, who was so overjoyed at my presence that she seemed utterly happy and serene.

About midday we heard unwonted uproar and shouting. 'What does it mean?' said my father. 'Can it be your Colonel arriving to the rescue?' – 'Impossible,' I replied. 'He will not be here before evening.' The noise increased. The tocsin was sounded. Mounted men were galloping across the courtyard. At that moment Savelich thrust his grey head through a narrow opening in the wall, and my poor old servant said in a pitiful voice: 'Andrei Petrovich! Piotr Andreich, my dear! Maria Ivanovna! We are lost! The bandits have arrived in the village. And Piotr Andreich, do you know who has brought them? Shvabrin – Alexei Ivanich – may the devil take him!'

When Maria Ivanovna heard the odious name she clasped her hands and remained motionless. 'Listen!' I said to Savelich. 'Send someone on horseback to the ferry to meet the Hussar regiment, and tell him to let the Colonel know of the danger we are in.'

'But who is there to send, sir? All the lads have risen, and all the horses have been seized. Oh dear – there they are in the courtyard already! They are coming to the granary.'

As he said this, we heard several voices on the other side of the door. I signed to my mother and Maria Ivanovna to retire into a corner, drew my sword and leaned against the wall close to the door. My father took the pistols, cocked them both and stationed himself beside me. The lock rattled, the door opened and Andriushka's head appeared. I struck it with my sword and he fell, blocking the entrance. At the same moment my father fired the pistol in the doorway. The crowd that had been pressing round ran away, uttering curses. I dragged the wounded man across the threshold and closed the door.

The courtyard was full of armed men. Among them I recognized Shvabrin. 'Don't be afraid,' I said to the women. 'There is a hope. And, Father, don't shoot again. Let us save the last shot.'

My mother was praying silently. Maria Ivanovna stood beside her, waiting with angelic calm for her fate to be decided. Threats, abuse and curses came from the other side of the door. I stood at my post ready to cut down the first man who dared to show himself. Suddenly the brigands were silent. I heard Shvabrin's voice calling me by name.

'I am here. What do you want?'

'Surrender, Griniov: resistance is impossible. Take pity on your old parents. Obstinacy will not save you. I shall have you!'

'Try, traitor!'

'I am not going to risk my own skin to no purpose, or waste my men: I shall set fire to the granary, and then we shall see what you do, Don Quixote of the Bielogorsky fortress! Now it is time for dinner. Meanwhile, you sit and think it over at your leisure. Good-bye. Maria Ivanovna, I make you no apologies: no doubt you are enjoying yourself in the dark with your knight.'

Shvabrin went away, leaving a guard at the door. We were silent, each thinking his own thoughts and not daring to communicate them to the others. I pictured to myself all that Shvabrin was capable of doing in his malice. About myself I hardly worried. Shall I confess it? – even my parents' fate terrified me less than Maria Ivanovna's. I knew that my mother was adored by the peasants and the house serfs. My father, too, was loved, in spite of his severity, for he was a just man and knew the true needs of his serfs. Their rebellion was an aberration, a passing intoxication, and not an indication of discontent. It was possible that my parents would be spared. But what of Maria Ivanovna? What fate was that dissolute and unscrupulous man preparing for her? I did not dare dwell upon this awful thought and made ready (God forgive me) to kill her rather than see her a second time in the hands of a cruel enemy.

A further hour or so went by. Drunken men could be heard singing in the village. The sentries on guard at the granary door envied them and vented their spite by reviling us and trying to terrify us with promises of torture and death. We were waiting for the sequel of Shvabrin's threats. At last there was a great commotion in the courtyard and we heard Shvabrin's voice again.

'Well, have you bethought yourselves? Do you surrender to me of your own will?'

No one answered.

After waiting for a short while Shvabrin ordered his men to bring some straw. In a few minutes flames appeared, lighting up the dim granary. Smoke began to force its way through the cracks in the door.

Then Maria Ivanovna came up to me and, taking me by the hand, said in a low voice: 'Come, Piotr Andreich! Do not let both yourself and your parents perish on my account. Shvabrin will listen to me. Let me go out!'

'Never!' I cried heatedly. 'Do you know what is in store for you?'

'I should not survive dishonour,' she answered quietly. 'But it may be I could save my liberator and the family which has so generously cared for a poor orphan. Farewell, Andrei

Petrovich! Farewell, Avdotia Vassilievna! You have been more than benefactors to me. Give me your blessing. Farewell to you, too, Piotr Andreich. Be sure that ... that ...' She burst into tears and buried her face in her hands ... I was as one out of his mind. My mother was weeping.

'Do not be foolish, Maria Ivanovna,' said my father. 'Whoever would dream of letting you go to the brigands? Sit here now and be quiet. If we must die, we will all die together. Listen! What's that they are saying?'

'Do you give in?' shouted Shvabrin. 'Another five minutes and, you'll see, you will be roasted.'

'We do not surrender, you villain!' my father answered firmly. His fearless, deeply lined face was astonishingly animated. His eyes flashed under the white eyebrows. Turning to me, he said: 'Now is the time!'

He opened the door. The flames leaped in and twisted along the beams which were caulked with dry moss. My father fired the pistol, stepped over the burning threshold and shouted: 'Follow me!' I took my mother and Maria Ivanovna by the hands and quickly led them out into the air. By the door lay Shvabrin, with a bullet through him fired by my father's decrepit hand. The crowd of brigands who had fled at our unexpected emergence instantly took courage and began closing in upon us. I succeeded in dealing a few more blows with my sword; but a well-aimed brick caught me full in the chest. I fell to the ground and lost consciousness for a few seconds; I was surrounded and disarmed. Coming to myself, I saw Shvabrin sitting on the blood-stained grass with my family standing before him.

I was supported under the arms. A crowd of peasants, Cossacks and Bashkirs encircled us. Shvabrin was dreadfully pale. He was pressing one hand to his wounded side. His face expressed suffering and hatred. He slowly raised his head, glanced at me and said in a weak, hardly audible voice: 'Hang him ... and all of them ... except her ...'

The crowd surrounded us at once and dragged us to the gates. But suddenly they left us and scattered: Zurin and a whole squadron of hussars with drawn swords were riding in through the gates.

The rebels fled right and left. The hussars pursued them struck out with their swords and took them prisoner. Zurin jumped off his horse, bowed to my father and mother, and warmly clasped me by the hand. 'Got here just in time!' he said to us. 'Ah, and your betrothed is here too!' Maria Ivanovna coloured to the ears. My father approached and thanked him calmly, though he was obviously shaken. My mother embraced him, calling him our delivering-angel. 'Welcome to our home!' said my father, leading him into the house.

Zurin stopped as he passed Shvabrin. 'Who is it?' he asked looking at the wounded man. 'That is the leader of the gang in person,' replied my father with a certain pride which betokened the old soldier. 'God assisted my feeble old hand to punish the young miscreant and avenge the blood of my son. –'It is Shvabrin,' I told Zurin. 'Shvabrin! Charmed! Hussars take him! Tell the leech to dress his wound and watch over him like the apple of his eye. Shvabrin must certainly be sent before the Kazan Secret Commission. He is one of the chief criminals and his evidence will assuredly be of great importance!'

Shvabrin opened his eyes wearily. His face expressed nothing save physical pain. The hussars carried him away on a cloak.

We went into the house. I looked about me with a tremor recalling the years of my childhood. Nothing had changed in the house, everything was in its old place. Shvabrin had not allowed it to be plundered: low as he had stooped he had preserved an instinctive aversion to the dishonouring greed for booty.

The servants appeared in the hall. They had taken no part in the rebellion and whole-heartedly rejoiced at our release. Savelich was triumphant. I must tell you that in the commotion caused by the outlaws' attack he had run to the stable where Shvabrin's horse was, saddled and led her out quietly under cover of the general hubbub and galloped off unobserved to the ferry. He came upon the regiment enjoying halt on this side of the Volga. Hearing from him of our danger, Zurin had sounded the trumpet call to mount, ordered his men forward at the gallop and, thank God, arrived in time.

Zurin insisted that the head of Andriushka, the village scribe, should be exhibited for a few hours on the end of a pole by the tavern.

The hussars returned from their chase with a number of prisoners. These were locked in the same granary where we had endured our memorable siege. We all went to our rooms. The old people needed a rest. Not having slept the whole night long, I threw myself on to the bed and dropped fast asleep. Zurin departed to make necessary arrangements.

In the evening we all gathered in the drawing-room round the samovar, chatting gaily of the peril that was past. Maria Ivanovna poured out the tea. I sat down by her side and devoted myself exclusively to her. My parents appeared to view with favour the tender feelings we had for each other. To this day that evening lives in my memory. I was happy, completely happy – and are there many such moments in this poor life on earth?

The following day my father was told that the peasants had assembled in the courtyard to ask for his pardon. My father went out on to the steps to talk to them. As soon as he approached, the peasants fell on their knees. 'Well, you foolish ones!' he said to them. 'Why did you take it into your heads to rebel?' – 'We are sorry, master,' they answered in one voice. 'Sorry, are you? You get into mischief and then you are sorry! I forgive you for the happiness God has given me of seeing my son, Piotr Andreich, again. Very well, so be it: a sin confessed is a sin forgiven.'

'We did wrong, of course we did!'

'God has sent us fine weather. We ought to be getting the hay in; and you, you pack of donkeys, what have you been doing these last three days? Elder, put everyone on to hay-making. And see that by St John's Day[1] all the hay is stacked, you ginger-headed rascal! Now be off!'

1. June 24.

The peasants bowed and went about their work as though nothing had happened.

Shvabrin's wound did not turn out to be a mortal one. He was sent under escort to Kazan. From the window I watched them laying him in the wagon. Our eyes met. He bent his head and I made haste to move from the window: I was afraid of looking as though I were triumphing over a broken and unhappy enemy.

Zurin was obliged to continue farther, and I decided to accompany him, in spite of my desire to spend a few more days with my family. On the eve of our departure I went to my parents and, in accordance with the custom of the time, bowed down to the ground before them and asked their blessing on my marriage with Maria Ivanovna. The old people lifted me up, and with tears of joy expressed their consent. I brought Maria Ivanovna, pale and trembling, to them. They gave us their benediction. I cannot describe what I felt. Those who have been in my position will understand in any case; as to those who have not, I can only pity and advise them, while there is still time, to fall in love and receive their parents' blessing.

The following day the regiment was ready. Zurin took leave of my family. We were all convinced that military operations would soon be over. I was hoping to be married within a month. As she said good-bye, Maria Ivanovna kissed me in front of everyone. I took my seat in the carriage. Savelich came with me once again and the regiment marched off. For as long as it was in sight I looked back at the country house that I was leaving again. I was troubled by a gloomy foreboding. A voice seemed to whisper that not all my troubles were past and done with. In my heart there was a presentiment of another storm.

I shall not describe our campaign and the end of the war against Pugachev. We passed through villages he had pillaged, and were obliged to take from the poor inhabitants what little the rebels had left them.

The people did not know whom to obey. Law and order

everywhere came to a standstill. The gentry were hiding in the forests. Bands of brigands roamed the countryside, robbing and plundering. Commanders of isolated detachments sent in pursuit of Pugachev, who was by then fleeing in the direction of Astrakhan, chastised the guilty and the innocent at will. The whole region where the conflagration raged was in a parlous condition. Heaven send that we may never see such another senseless and merciless rebellion *à la russe*! Those who plan impossible revolutions in Russia are either youngsters who do not know our people or positively heartless men who set little value on their own skins and less still on those of others.